Crystal Spirit
Roger Granelli

seren

Seren is the book imprint of
Poetry Wales Press Ltd
Nolton Street, Bridgend, CF31 3BN, Wales
www.seren-books.com

© Roger Granelli, 1992; reprinted with revisions, 2004

ISBN 1-85411-332-1

The right of Roger Granelli to be identified as the author of
this work has been asserted in accordance with the Copyright,
Designs and Patents Act, 1988.

A CIP record for this title is available from
the British Library

All rights reserved. No part of this publication
may be reproduced, stored in a retrieval system,
or transmitted at any time or by any means
electronic, mechanical, photocopying, recording
or otherwise without the prior permission
of the copyright holder.

This is a work of fiction. The characters
and incidents portrayed are the work of the author's
imagination. Any other resemblance to actual persons,
living or dead, is entirely coincidental.

The publisher works with the financial assistance of the
Welsh Books Council.

Printed in Plantin by Bell & Bain Ltd, Glasgow.

Newport Community Learning
and Libraries

Z658015

Newport Community Learning & Libraries
Cymuned dysgu

Crystal Spirit

For Hydref

Your name and your deeds were forgotten
Before your bones were dry,
And the lie that slew you is buried
Under a deeper lie;

But the thing I saw in your face
No power can disinherit:
No bomb that ever burst
Shatters the crystal spirit.

George Orwell, *Homage to Catalonia*

Thanks to Morien Morgan
for the informative chats and the encouragement.

Lines from *Homage to Catalonia* quoted by permission of
the Estate of the late Sonia Brownell Orwell
and Martin Secker & Warburg Ltd.

1

At the age of seven David smelt death for the first time. He felt the panic and fear it brought, and savoured its excitement with a heart free of the future. He enjoyed it. David witnessed the aftermath of a mining accident, a small affair, three men killed in a roof fall, a dozen others with smashed limbs. It was the second week of the summer holidays, and already he was bored with freedom, the grey weather, and the lack of friends.

He had wandered after his mother to the pithead, in defiance of her strict orders. The doleful shriek of the pit's whistle pulled the women from their kitchens with its promise of bad news; they were honed by its regular stabs at their lives. David could not resist it either. He hid behind a wall, and saw his mother there, one of a frenzied, milling crowd of women, half-crazy with fear, and desperate with hope. They held each other, as if they shared one collective heart, and comforted each other with words, and every woman wanted it to be someone else's man. David watched as they brought up the bodies, inert crumpled mounds, covered in coal sacks. There had been no explosion, and no gas. Knowing this, the crowd settled itself for a lesser mourning.

Daniel Hicks, David's father, came up with the rest, his face as white as a cloud beneath the black smudges. His mother ran to embrace him, the first and last time David ever saw his parents do this. He sneaked back past the throng as the crowd walked back to the terraces, to be waiting innocently on the doorstep. The streets emptied of people, leaving those without work to scuffle about on corners, and talk about the new widows.

This was the strongest image of David's early childhood, the pit-monster, and the havoc it wrought. It came often into his head down the years, at times of stress, sadness, or even quiet happiness, a watershed that set his youth against the ways of the valley, and its work. He thought of it half a century later, in another country that held so much past for him.

David sat alone in the corner of the café. Opposite him was a table of young men, talking softly with heads locked together, a conspiracy of youth, the whispers of boys about to wave goodbye to their childhood. From his side of the room David strained his good ear to catch slivers of the conversation. He heard sweet voices, the talkers were educated and polite, and visitors, like himself.

It was siesta time, in a village as hot as a forge, and deadly still. Only the talkers, and a few flies, disturbed the silence. Drones and murmurs lulled David into a doze. While he slept the flies alighted on the sticky spillage of wine on the table, and scorned David's twitching hand. They knew it was old and slow, and no threat to them. In the street outside the sun blazed fiercely, in control of this place. It slashed its way through the café door to display itself on the wall in a scimitar of light. Its glare dashed David's eyes, rousing him to light a cigarette. He sucked at it, and watched the smoke turn from powder blue to dirty grey, made filthy by a voyage around his lungs. It swirled into the rays of the sun and twisted itself into patterns. A rasp started deep in David's throat and grew stronger as he gasped in clouds of the hot air.

The boys in the corner stopped talking and studied David. He heard the word '*Ingles*' and smiled across at them, to excuse his disturbance. The smile drew one to his table, a short and solid eighteen year old, a Spaniard out of the traditional mould.

'Can I have a cigarette, *señor*?', the boy asked, in good English.

'Take one,' David said, in rusty Spanish. The boy took a cigarette from the packet and lit it with a flourish.

'*Gracias*,' he said, pleased with David's Spanish.

'*De nada*', David replied, tasting the foreign words on his tongue. The boy rejoined the others, who glanced over and mused on David's origins. Tourist Spain was many miles and lifestyles away, and foreigners did not come to this place without reason.

David got up from his chair. It was time to take his chance in the afternoon heat. On the table he left a pile of coins, for the flies to investigate, and the landlord to collect when he awoke from his slump over the bar. David's back had stiffened on the café's rickety furniture, the sun would be good for it, he hoped. He turned towards the group and said 'adios'. There was a murmur of response; he heard one say 'what does that old man want around here anyway?' The smoker answered 'who knows – see how he goes out into the sun at this time.' David left, amused at the round of sympathetic clucking and judgement rising in his wake.

He walked steadily up an alley of cobblestones, poking the uneven ground with his toe, and waking the cats that slept in the shadows. They slunk away from him, hating this alien disturber of their sloth, looking back at him with their moon-like eyes. The sun drummed on David's back as he walked. He felt his shirt moisten and stick, but the heat did not bother him overmuch. It never had – a hat, and the ability to take one's time were good foils.

The village David passed through was little changed since he was last in it. There was little to change, the sea was a day away, and there was nothing of value here, except the people, as permanent as the rocks their homes rested on. There was nothing to develop, or speculate over, and little of interest for any stray tourist, but for David memories sprang from its stones like water after a summer storm. They pricked his mind with images as sharp as pins; layers of recollections churned in his consciousness. He realised they had been stored there for longer than most of his comrades' lives had lasted back then, in that time of great dreaming, and killing.

Life had twisted around David much since those days, but he was formed by that tumultuous experience of Spain. The core of him had learned to stand up then, to think for itself, and David had thought the same ever since, he realised, and had dreamt the same. The years had aged his body, but his mind was still fresh, and he would clutch those crazy times again, if he could. Thoughts and ideas did not grow arthritic, like his body, not if they kept true and constant. David had gained this wisdom with age, and he savoured it now, as he trudged up the winding gradient of the sleeping village.

It took him an hour to gain the top of the hill, his steps slow and even, his mind crowded with thoughts. He knew events were turning in a half-century circle for Spain, but there would never be that whirlwind of change again; too many had died before, with hasty handed-down ideas vibrant in their peasant heads. David looked down on the houses from his high perch on the slab of rock that was the hump-backed guardian of the village. The people lived under it, their homes loosely contoured about it, squeezed between its folds in a nest of alleys, cul-de-sacs, and streets that just petered out, as if their builders had acknowledged the sovereignty of the rock. Romans might still be at home here: the sea of serrated red tiles, and the white glare each cluster of houses gave off would be familiar to them. The impossible architecture of the place reminded David of his own home, another village carved out of a valley.

The air was fresh on the hilltop, and David felt lighter himself, a whiff of being young again came to him, fleeting and exquisite with the promise it could never fulfil. On all sides the landscape was dried to dust; it stretched away to the horizons like a red blanket. The first time David saw it it had been so strange, opposite in every way to the wet green of his upbringing, an African land, slashed with cruel light, pulsing with heat and death, and scornful of human life.

David took some tobacco from his tin, the local cigarettes he abandoned in their soft packet, they were no more to his taste now than they had ever been. As he tapped out his thin smoke he saw his image in the tarnished tin. His face had not aged too badly, it was never fleshy, and had stayed free of lines, despite a lifelong frown of inquiry. It was stretched a little tighter now, etched with crows' feet around the eyes, but they were clear, not rheumy with a tiredness of life, and they were still the brown of old hazelnuts. David put the tin away, laughing at his vanity. He lay back and looked at the building that had brought him up the hill, and to Spain itself. He felt himself part of a film, he knew the scene he was creating, old man, old memories, a return, how many had started like this? Always he had avoided going over this part of his past too much. There was the danger one might inhabit it permanently, a prisoner of what might have been, like some of his old comrades, men mourning through their lives for their busted idealism. But now, as he closed his eyes, he obeyed the instinct to map it all out, once and for all. He had all the time in the world.

The valley was much like any other in the coalfield, smaller than some, but no less torn by the coal it lived on – lived on, breathed, wore about itself like a black cloak; it was steeped in getting it out of the ground. Before the pits there had been few people, some hill-farmers and their sheep dotting the hills. The sheep were still around, but they grazed on the edge of the black slopes in

David's time, spilling over the tips like grey flakes of snow.

David's family lived in a cramped terraced cottage, one of the thousands that ribboned the valley's floor, following the contours of the river like stone snakes, thin lines which came together every few miles to form the fatter wedge of a community. They are still there today, renovated, and brightly painted to the whims of their new owners, the generation freed from coal. Viewed from afar they appear toy-like and defiantly hopeful; in the Twenties they all looked the same, a grey uniformity of slate and stone, built and owned by the pit's overlords. David's was no different to the others, it had a few box-like rooms, a best one at the front, for funerals and weddings.

David was one of three children, a modest family for the times. He had two older sisters, Ruth and Mary; Daniel and Helen were his parents. There were too many years between the girls and David for there to be any friction between them, he was the mascot kid brother, spoiled and fought over, placed on a male pedestal from an early age. And his father was old, approaching forty when David was born, too old for David, who saw him as a match for other boys' grandpas, and let this perception create a chasm between them which he never cared to breach. Daniel, like most of the men in the street, mined for coal at the nearest pit; he managed to hold onto his job through the hardest of times, a steady, self-effacing worker.

Coughing. It was David's first memory of his father. He heard it now on the Spanish hilltop, echoing clearly down the years. It was Daniel wheezing through the night, his chest like a bellows being gently tickled. At intervals he would stop, and there would be an explosion of coughing as his system cleared itself, then silence for a while. When David shared his parents' bedroom he sometimes tried to stay awake, to see if his father would continue all night, but sleep always came, and the mystery remained unsolved.

Daniel's nights belied the calm of his days. He believed in the quiet life, in keeping his head down, and getting on with his work, no matter what. He was friendless, a lone man of middle size, with little to distinguish him, apart from his shock of black hair. It stood up like a tarbrush on his head, questioning his soft spirit, the resigned hunch of the shoulders, and the habit of 'tut-tutting' under his breath. David sensed the inner man, but it rarely made

11

an appearance in front of him apart from one best-room chat. In the house Daniel mixed despotism with detachment, and was usually bested by his wife's strong will and implacable patience.

David always knew his father was not much interested in the family as a whole, he could not share much of himself. Life seemed something to be put up with for Daniel Hicks, a journey towards an inevitable end. As a child David took this attitude for granted, not caring if there was a reason, not seeing any further than himself.

Helen Hicks was taller than most women in the village, thin and upright in stance, with high cheekbones, a severe figure to those who did not know her. Her hair was greying from David's earliest memory, it was a soft brown, as fine as sand, with age seeping through it like smoke. Helen was from mid-Wales, lured from the countryside as a young girl in search of work. Like her husband, she was an elusive figure in the street, unconcerned with mixing or aping the norm. David was proud that his parents were different, but at times he hated them for it; he was allowed to lead an awkward and often lonely childhood. For his first eighteen years he walked a tightrope between wanting to be accepted, and being glad that he was not.

'He would like money, your father would,' Helen was fond of saying, when there was tension in the house, 'he would be alright then, with money.' Daniel's answer was a shrug of dumbness, and a slump into his armchair. David could not understand the accusation then, it seemed a natural enough aspiration, a rich father would have suited him well. At these times his mother referred to the Big House, often a target of her vitriol. It was the villa of the local colliery owner, a heavy fortress of stone that looked down on the village from its high site. The Rees family lived in it, they had resisted the combines that were buying up the pits, and maintained a patriarchal hold over the community. David remembered the Sunday walks over the hills, and the plod past the villa on the way home. Eyes were attracted to it like moths to a night lamp, some hostile, some envious, but none unaffected by its presence. 'That's the way to live, boy,' Daniel once muttered to him, 'looking down on the likes of us buggers.' Daniel talked occasionally of bettering himself, with money David assumed, but he never did so. The men of his generation had no means to do so, the only way out of the valley was to take the King's shilling.

It was after a Sunday tramp that David had his one talk with his father. He was halfway through his primary years.

'Come into the front room, boy,' Daniel said to him, 'away from all these women. I want to say something to you.'

The mystified David followed his father, searching his mind for wrongdoings. They sat opposite each other, in front of the cold grate, Daniel rolling a sliver of tobacco into smudged papers.

'You have got to have an education, boy. That's what I want to say. I don't want you down the pit. Go down there, and you'll stay down, like me.'

'Yes, dad.' An education. David's mind spun. And not to go down into the belly of the pit-monster.

'Aye,' Daniel continued, 'you'll be the first boy in this street to escape it.'

The first boy! David looked up at his father. Daniel sucked on his roll-up, rubbing one hand against the other.

'Don't know how we'll manage, mind, money gets tighter and tighter these days, but we've decided, your mother and me. You will come down the Hall with me on Saturday, join the library. Read, that's what you must do. It's free, if you're in the union, and it's all there, see. Everything under the sun they have on those shelves, so read your head off, and if you get a chance, grab it, and make the bloody most of it.'

David stared at his loquacious father. What strange man was this, talking to him with enthusiasm? Daniel tapped him on the shoulder, 'things will be better for you boy, they have to be.' David squirmed under the rare touch of his father's hand, but he felt affection surge out of it, and was confused. His mind was read.

'I know I don't say much to you, never will probably, words are hard for me, ask your mother.' There was another squeeze of his shoulder and his father left him, sitting in the dusk of an unlived-in room, wondering.

Daniel was true to his word, David joined the library and his father reverted to his distant role. David could not yet see that it was the stern duties of his work as provider that made this so. Whilst he doused the sleep from his eyes his father was under-ground, taking his first swing at the black wall, bent double, or on his knees grubbing, as often as not. When David got back from

13

school he was shooed away, so that Daniel could wash and eat in peace. David's young life was caught in a conspiracy of class and environment, normal for the time, and for the village. His mother had to serve as both parents, doling out love and discipline as best she could. For David she was always there, a solid presence, and neither party thought any more about it, mother and son each blind to the dangers.

David was a ready initiate into the art of reading. When others ran riot in the streets, he stayed in, poring over his books, tracing their words in the inadequate lamplight, seeking out the new ones in the dictionary his father had procured for him. From boys adventures he advanced rapidly. *The Coral Island* gave way to Dickens and Scott. He took comfort from Dickens's solid Victorian world. Much he did not understand but there was always a kinship there, even bleakness was heartening when experienced before the kitchen hearth. He imagined the characters: he was Pip, Oliver, and the Dodger; David was proud of his knowledge of the grown-up writer. The books were part of him, belonged to him, he liked to smell each new one, and run his hands along its binding. Mustiness became a mellow friend, it was always there and willing to share itself. Books were his childhood.

David's sisters left home when he was still young. They went into service, encouraged, if not forced to do so, by their father. 'Women should do women's work,' Daniel pronounced, 'Nowt else for them to do, anyway.' Mary went up to Surrey, a leafy, green and foreign land, David was told. Ruth went to work at the Big House, much to Helen's dismay, especially as Daniel had arranged it. It led to one of the few rows David ever witnessed between his parents. He looked up from one of his books to follow the action.

'Bowing and scraping to them.' Helen stood over Daniel, wringing a tea-cloth in her hands, her words half-choked sobs. 'How could you, Daniel, not enough for you to be scraping the earth on your hands and knees, now our Ruth has to join you, waiting on the Reeses hand and foot.'

Daniel's face reddened. 'Shut your row, woman, you're getting as bad as them down the Hall. What else could the girl do, eh? We need the money the girls will send home, for the boy here to stay on at school.'

David looked down at his book as his father walked around the table. 'Look, he is reading now.' His hand rested on David's shoulder. He saw the blackened nails embedded in the fingertips in broken mounds, and the collection of thin blue scars that made the hand like a fern.

'Let's have a bit of peace now,' Daniel said.

Helen turned to the stove, and stirred something vigorously.

2

'Crushed like a pancake old man James was,' one of the boys shouted out in the school yard, 'his eyes popped out like a fish's. My dad said.' David looked to see if Tony James was in earshot, but he had secreted himself in a corner somewhere. His father had been killed underground. Tony shared a desk with David in the primary school and all morning he had cried next to him, an almost noiseless whimper that the teacher ignored. It was a week after the fateful day but Tony cried on, he was ashamed of his father's death, and the way it marked him out. Now he was different, and known, and this made him cry. David learned a lesson from Tony, he vowed to himself that he would never stick out like Tony had.

Books took an even greater hold on him from this point, and they paid early dividends. David won a scholarship to the County Grammar School, the first boy in the village to do so. His success boosted Daniel, he saw the family sacrifice vindicated, and boasted of his son, on the rare occasions when he talked. 'My boy is down the County' would become a catchphrase, and David would be pushed on, kindly yet constantly by the family. It was an arrangement that suited him, he would be the one to escape drudgery, but they would all share in his freedom.

A decrepit school bus delivered David to the school on a wet Monday in September 1928, a frightened new boy, crisply turned out in blazer and cap, with grey short trousers and socks, comforted by the smell of his leather satchel. David's uniform had all but crippled the Hicks's finances. The building that greeted him was gaunt and cheerless, three storeys the colour of his socks, built at the turn of the century. It sat on the hill like a toad, a much greater world than the one he was used to.

David always remembered polished wood, wet clothes steaming on massive iron radiators, stale air pungent with sweating bodies and multiple farts. In his seven years there David saw only one woman, Mrs Dagg, the caretaker's wife. Dry Mondays were looked forward to, the time when Mrs Dagg hung out her washing in the garden of the school house. Boys strained necks for a glance at this ritual, praying for a flash of leg, or the wiggle of a buttock. Mrs Dagg became the beacon of David's burgeoning adolescence: he experimented with her many times in his mind; when the sun shone he looked down on that blonde head or saw the ample backside fight to get out of the too-tight skirt, like two angry fists clenched. He imagined Zola's women, and the new heroines of the cinema screen, and let his fantasies run, enjoying the excitement, and the residue of shame they left. Sometimes Lewis-Jones, the headmaster caught and caned a Mrs Dagg-watcher; David saw them returning from his study, their cramped walk back to the classrooms agonisingly long, announcing their fate to the whole school, and their classmates' averted heads. It made David wary in his spying.

He did reasonably well at his studies, and was considered diligent and dull, an honest plodder, in the shade of the brighter boys. Being in the background suited him, he read outside the schools' thin curriculum, advancing to Conrad and Lawrence, James and Mann, Whitman and Thoreau, and the new writers of his times. There was no plan to his reading, he ranged like a pig amongst husks, snuffling out whatever caught his eye on the library shelves. He looked for loners, outcasts, losers, anyone he could imagine into his own comfortable life. When Conrad wrote of the dark patterns of men David joined him; he inhabited his sultry lands as surely as if he had been Jim, or Kurtz, or the impenetrable Nostromo.

He began to write for himself, short stories about the valley, descriptive pieces that became cameos of his neighbours. Onto the page he worked immaturity, frustration and snobbishness, writing about things – work, for instance – of which he had no experience. The daily grind of the miner was a favourite theme, sometimes they were dignified workers, bonded together with honour, and dignity; then they were brutal, low-thinking men, sodden with drink and a thousand vices. Without knowing it, David wrote of his own dilemma: the need to belong and be a part of things coupled with his conceit at thinking himself better and different to the place that spawned him.

At seventeen David knew immeasurably more than any Hicks before him, and had been at the County school "an age", as his father put it. Daniel Hicks was saying it as he keeled over down the Hall, according to the men there. 'One minute he was going on like, about that boy of his, then the next, bang – he was down on the floor, gasping something terrible. We could do nothing for him. He just slipped away.' Daniel was the first Hicks to die of a burst heart, a disease for the changing times.

Helen was calm, through all the ensuing events she was not seen to cry once. 'A cold woman, that one' some muttered behind their hands. David remembered his mother sitting in the parlour. There was a far-away look in her eyes; she might have been trying to see where Daniel was now. David noticed what was in her hands, a blurred photograph of his father, taken years ago, when he had been young, and fresh. Helen turned it in her hands and gazed at the fire. As David turned to leave her she heard him and beckoned him into the room.

'At least he did not die down there, in the dark,' Helen tapped the floor with her foot, and drew David to her, holding him against her waist. He was old enough to be shy of her, but did not pull away. 'You are the man of the house now, David *bach*,' she murmured softly. 'Yes, ma'. He could not think of anything else to say.

Mary returned from Surrey and Daniel was buried in the drizzling gloom of an April morning, a bitter day of a winter stubbornly resisting its end. Daniel's bachelor brother Billy had made the arrangements. There was not much of a turn-out: a few men from the pit, and the family. They stood around the grave like sodden penguins, and listened to the Reverend Iolo Hughes cough his way through the service, feet apart on the slanting, greasy surface of the graveyard. The chapel clung to the side of the hillside, casting its shadow over the group. David tried to avoid the Reverend's spittle, and stood next to Billy until it was over. They each threw a handful of earth onto the coffin, making soft rattles like fingers drumming, then turned to trudge back down the hill. Daniel was left in the ground, his desire for peace granted at last. The graze of the gravediggers' shovels accompanied their departure, and the lone caw of a crow wheeling across the sky bade an eery farewell to David's father.

Billy tapped David as they walked. 'Well, I hope you've learned a lot down that fancy school of yours, boy. I'd see if I could get you a start down the pit, but there's no chance, things the way they are. There was twenty down, day after your father went, all after his place.'

Billy's words put more of a chill into David than the occasion or the weather. Was that what they expected him to do, go down the pit? It would make his years in school meaningless, and betray his father's hopes. Thoughts of any approaching responsibility filled him with dread; he felt panic rise up inside him, and struggled to control it.

The small group of mourners sat in the front room of the Hicks house. Billy had provided some beer, which he offered to David, and the few other men. David drank for the first time, and was disappointed by the flat bitterness of the liquid; it belied its soft colour, he thought. He sat in a corner and watched the men get a little drunk. His cheeks reddened with the flush of alcohol, and he found it hard to follow the disjointed talk, only snatches of it registering. 'Alright, wasn't he, bit of a loner mind, there would have been more come, but he wasn't much for the union'. Helen served thin sandwiches, and took no part in the talk.

'Not much for the union.' David thought on that. His father had appeared to be indifferent to the stormy politics of the valley, even to the point of disdain, although he was always affected by the strikes, lock-outs, and once by a demonstration in which he had been inadvertently caught. A policeman had crashed a truncheon onto Daniel's back as he tried to get through a crowd of angry men. This was what David had always thought but he knew now he could not be sure. There had been that one slight talk with his father, and what else? He did not know him, and felt the waste of this now. It had been easy to ignore the distance which existed between him and his father: there would always be time to get closer later, he had told himself, perhaps when Daniel had retired. He had put off any sharing of himself, denied his father any part of him. The beer sharpened David's self-awareness, why did he find it hard to think of his family as people? His parents were figures, playing the roles he expected of them, they revolved around him, it came to David that he had never thought about their happiness, or hopes. As he toyed with his glass he suspected he was selfish to the core. He shrugged, and tried to push guilt to the far reaches of his mind. It was Daniel's shrug.

These were David's rough memories of his early years. Try as he might he could not recall much about playing games, joining in, being a part of anything. All that came later, too late for it to be woven into childhood. He had passed a curious, and somewhat

19

blank first sixteen years, but he had accepted them now; distance had given him an understanding of his younger self.

He was fully grown by the time his father died. Tall and gangly, a good head above most of the men in the village, where ill-fed boys rarely grew taller than a policeman's shoulder, and fat was as rare as fresh meat. His hair, brown and thick, fell like a thatch over his forehead, a reaction against the cropped heads of his neighbours. Spots of colour highlighted his pale skin, intensifying when angry or nervous. He might have been taken for a consumptive, but had never been seriously ill, his constitution strengthened by his schooling. When other boys of his age were coughing up their first dust David was running around the playing field, chased by the voice of Butch Morgan, their violent Games Master. He had one distinguishing feature: at twelve he had tumbled down the bank of a brook and cracked his teeth on a fence post. His teeth grew unevenly after that. When he tried to clench them there was a gap on one side, as if each row was trying to escape the other. David was conscious of it, and rarely smiled, hiding his mouth behind his hand when nervous, so that his words came out in jumbled bunches.

To David's relief the Hicks women wanted him to stay in school. His sisters were proud of his privilege, and he basked in their adulation. Boys half his size trotted to the pit before dawn, while he lay abed, dreaming of the good life.

3

Throughout his first year in the sixth form David worried about the family finances. A solution arose in August when he managed to get a Saturday job at Vincent's Emporium. He was to serve in the shop, and help with the order book, when necessary. It was a compromise: David could stay on in school, and bring home some money.

Vincent was a prominent local businessman, with two shops, one at each end of the valley, standing like sentries to gather in the money of the unwary. 'If he misses you with one he'll get you with the other bugger,' local folk were fond of saying. Vincent was deaf to any pleas for credit and striking miners got short shrift from him. Vincent set his web for the small but growing middle class of the valley. Education secured the job for David – Vincent liked the idea of a grammar school boy serving in his shop.

David presented himself the first Saturday of his holidays, squirming in the tie his mother had begged him to wear. He stepped into the Emporium, to be greeted by Vincent.

'So there you are lad,' a hand was thrust in his. 'Well, not badly turned out, I must say. What do you think, Mrs Vincent?'

His wife sniffed down her nose at David and polished her counter. 'Don't ask me. You wanted the boy, can't think why, I'm sure.'

Vincent led David to one side. 'Don't mind her, lad. Likes to think she's a bit of a queen in the shop, she'll get used to you.'

David said nothing, but a fist of embarrassment knotted in his gut.

The Emporium was a large hollowed-out dome packed with the bric-a-brac of a general store, everything from laxatives to ladles. Vincent piled his goods on tall shelves, reached with a sliding ladder. Racks hanging from the ceiling held more items, things rarely requested. On one side of the shop was the food, rows of gleaming jars and glass cabinets displaying meats and cheeses. This was Mrs Vincent's domain; she left her husband, and now David, to deal with the hardware. David sold equipment about which he was totally ignorant at first, but he quickly learned to copy Vincent's sales pitch, becoming adept at faking knowledge. Eventually he took to inventing facts about the stranger implements and found that customers lapped it up. David dealt in illusion, and survived.

Despite its brisk turnover the Emporium reminded David of a mausoleum; he imagined it frozen in time, and exhibited to future generations. There was an air of decrepitude about the place, it clung to the past, like its owner. It became David's Saturday prison, and he resented every minute he gave it, walking the half-mile in the morning with a heavy tread. He saw the shop as the price he had to pay to stay out of the pit. There was a bonus however: Vincent had two daughters.

Charlotte and Emma Vincent were both beautiful, visions of loveliness for the village boys to lust after but never have, for they were Vincent girls. Emma aroused feelings in David which had simmered below his cool surface since his Mrs Dagg days. She was a few months older than him, in the last year of the Girls' Grammar School strategically placed at the opposite end of the valley to the Boys, invested with remote mystery by David's classmates. Emma was almost as tall as David, her figure bearing none of the signs of drudgery that so weighed down the village women. Her hair was flame-red, her eyes a blue-green that never ceased to dazzle David with their promise. Mrs Vincent was part Irish, and Emma echoed this.

Emma's sister was twenty-one, and engaged to marry Edward Rees, the son of the pit owner. She cut a distant figure and rarely came into the shop. When she did she never acknowledged David's presence, he was the paid help and that was that. David quickly judged Charlotte to be cold and shallow, but she was undoubtedly a beauty, her haughty face touched off with sparkling teeth and perfect skin.

The Emporium stayed open until nine on Saturdays, Vincent gleaning money to the last. 'People always want things late,' he told David, 'the women pop out, see, when their husbands are swilling ale. They always manage to keep a little back from them, and then they buy things they don't really want, just to spend it. And we're here to help them do it, boy.' David listened in misery to the hard-headed merchant. He wanted to see the man as a stupid grasper, insensitive and tasteless; but David was learning to be wary of easy judgements. It was comforting to see Vincent as a caricature of all that his books encouraged him to despise, but David thought of the mystery of his father, and tried not to let his own weaknesses cloud his opinions. This was always hard for him. Throughout the day Vincent grew rounder, his eyes more greedy. His corpulent frame solidified over his counter and time went very, very slowly. David got used to watching the last hour tick away, hearing each minute drop with regularity. Then he was free, and walking home, with his shillings safe in his pocket. Like Vincent, he did it for the money.

David worked through the winter of that year until he was nearly eighteen. He was in the last term of his schooling and his height had levelled off at just under six feet, the tallest Hicks ever. His school work had not troubled him for a long time – and he was no longer the only 'pit boy' in the school, other bright lads had filtered through into the junior forms. Ruth and Mary had not married, and Helen continued to take in all kinds of sewing work. With David's pittance and the girls' regular money, they managed. The pennies his mother gave him back from his day's pay David saved, he shared her trait of thriftiness and added copper to copper, saving for a good jacket. He had always wanted one. Although David was loath to admit it to himself he shared his father's longing for elegance. His mother scorned it, and turned on him angrily one Saturday night when he told her the sum required.

'Too much like your father, you are. Full of big schemes, he was, dressing up whenever he had the chance. Only they never got out of his head, those schemes, dreams, that's all they were. Don't you be following him, David Hicks, getting too big for your boots, just because you've had a bit of learning.'

David was taken aback at his mother's anger. 'I just want to look smart, ma, no harm in that, is there?'

'H'm. Maybe, if that's all it is, but don't go copying those toffs that come in the Emporium. You can better yourself without following the likes of Eddie Rees.'

She stormed of into her kitchen, leaving David to eat his supper alone. It was the first admonishment he had received from his mother for a long time, and came as a minor shock to him, a kink in the long chain of praise the women in his family had given him. He wondered what his mother really thought about things, then shrugged it off. It was easier to think of the jacket, the one in Sealey's window. His father had bought a suit there once, not drinking for a year to pay for it.

The jacket was part of David's plan to impress Emma Vincent. Emma helped him serve in the shop when Vincent popped out in the afternoon. After a shy start they began to talk, at first the usual feelers of adolescence, then, when confidence was gained, David talked freely of his books and stories. He enjoyed displaying his knowledge, and Emma seemed pleased to listen, when they could avoid the hawk-eyes of her mother.

Emma did not have the perfect symmetry of her sister, but there was an infectious quality in her smile, it was natural, without deceit, and David savoured it in the starchy atmosphere of the shop. He was attracted to qualities in Emma he found so hard to instill in himself. Her frank honesty beguiled him.

By May David was ready for his jacket, a brown single-breasted affair, a little sombre, but refined, he thought. He was fitted out for it on a Friday evening, after school. 'Fine big lad you have grown to, David,' Meredith Sealey lisped. 'There, that's a good fit, that is, perfect. Aye, make something of yourself, you will, take pride in your appearance. I've said as much to Mr Vincent, you're not like that lot down the terraces.' Sealey ignored the fact that David was one of 'that lot'. He fussed around David, intending to keep his customer for life, standing on his toes to give the jacket one last flick with his stubby hand. 'Can hardly reach you, *bach*.'

David's purchase was wrapped, and an account made. He would be another six months paying for it, a debtor at seventeen. This fact would be abhorrent to his mother but David was excited, the jacket was a symbol of the future, and now he possessed it. Sealey peered into his books, his nose close to the print. With his round spectacles he looked like an owl searching for prey. 'Here it is,' he said, 'your father's old account. Good suit, that was, he liked a bit of style, Mr Hicks did, for a miner.' With a flourish the tailor grasped David's hand and led him to the door. Sealey's palm was moist, the sweat of a sale was upon it. David had noticed with Vincent how the anticipation of profit excited, held him in its sway.

Helen held the jacket up to the fading light and felt its lining. 'Well, it's well made anyway. You'll look a right little gent in this, won't you?'. Her tone was chiding but not angry, she had come round to David's purchase, and shared a little pride in it now.

Uncle Billy was slumped down in David's armchair, smoking like a chimney, and exuding the beer fumes of the early evening. Since Daniel's death he had taken to visiting more.

'Duw, Duw, bit of a toff, aren't you boy?' Billy chuckled.

David reddened and said 'It's just an ordinary jacket, Billy.'

This made his uncle laugh all the more, a booming noise that ended in a cough.

'Killing yourself you are, Billy Hicks, all that drinking and smoking,' Helen muttered.

'Now then Helen girl, don't start. It could be worse, I might be wearing a jacket like that.' Billy collapsed into another fit of laughter and David walked out in disgust – and with a secret delight at the stir the jacket had caused.

'You shouldn't tease him like that, Bill,' Helen said.

'Oh, it won't hurt him. He's had it pretty easy so far, you know. It won't always be like that. Anyway, I was only joking, it's not a bad bit of cloth, actually.'

'You think I've spoiled the boy, don't you?'

'Well now, that's not for me to say, is it? I know one thing though, he'll have to shape up pretty sharpish, he's almost eighteen. God, I was an old hand down the pit by then.'

'I don't want him to go down there, ever.'

'Aye, maybe you're right there, girl. Right then, I'm off, I can hear the Anchor calling.'

'Drink. I don't know, don't you think of anything else?'

'Of course I do, lots of things, but I daren't tell you.'

Helen slashed at Billy with her tea-towel, but he was too quick. He turned as he was in the doorway. 'You know Helen, seeing the boy in that coat, took me back a bit, looked so much like Dan in it.'

'Yes, I know.'

There was a pause and Billy shuffled his feet.

'Right then,' he said. 'See you soon.' He opened the door. 'And let me know how David gets on with that jacket.'

'What do you mean?'

'You don't think he bought that thing just for himself, do you? If I know a thing about young chaps there'll be a girl somewhere, mark my words.'

Billy was gone before Helen could answer. She dismissed the notion, David had not bothered with girls at all, there had never been any mention of them, and he was far too sensible in his studies. Helen told herself this as she washed up, ignoring the tiny stab of jealousy that pricked her.

In the shop David hid his loathing for his job well; Vincent thought him a good asset, and did not perceive his distaste. David worked on the old man with a show of diligence, until he felt confident enough to ask if Emma could accompany him on a Sunday walk. They had talked furtively about it for sometime, but Emma did not think her father would consent to it. David tackled Vincent in the afternoon lull, when his wife was absent. Vincent stood back with his hands cupped in his waistcoat, his favourite debating stance.

'Walk out with our Emma, eh? Well, well, I don't know boy, Mrs Vincent would be dead against it, I'm sure of that. Emma, come here, what do you say to this young man?'

Emma stood before her father, eyes down.

'Would you like to walk out with David here?' Vincent was not angry. David took heart from this.

'Yes, I would dad,' Emma answered.

'You would, eh? Why?'

The question flustered Emma.

'We have a lot in common, Mr Vincent, with school and everything,' David said. Vincent was hooked on education, it was a favourite theme of his.

'Aye, schooling, that's true. Don't think I haven't noticed your little chats, poetry, all that stuff.' He stalked around the Emporium, a restless ringmaster revelling in his power. 'I'll think about it, I'll say no more than that for the time being.'

A few weeks later Vincent assented to the request, just as David had felt he would. His star was rising steadily with the old man.

'I'll be watching you, mind,' Vincent said, 'and Mrs Vincent will be watching me, I dare say, but you can go. But not for too long.'

They decided on immediate action, and planned a walk for the next day, taking advantage of the first sunny weekend of Spring. After his Sunday dinner David walked up to the Vincent house, wearing the jacket for the first time. The mud of the streets had dried to a fine black dust which stuck to the toes of his polished boots, and the air was warm on his face. He looked forward to it freshening on the ridge of the valley. They intended to walk to the top of it.

Emma's house lay two hundred yards below the Rees villa, a scaled down version of the Big House. David saw his image in the veneered oak as he braced himself to knock. He flicked his hair back from his forehead and the door opened and Emma greeted him with a shy smile. David returned it, and brushed his jacket nervously.

'You are right on time,' Emma said.

'Of course. Your father wouldn't like it if I wasn't.'

Vincent appeared behind Emma, cigar in hand. 'Make sure you are back by five, now,' he warned.

'Yes, of course, Mr Vincent.'

Three hours. That was a lifetime after the clandestine minutes they had snatched in the shop. Vincent watched them go, and from a window his wife also watched, glaring out at David like an angry crow; David wondered how Vincent had managed to persuade her.

Emma looked fine; her hair shone redder than ever in the open, she wore it long and loose today, shaking fire every time she moved her head. She walked almost on a level with David, easily the tallest girl in the village. David thought his jacket went well with her dress, a light grey one to welcome the summer, setting her eyes off perfectly.

They were bashful for a while, this was not the same as sharing the Emporium counter. 'We've picked a lovely day,' David said, 'perhaps we'll have a good summer.'

'Oh, I hope so, it's been so gloomy all winter.'

'Yes, the valley gets like that, doesn't it?'

David felt his talk so lame. He wanted it to be like the books, he wanted to flash ideas at Emma, to be different. 'I always feel I am hemmed in, by these.' He pointed to the hills around them.

Gradually their lost their shyness and talked easily, David letting his tongue loose, as they enjoyed the treat of sunshine. He led Emma out of the village by a back lane, and up the steepest slope of the valley, the Tump, as it was locally dubbed. It took them an hour to reach the top, where they sat in the thin grass, regaining their breath.

'It's the highest I have ever been,' Emma said.

'Oh, I come up here lots of times in the summer. It's a good spot for reading, and thinking.'

'Yes, it would be.'

'Look at the view, Em.'

The abbreviation came easily and naturally. David waved his arm about him as if it was his land he was showing off. He did indeed view the Tump as his kingdom, a place where people rarely came. They worked too hard to do so; this was an idler's place, a thinker's perch.

There were two worlds on view. Beneath them the valley sprawled, curving and twisting to the course of the river. David imagined a serpent warming itself in the first hot rays of the sun. The villages were its eggs, mottled with terraces. A sooty pall hung over it, fed constantly by the smokestacks that scattered the valley floor. Tips covered the lower slopes, advancing up the ridges in soft black waves, until forced to give up their hold on the steep sides. 'Nigger tits' the boys called them. The river caught the sun and gleamed silver for a moment, like a thread of silk. This day is a liar, David thought.

'You'd think the place was clean from up here,' he said, 'you can't see the filth.' There were eight pits in the valley, each one much the same, their winding wheels standing out like beacons. They were the cairns of the present. It was David and Emma's world, but they were high enough to see another one.

The sky was clear above the valley floor, free of the haze that clogged the lower reaches. It led their eyes down to the coast, a dozen miles away. They saw a soft grey band wavering on the horizon, dotted with black smudges that moved slowly across it, like beetles. These were the ships that came for the coal. David knew there was space down there, away from the hills, but it was a foreign land. Until the Federation began seaside trips, a few years back, few valley folk had ever seen the coast.

The sight of the sea always set fire to David's smouldering dreams. Emma was still beside him, he could feel the rise and fall of her breasts as she breathed in the untainted air. He felt a flush of desire as he put an arm around her, ready to snatch it back at once. She gave it a welcoming squeeze, and he pressed hers, more confidently.

'Wouldn't you like to get away from all this, Em?' David nodded his head at the valley. 'Look at it, one big slag heap.'

'I don't know, it's not all bad, it's nice up here, and – '

David did not let her finish. 'But there's so much to see in the world, so much to do. Nothing changes here, only the tips grow. There's no future for a man here.' David expected Emma to agree with him but she answered differently.

'My father has made a future here, with his shops. He says a person should stay put, make something of himself on his own patch.'

David bit his tongue, but it made him burn to hear her echo Vincent's sentiments. Charlotte was a true Vincent but Emma, his Emma, he wanted to be different, to be like him. Emma talked on freely now.

'We've had an education, David, we've been lucky, not like Dad, he has had to work so hard for what he's got.' David felt himself getting angry.

'You should think of going into business here David, after school. Perhaps my father would help you, he thinks a lot of you, you know. He would not have let us go for a walk otherwise.'

'Business. Is that how you see me, a future man of commerce? That's the last thing I want to be, Emma. I want to see some of the world, get away from this place.'

'That's for the likes of Edward Rees,' Emma said softly.

'Why should it be, though? Why should they have it all? Don't tell me he's ever worked hard. Anyway, aren't we all born equal, that's what Hughes is always saying down the chapel.'

Emma sat besides him like someone waiting out a storm. David felt frustration, and disappointment. Emma reminded him of his father, she had the same passive acceptance of her lot, leaving the living to someone else. Yet she made him feel inferior in a way he could not fathom. It was as if she had been given something he had not, an inner calmness protected her. She did not want too much. In the Emporium Emma had seemed so much in tune with him, now she talked like the shopkeeper's daughter she was. Selfishness fed David's mood, he wanted Emma to live up to his fantasies and amplify his own hopes. He thought only to take from her.

David shrugged and lay back, his anger subsiding into silence. The sun caught in Emma's hair, sifting it with light, he felt her shoulder warm against his as she looked out to the far sea, eyes wide and bright with her thoughts. He ran his hand through the luxury of her hair and she leant against him, easily. They had walked out together many times, David felt, their time in the shop had given them a head start. He pulled Emma's head towards him and they kissed for the first time, a gentle brush of lips that frightened her at first. She stiffened and drew back, but David pulled her to him, and kissed her again. Emma's body sunk under his, undulating against him like a warm wave. He crushed hers with his own, surprised at the ease of her surrender. Lost in the maze of Emma's hair David felt released for the first time in his life.

Emma breathed heavily and moaned that it was wrong, but David smothered her warnings. He felt the need to dominate her, he wanted total power over this girl. He began to fumble in her clothing, looking for things to unfasten. Emma fought him, then welcomed him alternately, struggling to control her own aroused state. David managed to caress her breasts, delighting in their warmth and softness.

'I won't end up no shopkeeper, and you won't be no shopkeeper's wife,' he gasped. Emma seemed to come to her senses with these words. With a strain she pushed David away.

'Stop, please David.'

David tried to hold her again, but he halted when tears came to her face.

'I know you want to, why shouldn't we?' he said.

'It's wrong. This shouldn't be happening,'

Emma put her hands to her eyes, hiding them from him. David felt the stab of guilt as he calmed down.

'Don't cry, Em. I'm sorry, I got carried away. I like you so much.'

He reached out a hand and held one of hers.

'If my father ever found out,' Emma murmured.

David smiled inwardly at the thought, he was exhilarated, a little shamed and afraid, but exhilarated. He knew Emma would be his now, it was just a matter of time.

'I think I love you Emma,' he said quietly.

At first he thought she had not heard him, there was a keen wind whistling off the top of the Tump. Then she turned and leaned against him.

'Oh David, you hardly know me.'

'Yes I do, all those Saturdays together, and now. I know that I love you.' It was easier to say the second time, his mind told him not to say it, but he ignored it. 'Don't you love me?' The question brought a fresh wave of sobbing. 'Well?'

'Yes,' Emma said, after a while, 'yes, I do, David.' They embraced without moving or saying anything for a long time, the wind cool on their backs.

'We had better get back,' Emma said, 'or we'll be late.'

'Yes, alright.'

David stood up, and put his jacket back on. It had lain under Emma, and was now crumpled, and stained with grass. Emma tried to smooth it out with her hand. 'Not new now, is it?' David muttered, hardly able to conceal his annoyance. They walked back down the Tump, Emma excited and talkative, David lost in thoughts of himself.

Vincent was waiting for them on the doorstep. David feared a ticking off, but the old man was amenable.

'Had a nice time, then?' he asked.

'Yes thanks, Mr Vincent, we took advantage of the weather.'

'Aye, its been a grand day, don't have many of them, do we? Come inside boy, for a second.'

Vincent ushered him in, and Emma slipped away into the house.

'I'll see you soon, David' she said formally.

'Yes, see you soon,' he answered.

David was left with Vincent's arm on his shoulder. He glimpsed a gloomy interior from his position in the hall. Large ornaments perched at various spots, to catch a visitor's eye. There was carpet everywhere, the most David had seen.

'Look David, I want to have a little chat with you,' Vincent said. 'Bit of business, you might say. You'll be finishing down the County soon, done very well too, by all accounts.'

David was surprised at the old man's interest, two conquests in one day.

'I want to have a chat about your future, our future, you might say.'

'Yes, of course, Mr Vincent, I'd like that.' Lying was becoming easy.

'Good, good, I'll say no more then, not now, Mrs Vincent will want me for tea. I'll see you next week, in the shop.'

'Yes, goodbye, Mr Vincent.'

That night David sat in his father's old armchair, close to the fire, which spluttered a red glow through the parlour, like the pithead at night, or the sun dying at the end of this Sunday. He was lulled into a doze by the rhythmic clicking of his mother's knitting needles. She sat close to him, humming away, content. The climb of the Tump and the sight of the sea brought back memories of David's first and only trip to the coast, one sticky morning in August, ten years ago. He preferred to think of this rather than his behaviour with Emma.

They had set off in a special train, organised by the Miners' Federation. It was the one time David could remember his family doing anything together. His father wore his best suit from Sealey's, despite the hot day, and his Sunday cap, which rested precariously on his shock of hair. Ruth and Mary wore bright frocks and excited faces, but his mother looked the same as always in her thin coat of quiet brown.

It was a day of new experiences for David, a day when he felt his first rush of freedom. He remembered being ashamed of his father. All the parents joined in the games except his, and when the men went off to the pubs Daniel remained, sitting stiffly on the newspapers he had brought, in waistcoat and trousers. His sisters took him along a flat beach, which spread out endlessly before his young eyes, like a yellow fan. There were dunes at one end, and a cluster of black rocks at the other. They looked for creatures in the pools, probing the murky surfaces with sticks, ready to jump back with a squeal if any salty denizen challenged them.

There was so much space here for a boy to lose himself in, there was no coal dust and they could see and feel the sun clearly. It was like being on the Tump all the time. David envied those who lived here, and the lives they must lead.

'Why can't we live here, ma?' he asked, when they got back to their spot. 'It's great here. Can't we live here?'

'Hush, David, your father is sleeping. We live where we live. There is no work here, no pits.'

'But people live here, don't they?'

'Quiet now, or we won't come again.'

That day passed too quickly, the train pulled David back to his dark valley, disgorging the trippers onto a drab station platform. The village welcomed them back with great gouts of smoke from the chimneys, and a fine black rain began to fall. It poured over them, claiming its children once more.

4

David made more trips to the Tump with Emma as spring turned to early summer. His relationship with her was established, no longer village gossip. Their Sunday walks took on a pattern, the climb to the ridge, the sinking down into their favourite hollow, a little argument sometimes, then the lovemaking. David wore Emma's resistance to a thin thread of denial which he finally snapped in July.

David had sat the last of his examinations, an English paper which he breezed through. Emma was a great boost to his ego and confidence. He was coming to the end of his seven years of grammar schooling, and life was almost sweet for him, full of promise without commitment.

They ignored the threat of rain and hauled themselves to the top of the Tump. Emma was full of future plans, arranging things neatly, nest-building. When David was silent she took it for agreement. David was to have tea with the Vincents the following week, and Emma saw this as a formal assent to their pairing.

'I'm sure Dad wants to offer you something in the business,' she said, as they settled into the grass, 'he has dropped a few hints recently.'

David feared Emma was right, although the old man had not had the promised talk with him. He sat with his hands hunched around his chin, looking out to the coast.

'You are very quiet,' Emma said. She touched his hair with her hand, causing David to turn round. His face was flushed

'Emma, I want you so much I can't stand it any longer.' He gripped her hands in his own.

'It's not easy for me either, but we must wait. We aren't even engaged yet.'

'But I can't wait, Em, not any longer. It's torture.'

He pulled her to him and kissed away her complaints, and this time he did not stop. He undressed Emma surely, having learned where everything was now. When she fought him he stopped, then went on, until his goal was reached. Emma stopped resisting and returned his passion, matching David's fervour with her own as they wrestled in the hollow.

Emma cried out words in David's ear but he was deaf to them. He knew he should be careful but something inside spurred him on: throw all care to the wind, it said, go on, go on. Emma screamed like the keening of the wind, light breaths of pain and love came after, sighs that gradually faded to silence. David felt such power as he looked down on Emma's moistened face.

'That was wonderful, Em,' he murmured.

'You should have been more careful, I told you to. Didn't you hear me, I told you so many times.'

'It will be alright, don't worry.'

David sat up and pulled his jacket about him. Emma asked him that question again. 'You do love me, don't you David?' She rubbed her face in his shoulder. He felt the faintest core of doubt in her, intuition perhaps.

'You seem so remote now, as if you were someone else,' Emma said.

'Don't be daft, I'm here, with you. Of course I love you, I wouldn't have done it otherwise.' She will believe me because she has to, David thought.'

They descended the Tump, David in triumph, Emma fearful and in love. A fine drizzle followed them back to the village, soaking them slowly.

'Bye bye, Em,' David said as they reached her home, 'and don't worry. I'm glad we did it, aren't you?'

Emma did not answer as she went quickly into the house. 'See you in the shop,' David called after her.

He walked home with a spring in his step, whistling a tune between his teeth. He greeted his mother cheerfully and sat down in the armchair, still whistling.

'Had a nice day then, David Hicks?' his mother asked.

David handed her his drenched jacket. She tut-tutted. 'You'll ruin the cloth, getting it wet like this. Not like you lad, you are usually more careful.'

'Yes ma, I am, aren't I?' David put his hands behind his head and stretched lazily.

A week later he presented himself for tea at the Vincents. It was an awkward affair for him, sitting at a table almost as big as the Hicks's kitchen. He sat opposite Mrs Vincent and Charlotte, like a vulture's dinner, but he had the confidence to deal with them now, and he had his secret. The room was ornate with trinkets, they filled every available space, acquisitions of Mrs Vincent. Vincent himself was friendly and welcoming, full of 'my boys' and beaming smiles. Emma was shy in the presence of her parents.

David watched Vincent shovel food into his mouth, trapping morsels on his chin, a crumb of sandwich, the currant of a cake. You have not the slightest inkling of what I have been doing with Emma, David thought, none of you have.

'The future', Vincent spluttered, 'that's the thing, my boy. To look forward. We have been through bad times, but we are coming out of them, slowly. In a few years things will be really moving again. You are just the right age to take advantage of it, David.'

'Yes, Mr Vincent.' David sensed the old man wanted a son to celebrate in his commercial glory.

'Come into the study with me, we'll have a smoke, and a chat, away from all these women, eh?' Emma gave him a smile of encouragement as he followed Vincent out of the room.

In Vincent's male sanctum they sat in club chairs, which were hard and smelt of new leather. David accepted the cigar he was offered. 'You're old enough for one now, lad. Be a man soon.' David copied Vincent and cut off one end. He inhaled directly Vincent lit it for him, and sucked the smoke into his lungs. It was as disappointing as his first beer, and he almost gagged, yet David knew he would be a smoker. He liked the feel of the cylinder between his fingers, it felt friendly, like a pen, and it was a good prop to hide behind.

'Now look, David,' Vincent said, 'you've been in the shop for a twelve month, just about. I've watched you carefully, and I think you're a natural, boy. Great with my regulars, you are. Oh, I know you are set on that teachers place, but there's a good future here for you. I've plans, big plans, there's room for more shops in this valley, my shops. People always need what I sell, I've made sure of that.'

'I'm sure you have, Mr Vincent.' David coughed on his smoke, and felt his eyes water. Vincent laughed.

'Bit of strong stuff that is, from Cuba, the very best they are.

Anyway, the long and short of what I am saying is that I need a good man, see, someone with a knack for the business, and an education. You fit the bill well, David.'

Vincent halted, and sucked on his cigar. The irony of what the old man said was not lost on David. He smiled at Vincent, satisfied with his deceit.

It would soon be time for him to cut loose from Emma, and her father. Lewis-Jones would give him a good testimonial, as the boy who wanted to better himself, and his mother and sisters would help, as always. In Vincent's study David dreamed of the milestones he would reach.

'Well, what do you say?' Vincent said.

'I don't know what to say, Mr Vincent. I'm very flattered. I have thought of the training college, my mother thinks that a good idea, but I'll talk to her about your offer.'

'Alright, but don't take too long, mind.'

David was satisfied with the outcome, he had not promised anything. He crushed the butt of the cigar into an ashtray and left the house. Emma joined her father at the front door, to bid him farewell. Her eyes asked if everything had gone well, and his answered yes. Vincent was buoyant, and clasped them both with his hands.

'This young man of yours will make a fair businessman, lass.'

'I'm sure he will, dad.'

David stopped to wave back at the gate. There was no sign of Charlotte, or Mrs Vincent.

A dry July met David's release from school. He passed all his papers without difficulty. Helen was proud of her scholar son and even told the neighbours about his success, but they were not much interested, and received the news blankly, without jealousy. The street had grown used to the different ways of the Hickses, and their book-reading boy who worked down the snotty Emporium. What David had learned did not touch their lives at all.

Mary returned for a few days holiday and it was decided to have a small party – unheard of in the Hicks household. After much debate in the kitchen David was persuaded to ask the Vincents. He winced at the thought of having them in the house but went along with his mother's wishes. Until now he had kept Emma away from her – they had met a few times in the shop, that was all. To have Emma in his house for a whole afternoon would be dangerous. The party would be the largest family gathering since Daniel's death. Billy was invited, to David's dismay, for he was becoming active in local politics and was Vincent's antithesis in every way.

'Does Billy have to come, ma?' David said, as Helen made her plans for the event.

'Of course he does, he's the only uncle you have, and he has been good to us since your father died.' David paced the kitchen childishly.

'I know what's wrong with you, David Hicks, you are ashamed of this house, and the people in it. Ashamed of your mother too, are you?'

'Don't be silly ma, it's not that; it's just a lot of fuss, that's all.'

'Well, you had better get used to fuss, young man. You are courting now, and you can't have one without the other.' Helen dismissed the matter with a wave of her ever-present cloth, and David did not pursue it.

To David's surprise Vincent readily assented to the get-together.

'Aye, why not,' he said, 'chance to meet everyone, eh?'

He shouted across the shop. 'Hear that, Mrs Vincent, we've been invited to David's house this Sunday, to celebrate his results.' His wife sniffed and glared at David, then floated to the storeroom with a ruffle of her skirts. Vincent winked, 'Takes her time to get to know someone, she does, it's all been a bit of a surprise for her, you and our Emma.' A shock more like, David thought.

'Can you come at four then, Mr Vincent, four tomorrow?'

'Aye, we'll be there, lad, chance to give the new motor an outing. Right, go and serve Mrs Pritchard over there.'

Sunday turned out to be a rare day for David. Helen had a notion to go to chapel, a place seldom visited by the Hicks. She preferred the humblest place of worship in the village, a squat building of corrugated iron, known to everyone as the 'shed'. It was a baptist chapel that hugged the bottom of a coal tip. The chapel had lost its absolute grip on the village long ago, but still drew respectable congregations, when a notable preacher visited.

They sat at the back, on a hard wooden bench designed to make people squirm. Helen and his sisters sat inside of him, allowing him space to stretch out his long legs. They listened to

Iolo Hughes blast the ungodly. Iolo was a tiny man, clothed in a black suit that smothered him, his well-scrubbed head barely able to struggle out of it. But he had the voice of a giant, a quivering baritone that boomed around the tin walls like a gong being struck.

The preacher's message never changed, and few people escaped his diatribe. The rich were hammered because they were rich and worshiped at the feet of Mammon; the poor caught it for the drunken, lustful lives they led. Everyone was ripe for saving. The preacher cast his bloodshot eyes around his flock as he spoke, looking for the particularly sinful, the boys still drying-out from Saturday night, the suspected adulterers, the husbandless mothers. He noticed the Hicks family and gave Helen a nod of acknowledgement. Iolo made a point of talking to them after the service.

'Good to see you here, Mrs Hicks, and with all the children. David too, you're a rare visitor, *bach*.' The preacher thrust his face within inches of David's. 'I hope all this education has not taken you away from the Lord, boy. Learning's a wonderful thing, but it can lead to unclean thoughts, cynicism. People get to think they know more than the Almighty himself.'

'Of course not Mr Hughes,' David answered.

'Glad to hear it, glad to hear it. Remember, a man without God is a rudderless man, drifting through a sea of evil, to nowhere.'

David tried to avoid Iolo's spittle, and suppressed a smile at the old man's fervour. The preacher said goodbye with a flourish of his hat. David watched him stride off to the next village, a jackdaw, looking for worms.

At the appointed time the Vincents arrived in their Riley motor car, causing a minor stir in the street. People were used to the ancient two-seater of the Doctor, but had never seen anything as grand as Vincent's new car. Children gathered around it, whistling, one tried to touch the gleaming coachwork, but Vincent stopped him in his tracks with a bellow. David ushered his guests inside, quickly. Mrs Vincent passed through the door, wearing a hat that resembled a bowl of fruit. 'Charlotte has a prior engagement,' she told David tartly. Vincent grinned, and pushed Emma before him. She looked lovely in a dress of pale yellow, but her face was tired.

'Nice to be visiting you, lad,' Vincent said, souring his wife's face further, and in a lower voice, 'eh, the car will be alright outside, won't it?'

'Yes, I don't think anyone can drive around here, Mr Vincent.'

They went into the front room, where a fire blazed in the grate, despite the season. Vincents and Hickses sat down like two opposing teams, and David formally introduced everyone, although they had all met over the years. The village was not large enough for strangers. Helen had provided the best food she could afford, rows of neatly cut sandwiches lay before them, with a mound of cakes on either side. Vincent glowered at Billy, who was already seated. Billy stoked up his pipe, Vincent replied by lighting up one of his Cuban cigars. Both reached for the bottled beer.

David let the conversation drift around him without concentrating on what was being said. He supped his beer, which he found he was getting a taste for, and kept silent. There were brief inquiries into family histories, a little gossip, then the eating began. David was surprised at the way Helen handled the Vincents, she was confident and not awkward as he had expected. She treated the Vincents as equals, not the betters they tried to be. When Mrs Vincent listed her possessions she listened politely.

Emma was pale and looked strained, as if she had gone without sleep. David put it down to the occasion, and gave her a half smile, which she returned. Vincent was on about his favourite theme, as soon as the food was consumed. 'We must look forward,' he said, 'there's a lot of prospects in the valley if people are allowed to get on with things'. Vincent glanced at Billy when he said this, but the old miner remained silent as the shopman gave his views on business, politics and anything else that came into his head. Billy drank steadily throughout, glancing up from his mug to cast a wry smile about him from time to time. Although they would never admit it, Billy and Vincent were men out of a similar mould, both with an unshakeable, prickly belief in their vision of life.

'Well Mr Vincent,' Billy said, 'that was a nice little speech you've given us, unasked for, I might say.' He ignored Helen's warning stare. 'What you said earlier, about people being allowed to get on with things, you mean letting the rich get away with murder, don't you? Free enterprise, aye, the freedom to fleece the poor, fix the pits, do anything they want. I don't blame you for wanting that – you are on the right side of the fence, aren't you?'

'I resent that, Hicks,' Vincent said, 'but it's the type of talk I expect from you. I've heard of your doings in the village. Troublemaking would be a good word for it. Moscow Billy they call you now, don't they?'

Billy gave a mock salute, and started to reply, but Helen stopped him.

'Bill, we don't want this political talk here, keep it for down the pub.'

She wiped the drops Billy had spilled onto the tablecloth, and both men's anger subsided. They sat quietly, and a little shame-faced.

'You can bring the dessert in now, Mary,' Helen said.

David became sleepy as the room grew stuffy with heat and smoke. Soothed by the beer, he dozed off. After a few minutes he was startled into alertness by Billy digging him in the ribs. 'Here's a fine one, passed all his exams and can't even stay awake.' All eyes fastened on David, making his face glow. He saw the reproachful look Emma gave him from across the table. Helen came to his rescue. 'He has been working very hard this year.'

After this David tried to pay more attention. He learned of Edward Rees's trip to the continent, and felt a surge of jealousy that Rees should be living out his own dreams of travel, and escape. Vincent brought him into the conversation.

'Isn't that right, David,' he said, 'what I was saying about the future?'

'Yes, Mr Vincent.'

David caught Billy's half-sneer in the corner of his eye.

'Look ahead, Mrs Hicks, that's what I've been telling your boy in the shop, he's had an education, that's very useful, very useful indeed. Now he must make something of himself.' Vincent paused, anticipating Helen's agreement.

'I'm sure he knows that, Mr Vincent,' she said.

'Aye, aye, but young men need guidance. David could do well in the business, I've told him as much. Could do very well.'

Billy interrupted. 'As a shopkeeper, you mean?'

'Well, what better start could he want? I suppose you think going down the pit is better?'

'What I think is better is letting the lad steer his own course.'

Helen began to serve more tea, noisily, and things calmed

down again. The end came rather limply. Billy and Vincent were a little drunk, much to the disgust of the women. Mrs Vincent looked at her husband with eyes that said he would pay later. She made no attempt to hide her relief at leaving, and made no reciprocal arrangements with Helen.

'Very nice, Mrs Hicks,' she said, as she drew her family through the front door, like a hen herding chicks, 'very nice I'm sure.'

When Emma passed David she whispered, 'I must see you tomorrow, please come tomorrow.' David smiled a lazy smile and said he would, but he did not pay much attention to the urgent tone of her voice.

Billy left with the Vincents, patting David as he lurched into the street. 'Now watch it boy,' he joked, 'Vincent will have you dishing out the butter permanent, with a nice little pinny on too.' Billy laughed his way up the street, then turned to bid them a beery farewell. He doffed his cap at Mrs Vincent, who feigned not to notice. The Vincents huddled into the Riley and Vincent crashed the gears as the car heaved up the street, catching the sun on its top as it went. David saw Emma turn and look back through the window, he raised his arm, then let it drop again.

'That Billy,' Helen muttered, 'get himself into trouble with that mouth of his, one day.' David left the women to clear up and sat in his armchair to resume his snooze. Peace descended on the house, David let it soak into him with relish.

The next morning he went for one of his solitary walks along the valley ridge. The day was fine, with a fresh wind making walking comfortable. He reached the Tump quickly, and stopped there for a while, in the usual hollow he shared with Emma. She was working full time in the Emporium now. Her schooling had come to naught, David thought. His days were free and idle, a brief taste of breathing space for him to savour, long days dawdling in the sun, with books.

It was shaping up to be the best year he could remember. School was over and there was a letter from the training college in his pocket. He had been accepted to start there in September. He had not told anyone yet, he wanted to enjoy the news throughout the day. Emma would have to know, that would be difficult, but David let that irksome thought drift from his mind, and concentrated on his poem.

Attempts at verse were his new interest. They followed on naturally after his stories. He had a set pattern: first a delve into some anthology to get in the mood, then the sharpening of pencils, a few licks, and a few lines. If the words did not come he gave up easily, so he did not write much. He read the work of others, and dreamt of what he might write, later.

David lay on his back and watched a buzzard circle overhead, arcing the sky with a delightful curve, masterfully descending the air currents. It was a consummate airman. It would kill that morning; something small and furry would shriek its last as the talons struck. He thought himself up there, with the bird; he borrowed its power, and flew with it.

Obeying Emma's request, David dropped by the Emporium on his way back. She was helping her father count the stock, putting down the numbers he shouted by the names of the goods in the ledger. Vincent clung to the ladder like a giant spider. He climbed down and shook the shelf-dust from his clothes.

'Nice little do yesterday, David. Get everything down, Emma?'

'Yes dad.'

'Good. Well I suppose you want to take a stroll with your young man. Better get off then before your mother gets back. Half an hour only mind.'

Vincent continued his counting, licking his pencil as he went. There was a bubble of spittle around the old man's mouth, David had an image of a weasel raiding a nest, yolk dripping from its fangs.

It was a pleasant afternoon so they walked over to the weir, a black waterfall that directed the sludge of a river through the village. The water, where salmon had once spawned, was now little more than liquid coal. Emma was tense, and shivered a little, despite the warming rays of the sun.

'Well, what's up then?' David asked, 'you were a bit quiet yesterday.'

'I told you to be careful, I told you to. What are we going to do?' Emma blurted out these words to him in a jumble, and tears quickly followed them. David looked around to see if anyone was watching, but they were alone on the footbridge. He felt an emptiness in the pit of his stomach as he watched the swirling water dash on the rocks below.

'What do you mean?' he said, without meeting Emma's eyes.

'You know what I mean. You said it would be alright, you were being careful. It was wrong, David, we were doing wrong.'

She was sobbing heavily now, trying to hold onto David. Her breath came in gulps.

'I'm going to have a baby, David, our baby.'

He did not know what to say to her, his senses reeled, he wanted to tell her she was mistaken, he wanted to run. For one crazy moment David thought to deny the baby was his. A baby. He felt such panic. The girl a few doors down had one last year, without knowing the father. He remembered the sneering gossip, the self-righteous judgements. That girl went away somewhere. David thought of his plans and felt very sick, and all the time Emma was crying. He patted her arm, but could not bring himself to hold her. His own guilt made her repulsive to him, but he tried to hide it the best he could.

'Don't worry, Em,' he said, lamely.

'What are we going to do?'

'I don't know, I must think.'

'We'll have to tell my parents, your mother.'

'Yes, yes, but not yet.'

'If only we'd waited. We should have waited. David, you seem so far away, like a stranger almost. You will stand by me, won't you?' She crushed herself to him, and he held her now, gingerly.

'Of course I'll stand by you. Don't be daft. It's the shock, that's all... stand by you, what type of man wouldn't?'

Emma searched his face anxiously.

'Come on, we'd better go,' David said. He tried to look supportive as walked back, but he felt the valley mocking him. The hills that had pointed away to his future that morning closed around him, their ridges scarred fingers that held him tightly in their grip.

He left Emma at the Emporium and made his way home. As he neared his house the dread intensified, and again David felt the urge to run. In the kitchen Helen picked up his mood, and watched him closely.

'Everything alright, *bach*?' she asked, as she stirred a teapot.

'Yes.'

'Haven't had a row with Emma, have you?'

David seized the opportunity.

'Aye, a bit of one. Nothing really.'

'I thought so. Well, don't look so downcast, David, you are bound to argue now and again. It's nothing to be ashamed of. Come on, eat your tea.'

Helen hummed to herself as she fussed around the table, clicking her tongue at David's lack of appetite. She was proud of her son, and content at the way things were going. In a few years he would be a teacher, a professional man, happily married, and giving her grandchildren. The house had been quiet for such a long time, and Helen worried that her daughters were heading for spinsterhood. The valley was no place for women on their own.

She looked at David sitting in Daniel's old armchair, and saw the frightened little boy she had cajoled to school, she felt the grip of his hand in her skirts. David was past eighteen, an age when most of the village boys were hardened workers, and some of them married. He was not like them. Her boy was going to amount to something, as Daniel had always wanted.

The next few weeks David lived on his nerves. Desperately he continued to prepare for college, telling himself it was not hopeless, and he continued to reassure Emma. The more desperate he became, the more his tongue ran away with promises of commitment, and love. Emma's condition would soon be known to all, and her presence was unsettling, she was beginning to sense his diffidence, and hear the increasingly hollow ring of his words. Vincent was also pressing for an answer, David found it hard to keep stalling him. He promised a decision by the end of August. One night, it went from the shop weighed down with the need to tell of his plight. It was too much to bear alone, and David felt keenly for the first time his absence of friends. He changed course and cut across to Billy's house, a ramshackle cottage close to the pit. It caught all the smells and rumble of the workings, as if the house itself was underground. Billy, just opening the door with his hat on, was surprised to see David.

'David boy, we are honoured, I must say. I was just going down the Anchor for a few pints, coming?'

David shook his head and stood on the doorstep. Now that he was there he did not know what to say to Billy. He feared his uncle's wit.

'Well, don't just stand there, like a man who has found a penny and lost a bob, get yourself in. I can see you want a chat.'

Billy ushered David into a tiny kitchen, where the air was heavy with coal and tobacco smoke. Old, unwashed clothes were strewn around, singly and in heaps, entangled with newspapers and walking sticks. Miners' gear, dogeared books from the library, cheap editions of Lenin, Marx and people David had not heard of, piled up on the table. It also supported a pot of jam and half a loaf of grubby bread, patterned with coaly fingerprints. Bread, beer and jam made up his staple diet. Billy's home had not the slightest shred of organisation, but David found it welcoming in his present state of mind. There were no rules here, he felt.

'Bit of a mess, I s'pose, isn't it?' Billy said. 'Don't tell your mother mind, I don't want Helen down here checking up on me!' He pushed his mongrel Betty off a chair and dusted it down for David. 'There you are, park your backside on that, best chair in the house.'

The dog growled at David and slunk under the table, watching him carefully with doleful eyes.

'Betty is the same as me,' Billy said, 'not used to people calling. Right, let's have it then, what great weight has dropped on you?'

After a faltering start David found himself telling Billy everything. He felt relief when his secret poured from him, but it did not last long. Billy was not surprised by the news.

'Aye, I thought it might be something like that. Got Emma into trouble, eh? I could see that coming a mile off. Going to cause a lot of bother this is, boy.'

David nodded miserably as Billy paused to dig out his pipe.

'What shall I do, Bill? I don't know how to tell ma.'

'Aye, that's going to be tricky.' Billy stopped fiddling with his pipe and looked hard at David. 'David, I think it's time you heard a few home truths, things that stick out a mile outside your house. First off, you've been spoiled rotten, for as long as I can remember. First by Daniel, then your mother, even your sisters. Never been such a blue-eyed boy in the village. Maybe I should have said something long ago, when your father died, but Helen is a strong-willed woman, and you aren't my boy. I've watched you over the years. It started with all that book-reading, nothing wrong with that, I do a bit myself now, as you can see, but you do damn-all else. You put on all these airs and graces as if you are something out of a bloody book yourself. You can't wait to get out of the valley, can you, and turn your back on your own kind? You despise old man Vincent but you don't mind being around him if it suits your purpose. You've become a devious little bugger, boy, and a proper little snob to boot.'

David felt his face flush as Billy paused to light up his pipe. This was not what he had expected, no-one had ever talked to him like this before.

'Life has a funny way of upsetting the applecart,' Bill continued, 'as you are about to find out.' David sat in silence, with his head down. 'Look lad,' Billy said, 'you are a silly bugger more than a bad bugger. You have learned a lot of things down that school, but you know nowt about life, not yet. Your education is a good thing, it could be useful to the people here, your people. Perhaps you will think on this now, for you won't be going anywhere, be sure of that. Marriage is the only course now, your mother and the Vincents will see to it.'

David heard Billy's words like a man receiving the ultimate sentence; each comment was a barb that skewered his insides.

'Feeling mighty sorry for yourself, aren't you?' Billy said. 'Thought I'd give you an easy ride. You were well overdue for a bit of truth David, hurts doesn't it? I think I'd better come over with you now, see Helen. Come on, let's get going.'

They walked to David's house as the dusk gathered. Billy pulled Betty along besides them, reining her in each time she strained at the leash. He rarely took her to the Hicks house, for she was getting old and smelly, and a bit moth-eaten, like Billy himself. He was taking her now for moral support. He feared Helen's reaction as much as David, just as he felt more for the boy than he had shown. After all, he had been quite a lady's man in his time, only he had got away with it – that was the only real difference.

Billy thought the situation interesting. It might be the making of the boy. The movement needed people like him, educated, with a gift for words. Knowledge had begun to fascinate Billy, but he knew most of it was out of his reach. He read slowly, tracing words with his fingers and taking an age to understand his books, if he understood them at all. David could do it easily, all the long shelves of the library were open to him. He envied the boy that. David walked by his side with his head down, this way the fine dust was kept out of his eyes, and he could hide his shame.

Helen was in the kitchen, making bread, when they let themselves in. She was up to her elbows in a bowl of dough, kneading it to the rhythm of her song. They stood before her like recalcitrant boys.

'What have you two been up to then? Must be something, from the look on your faces.'

David looked at Billy, Billy looked at Betty.

'Well, come on now, can't be all that bad, can it? You haven't been taking David down that pub of yours, have you Billy?'

'No, nothing like that, lass. It's about David and Emma, see.'

Helen did not seem surprised, but she stopped her work. 'Oh, I see. I think you had better tell me yourself, David.'

He looked at the floor and blurted it out. 'Emma says she is going to have a baby... our baby...'

David found the strength to look at his mother, and saw sadness in her eyes, but no anger. An outburst would have been easier to bear. Helen went to the sink to wash her hands, turning her back on them as she spoke.

'Well, I hope you love the girl, that's all, because you will have to stand by her now, David. God knows how you will manage, you haven't even got a job. She's a good girl, Emma, a warmer heart than the rest of her lot. She must be very worried, with that mother of hers. There's no warmth in that one, no forgiveness either, I shouldn't think.'

She wiped her hands on her apron. 'Mr Vincent will have to be told straight away. The longer you wait, the worse it will be. How long have you known it?'

'About two weeks.'

'Things have gone on too long already, then. We had better go up there, there are arrangements to be made, people to be faced. I hope Mr Vincent won't take it too hard. You'll need work now, David, as soon as possible.'

For once Billy had nothing to say, he stood before Helen, trying to hide the dog Betty.

'I don't know why you are looking so hopeless, Billy Hicks. Men! Stick together don't you, like children. Come on. No time like the present.' Helen put on her coat and David followed her while Billy made his way home. David felt his future slip away from him, like a greasy piece of coal.

5

David endured his confession and, with his mother there to deflect some of the Vincents' outrage, he survived. Vincent took the news quite well, but his wife predictably raged against it, spitting malice and a plethora of 'I told you so's at anyone who would listen. Vincent weighed up his anger with the prospect of David being a good business catch, the man was not a prude, or a snob, despite his aping of the rich. Emma was calmed by David's acceptance of marriage.

He lurched through the next few weeks in a haze of despair, hidden by as calm a front as he could present. Fear and frustration never left him, but he could protect himself in a cocoon of mental lassitude. With Vincent and Iolo Hughes he was contrite, and enthusiastic towards any business ideas Vincent suggested; and he was loving to Emma, listening with outward brightness as she talked of their future. Her fears had been allayed when he came to the house that night, she saw a path of secure happiness stretching before her, despite her mother's attempt to spread poison upon it.

Vincent had it all planned. David was to run the other shop at the far end of the valley. The two rooms above it would be their home. They would live within earshot of the till. David listened gloomily as Vincent told him of his decision.

'It will be the perfect start for you, boy, the place has a lot of potential, but needs bringing on a bit. The man there now, Dawes, is too set in his ways. Make a go of it and we can branch out a bit, eh, son?' Vincent had adopted a paternal style soon after news of the baby.

Huw Dawes was promptly given his notice by Vincent. The man had three children and scant prospect of other work in the valley; but there was no sentiment in Vincent's idea of business, although Emma did get him to promise to re-engage Dawes when her time came.

They married in late September, on the last warm Saturday of the year. It was a small ceremony sandwiched between larger weddings. To Vincent's chagrin Billy was best man, David had no-one else to ask. Helen, his sisters, and the Vincents were the only others in attendance. It was a far cry from what Mrs Vincent had planned for Charlotte, and Vincent himself was torn between the need for haste and a showy affair.

'She'll be showing, if we take time to arrange something grand,' he said.

'People will know anyway. They'll be suspicious at a piddling little wedding like this.'

Mrs Vincent had a point, David noticed the curious onlookers as they attended the chapel. It would not take long for tongues to wag and begin tapping the village telegraph, but at least fuss had been avoided, and for that he was grateful.

They stood before Iolo as he intoned his way through the service. Emma was beautiful in a dress of the softest cream, believing that she had David's heart. David said 'I do', but avoided the piercing eyes of Iolo. Then it was over, and he had a wife, and a career, and all that went with them.

After a strained reception at the Vincents, David and Emma travelled down the valley to the main town at the end of it, where they stayed that night, in the one grand hotel. It was a place built in the twenties to serve the increasing traffic of commerce and it reminded David of the Vincents' house: over-large, built to impress, with mock pillars and arches leading nowhere, painted in reds and purples. His mood matched its opulent seediness.

Emma was shy of him that night, they slept in a bed with red covers, in the bridal suite paid for by Vincent. David was conscious of eyes everywhere in this place; they were acting out a scene many couples had done before them, for the amusement of the staff and other guests. It was the start of David's penance.

'Everything has gone so quickly, hasn't it?' Emma whispered to David, at breakfast. They ate in a large dining room with a few commercial travellers, and an old man who sat alone gazing at them. 'Who would have thought we'd be here, like this, as man and wife, a few months ago?'

Emma referred to them constantly as 'man and wife', she liked the phrase and rolled it around her tongue confidently.

'What are you thinking, David?' She squeezed his hand with her own. He saw the old man smirk.

'Oh, just that,' he answered, 'that it has all gone so fast.'

'You are glad aren't you? You don't mind about not going to the training school?'

'That was just a dream, Em. I don't think I was ever meant to leave the valley. It's as good a place as any other, after all.'

'Good.' She squeezed his hand again. 'I used to get worried when you talked of all those foreign places. I thought they might take you away from me. Now we can settle, and make a good life together.'

David stirred his coffee, making a tiny vortex in his cup. Emma had not an ounce of deceit or malice in her, he thought, she was one of those rare people who are good and do not know it, for they see good in everyone else. They left the hotel after breakfast and moved into the shop that same Sunday.

Vincent's far shop, as he liked to call it, was in the last village of the valley. Beyond it the terraces petered out into the hills, and the valley came to an end. The shop was on the corner of a row of cottages, overlooked by an old tip which reared above, taking what light there was, setting its seal on the community and welcoming David with its black gloom. Two cottages had been knocked into one to make the shop. Inside David could see the hand of Vincent everywhere. Double doors led to a smaller version of the Emporium, the same twin counters and layered shelves, and the clear circle of space in the centre, to keep custom flowing. A staircase spiralled from the shop to their quarters upstairs, their bedroom lay directly over the entrance, and the kitchen was alongside them, above the rear storeroom. Their new world was spartan, and cramped: David's perfect nightmare lay before him. What few possessions they had were sent along in a small removal van driven by a man who complained about it being Sunday.

David had brought his books with him; he scattered them around the bedroom like a man sowing seeds. Emma watched him.

'You have so many books, David. Have you read them all?'

'Most of them. Twice, some of them.'

Emma glanced at a few. 'I don't know what Dad will think, he's never had time for reading.'

'I'm still my own man, Emma. I'm married to you, not your father.'

Emma busied herself with unpacking their clothes, and did not say more.

David ran the far shop well, money matters came easily to

him, despite his inner protestations. He knew instinctively who was good for credit and who was not; he knew who to butter up, or to be firm with; who to leave alone. This facility for shopkeeping tortured him, he wanted to deny it to himself, but could not. 'You have the soul of a merchant,' he said to himself when depression struck. Sometimes his mood lightened, and he saw the shop as a haven, not a trap. It protected him from the crowd, and he had more time to himself than in most jobs, for the custom of the shop ebbed and flowed with the fortunes of the colliers. In quiet spells David hid amongst his pots and pans in the store-room, thumbing the pages of a book. It was easier for him in this village, where he was not known. When they had first arrived there was some interest. Emma's condition was soon discerned, but talk was dulled by their marriage. They were important, in their way. Theirs was the only shop in the village, and was depended on.

Emma grew larger, her hair took on a deeper shade of red, and her face shone with health. Her perception was dimmed by thoughts of the coming child. She put David's moods down to his reading, and she was not worried by them. For Emma marriage was the cornerstone of security, a foundation she thought absolute, and unbreakable. Her father provided some new furniture for the bedroom and Emma was content to rest there when she was tired, and help David when she was not.

Vincent checked on the shop often at first, but could find no fault with David. 'Good start you are making here,' he said, on one visit, 'got a head for it, see, just like I said. I knew from the start, told the missus. He's a natural, that Hicks boy, I said.'

Vincent leaned on the counter and beckoned David nearer.

'Well, how are you finding it all? You are the youngest shop manager in the valley, you know.'

'I think I've done all right so far, Mr Vincent.'

'Aye, you have that, and this is just the start. I've got plans boy, you wait and see. Right, I'm off, can't stop still these days.'

He huffed his way out of the shop, halting in the doorway. 'That display over there could be a bit better, change it around so people can't help looking at it.' David watched him get into the Riley, his mouth clamped around a cigar.

After a few weeks Helen came over to see Emma, with Ruth. They were a little nervous in the shop, unable to get used to

David being in charge, handling all the money. Helen fingered the groceries, and was as shy of her son as David was uneasy with her. She made his guilt flare up, and he was terrified she would sense his inner thoughts.

'How are you doing then, David?' Helen asked. 'It seems a big responsibility, all this.'

'I'm alright ma, don't worry.'

Helen looked at him closely. 'I'm glad you are. Emma is a good girl, you are lucky in that, and you won't be here forever. This is only the start for you.'

For David it felt very much like the end. Now his mother was sounding like Vincent. She pressed his arm gently as Emma came in with Ruth. She had been showing her the upstairs. David let them talk together, and busied himself about the shop, dusting down the tins with a cloth. In the steamy glass of the window he caught sight of himself, wearing the pinafore Billy had predicted.

Life was not getting better in the valley. The promise of the years immediately after the Great War had long ago faded and miners returned to the struggle for a living wage and a decent life. For most this was as far away as ever and mining for coal had grown more difficult. As new seams were tapped, colliers took greater chances to earn their slim bonuses. Accidents were common-place, and David felt undercurrents of bitterness lap against his counter. Vincent had failed to indoctrinate him with his orders to 'stand firm' against the pleas of desperate women; he had his own system of credit, which helped assuage his conscience. Emma approved the slate, as long as it was kept secret from her father. Gradually, the 'far shop' became a very different place to the Emporium.

Billy began to drop over some evenings, bringing Betty with him. 'I've somewhere to walk besides the Anchor and the Hall now,' he said, 'and Betty likes the broken biscuits.' He threw her one from one of David's tins. Billy was increasingly active in local politics; he called himself a Marxist now, like many of the miners' leaders. He shared his books with David, they took to discussing them long into the night, sat at the shop counter with the blinds drawn. This way Emma would not be disturbed, and their political trysts kept secret from any friend of Vincent.

David felt it a triumph over the old man, to have Billy and such books in his shop.

David learned many things from Billy, about the local organisations, and their struggles, the conditions in the pits, the Means Test, the hunger marches to London, events which had not penetrated his wall of self-interest before. He became a willing disciple of the zealotry of his uncle, and the individualism forged by his book-reading was tempered. David wanted to belong to something, and Billy sensed his keenness. He resolved to bring David into the fold, he would inspire the boy with commitment, passion, even. In his way Billy discounted Emma as much as David did, he knew his nephew, and he knew that the marriage would have stormy times ahead. Billy let David make points from his books, then knocked them down with his experiences. They became good friends.

The first thing David saw when he opened the bedroom curtains was the great slab of waste coal, poised over him like a black fist. Many mornings he stared at the tip as he lay in their iron bed, steeling himself to brave the cold and go down once more to his counter. The waste marked the end of their blind valley. No road had managed to find its way over the top, just a few sheep tracks crossed the next valley, wisps that tantalised David with their promise of another place. Sometimes he felt the tip mocking him, flaunting its triumph at him, while Emma slept against him, heavy and warm.

Once behind his counter David looked to escape whenever he could. When the shop was busy it was easier to cope, when things were slack, time slipped through his fingers like glue, as it had in the Emporium. He became adroit at judging the gaps between customers on cold Autumn mornings, and took to reading in them. A book would be unearthed, a page turned, a point mulled over, until the doorbell rang its warning. He came to savour the intervals of peace he had, and hated their interruption. His novels gave way to Billy's political tomes, and he read Engels and Marx, ploughing through stodgy texts with enthusiasm, making their points his own, as he had made Billy's his own.

With Christmas approaching Vincent decided they could take Huw Dawes back on for a few weeks. David welcomed it, thinking of the extra free time it would give him. Dawes was small, and sallow faced, with lips as thin as matchsticks, and a nose that curved down to them. On his upper lip he wore a pencil moustache, a thin strand of hair that was as fine as the dust on the streets. He was slightly lame in one leg and scuffed the floor when he walked. Dawes worked well, and was always willing to do more than his share. David wondered how the man could bear the humiliation of returning to work under him, until he came to realise that a man with a family will do almost anything to provide for them. Dawes's humility was enforced by the times. The sound of Dawes's boot striking the floor became one of the recognised sounds of the shop, like the ring of the till as it snapped shut, and the tinkle of the doorbell. They were symbols of drudgery for David, they called out to him through the storeroom walls. He was increasingly to be found in this refuge, taking less and less trouble to hide his sloth.

The weather grew steadily colder, customers were often blown into the shop, half-frozen. They did not have the clothes to keep out the cold, many wore the same things all the year; they had no choice. Boys from the poorest families went blue-legged from November to March, their short trousers pathetically inadequate. David hated the blasting winds and icy rain of winter. His thin frame was easily pierced by the elements, and he did not stray far from his stove.

Emma persuaded David to go to her parents for Christmas dinner, much to Helen's disappointment. He spent Christmas Eve steeling himself for the ordeal, and dealing with the last surge of shoppers. Emma suggested going to the chapel in the evening but David talked her out of it.

'Let's stay here, have a glass of that sherry you've bought,' he said, 'it's too cold for you to be going out.'

Emma smiled at him. 'You like everything so quiet, don't you? No-one else around.'

'Yes, I suppose so. Anyway, there's be plenty of socialising tomorrow, with your lot. Edward Rees won't be there, will he?'

'No, I shouldn't think so.'

'Good. That would be too much to bear.'

One glass led to another until David had worked his way through the sherry. He got drunk gently, as the revellers outside made their ways home. Their wild attempts at song echoed through the house, then dwindled away, leaving David as empty as the bottle he clutched. Emma was not an arm's length away, but he had never felt so lonely. Her voice came from a void. Dimly he could hear her talking on about the baby, and the house they would have one day. David thought of the price he must pay, and slept.

Christmas morning they exchanged gifts, some clothes and a new dictionary for David, a new dress for Emma, chosen secretly by Helen, and baby things. Somehow Emma had managed to get him into bed. He awoke there sticky with the dregs of the sherry in his mouth, but strangely without a hangover. That, and the Vincents, would have been too much for David to bear. At one o'clock they were at the villa, sitting down to the grandest spread David had yet witnessed. Mrs Vincent had tried to rival the Reeses' famous dos. The table was crowded with dishes offering the widest choice of foods.

They were served by a girl from David's street, one of the two maids Mrs Vincent employed. Mrs Vincent showed her little Christmas cheer, and the girl served timidly, anticipating the sharp edge of her mistress's tongue. David ignored his queasy stomach and took a long draught of the wine Vincent offered him. New sensations were coming quickly for him. The wine combined with the ghost of the sherry and David felt his face flush, and the room swam a little. Drinking was getting to be a habit.

Mrs Vincent had on a dress with a high collar; as David's eyes clouded, she took on the look of a cobra, he half-expected her to spit at him, or puff up. Besides him Emma was quiet, and ate little. He put her mood down to her condition, and concentrated on his own food. After it David sat back, and smoked the cigar Vincent offered him. Vincent enacted the ritual of the study again. David followed him, giving an encouraging smile to Emma. He avoided the stare of the cobra.

The air in the study was cooler, unlived-in, and David felt the calming presence of books. Vincent had plenty of them, bookcases lined with quality editions, titles no-one in the house had read. On the wall was an ancient chart of a sea Vincent had never sailed on, next to it was a painting by an artist whose name the old man could not pronounce. The room was phony. It leapt out at David and said 'welcome brother'.

Vincent sat down in his club chair and gazed at David through a cloud of smoke.

'Settled in well, haven't you, lad. Just like I said.'

'Yes, everything is fine, Mr Vincent.'

'Good. Dawes not giving you any bother, is he?'

'None at all.'

'Let me know if he does. He probably bears a grudge, that one. Well, how do you find it, running your first shop, exciting, eh? When I was your age I was sweeping the floor of one, for a few pence a week.'

'There's a lot to learn,' David said.

'Of course, of course, but you are learning it. Huh, I almost said you were a chip off the old block, then, eh, son?'

David knew that Vincent would not require much conversation from him in this mood, just the odd nod of agreement would be enough for the old man to ramble through his usual pet speeches. Vincent saw the future turning his way, rows of Emporiums lining the valley.

'I'll be a grandfather soon, my boy,' Vincent said, patting his girth in satisfaction, 'never thought that would happen so quickly, neither did you, eh?' Vincent laughed, and slowly slipped into sleep.

They got back to the shop late in the afternoon, in a taxi Vincent had arranged, the only one in the valley. Their rooms were cold and unwelcoming, but they were glad to get back. David turned up the stove and they sat before it for some minutes, without talking.

'I think I'll go to bed now, David,' Emma said, eventually, 'I'm so tired.'

'Yes, alright. I won't be long, I want to finish something I was reading the other day.'

'Books!' Emma said the word with great sadness, as it was a one word judgement of David's character. She brushed past him, heavy with their child, and left him alone in the room.

The alcohol was leaving David, and the aftertaste of the cigar was bitter. He sat amongst the tools of his trade, rows of glass jars gleaming in the gaslight, oversized jewels of gloom. If only they were precious to him. David threw his book down, and cursed his goods, he did not want to be in this place. A boy's frustration welled up inside; he wanted to cast it out, but could not. The book on the floor told of another way to live. Solutions dripped from its pages to seduce the dreamer, and snare the unwary, men who wanted something better, empty men needing to be filled with promise. It offered hope, a new religion to follow, and David imagined it pulled on his heartstrings, too.

David's eyes turned up to the ceiling, and he thought of Emma. He remembered the sense of power he had felt on the Tump, his body gave a jerk of awareness. He had the ability to excite with dreams, but not with reality. For the first time he tried to imagine a child, and how he would react to it. 'It' was the only way he could think of the baby, never 'him' or 'her'. The idea of another person to worry about brought panic, and jealousy.

Emma was ill in the morning so David put off the planned visit to his mother. She stayed in bed, overcome with tiredness. David thought of sending for the doctor, but Emma did not want that.

'It's just the baby making me tired, that's all, it's normal.'

'Your father would want me to call the doctor.'

'No, leave it, I'll be all right tomorrow. Let me sleep now.'

David was restless, and could not settle to any book. He was grim, and brooded, as he usually did over Christmas. A wind whipped off the tip and gusted through the village, scattering bins, and wheezing in the roof like his father's chest. He gave up any attempt to read, and settled down in front of the stove. David slept below and Emma above. They were the only people in the world, he felt, drifting through their lives quite separately.

He awoke cold and irritable, and felt sorry for himself. Upstairs Emma was in bed, asleep. David saw that her health of a few weeks ago was fading: her face was as pale as the sky outside, her hair was dulled, and there was a film of sweat on her brow. David sat on the edge of the bed for a time, then got up to leave her.

'Don't go, David, I want to talk to you.'

'Oh, I thought you were sleeping. Sorry I woke you.'

'You didn't. I was not really asleep, I wanted you to watch me, that's all.' Emma sat up in bed, pushing the hair from her face. 'What's wrong, David? What's wrong with us? You are so remote, I can't seem to reach you'.

David looked out of the window. 'Nothing. Christmas is always a funny time for me.'

'Don't blame Christmas. I think every time is a funny time for you. You don't even notice me anymore. It hurts so much, you're making me ill'.

She reached out for David's arm, and pulled him around to face her.

'You're imagining things worse than they are, Emma. Being pregnant makes you like that.'

'You use anything as an excuse, don't you, anything to get out of really saying anything. Oh David, you think you are so intelligent, the only one who thinks, who sees things. You think you know it all, but you don't. I know you did not want to marry me, I tried not to think it, but I always knew it, deep down. And I thought you loved me. The baby was a shock to you, I thought, mixed you all up, you would come round when we were married, be a good husband, and father.'

Emma was sobbing now, a bitter moan that shook her body. David reached for her hesitantly, but she pushed him away.

'You don't love me, admit it. You are embarrassed by me, embarrassed to be close to me, as if I had the plague.'

David was startled by the outburst. He did not know what to say to Emma, he wanted to reassure her and deny her words, but his tongue was still.

'Aren't you going to say anything?' Emma begged. 'Tell me I've got it all wrong, tell me you love me.'

David's mouth was locked up with guilt and cowardice. Emma hid her face from him, trying to escape into the folds of the bed. He let himself out of the bedroom as quietly as he could, anxious to avoid any more words.

Hurt had conquered Emma's timidity. Their relationship, or lack of one, was out in the open. David went back downstairs to stoke up the stove, wishing his life could be re-arranged as easily as the embers he pushed around with the poker. There was a rap on the front door, jarring David from his thoughts. He opened up to find Billy on the steps, well-filled with beer, and a couple of bottles in his hand.

'Hello Happy, been enjoying the season, I see. Got a face like the Ghost of Christmas Past. Glum. I've brought you the only type of Christmas spirit you can rely on. Here, let me in.'

Billy swept past to settle himself in front of the stove, in David's chair.

'This fire is almost out. Come on, let's get a bit of shape on it.' David tended the fire, restocking it with coal, and using the bellows until it roared again. He was glad Billy had called.

'How's your first Christmas as a married fella, then? Here, we're not disturbing Emma? Where is she, anyhow?'

'She's asleep. Resting.'

'Aye, she isn't that far away now'.

They sat supping the beer for some time, then Billy got into his gossip. 'That last march didn't get very far. Half the boys were not strong enough, the way things are. And London is a bloody long way for tramping. Still, it's something to do, keeps us fighting. That's the thing see, Dave, to keep going. If they are going to grind us down to coal dust might as well go shouting about it, eh?'

Billy heaved a boozy sigh, and looked for his pipe. David saw a lonely man not far off old age. Billy had not much to go home to, an empty house, a smelly dog. David did not want to end up like him, yet he envied his freedom.

'About time you came down the Hall,' said Billy, 'met a few of the boys, isn't it?'

'What do you mean, Bill?'

'You know, start mixing, like, get to know your local scene.'

'I don't think they would welcome a shop keeper down there.'

'Don't worry about that, I'll vouch for you. Anyway, everyone knows you had to get married.'

David winced.

'Come on, David, I know your heart is not in this place.'

'What about Emma?'

'What about her? She'll be glad to have the house to herself, of an evening.'

Billy dozed off, flushed with the fire. David took the glass from his hands, and finished it off. Billy's offer appealed to him, he did not want to be on the outside of life any longer and it would be a means of escape from the shop. Billy tottered home late that Boxing Night, lending his voice to the midnight chorus of the other drunks. He shouted snatches of songs dimly remembered, pidgin Welsh floated up into the air, soaked with sentimentality. Most of the valley men resorted to it, from time to time. David checked on Emma, who seemed asleep. In the small hours, when he was certain she was he crept into bed beside her, and was not too ashamed to snuggle up to the warmth of her body.

The change in Emma became final after that Christmas. She did not attempt to talk to David again; she drew into herself, cut him out. Knitting clothes for the baby occupied her time in the day, and she stayed upstairs. David was worried, but Emma's reclusiveness made it easier for him to take up Billy's suggestion. Their marriage was a sham, and all he had to do now was be himself, it seemed. One part of David knew he was breaking Emma's heart, the other told him things were better this way, Emma could realise how hopeless he was as a husband, and do something about it. As for the child, David preferred not to think about that at all. He set his sail towards the course Billy was charting for him, like a blind sailor approaching reefs.

6

The life of Billy Hicks revolved around two places, the Miners' Hall and Conti's, an Italian café in the village. In winter Conti's was the chosen place, for the warmth its stove provided. It was in the middle of the main street, built out of altered cottages, like the far shop. Inside, its floor sloped upwards towards a den at the back, a hollowed-out space that housed the stove, a huge iron affair that was a beacon for the men who congregated around it. Apart from Conti's teetotal rule, Billy was in his element here. With his fingers curled around a battered mug of Bovril, he lectured anyone who would listen on the evils of Capitalism, his eyes gleaming with fervour through the thick smog that gathered in the den. When David was first introduced the Conti regulars were not sure of him, but a word from Billy was enough to win them over. After a few weeks David became an accepted member of the group.

Conti was an Italian-Welshman, tiny, and prematurely grey-haired, lost in the large three-piece suit he habitually wore. It enveloped his scant body like a cloak, giving him a theatrical air, and he had the habit of twirling a watch chain like a clown though there was never a watch on the end of it. Maria Conti was as stout as her husband was thin, much younger than he, sent over from the old country for work and marriage. In the evenings she did most of the work, bustling around the tables with a few children in tow. No-one knew exactly how many made up the Conti brood, but they were a small army of black haired children and one blond one, a boy Conti viewed with suspicion, called 'the angel' by Maria. Being such a father did not affect Conti much, he made himself available to join in the talk of the stove, casting cynical remarks from the safety of his counter. He was a rock to the shouts and scolds of Maria, and shrugged off her accusations of laziness. He liked to point to the clock and say he wasn't open all hours, didn't he provide for her and the many, many *bambinos*? Conti's opened before dawn, and shut after the pubs had spilled their loads.

Most of the men David met there were in their thirties and forties, all were older than David. It was a new world for him, one of enthusiasm, humour and spirit. His image of miners had been a grey one, men down-trodden by a system they struggled to survive in. His father's thoughts of miners being their own worst enemy had registered in his mind at an early age. In Conti's, David was slowly changed; and he was ripe for changing. Soon he saw these men as individuals.

David learned from the Conti talks, he kept his mouth shut and listened to the opinions being expressed. He saw how the arguments of his books were forged differently on the street and learned of the fierce rivalry of different ideologies. Billy's Boys, as they liked to be called, were all shades of the Left, but they tolerated each other. Billy tried to teach unity, and decades of strikes had welded them into a solid force. No blackleg union had yet penetrated in the valley, and the village held up better than most under threat.

Billy had the prime seat, next to the stove, and the Boys were arranged in order of importance and standing, a Socialist caste system. David got to know one man particularly. Thomas Price was a blacksmith in the pit, a widower who had lost his wife Mary three years before, a man of medium height, square shouldered, and stocky, a frame moulded by a lifetime of wielding a heavy hammer. 'The pit pony', Billy called him. Tom was taciturn, with a morose air, qualities which attracted him to David. His face had a nut-brown skin, etched with powerful headlines. Two blue-grey eyes stared out intently, without blinking for long periods, it seemed, as if Tom was constantly thinking, weighing things up. He lived alone in a neat and gloomy terrace, close to the shop. David encouraged Tom to visit him. At eighteen he had his first friend.

David's evenings at Conti's, and occasionally the Hall increased throughout January and February, until David was around the stove most nights. He saw out a hard winter fed by its heat and the talk around him, the new disciple. The cold of his late walk back to the shop was shut out by the ideas and dreams that circulated inside him, fuelled by bottles of beer when he got back to his own stove. Sometimes there was a sliver of foreboding as he shut the shop door after him, quietly, with a glance up the stairs. But there had been little said to Emma since Christmas, and he preferred to let things stay that way.

In the day Dawes increasingly ran the shop, saying nothing and seeing everything. As Emma's time drew near David went down to the Hall in the day also; when she needed him most he drew steadily away from her. One night she was still up, waiting for him by the fire.

'Oh, still awake, are you?' David said. 'Aren't you tired?'

'Yes, I'm tired, but I couldn't sleep.'

David sat beside her, and rubbed the frost from his hands. 'Brr... No end to this winter. I hate it.'

'It's not far to walk from Conti's, and it's warm there, isn't it, with that old stove of theirs?'

'I didn't know you'd been there, Emma.'

'I have a few times, in the afternoons.'

'Oh.'

'Mrs Conti says you are one of them now, one of that political lot.'

David sighed. 'That's right, though I don't think the boys would like to be called a lot.'

'There will be trouble if Dad finds out, if he hasn't already. You know what he thinks about all that, and you are letting the shop go. Dawes is doing your job.'

'You've never said anything about it before.'

'I know, but it's getting that you are down that café every night. It must be obvious to the whole village there is nothing to keep you here.'

'It's just that I am very interested in politics, you know that.'

'Do I? Perhaps you are looking for any reason to get away from me. I don't see that you are anything like your uncle, or that Tom Price.'

'No, I'm my own man, Emma.' He smiled. 'I don't have to be like them, Em, the movement is for everyone. I'm trying to be part of something I believe in.'

'Yes, I think you are trying to be a part of something. You don't believe in me, in us, that's certain. Politics, that's just an excuse, David – you hide down Conti's, like most of them.'

Emma threw down the knitting she was holding and left him. David heard her moving around in the bedroom. Emma knew him now, she saw the thinness of his character, and its impenetrable selfishness, but she had not stopped loving him. Emma thought of the child inside her to try to ease the feeling of rejection, but it was hard. She hoped the baby would improve things. It must be a boy, she thought. Girls had such a hard time in the valley, a round of serving family, employer and husband, until old age came on stealthily, to snuff out vitality, and wither the spirit. Most days now she lay in bed, listening to the sounds in the street, blurred voices fading away from her, snatches of talk carried off by the wind, the day punctuated by the ring of the doorbell. She was more tired than she should be, and a doctor attended her regularly, engaged and paid for by Vincent. He prescribed a tonic, and said the first was always the worst.

It was only a matter of time before Vincent learned of David's new allegiance. He exploded into the shop one afternoon, spluttering with indignation and anger stoked up by the bumpy ride he had made over the frozen roads. Vincent ushered David into the storeroom, where books were strewn around. As soon as the door was closed he turned on David.

'Is it true?' he shouted. 'Have you been down Conti's, mixing with those Bolshies? God, I could hardly believe it at first when the wife told me. I thought you had more sense, a shop-keeper messing around with Communism. My own bloody son-in-law. What the hell's going on, boy?'

David was calm in the face of this onslaught, he had expected Vincent, sooner or later.

'Nothing is going on, Mr Vincent. My private life does not affect the shop. I talk to my friends in the night, that's all.'

'That's all, be buggered. You've been letting the shop go, and even if you haven't it's still treachery, that's what it is, treachery. You have betrayed me. I never knew you thought like that bunch, never suspected.'

'I do share the same beliefs as my uncle, and the others.'

'Beliefs. Hah, you are just a lad, what do you know about beliefs. Most of Billy Hicks's beliefs come from a bloody beer bottle.'

David's calmness infuriated Vincent further. He had expected denial, or contrition from David, not this. The boy stood there as bold as brass, with his Emma lying upstairs, pregnant.

'You are going very red in the face, Mr Vincent, do you want to sit down?'

'Don't get cheeky with me boy, I won't be made a fool of, Hicks. I started you here, and I can finish you just as quick'.

David kept his voice as even as he could. 'I don't think you should go making threats, that would upset Emma very much. She married me, she chose me, and she is carrying your grandchild.'

Vincent was taken aback. 'Why you impudent young sod, I'll knock you through that wall...' Vincent did not move. 'Well, it's all coming out now, I should have listened to the missus, she said your were a jumped up little brat. Listen boy, don't think I don't know how you have been treating our Emma. She'll be back with us, where she belongs, and the child too. You'll be out on your arse. Go and look for a job down the pits, see how far you get there.'

Vincent had shouted himself out. He leant on a shelf, breathless.

Emma came into the storeroom, a dressing gown draped around her.

'What's the matter, I could hear the row upstairs. I heard you shouting, dad, what is it?'

'That is what it is.' Vincent waved a hand at David. 'You are married to a damned Communist girl, a bloody bolshie.'

Emma sighed. 'Politics, is that all?'

'All? It's everything. All my life I've tried to get ahead, from nothing I started, and I done it. You've wanted for nowt, none of you have. The Vincents have amounted to something in this valley. Don't you see girl, I can't have a Red in the family.' Vincent sat down heavily on a barrel.

'Oh dad, David is not a Communist, don't get so excited about it, you'll make yourself ill. David has run the shop well, you said so yourself, he just likes to go down Conti's to talk, that's all. It doesn't mean he thinks the same as them.'

David kept quiet and let Emma defend him. She padded out the sparse truth in a way that amazed him. Vincent's resolve weakened, his love for his daughter was greater than his anger for David.

Emma stopped speaking and there was silence for a moment. The men glared at each other, two rivals. Then David spoke.

'Look, I won't go to Conti's anymore, if it's going to cause so much fuss.'

Vincent looked at him suspiciously. 'Bit late now,' he muttered.

'Dad,' Emma said, 'that's not fair, David's trying to be reasonable, you must do the same'.

The old man chewed on this.

'Hmpth. Alright, I suppose I'll have to, with the baby coming. It's a mess though, Emma, you talk to this husband of yours will you, make him see a bit of sense, if he wants to keep this shop.'

Vincent left the shop quietly, pushing his way past Dawes, who hovered near the storeroom door, his ears on stalks. The Riley roared off up the street, slipping dangerously on the thin layer of snow. David went up to the warmth of the kitchen, leaving the shop to Dawes. Emma was in his chair, the glow of the fire caught in her hair, making it fine red gauze. David sat beside her, and felt her shaking. She did not speak, so they sat there mutually silent, watching the intrigues of the fire. There were tiny explosions as gas escaped from the coal in a soft hiss, the fire re-arranging itself as coals burnt away. Emma's hands reached for him, questing, wanting hands. David patted them and did not look at her.

'You always touch me like that,' Emma said, 'as if I'm a pet or something. Why don't you talk, David, you say enough down Conti's, I'm sure.'

David turned to face her. 'Not really, I must be the naturally silent type. Thanks for sticking up for me with your father, you did not have to you know.'

'I did it for the baby, I don't want it born with you at war with Dad. What about our child, David, will you ignore him, cut him out of your life, as you have me?'

'No, no, of course not'.

'I don't believe you anymore.'

'Give me time, Emma, everything has gone so fast, sometimes my head reels with it all.'

'And you think mine doesn't? That first time on the Tump seems like yesterday and its formed my whole life. I'll be a mother soon, and you a father, and you are still thinking about yourself. You're a bastard.'

David thought he had misheard her, yet for the first time since Christmas David had some feeling for Emma, a faint echo of the love she felt for him. Emma sensed it, and was desperate to rekindle the spark. She leant towards David, and he held her, awkwardly at first, then losing himself in the warmth of her hair.

He felt the child, and smelt the sweet, indoors smell of Emma.

'It will not be long now,' she whispered, 'and I'm afraid David, I am so tired, and you leave me alone so much.' David sifted her hair until he felt her calm. I can do this much, at least, he thought, for someone much better than I am. Another coal split asunder in the fire, a piece of it fell out onto the grate, where it glowed red until it returned to black rock. David pushed it back into the inferno.

To compensate for David's self-imposed exile from Conti's, Tom and Billy visited the shop several times a week. They did not chide him for his decision.

'Wait until the baby is born, you will have more scope then,' Bill said. Tom had lost his job at the pit, sacked on a pretext by the owners, he claimed.

'I was getting a bit too political for them, I think. A trouble-maker, they said I was.'

'Aye,' said Billy. 'They use that word to describe anyone that shows any sign of backbone.' It was the dole for Tom now, the beginning of an existence eked out on pennies. He had hidden the few worthwhile possessions he had in Billy's house, safe from the prying eyes of the Means Test man. His one exotic item, a grandfather clock, was hauled down to Billy's shed, where it stood covered in sheets. Billy was charged with the duty of winding it, and it continued to give good time, chiming out the hour to the emptiness of his yard.

David talked with the two Boys in the storeroom, sat on barrels with beer and tobacco. Tom was going on a march to London soon, one hundred and seventy miles of hard road, and Billy was helping to plan the route. He was an old hand at it, he knew the best places to stop, the towns where they could expect help, and sometimes shelter. David envied his friends, they were seasoned campaigners, with strong wills and clear hearts, who knew where they were going. A year ago most of the valley had been on the march, thousands of people walking in protest to the main town.

'That showed what can be done,' Billy said, 'if we organise properly. I'll never forget when we unfurled the banners, my heart was bustin' with pride, man,' Billy chuckled. 'No wonder they call us Little Moscow down here, eh lads?'

David remembered that mass march, it had been impressive, but it had not changed anything, it seemed to him.

'Miners are still being thrown out of work, Bill,' he said, 'and no-one is better off. The bosses always have the strength, and that seems to beat miners every time.'

Tom nodded in agreement, encouraging David to continue. 'They won't let us have anything, Billy, not willingly, why should they? We'll have to fight in the end, it will be the only way'.

Billy lit his pipe, and looked at David thoughtfully. 'Well now, David *bach*, getting the bit between your teeth at last, eh? Good. But there's all sorts of fighting, see, not so long ago there was no dole, remember. We have won things, we have a start, something to build on now. And look, you say about numbers, isn't that what won in Russia?'

'Aye Bill, but you can't compare the two. Russia was a totally different animal, that could never happen here.'

'Why not?'

'The people are not the same, this stiff upper lip business. We are too clubby, at the end of the day.'

'Good point, David,' Tom said.

'Oh, ganging up on the old man, are you?' Billy paused. 'Well, maybe you are right, there might be a fight coming. We'll see what happens down in Spain. Have you been reading about it?' Billy held up the paper he had brought with him. 'There's trouble brewing there, mark my words. The Spanish workers want the same as us. I was talking to Juan Davies the other day, you know, that one up at the iron ore, him who came over years ago. Knows all about it, Juan does. They are treated worse than animals over there, he says, the peasants got nothing, they work in the fields from dawn to dusk for bread, filling a rich man's pockets even fuller. We are far better off than them. Juan thinks there will be a civil war; looking forward to it, I think he is. Well, if there is a do perhaps we can learn from it, it might show us the way here.'

Spain. It was a country David had thought little about, although the situation there had been discussed several times in Conti's. The boys liked to follow the struggles in foreign lands, to look outwards, Billy said. In Spain, the Popular Front, a loose coalition of the Spanish Left had just won a victory in the national elections. To celebrate this, Billy organised a talk on the subject of Spain, hoping to gain the interest of those who did not see further than their own skyline. For most in the valley, Spain was a far-off mysterious place, hot, alien, and very hard to imagine.

On a Saturday afternoon David slipped away from the shop to attend the talk. Juan Davies and a few other Spaniards addressed the crowd. They were men who had come to Wales to work in the iron industry. David was impressed by the force and simplicity of their beliefs. Their words were naive and dreaming, his education told him, but they still inspired, as dreams briefly made real do. One young Spaniard was full of fire, exhorting his audience to help his Spain. 'Our struggle is your struggle, boys,' he shouted, part matador, part Welsh preacher. All talked eagerly of going home, to take part in the struggle they thought would inevitably follow the elections. Juan was more cautious than his fellows, his older memories balanced his optimism. He had fled Spain at the turn of the century, and was now almost Welsh, a grizzled, tousle-haired old man whose powerful torso sprouted from stubby legs, like a troll. Davies was his adopted name, no-one could pronounce the others, and they were too many for one man.

'I never thought the people would get away with it, Juan,' Billy said after the meeting.

'We shall see,' Juan answered. 'Many times before we have tried to change things in Spain, but have not done so. We shall see what they will do now, those with the power.'

Spain was in the news increasingly. While national papers told of Communist atrocities, and attacks on the church, David's journals spoke of the deliverance of the people. It was at hand, they said, first in Spain, and then anywhere where men followed the lead given. David relished the idea of studying the events from afar, involved in thought and allegiance, while safe in his kitchen armchair.

7

The winter proved mild after Christmas, an early spring was promised by the constant rain that drenched the valley. Each cloud that scudded over the village dropped its load, sheets of water hung from the skies like grey blankets, blotting out all landscape. Emma had been in bed for a week, and was very near her time. She was overcome by a lassitude caused more by David than her pregnancy. Vitality had been sucked steadily from her by worry, and the hurt of a love not returned. At a time when she needed the most support she suffered this most exquisite of tortures. Her eyes had enlarged into two dark pools, stagnant rather than shining, and she was strangely small for one so heavy with child. When he looked on her David saw his guilt mirrored in her eyes, but could do nothing other than smile, and offer weak encouragement.

An elderly lady, Winnie Rowlands, was engaged to sit with Emma. She was a retired midwife, called back to her trade by Vincent. Her fussy nosiness irritated him, so he stayed out of the way as much as he could, reading in the storeroom, and helping Dawes if the shop was busy.

On a Thursday, in the second week of April David was stirred from a book by the fraught voice of Miss Rowlands crying down the stairs, 'It's started Mr Hicks, it's started.' David went up to investigate but the old woman stopped him at the door. 'Best not come in, sir, not yet. Send for Mr Cobb-Evans, that's what you must do. David did so, half glad that her wizened hand barred him from his own bedroom.

Sour-faced Cobb-Evans rarely attended births in the village, the miners could not afford him. They made do with the patchy knowledge of whatever woman was available. The doctor was a friend of Vincent, and, like Winnie Rowlands, had been engaged by him. He arrived in the afternoon, as the light was fading, red-faced, and squeaking in new leather shoes.

'Right then, Mr Hicks,' he said, 'things are happening, are they? Not before time, she's a bit late you know, a bit late.'

David followed the doctor up the stairs, and this time he was not stopped. They allowed him a few minutes to sit with Emma, as Winnie helped Cobb-Evans with his preparation. He was shocked at Emma's state. Her face shone with sweat, her hair was a sodden red rag, and her body quivered with pain. David took her hand and she looked up at him weakly. Emma's hand felt clammy, tiny and desperate in his.

'It's so close, David,' she whispered, 'and it hurts so much. There's something wrong, I know there is.'

'No there isn't. Don't worry, it will all be over in a while, and you'll have a lovely baby, we'll have a child.'

Cobb-Evans's hand was on David's shoulder, 'That's right, lass, you listen to your husband, everything will be alright. You go down now, Mr Hicks, we'll call you later.'

Emma felt a crushing weight on her spine, as if some force was inexorably trying to rend her in two. She gritted her teeth to withstand the pain and tasted blood on her lips. Through a haze she saw David leave the room, he turned to smile that lazy smile of his, to encourage, but she saw fear in it, and that made her feel desolate, and alone. Cobb-Evans was fussing over her, and she heard Winnie cooing in the background soft Welsh words she did not understand, but which comforted her. The old woman stroked her hair as the baby grabbed at her, and squeezed with tiny, iron fingers. Emma stifled a scream and thought that the pain must be her punishment, it had gone on so long, she did not know how long, time had been lost in it.

They were encouraging her now. 'Push, girl, push,' the doctor said, 'come on, just a bit more. Push harder.' She wanted to get rid of the pain, to cast it away from her body. Cobb-Evans bent over her, lamplight catching on his face, turning beads of sweat into diamonds. He was in his waistcoat, with his shirt sleeves rolled up, poised over Emma like a vulture about to pluck a piece of flesh. Emma felt something flow from her, and screamed once, a scream that struck the farthest corners of the shop, jolting David upright in his chair. The pain was taken away, she felt light headed, and sick. Her two helpers were veiled by a film of sweat, they looked like figures in a dream, but she knew this was real. They were bending over something, hiding something from her. It must be the baby, why didn't they show it to her? They faded away.

Cobb-Evans left the bedroom and went down to David. He

heard his heavy tread on the stairs, each one creaked in turn. He was afraid to move out of his chair, Emma's scream meant evil news, he felt it strongly. The doctor stood before him, warming his back on the stove. His face was the colour of the coals, contrasting with the grey fuzz of his sideburns. Cobb-Evans cleared his throat and looked hard at David.

'Your wife has been through a great deal, young man, a great deal, I'm afraid.'

'Is she dead?' David spoke into his hand.

'No, no, she will be all right, after a long rest. It was just too much for her, bearing a child. She's such a slip of a thing. No, it's the baby, lad, that's what I meant to say. We couldn't save it.'

'Oh.'

'Yes, it was a little boy, died as he came from her, poor mite. There was nothing I could do to revive him. An act of the Lord I suppose it was.' Cobb-Evans shook his head grandly, and looked at the floor. 'Of course, Mr Vincent is going to be shaken by all this, mind.'

David recoiled at the mention of the name. What about Emma, what about him?

'You must make arrangements for the child,' Cobb-Evans said, 'Miss Rowlands knows the procedure. I'll telephone Mr Vincent when I get back, I expect he'll be down shortly.'

Cobb-Evans got his own coat and hat before David managed to rise from his chair. He showed the doctor out into the street, into an evening as black as the death that had visited them. As he started his car Cobb-Evans beckoned to David with a finger. 'The girl doesn't know much about it yet, mind. I gave her a bit of laudanum, she's dopey now, asleep. Best to break the news easy when she comes out of it.'

'How do I do that, doctor?'

Cobb-Evans ignored the question. 'It's a terrible thing for a woman,' he muttered, as he slipped the clutch of his car. David stood in the shop doorway for a long time, letting the splutter of the car dwindle away and die before he turned back to the ghastly silence of the house.

He climbed the stairs to the bedroom, where Emma lay asleep. Her face had the pallor of one long ill and indoors, and the air of the room was heavy and sour with death. Miss Rowlands had changed the sheets, and the baby was gone from the room. David did not ask where, he did not want to see it. He felt the reproach-ful eyes of the old woman upon him, the sisterhood was already working, and soon the news would be throughout the village.

David held Emma's hand while she slept; he needed to feel her warmth, to assure himself that it was not her who had died. Emma slept deeply, her bosom rising and falling gently under the sheet, her face half buried by them. He felt tenderness for her in this dreadful hour, and wished he could give her back the child. Winnie Rowlands went home, eager to tell her story. Until the world descended on him David sat by Emma, pushed the hair from her face and savoured the short peace, soothed by the ticking of the dresser clock.

The Vincents arrived in the early morning. The old man faced David in shock, he did not quite believe the news, would not believe it.

'What have you done to our Emma, Hicks? I want to see her,' Vincent said. He stormed through the door but David blocked the stairs.

'You can't see her now, Mr Vincent she's sleeping. I'm not having her disturbed. Keep your voice down, please,' David said.

Vincent faced him in total enmity, tears streaming down his face. David never thought the old man would do that. The cobra hissed behind him, Mrs Vincent at her malevolent worst.

'Keep his voice down. You cheeky young swine. Not content with ruining our Emma, are you, want to deny us seeing her now, is that it? Well, perhaps the girl is better off, not having to bring up a boy of yours. What sort of father would you make?'

David faced this onslaught as calmly as he could, but he wished there was someone there on his side. It was always the Vincents who could travel quickly in their motor car, able to be told quickly on their telephone. Seeing that David stood firm Vincent lowered his voice.

'Was the baby, the boy, born dead?'

'Didn't the doctor tell you?'

'I don't know, I couldn't take it all in.'

'No, he wasn't, he died shortly afterward.'

'Don't talk to him tidy like that,' Mrs Vincent said, 'you'll pay. David Hicks, you'll pay for everything.'

'Come on Margaret, no use staying here now.' Vincent pushed her back out of the door. She buried her face in a handkerchief, like a Dickensian matron, full of lace and poison. The shop still was not shuttered. David pulled down the heavy blinds and fastened them with the worn cord, wishing he could bring down the curtain of this chapter of his life just as easily.

He went back up to the bedroom as quietly as he could, avoiding the creaks of the stairs. The silence that hung over the place. was so intense he dared not disturb it. He sat with Emma the rest of the night, a blanket draped around his shoulders. The dark was lightened by a glistening Spring frost, and half a moon. David watched it come up over the tip to pepper the village with its ashen glow. He dreaded the dawn, and the waking of Emma.

Emma's cheek was warm to David's touch, something inside made him long to get into bed with her, to share that warmth, but he dared not touch her emptied body. He sat until the first smudge of dawn filtered through the drapes, as grey as his mood. Emma stirred, roused by the trudge of the miners in the street. David looked down on them, onto cropped and capped heads. Their hob-nailed boots made a monotonous clack on the road, an even sound. One long chain of men being pulled to a dark place of work.

Emma reached out a hand for him, and he took it. 'Was it a dream,' she asked, 'an awful dream?'

She looked around the room, eyes wide. David winced as they fastened on him.

'No, it was not a dream, Em. You... we lost the baby. It was very difficult for you the doctor said. I'm sorry...' David trailed to a halt, he wondered if Emma had heard him, then she shuddered, as if trying to shake off something unwanted, and he felt her fingers dig into his arm.

'I knew before I passed out,' she said, 'it was my last thought, that it had all gone wrong, there was so much pain. But I wanted it to be a dream.'

Tears came as he held her, waves of sobs racked her body for several minutes.

'Was it a boy?' Emma asked quietly.

'Yes,' David answered, 'it was a little boy, Em.'

'I thought so.'

David was relieved to hear Winnie Rowlands knocking on the shop door. He pulled himself away from Emma to let the old woman in.

The events of the next week swirled around David, much like his wedding had. Whenever he was forced into the company of the Vincents the air was stinging with hostility. His own family did not say very much. Billy brought him a bottle of whiskey, his mother came to see Emma, and was kind to her. Vincent made the arrangements for the funeral and David did not argue. The baby was buried a few days later. A pint-sized coffin was laid in a hole in the Vincent plot, and the shaking voice of Iolo once more attended. 'Receive, oh Lord, one who never knew the sins of this world,' he thundered, head tilted towards his heaven. The women huddled around the grave, Mrs Vincent wore a dress of black satin, and stood away from David's people. David stood opposite Vincent; they were just a few feet apart but there was a gulf between them. Emma was too weak to attend, and David was glad of that, it would have been another strain on his nerves.

Vincent came up behind David as they walked from the graveyard. 'You don't know me lad, don't know me at all. Believe what's easy, you do.'

David half expected him to strike out but Vincent squeezed his arm, almost with affection, then he was gone, following his wife to the car. There was to be no gathering afterwards.

'What did he have to say, then?' Billy asked.

'I don't know,' David said, 'I didn't understand him.'

Billy was the second man to squeeze. 'Never mind, butty boy,' he said, 'it was meant to be, meant to be.'

Meant to be. How often had David heard that said in the face of adversity, it was the catchphrase of the valley, a simple salve for weak and strong alike. It enabled the village to carry on, accepting its lot, by and large. David wished he could do likewise. He remembered a character in Lawrence, a reader and loner like himself. 'Those books will put you on your back,' his mother had said, and David saw the wisdom of that statement now. So far his learning had led only to bitterness, and estrangement, he felt a fledgling despair that no-one his age ought to feel.

The Vincents chugged past in the Riley. 'Old bastard' Billy muttered under his breath; David nodded mechanically in agreement, but he remembered that squeeze.

Emma kept to her bed for the next two weeks, and David spent more time in the shop. He got in the way of Dawes, but they tolerated each other. Each knew who really ran the shop now, and David knew it would not be long before Vincent made some move against him. His wife would make sure of it, her tongue would twist like a dagger in the old man's guts, keeping the wound keen. Emma did not speak about leaving him, she did not speak much about anything, so David was left to guess her thoughts. Emma was reluctant to leave the bedroom, all the confidence had drained from her. She had been robbed of her child, her one possible salvation, and David would not provide another, Emma was sure of that.

David renewed his visits to Conti's, and his welcome there was warm and genuine. He was greatly touched by it. The Boys kindled a spark of belonging in him, and David accepted it in a way he could not do with Emma. Mrs Conti fussed over him for a few days, dabbing at her dark eyes whenever she thought of the *bambino*. After a while she returned to normal, and admonished David for not being with his wife.

David realised how much he had missed the talks when Tom Price was asked to speak on the march to London. He did so shyly, in faltering tenor's voice. He told of the endless tramping, the acts of kindness they received on the way. His voice hardened when he spoke of London.

'Didn't want to know us there, boys,' he said, 'we was treated like tramps. One chap came up and called us layabouts, why don't we get a job, he said. I asked him for his, and he got funny then, called us rabble, scum, that sort of thing. We had to stop Hughsie from thumping him one.'

The Boys laughed.

'Aye, but there was not enough of you,' Billy said, 'men going up in dribs and drabs again, no-one notices that, might as *well* be bloody tramps. What we want is a mass march, like what the boys up north are up to.'

'Maybe, Bill, but they don't achieve much even then, do they?' Tom turned towards the Boys. 'We are squashed everywhere, whenever there is a demonstration the police are on you, moving you on, pushing you around. Look how they protect the black-shirts, Mosley is treated like a bloody lord when he moves around, they even gave him an armoured car once.' Tom stopped, suddenly aware that he was addressing the men.

'Well Tom,' Billy chuckled, 'that walk has certainly done wonders for your tongue, that's for sure. And talking about

Mosley and lords, there's plenty of them that would like to see him in power here, don't forget. They are watching what happens in Europe, like we are. We are all waiting for our cue, so be ready for it, boys.'

Billy's exhortation ended the discussion, the Boys ordered another round of tea, and grew silent as they collectively mused to the splutter and hiss of the stove. Conti came from behind his counter and poked it.

'Issa rubbish, this thing,' he said. He caught his hand on a hot plate and cursed in a flurry of Italian.

'Be quiet, Conti,' Maria shouted across the den, 'you fool.' Conti took no notice, and chastised the stove with his tablecloth, whipping it like an angry hairdresser, to the winks and encouragements of the Boys.

David asked Tom back to the shop for a nightcap. He had taken to drinking whiskey in the evenings, before bed.

'Are you sure it's okay?' Tom asked, 'so soon after... you know.'

'Yes, it's alright, Tom, we'll be on our own in the kitchen.'

As they drank Tom talked of his wife for the first time.

'I could never afford the proper treatment, Dave, not on the pit's wages. I had to watch her slip away, day by day, she looked fifty in the end, like one of those flowers you see crushed in a book, all withered up. Used up.'

'What was wrong?'

'Oh, pernicious anaemia, they called it. It's not unusual in the valley, poor nutrition, the doctor said.'

'Were you political before that?'

'Oh aye, born to it. My dad was one of the early Federation men. No, I've always lived and breathed socialism, I didn't come to it because I had nothing else, if that's what you are thinking. Ann being taken so young just strengthened my resolve to try to change things, that's all.'

David poured Tom another drink.

'Could get a taste for this, I reckon', Tom said. He continued, 'anyway you can't really believe in anything else, if you go down the pit. I remember my first day down the Navigation, thirteen I was, just a scragend of a lad. I soon learned what type of world it was down there, you've done well to escape it, Dave.'

David grimaced.

'This shop hardly inspires me to think so.'

'Don't you believe it, man. It's clean here, you are not breathing in dust all day, till your chest feels like an old hinge. It was hot that day I started, and there was a lot of flying cockroaches in the levels. They stuck to your chest and sucked your blood, the little buggers. Couldn't get them off easily, either. That's what the bosses are to me, I soon came to thinking, bloody bloodsuckers.'

Drink loosened Tom's tongue, then tiredness took hold. He sat and dozed. The bottle had been half emptied, and the hour forgotten. David wanted to talk on, he liked Tom's company. He prodded Tom into alertness, and, in the manner of someone half-drunk he carried on talking, as if unaware of the gap.

'How are things between you and Emma now, David?' Tom asked.

'I've told you a bit about it,' David said, 'it's not better.'

'It's a terrible thing that you are not getting on; you can't live without love – I don't think so anyway, mine was taken away from me. Trouble is, you see marriage as a trap, don't you, I can tell that. All young fellas do, but it's only a state of mind, freedom is a state of mind, and a young one at that. I think a man can be as free in a prison as he can in a wilderness, if his mind is right. That's the only place it really counts, in here.' Tom tapped the side of his head. He clutched his glass with both hands, hands gnarled and blue-scarred. His fingers were calloused, ending in ball ends in which the nails were submerged. David remembered his father's, and looked at his own. They were white, and soft.

'You are very young, Dave,' Tom said, 'all mixed up at the moment, I think, but I tell you something, I like that Emma of yours, something good about her. You'll be a fool if you panic yourself out of keeping her.' Tom leant across in his chair and punched David lightly. 'Eh, something good might come out of your trouble, you might be free of old Vincent, be your own man. You'll stand by Emma, won't you?'

David drained the last of the whiskey and did not answer.

Vincent did not appear in the shop but he wrote to Emma after the funeral. He wanted her to leave David, and return to the fold. 'It will all be forgotten, in time,' he wrote. 'You will have the chance to meet someone else later, someone decent.' Vincent would be able to arrange a divorce easily enough. 'I have plenty to go on,' he said.

The old man was in a dilemma, David knew that. If Emma stayed with him, Mrs Vincent would see to it that she was cut off, perhaps even thrown out of the shop, if she had her way. But Vincent would never allow his daughter to suffer like that, so he was stuck. Emma was the key. She was in the shop again, helping Dawes. The letter gave David the opportunity to try to talk to her.

'What will you do, Emma, are you going back to your parents?' he asked.

'I don't know, David. I need time to think. Is that what you want?'

David shrugged. 'I don't know either, I don't want there to be a rift between you and your family.'

'Oh David, there is already. I can't see you and Dad ever being reconciled, neither of you would want it.'

Nothing more was said, so David let it drift. With Emma in the shop he had more time to spend in Conti's, or in his makeshift storeroom library. His sloth became increasingly public; he was no longer the manager of the shop in body, and he had never been in spirit.

David followed the events in Europe, viewing the rise of Fascist dictators pessimistically. In the Hall there were frequent talks about the fate of German and Italian workers, grim pictures were painted by a succession of speakers, but the news of Spain was better, and David began to immerse himself in the patchy details of the happenings there.

On the first Saturday of May David gave himself the day off. Billy had asked him to take part in a demonstration, his first. Local businessmen had invited Mosley to speak at the town at the bottom of the valley, a challenge Billy's Boys found impossible to ignore. Emma was nervous about David attending the rally, and Helen came over to voice her concern also, but David stuck to his decision. He was glad to leave the women in the shop, when Helen was with Emma he felt their collective disappointment in him, yet his mother's visits were good for Emma: her pain was softened by Helen's kindness.

David assembled with the others at Conti's, early in the morning. He was thrilled with the idea of protesting publicly. It was just a year ago that he had watched a mass demonstration flow past his window, the streets awash with people spitting out chants and slogans that caught him up even then. Now he was part of it. The Boys shuffled around outside the café in soft drizzle, like birds gathering before a flight. Excitement coursed through them as Billy gave a few instructions. There had been considerable violence when the blackshirts had last tried to penetrate the valley, this time Billy was even more determined to prevent the meeting.

'There will be a lot of them down there, boys,' Billy said, 'but there will be a lot of us too, and we've learned to play like them now, haven't we? Keep together, don't let the police split you up, 'cos if you get cut off from the main bunch and there's trouble, you'll get a hammering, and six months hard to boot.' None of the Boys had any doubts that there would be trouble, and some had suspicious bulges under their coats.

David travelled down the valley on a train filled with men firing themselves up for the fray, they were colourful and garrulous, like green soldiers going to war, in search of glory. He felt out of his depth with these tough miners, and stayed close to Billy and Tom when they marched from the station to the town when Mosley was to speak. The police were there to meet them, more police than David had ever seen before. He heard West Country accents, these were specially trained men, drafted into the valleys for such occasions. The protesters were herded into a tight knot of men, and more than a few women. They numbered five hundred. Mosley was already in the hall, they learned, smuggled in before the crowd had assembled. This fact was shouted through the people, stoking up the fire.

David jeered with the others as they approached the hall. Each car of dignitaries that arrived incensed the crowd. One of the Reeses was recognised, and a roar went up from the miners. A few stones thudded off the car, galvanising the police into action. They charged the crowd with arms linked, trying to push people away from the hall steps. They were attempting to expand the cordon they had established in front of the building. Billy began to shout, other leaders joined in.

'Are we going to let this happen in our valley, boys?' he bellowed, 'we all know what this lot stands for, but we're not going to stand for it, are we? Let's give Mosley a real Welsh welcome.'

The men around David hurled themselves forward against the closed ranks of the police. Their surge was strong enough to break the cordon. Both sides lost what control they had and fighting broke out, a series of small groups battling each other. The square looked like a huge ballroom where people whirled around, fighting instead of dancing. Policemen lashed out with truncheons, the Boys retaliated the best they could. David saw Billy lay out a sergeant with one mighty blow, before being engulfed in a melee of warring men. The ground under his feet seemed to shift, he was being swept along with the momentum of the crowd. Beside him a young woman was hanging onto a policeman, trying to gouge his face with her nails. The man lost patience and struck her away with his fist. Blood from her smashed face showered David, he felt its warm spots on his own. He went to help the woman but Tom pulled him away.

'Come on,' he shouted, 'let's get out of this, they have all gone crazy.'

Tom dragged David away from the main action into an alley, where the wounded of both sides were being laid out. David felt his own blood flowing from the back of his head as Tom sat him down.

'Looks as if you've had a bit of a bump there,' Tom said, 'let's have a look. Not too bad, a cut, that's all.'

David touched the wound gingerly; he had no idea how he had received it. As he looked at his bloody hand he felt dizzy and sick in his stomach. He had not bargained for this. He looked out at the scene, in front of the hall the police had succeeded in moving the rioters. Slouched against the alley wall David had a distorted view of the action, it was dreamlike, and distant, he felt he was not part of this mayhem. It was an Eisenstein film, milling people, swirling action, violence. Blood was being spilled uselessly, the blackshirts were in the town hall, and the demonstrators were no match for the trained police.

Tom pulled David to his feet. 'Come on,' he said, 'let's get away. They'll arrest us if we stay here.'

'What about Billy?' David asked.

'Don't worry about him, he can look after himself. Billy's got what he wanted, even if he's taken a beating for it, Mosley won't come back here in a hurry.'

As they left the fighting was ending. David heard isolated noises behind him, the wail of a woman, the scattered shouts of angry men, and the curses of the wounded. He never knew how he got home. Hills flashing by through the train window, being sick on the village platform, that was all he could remember. The rest was a semi-conscious blur of noise and fear. The war-cry of Billy echoed and re-echoed in his ears, he tried to stop them up with his hands, with Tom pulling him along. That woman had been pretty, David thought.

Emma bathed David's head when he got back to the shop. His wound was a superficial cut behind his left ear, bloody but slight. Emma tended it in the kitchen as Tom talked excitedly of the day's events.

'I hope Billy got away. Last time I saw him he was under a bunch of men. The police will be sniffing around you know, looking for the leaders, we'll all have to lie low for a while.' Tom did not notice Emma's reproachful glance, but David had regained enough sense to be worried by what Tom said. It had not occurred to him that he might get on the wrong side of the police. His worry was mirrored in Emma's face, he had given her another new torment. After drinking a bottle of beer Tom left them, anxious to be off the streets.

David went to bed, supported by Emma. He had a plaster around his ear, and blood on his shirt that he was now rather proud of. Although he had done nothing but naively follow the others David felt he had been blooded this day, initiated into the world of men. He got into bed and Emma pulled the blankets over him. 'Are you sure you are all right, David?' Emma leant over him, looking ten years older than he.

'Yes, it's nothing. I didn't think things would go as far as they did, mind.'

'You must have been the only one then. Will you still be going to Conti's, after this?'

'Yes, of course. More than ever, now.'

Emma nodded sadly and left him to sleep.

As Tom predicted, the police were active that weekend, picking up several of the Boys. Tom was questioned, but released, and no-one came for David. He spent Sunday in dread of the doorbell, but Tom was the only visitor. From him David learned that Billy had been arrested for inciting a riot, and assaulting various policemen. It would mean prison for him. David wondered why he had not been questioned, the police must know he had been there. It would have been an ideal chance for Vincent to strike, he thought.

Conti's was quiet the next week. The Boys were defiant but beleaguered, and the loss of Billy was greatly felt. 'At least we've warned off the Fascists,' one muttered, 'Billy will think that's a fair exchange for a few months in Cardiff nick.'

The Boys looked to Tom for guidance now, and calmly he took up the reins of leadership. As the one with the knowledge, David's own opinions were increasingly sought. He became Tom's lieutenant. He was not nineteen yet the Boys were willing to place some trust in him, at least in affairs of the head. David sat closer to the stove, and voiced his ideas more openly. He took the riot as a signal to throw away some of his caution. Under the glow of Conti's low-hanging lamp David began to talk, assertions turning into minor speeches as his confidence grew. Often he quoted his books, but the Boys did not know that.

Billy's trial came up early, and although urged not to by Emma, David attended with the other Boys to lend what support he could. The courtroom was next to the same town hall they had tried to storm, it still bore some of the scars of the battle. Billy was in the dock with five others, four men and a woman who David recognised as the one struck by the policeman. Her face was bruised and her nose misshapen and mauve.

Past records of the accused were read out as the magistrate summed up. Each defendant said his piece, except the woman, who remained silent throughout the trial. No-one really believed the crown's version of events that day, but no-one had any illusions about the outcome. A small verbal tirade against the state by Billy and the others was granted in exchange for a verdict of guilty. Billy was unrepentant. 'I'd do the same again, your honour,' he shouted, rather dramatically.

There was a ripple of applause from the gallery. 'You tell 'em, Bill', someone shouted. The magistrate looked up from his papers, and twitched his nose. 'Would you now, Mr Hicks? Well not for nine months you won't. Take him down.'

Billy had the longest sentence; the rest of the men got six months, and the woman, in deference to her sex it was said, was to serve three. No mention was made of her injuries. Billy led the six down to the cells, his face showing the signs of a beating. He winked up at David, and walked out proudly, leaving the Boys to make their way home muttering threats and promises.

Helen was shocked at Billy's imprisonment. She saw the

family breaking up around her, instead of strengthening. David's marriage was foundering in its infancy, her daughters were without men, there was no grandson to nurse, and the strongest one was behind bars. These thoughts coursed through her head as she walked up the street to catch a bus to the far shop. Her feet hurt on the uneven slabs, and the wind blew off the tip into her eyes. She screwed them up and kept her head down. House windows marked her way, she knew them all now, which ones held the plants, which were bare and in need of paint. The ones nearest the shop were in the best condition, as if some of the shop's affluence had poured out and over them.

Helen's visits were not common, despite her loneliness. There was too much sadness in the place for her, the emptiness was on display as much as the cheese and jams. She wished David had escaped the valley; that was what he had always wanted. Now he was caught, and was hated by his in-laws into the bargain. Huw Dawes looked up from the counter as the doorbell announced Helen.

'Hello Mrs Hicks, nice to see you again.'

'Nice to see you, Mr Dawes. How is the family?'

'Can't grumble. The missus is glad to see me working again, of course.'

'Of course.'

Helen went up to the kitchen, where Emma was waiting to have tea with her. David was down in Cardiff with Tom, visiting Billy, taking time off again. Emma greeted Helen at the top of the stairs; she was shy but friendly with her mother-in-law. Helen saw the strain in Emma's face, and knew that her son had put it there. Marriage had not made a man of David and both youngsters were stuck fast, and unhappy.

'Hello, Mrs Hicks, you are early,' Emma said.

'Am I? My old legs must go faster than I think. They were starting to ache a bit coming up from the bus stop.'

Emma made tea too weak. Helen liked hers dark and strong, a habit from older days, when fresh milk had been scarce in the valley. With cups in hand they settled in front of the stove; Helen stretched out a hand to it.

'Still need a fire, don't we, and it's summer, just about. Don't think we are going to bake too much this year'.

She put down her cup and got out her knitting. 'Nothing like it for thinking, and calming yourself.' Helen held up a half-finished jumper, 'I'll put buttons down the front of this, and send it down to Billy. It'll be cold where he is. And how are you feeling now, Emma, is the tiredness gone?'

'Yes, I'm quite alright now, thanks.'

'H'm, well, that's good, if you are. You still look a bit peaky, mind.'

'I'm alright, really Mrs Hicks.'

'Mrs Hicks. About time you stopped calling me that, it makes me feel like an old biddy. Call me Helen.'

'I will then, Helen... David has gone to see his uncle.'

'Aye, I know. Leaving you to it again, is he?'

Emma coloured, and looked at her hands. 'I don't mind. It's good for him to get away from the shop.'

'He's away from it most of the time, as I hear it. And you too. Is that what you both want?'

Emma was not used to Helen's directness yet, so opposite was it to David's reticence.

'You know how it is between us, I think,' she said in a small voice. 'Nothing seems to be working. It's all mixed up.'

'Yes, David is good at that. Don't be embarrassed, girl, I've got eyes to see, and ears to hear, even if he is my own son. Is there anything I can do to help?'

'No, thank you. It's up to David and me to sort things out, if we can... I don't think he's ever loved me. I think he felt I trapped him. I thought the baby would help us, but he was taken away from me.'

'Yes, you have had a hard start, Emma, awful hard. When I was young, younger than you, I remember my grandmother saying something. If you loved someone who did not return it then love him twice as hard, until he does. I don't suppose that makes much sense, but that's what she said, and I think that's how she got her man. But things were much simpler then.'

'Yes.'

The two women sat quietly in the kitchen, listening to the sounds in the shop below. The coals in the stove hissed, Helen's needles clicked together, like fingers being snapped faintly. Each grew broody with her thoughts. Helen liked Emma, her fondness for her growing, as David slipped further away from her. She felt the girl nervous in her presence, guilty about the baby perhaps, although Helen had never blamed her for that. David's own guilt and shame had rubbed off on Emma, those two old Welsh devils that flowed too strongly in the lifeblood of the village. As Helen aged she knew there were few blameless lives, and no-one was pure, especially those who claimed it. Perhaps some day she might tell Emma this.

Helen finished her last row and put the wool away. Emma had fallen asleep on the sofa. She looked a child as the light caught her face. Helen thought of her own youth and lost dreams; they had vanished so quickly when she had married Daniel. And she had hoped for so much more for David, for his character especially. Her own desire for an education had been snuffed out when she had to leave school to look after her brothers, secretly it had been reborn in David, and now his future seemed as blighted as that of any other working boy in the village. She left Emma without waking her, and made the painful walk back down the street. Her limbs complained more each week, dull aches that seeped out from her very bones. She felt age creeping in like a thief, to gnaw away at her in the night, stealing sleep, and conspiring with time to take her health. The young ones did not realise how little time they had, and how very precious it was.

8

The brown bracken of the hills was speckled with new growth by mid-May, what trees there were took on leaves again, and the air was fresher, with a little warmth to it. Even in the black valley there was a quality of renewal, encouraging people to be out and about. Each sunny day was seized on as if it might be the last.

David took advantage of the first fine Sunday to walk the ridge with Tom. They left early and climbed quickly, David struggling to match Tom's pace. Tom was a good walker: he kept low to the ground, head down against the wind. David watched him walk on ahead, propelling his sturdy frame up the slope, like a pit pony put out to graze. They passed several couples, competing with the sheep for the kindest hollow, as David had done, just one year before. He sucked in the air, and was invigorated by it, it was free of the streets, and work. Clouds raced across the sky as the day fattened out, and sunlight shafted through them, moving its rays up and down the valley, like a vast searchlight.

They gained the top of the Tump and stopped to rest. David saw the sea for the first time as a married man, this day it was a dull blue slash beyond the mountains. Old dreams were rekindled by its image, and once more David glimpsed other worlds, and other possibilities.

'What are you thinking?' Tom asked, 'got your head in the clouds more ways than one, eh?'

'This is a good place to think, Tom. It always gets my mind going.'

'Aye, mine too.'

They sat on the highest spot of the Tump, amongst a scattering of broken stones, clumps of grass, and the bleached bones of a sheep. The village was tiny below them. David shared cheese and bread with Tom, and they drank the bottle of beer Tom had brought, and lay back, letting the sun soak into them and suck the winter from their bones.

'I saw Juan Davies the other night, Dave,' Tom said, 'down the Hall. Said he was going home, to those mines they have over there, in the north, the um...'

'The Asturias, Tom, that's where Juan is from.'

'Aye, that's it, the Astoorias. He was telling us about the riots they had there a few years ago, a bit different from our go down the town, I can tell you. They sent the army in, butchered thousands of miners. Juan said they won't let that happen again. "We have a government now," he said, "a voice."'

'When is he going?'

'As soon as he can get a boat from Cardiff, he said.'

In Spain Azana was President, a liberal, David read. Socialists were doing well in France also, whilst Mussolini was flexing his muscles in Abyssinia.

'The world is taking sides,' David said.

'Aye, looks like it. Hasn't it always, though? We get to know about things now, with the papers, and the wireless. Who would have thought we could sit in Conti's and be told what was happening thousands of miles away?'

'I think the lid will blow off Europe soon, Tom. It has been shaping up for it since 1917.' David stretched on his back.

'Perhaps you are right, David. If it does we'll be in the thick of it all, I shouldn't wonder.'

Tom passed over the rest of the beer. 'Here you are, have the last swig.'

'How do you think Billy is doing?' David asked.

'Well, they don't treat the likes of us too good in prison, but Billy will be alright. He's too old a campaigner to worry about a short stretch inside. Right now he's probably planning the next demonstration.'

They slept for a while, David drifting into a dream in which he led men, like Billy, a dream in which everything worked out. He awoke crumpled, with a headache. Halfway up the Tump a sheep struggled over a low wall. It was anxious to join the flock and bleated repeatedly, a high, pathetic sound that did not seem to suit it.

David pondered on the sheep for some time, other placid animals had high-pitched voices that belied their bulk, pigs, horses, they all could scream. Dinosaurs had once roamed the swamps that were here, David thought, many-tonned creatures with the voices of sheep, perhaps. He scratched himself and sat up, rousing Tom as he did so.

'We had better get back, Tom, we've been asleep for an hour.'

'Have we, be damned. That's fresh air for you.'

'And ale.'

They began their descent, passing a young man and his girl on the way.

'They'll be going for our place,' Tom said, 'the grass is all smoothed down for 'em.'

Tom chuckled to himself as they walked. It was the most talkative David had known him.

'Do you know, Dave,' Tom said, 'I was up here with Billy once, and the dog, just sitting and talking, like us today. "That's the world out there, Betty," Billy says to her. "I'd like to bring all the village up here, one big outing. They can look at something other than coal tips and pit wheels then. I'd tell them that their lives could be changed, re-shaped, like that sea down there. A free-moving thing that is, a thing that calls no man Master. They don't have to put up with everything as they do, I'd tell 'em, they could change things, if they stuck together.'

David laughed, 'Unity. We'll have to carve it on Billy's headstone.'

'Aye, we will that, although Billy is right enough.'

Tom left David at the shop, declining the invitation for tea.

'No thanks, Dave,' he said, 'I'll get back now, feed the dog. Billy would never forgive me if I didn't look after her proper.'

Tom strolled off down the street. David pushed the door open and went back into his prison. Immediately he felt it clutch at him. He glared at the row of jars and they glared back at him. How he longed to dash them to the floor, but David settled for a sigh of self pity, and went in search of a book.

He climbed the stairs to find Emma back from her parents. Her eyes were red-rimmed, and under each of them was a furrow in her face powder. When David entered the bedroom she got up and went into the kitchen. Normally he would have left her alone but this time he followed her, sensing she would have news for him. He stood in the kitchen doorway as Emma filled the kettle. They were silent as tea was made, two strangers sharing the same room. Emma handed him a mug of tea. 'They want me to leave you, David, Mam and Dad.'

'Well we know that,' David said, 'that's obviously what they want. What did you say?' He sat on the kitchen table and sipped his weak tea.

A shiver ran through Emma as she answered. 'The usual things, it doesn't matter what they said. It's us. Things are getting worse. I think only one little bit of you cares about me, the rest, I don't know the rest, I don't know you, David, you won't let me. You hide, in your books, behind your friends, you are wrapped up in yourself. You live for yourself.' David slumped in his chair, hands cupped around the mug.

'I don't blame you for the baby,' Emma continued, 'he was both our faults, but I blame you for pushing me away.' Her voice grew very small. 'You must end it, David, before I go mad. Let me go, it would be better than this, you can do what you want then, you'll have your precious freedom.'

'Yes.' A lame one word response was all David could muster, and Emma had paved the way for him to say it. She was never prettier than now. He saw the slender lines on her neck as she talked and felt a spurt of attraction for her, in his moment of rejection.

'I'll not divorce you, David, I don't mean that, no matter how much Dad wants it. But we must separate, I need to be away from you. My father will have the shop back again, and Mr Dawes will run it, he has talked with Dad apparently. You will be able to go back to your mother.' Emma stood over David, fighting back bitter tears. He envied her strength; in her place he would have clung on, swallowing pride, and hoping, childishly, that everything would be alright.

'Don't you have anything to say except yes?' Emma asked.

'What you say is right, Emma. We had better split up, it would be best. I'm sorry.'

'Sorry.' Emma spat out the word with disgust and ran from him. David still sat with his tea, like a man in a trance. This was what he wanted, but he still felt empty, and sick with failure. The first chapter of his life was ending in confirmation of his weakness. He wanted Billy to return, he missed the old man's guidance. The riot had terrified him, he thought often of his face disintegrating like that woman's; thoughts of pain and death were often in his mind, when he should be cultivating his youth, and planning his future.

Helen accepted the news of the break-up of the marriage calmly and with resignation. Since her last visit she had seen it coming, she knew David had lost all heart for the arrangement.

She worried about him, for she did not know how to help him, but at least he would be home, with her. It would be another chance for him. She painted the boxroom at the back of the house. It still held some of his toys, home-made lead soldiers that Daniel had cast, and horses made out of pit prop shavings, and books. Books were all about the room, in boxes, piled up on the window sill, their pages yellowed at the edges by the sun. They were lad's books, David had taken the ones with the big words with him. She thumbed through a few, looking at the sketches, and the odd colour print, looking at her son's early dreams. They were books from years ago, when they could ill afford them. Helen remembered reading them to David, he could never get enough of stories, and now he was returning to this boy's room a married man, and she knew he would be up here like before, reading, dreaming, getting nowhere.

Helen aired the bed, and put a pot with some spring flowers in the window. Through a gap in the opposite terrace the wheel of the pit could be seen; David had always been so frightened of it, it was a dragon belching flames to him, every underground rumble was a roar, every whistle the cry of a victim. The boy had such imagination. She turned back the bedclothes, arranging them neatly. There was a blurred picture of David on the dresser, taken that time they went to the seaside. He peered seriously into the camera, his eyes screwed up. Behind him other children waited, anxious to have it done, and be gone. That had been a grand day, they had all had a glimpse of a different life. Perhaps Billy was right, Helen thought, perhaps they can change things in the valley.

It was settled quickly in the next few weeks. Vincent sent a man down to sift through the shop's accounts, but David had kept them well. Dawes assumed full control on David's last Saturday. His limp was less prominent, the man grew in stature as he fussed about the shop, his shop.

'You'll be off today then, Mr Hicks,' Dawes said. David could not tell if Dawes was laughing at him or not, he had always had the habit of standing at one's shoulder, and rubbing his hands together, Uriah Heep-like.

'You are manager again now, Dawes,' David said. 'Funny how things work out, isn't it?'

'Yes indeed, Mr Hicks. I was just telling Mrs Dawes the other day, we never know what life holds in store for us, I said. She took it very hard, you see, when I had to leave the shop, what with the children and everything. Now you are going. Who would have thought that now?' Dawes flicked at his counter, picking off a fly with his duster. David knew that Dawes had always thought it.

Two boys came into the shop, David recognised them as second years from the County School. They were fresh-faced, and clad in bright uniforms, their badges of difference in the village. They pondered over the sweets, gazing into each jar with judicial eyes, debating the best tastes and the best prices. They were like sweets themselves, sharp, well turned out, bursting with pride and mischief, confident that they were going places, and that it was their world. They settled on a purchase and paid David with grins on their faces, letting him know they knew all about him, and what he had done with Emma on the Tump. The door snapped shut and David had served for the last time.

David settled back into the family house easily, his own bedroom was an instant haven after the tyranny of the till. He was in a kinder place, filled with quiet, and books. It had always been like that, for as long as he could remember, yet the house was changed. David felt an air of reproach and disappointment in Helen, he was the one so much hope had been pinned on, and now he was back, and about to sign on the dole, something his father had always managed to avoid.

Going down the labour exchange was a very miserable experience. It was in the town of the riot, close by the place where David had been carried along, a gaunt building in the centre, known to everyone as the Grange. Men scuffed around outside it, watching each other, trying to sniff out news of any jobs. The air of the place was dismal, and final; a wave of hopelessness drifted towards David as he pushed his way in. Tom had accompanied him, to show him the ropes. 'You're in the knacker's yard now boy,' Tom whispered, cheerfully.

David's treatment by the clerk was a little worse than the norm, his background singled him out for it. Had he not been to the County, had he not run the far shop? Was he not married? These facts fuelled official indignation. David sat opposite his questioner, in a small cubicle, like a confession box. The clerk tapped on his notepad; the more he questioned the more he tapped.

David's sense of privacy was torn to shreds. Why was he here, why wasn't he still working, didn't he know how lucky he was?

The unemployed graded the clerks in terms of hostility, heartlessness and downright stupidity. David's man was Ronald Reginald Meredith, 'R.R.', the worst of the bunch by all accounts. He was small bodied but large boned, and had the look of a trussed chicken. Large collar bones struggled to escape the puny torso, and his face was prone to redness, making him look perpetually angry. It was a handy weapon in his work.

'You left your last employment, Mr Hicks,' R.R. said, with a pursing of the lips, 'left your wife too, it seems. That is bad, very bad indeed as far as we are concerned, a cardinal sin, you might say. To leave a job in times like these...' Meredith clucked his tongue for a few seconds, and scanned his notes. He moralised for a few minutes more, then made calculations on his pad. 'We will have to make checks, Mr Hicks, lots of checks, since you are separated from your wife – you are separated?' David nodded, 'and there are no children. You might receive fifteen shillings a week, subsequent to our inquiries being satisfactory.' The ring of Meredith's bell brought the interview to a sharp end.

David rejoined Tom in the waiting room feeling he had been stripped bare. Tom smiled. 'Join the club, boy. How do you feel? Don't answer, your face says it all. Bit of a shock, eh?'

'That Meredith is a swine.'

Tom chuckled, 'Maybe. From our village, too, but don't be too sorry for yourself, you had the usual treatment. "R.R" is not a monster, the job has made him like he is; they feel guilty, see, the blokes who work here. They are surrounded by the likes of us, people suffering bad. There is a big wall between them with work and them without, Dave. And the ones with don't want to look over the wall too much, they don't want to know. This lot here have work, it makes them mean, 'cos it makes them guilty.'

David looked at Tom gloomily.

'Cheer up,' Tom said, 'you have lost your job, your wife, have no prospects, you are a fully-fledged Conti Boy now. You'll get used to it, in time, and time is one thing you'll have a lot of – you can make speeches down the café, read on the Tump, do what you like, workers throw off your chains, eh? Make the most of it, that's all any of us can do.'

David was not listening to Tom, he still burned with the

grilling Meredith had given him, he was at the sharp end of struggle now, as Tom said. He took Tom's advice. His interest in Spain intensified, he read whatever he could get his hands on about it. People were being killed in the streets as various factions jockeyed for position. The country was moving towards civil war, there was no doubt of that. Juan Davies had predicted it, and now he looked forward to it.

'They have killed Calvo Sotelo,' Juan said, 'he was a big man for the Right, now nothing can stop a fight. Martyrs are good for the encouragement, no?'

Juan had arranged passage from Cardiff to Bilbao on a Welsh freighter. In his last days in the valley he became an honourary member of the Boys, his words adding colour to the brotherhood of the stove.

'I am a Basque, comrades,' he told them, on his last night, 'not Spanish. Is different, like you are not English, no?'

There was a gasp of denial from the Boys.

'What's a Basque then, when he's at home?' Tom asked.

This was Juan's cue to flow. He told them his was a different land within Spain, separate in language and culture. David saw that Juan thought the Spanish inferior, he hated them, for they ruled his people. In the heady, smoke-ridden air of the den it was easy for the Boys to compare their own predicament with Juan's. The old iron worker became a celebrity, he was someone for the first time in his life, and he loved the one brief swallow of importance it gave him.

Threatened by Maria, the Boys went down the Anchor, to send Juan off seriously. David followed on behind with Tom.

'Noisy tonight, aren't they?' Tom said. 'Haven't had much to celebrate recently, I suppose.'

'No, not with Billy inside,' David said. 'Let them go on a bit, Tom, we'll catch up. I want to take a bit of air.'

'If there is war in Spain it will be all or nothing for the likes of Juan, you know, Dave.'

'What do you mean?'

'Well, he will be fighting more for independence than politics, won't he? You could tell that back there, Juan's heart is still in those mountains of his, you could almost feel him come alive again, back in Conti's. There's a lesson to be learned from that.'

'What?'

'The strength you can draw from a cause, from having hope. Juan's got it back and he's twenty years younger.'

'Yes, he does seem to be.'

'Another thing I thought too, when Juan was talking. What the Left will be up against in Spain, like here only much worse I think. Remember that old saying of Billy, about the donkey that couldn't decide which bale of hay to eat and starved to death. Spain could be like that. From what I've read there will be too many viewpoints, too many people wanting to carve up the pie. They could end up shooting themselves in the foot, while the other lot gets on with it. They want a few Billy Hickses over there, to unite the buggers.'

'You've been thinking a lot, Tom'

'Aye, well Juan thinks we'll be following him out there, when the ball starts rolling.'

No-one had actually talked about going to Spain, and David thought it unlikely that anyone would do so. He was certain he would not.

At the Anchor the beer flowed until it was time for Juan to go. They put him on the last train to Cardiff, barely conscious, and kissing everyone. Before he fell into his compartment Juan stuffed a paper into David's pocket. When the train had pulled out and the Boys were walking away David stopped to read it by the station light. It had a smudged message under a sketch which he read: *This is where I come from. I do not know if I will be there when the fighting starts, I do not know if it will be of any use to you, but look for me everywhere in Spain.*

David was puzzled by the note, Tom would have been a better bet to meet in Spain, perhaps his pocket was the first the drunken hand of Juan had chanced upon. David kept the paper, tucking it into a fold in his wallet, then running to catch the others, to join them for the walk home.

If rain did not sweep down the valley David stayed on the Tump until dusk veiled the words on his pages. Sometimes he returned with headaches, exacerbated by stopping for tea in Conti's, and breathing in the Italian's indoor smog. On days like this Helen left a simple supper for him, which he ate in the kitchen, perhaps still with a book. Reading was within reach for the poor, it came free down at the Miners' library. The one his father had introduced him to was well stocked, and David had unlimited access to it, Billy had seen to that. It became his true place of work. When it rained he was in there, comforted by its smell of dusty knowledge. From Marx and accounts of Russia post 1917, David discovered the literature of Czarist times. He devoured the works of Dostoyevsky and Tolstoy, their depth, and their ability to surround simple themes with grandeur and never submerge them. He loved Dostoyevsky's guilt, Tolstoy's truth and his own elation at reading them in his barely literate village.

David spent so much time out of the house, or out of the way in it, he did not see much of Helen, and even less of his sisters. Sometimes he felt like a lodger. Helen's clandestine jobs were in full flow, putting precious pennies into the Hicks coffers, and cushioning David from poverty. She expected David to do jobs around the house, now that he had so much time, but he carried out the work entrusted to him with such consistent incompetence that she gave up, and let him be.

At the end of July Spain finally lurched into civil war. A rebel army was airlifted into southern Spain from Morocco to challenge the government, led by a Spanish general called Franco, David read. It was the first time that he had heard the name but it stayed in his head. A lifetime later he found out that Franco had been flown into Spain by a Welshman. The London papers were expecting a quick victory by the rebels, and looked forward to it. The status quo could then be restored, and British business in Spain protected. David sucked Conti's tea through his teeth and let his thoughts race. If the Spanish government could win through it would be a great example.

'Don't get your hopes up too much, eh?' Conti shouted from his counter. 'Workers unite – huh! The other side will have workers too, who else ever does the fighting? And don't underestimate the church, my young friend, many of the poor will be on her side, they care for their souls.'

Conti's words brought David's thoughts down to size. Sometimes he hated the Italian for shredding his dreams, but he always respected Conti's measured cynicism. No-one knew what the man stood for, what he believed in. 'Ice-cream,' Conti had once told Billy, 'why not, I can touch it, smell it, eat it, it makes me money, *si*, I believe in ice cream.' The Boys thought that Conti was just out for himself, but David reserved his judgement.

Once, when no-one else was about, Conti had begun to

expound his own views. 'People are mixed up, that's what I think,' Conti said. 'Good, evil, balance in here, and here' Conti pressed his heart and head. 'People have always been rotten, and they've always been good too. And so it will always be, one side sweeping against the other. Never will one thing be triumphant for long, for then the world would stop, I think. That's how the Almighty wants it, he gives us the choice. Choke with goodness, or sink with evil.' Conti laughed, flashing his teeth at David, taunting his frustration. 'It's complicated, no, this life, David.'

'You seem to see clearly enough, Conti.'

'Maybe, but I am only the keeper of a café, not even in my own land. You boys, Socialists, Communists, I don't know what, you see everything as great movements, fine thoughts, feelings that will sweep the people forward, you can't understand why they don't flock to you. I will tell you why, they are too busy, working, loving, dying, being tired, it is too painful for them to follow causes, and dreams die young. You boys, the ones who come here, you have time, so you have thoughts. Dreams come back for you, maybe. It is always the same for those who are idle, that is why it is such a dangerous thing for a working man. You David, are different, you have an education,' Conti rubbed his chin, 'perhaps that is the worst thing of all'.

'Conti, stop talking and work,' Maria shouted.

Conti shrugged, 'I am only a café man.' David felt power in Conti but was able to resist his reasoning as his self-confidence as a Boy grew. Very slowly he was becoming his own man.

There was terror in Spain: the Hall's reading room was full of news of it. David spent wet afternoons looking at newspapers. Either priests and nuns were being murdered by mobs of barbaric Red butchers, or the Socialists were freedom fighters, struggling against barbarians. It depended on which paper he read. Spanish workers were being armed by a reluctant government, as the rebel armies threatened. Some would use their guns to exorcise old hatreds, David saw the inevitability of that, but any crime of the left would be repaid a thousand times, he felt, by Franco's mercenary army. In the months that it had interested him David picked up a scattering of Spanish history. He saw the irony of Franco using an ancient enemy, the Moors, to fight his brothers. Conti would love it, the self-proclaimed saviour of the church using the pagan to do his dirty work.

There was growing talk of men going out to fight for the republic, the livelier Boys said they would do so. But apart from the hunger marches, none of them had ever crossed the Welsh border. No working man had a passport, and no-one had the slightest idea of how to reach Spain. The Boys longed for Billy's release.

Since Billy's imprisonment, politics had not been mentioned in the Hicks household. David never talked to Helen about it, and her only question these days was whether David was seeking work. He always assured her that he was. He had to attend the Grange often and once a man had called at the house without warning, checking its contents like a malevolent magpie. David never got used to the labour exchange; he dreaded the shuffling queues of men sucking on cigarette stumps, pale faced thin men, with faces more tired than the miners returning from their shifts, the tiredness of boredom and depression. The shame of idleness settled over them in a cloud as the months, and then the years, passed by. After signing on they hung around the edges of the Grange, watching for any action, watching for anything, commiserating with each other, comparing empty life with empty life.

Autumn crept quietly into the valley, David saw the sun turn softer and yellower as it set over the tip. What heat summer had given was replaced by chill nights, and crisper mornings. The valley's attempt at greenery faded back into the rocks, copses turned russet, and shed their thin crop of leaves. The village braced itself as the winds grew keener, and came from the east.

David had not seen Emma at all since they had parted, and had not felt any great desire to. Meanwhile, the news from Spain was not good. It was hard to form a clear picture from the confused stories told in Conti's, but one thing was certain, the rebel forces were advancing, and gaining ground rapidly in the south of Spain. Blum, the French premier, had closed his border to republican arms supplies. This was a big talking point with the Boys, Blum was a Socialist, and led a Socialist government, but he would not openly help his Spanish counterparts. This dismayed the Boys, but Conti was jubilant.

'See,' Conti teased. 'What have I always told you? There is no difference, Socialist, Capitalist – all the same, all out to feather their own beds. Politics, she is a whore, eh, don't expect any loyalty from her.'

'Shut up Conti,' Bernard Davies shouted, 'stick to your bloody ice cream, why don't you?'

'Settle down, Bernard,' Tom said, 'he doesn't mean half of what he says. Here, Conti, let's have another tea all round.'

Tom talked quietly to David amidst the general hubbub. Increasingly he voiced his intention of going to Spain. 'I have nothing to lose, David, and everything to gain. It will be one way of knowing what's really going on out there, and a chance to do something we can't over here.'

'Do you think going will do any good?' David asked.

'I dunno, we're not soldiers, are we, but this war could be the one to change things. And if I didn't go I don't know what I would think in later years. Staying put might be hard to live with.'

'Billy will be out soon, he'll have good advice to give, no doubt.'

'Aye, we'll see what Billy says.'

The next morning David saw his first clear photograph of Franco. The general was now the undisputed head of the Insurgents, the new name given to the rebels by the newspapers. He was surprised at Franco's ordinariness, a small pear-shaped man, standing amongst his officers like a batman. David pencilled a moustache onto Franco's face. The man could be Hitler's brother, he thought, he was similar to the other Fascist leaders, they were walking opposites to the racial ideals they promoted. With his own smudge of moustache Hitler was the evil clown, Mussolini the bully-faced marionette, and Franco, with his slicked-back, greased-down hair, looked like a money collector, with an eye for the ladies. And these men led millions, were loved by millions. 'There you are,' Conti said, 'if the world can follow *them*, what hope have you?'

The first recruits for Spain were beginning to leave the valleys, in twos and threes. Most were married men, in their thirties and forties, leaving families behind them. Few wives understood. Large towns were falling to Franco, Madrid itself was seriously threatened. 'The war will hinge on that city,' Tom said. 'If Madrid falls, they will have won, you can count on that.' David did, gloomily. In the den there was a rumour that a man had left his wife to do the shopping, and had ended up on the way to Spain. Maria thought this a monstrous act, but the Boys were enthusiastic. 'Shows courage on the home front too,' someone shouted. Maria was amongst them, careless with her cloth. 'Idlers, leavers of women and *bambini*! I wish you would all go over there, and leave me in peace.' Torrents of Italian poured from her, making her bulk quiver and the children about her tremble. She turned her wrath on Conti, who ducked behind his counter, just avoiding the hurled cloth. The Boys enjoyed the theatre, a time when Conti's cynicism was chaff in Maria's storm.

'You see, boys,' Conti said, when Maria had disappeared into her kitchen, 'you see how fire and fury always wins the day. Words are nothing, how can you reason with the power of an angry Maria?'

As the trickle of men going to Spain increased into a small but steady flow the British government invoked the Enlistment Act, which forbade Britons to fight in foreign armies. Despite this, the Communist Party was actively trying to recruit men to fight. The Boys learned of the International Brigade of volunteers. The name stirred them, it had a wide, united feel to it. Men were coming from many countries to help the Republic. The Boys turned all their attention southwards, and Spain took a hold on the consciousness of the Conti group. They waited for Billy to spark off their action.

David went again with Tom to see his uncle. They found him greyer, but his eyes still sparkled, and he greeted them earnestly.

'Hello boys, good to see you again. I haven't had any visitors for a while.'

They shook hands and sat on a bench opposite Billy. There were a hundred other people in the room, creating a low murmur of sound as hushed voices tried to avoid the flapping ears of the screws. Tom told Billy the news. He was excited by the International Brigade, and declared he would join as soon as he got out. 'I won't have any trouble going, an old soldier like me.'

They looked doubtfully at Billy's whitening hair, but he laughed at them.

'Think I'm too old, eh? It's the two of you that should worry. Never fired a gun between you.' Like Juan, Billy did not seem to doubt that David would be going to Spain. He gave them an address in Cardiff they could go to for advice. 'But don't do anything till I get out, don't go drawing attention to yourselves. The police will have their fat noses into all this, and they'll stop you leaving the country if you show your hand. I'll be out before

Christmas, in time for your mother's grub, Dai *bach*.'

Their time was up, Billy was marched back to his cell with the others, and Tom and David were let out of the gaol, its heavy door clunking behind them as they stepped out into the keen air. It was fresh after the stale visiting room, which reeked of cooped up bodies. It reminded David of school, and his thoughts were wrapped up in his short past as they rode the train back up the valley. He saw Mrs Dagg putting out the washing again and felt the traces of those lusty thoughts. Emma came into his mind, but he smothered her image before it could disturb him, and fixed his eyes on the distant lines of the ridge, solid and black in the dusk.

There was to be another march to London, and this time David wanted to be part of it. Tom and four other Boys were going, and another dozen men from the valley. Helen was concerned but did not make any move to stop David, although he was anticipating one.

'Do you think you can walk that far, David?' Helen asked. 'The roads are hard, you know, not like our hills here.'

'I know that ma, but I want to go, I want to be part of things.'

Helen looked at him. 'I see. Make sure you wear your father's old boots then, you're the same size.'

'I don't want them, I'll be alright with my own.'

'Alright then, you know best.'

The marchers set out on a Monday morning. They would walk through the south of England to Reading, then on to the capital. It would take a week. A small crowd saw them off, well-wishers and the curious, and a few bored policemen who had seen it all before. David was the least shabby of the walkers and the men from the next village were puzzled by the presence of the smart youngster. David heard one ask Tom about him. 'Oh, he's alright,' Tom said, 'he's a bit of a college boy, but he's one of us.' The valley liked labels, and David would be forever the 'college boy'.

After pats on the back and shouts of encouragement they set off into the biting, late autumn wind. The police walked behind them until they left the village. David was soon tired, his hillside strolls had not prepared him for the wear the hard roads brought to his legs. Long before they reached Newport, a mere twenty miles away, he was in trouble. His calves felt as if hot needles pierced them, and his soles were spongy with blisters. He tried to walk on different parts of his feet but it was no use, each tread got worse. David was ashamed and angry at his pathetic state. His comrades were getting into their stride, they walked far more freely than he in their hob-nailed boots. To his relief they stopped at a café Billy had recommended to them, a few miles from the border. They had been walking for five hours. By this time Tom was supporting David.

The men sipped tea whilst David sat slumped in a chair, away from them.

'Come on, college boy,' one of the Boys said, 'we 'ave hardly started, man.'

'Lay off him, Bernard,' Tom said, 'he's having a go, isn't he? Here, let's have a look at your feet, Dave.'

David refused at first, then let himself be coaxed round. The men gathered around his chair as Tom removed his shoes. His socks were bloody from chaffing, and blisters the size of pennies were on each heel. The Boys whistled their approval.

'He's got blisters like saucers. Those shoes are no good for walking, bloody carpet creepers, they are. The lad is not tough enough, he shouldn't have come.'

Tom glared up at the circle of faces. 'Shut up, you lot,' he said, 'leave the boy alone.'

Tom's defence made David feel worse, he felt his face burn at the jibes. He knew he was not one of them, not yet. Frustration flooded his mind: he was hard only in his dreams, only when he dealt in thoughts. The reality of a long walk defeated him.

Tom tapped his shoulder, when they were left alone at their table. 'Never mind, *bach*, you'll have to go back, I reckon, you can't do much more walking with feet like that.'

David nodded miserably.

'Have you enough money to get back on the train? It's only a mile to Chepstow station.'

'Yes, you know me, Tom, always got a little extra, haven't I?'

'Right then, I'll come with you to the station, then I'll catch up the lads.'

'No, it's alright Tom, I can manage to do that myself, at least.'

There was a moment's awkward silence, then Tom got up to leave with the others. 'I'll see you in a few weeks then, David, if we stay out of trouble. Goodbye now.' Tom went to leave. David called him back.

'Tom, take this food, I won't need it now.'

'Are you sure?'

'Of course, go on take it.'

Tom took the bundle Helen had prepared for David.

He watched them go, a small band of ragged men, moving like a cloth snake up the road, getting soaked by the rain that was falling. After more tea David walked slowly and stiffly back to Chepstow. He got back to the valley late that night, cold, hungry, his feet racked with pain. He was returning home shamefaced, without his comrades, avoiding people. He had still not got out of Wales.

Helen was glad, and not unduly surprised to hear David's key in the door. She did not get up, she knew David would not want her at this time. If he did there would be a tap on her bedroom door. There was not, so she tried to sleep again.

In the morning Helen took David a cup of tea. He was fast asleep under the covers, with just the top of his head braving the frost. It smeared the window with intricate patterns, like cobwebs. David looked such a child here, hiding from the world in a secret place. Helen sighed as she pulled back the covers, waking David with a tug of his shoulder. He tried to brush her off, to dream her away, then his eyes half opened, screwing up into slits against the light. For an instant he looked animal-like, a creature disturbed, and ready to bolt from a place it thought safe.

'Well, what happened then?' Helen asked. 'Haven't got into any trouble, have you?'

'No, nothing like that.'

'What then?' She saw him wince as he moved his legs.

'It was those damned shoes. They've cut my feet to ribbons. I couldn't walk more than twenty miles.'

'Let's have a look.' Helen clicked her tongue at the blisters. 'You should have told me last night, these feet needed tending then.'

She probed them gently. 'I'll get a bowl.' Helen went back downstairs to heat some water, and David hunched back under the sheets.

Tom returned to the village ten days later, he had made it to London with the others, where he had met men going to Spain. They had strengthened his resolve to do likewise. 'They were good chaps, Dave, really committed. They reckoned thousands are going out there, even Americans, it will be a real people's army, those Brigades. And Spain will be the graveyard of fascism, that's what they are saying.'

'But Franco looks to be having a lot of success, Tom.'

'Ah, it's only the start. He has been stopped outside Madrid, and the volunteers played a big part there, apparently. The tide will turn, once our side gets organised. Franco had an army to start with, that's been the difference. But the Republic will learn quickly; needs must, as they say.'

Tom said little about David's failure on the march. 'Just as well you came back, really,' Tom said. 'It was bloody hard, tramping those roads, still, it's a gesture, isn't it, something to keep the boys' spirit up'.

'Did they talk much about me when I went back?' David asked.

'No, of course not,' Tom lied, 'you could hardly carry on with feet like you had, could you? Still, we'll have to get you toughened up a bit, Dave. I hear a lot of men are walking into Spain, over the big mountains they have down there. Got to be fit to do that, they are not like our titchy Tump.'

'I haven't said I'll go to Spain, Tom.'

'No, I know, but all the Boys are thinking about it, aren't they, so I thought you must be too.'

David shrugged and Tom did not press him for an answer.

Billy Hicks was released a week before Christmas. There was a welcome home party for him at the Hall, and Billy celebrated his first night as a free man by drinking himself into a fine stupor. He was ceremoniously carried home by the Conti Boys, his inert, snoring body raised aloft, as if he was in his coffin, and the Boys his drunken pallbearers. David and Tom stayed at Billy's that night, they were incapable of shifting themselves further.

David was relieved to have his uncle back again, like the others he had missed the firm hand he provided. They all grew a little when the old man was with them. Watching Billy assume his place at the head of the stove, and exhort his willing troops David suddenly knew he would be going to Spain, the certainty of it came on with a rush, making him feel clammy, and nervous. He would not be able to bear being left alone in the village, it would be too lonely without Tom and Billy, and he could not face another failure. David decided to let himself be carried along with the others, making their determination his, their pride his, until the time might come when these qualities were present in himself. He read about men volunteering for ambulance service, and hoped he might do that. Prospects of actually taking up arms could not be countenanced. The riot had exposed a rich vein of fear running through him. David dreaded this, it might be cowardice, and the march had demonstrated his lack of stamina.

Whenever he could, David took to the hills in his father's boots, which fitted him well. At first his feet suffered, but he stuck to it this time, fighting the unyielding leather, until his boyhood walks tripled in length. He learned how to pace himself, and keep going, he copied the rhythm of the men on the march. Gradually he toughened up, his soles grew callouses of protection, and he braved the winter. Icy drizzle sifted through each layer of clothing without fail, to settle into his bones, but he put up with it.

After these solitary route-marches David settled in front of the parlour fire, idly poking the coals around, stupefied with tiredness. Helen once shouted at him, in exasperation.

'David, why do you go out on such days? You get soaked through each time. You'll catch your death.'

David looked at her in surprise. 'It's alright, ma, it's good for me. I need toughening up.'

'Toughening up! Yes, you need that alright, and much more besides.'

9

Billy decided to leave for Spain on Christmas Eve, under cover of the festivities. As he had predicted, he had no trouble in getting accepted by the Party. The Boys were to be denied his presence once again. Billy announced his intention in the back room of the Anchor. 'I will get over there when everyone is busy. Hah, don't look so glum, you lot, I'm not your mother. I've told you all how to go about getting to Spain, the rest is up to you.' The Boys spirits sunk, but Billy was unrepentant.

Helen feigned disinterest in the news. 'Your uncle will be all right,' she told David, 'he has more lives than a cat, that one, though what he thinks he's doing, I don't know. He should stick to his own, to what he knows.' Helen packed a bag for Billy, food, tobacco, and some of Daniel's old underwear. Secretly she hated Billy going, and over Christmas at that, but she was also glad that his stormy influence would be taken from David. Perhaps the boy would be able to settle down without him. It never entered Helen's head that David might follow him.

Billy was going up to London by train, then on to Paris, crossing the channel on a weekend ticket. No passport was needed for this. Victoria station would be crawling with police, they heard, on the look-out for would-be volunteers. The Party gave Billy enough money to get to Spain. He said his farewell in Helen's parlour, sharing a flagon of beer with David and Tom.

'You can follow on a bit later,' Billy said, watching the door for Helen. 'Don't worry about that Enlistment Act, or that they only want military blokes over there; they'll soon take anyone that arrives, I fancy, the way things are going. I'll write back when I can.'

'Shall we come with you to the station, Bill?' Tom asked.

'No, better not, don't want any show, do we? No, I'll slip away on my tod, catch that last train when everyone is still in the pubs.'

Helen came in with a bag of mince pies. 'Helen *bach*, only an old idiot like me would miss your Christmas dinner, eh?'

'No one is disputing that you're an old idiot, Billy Hicks. At least you can eat these on the way.' Helen stared at Billy sternly, and they hugged each other. Billy shook hands with David and

Tom and was gone, pushing his way out of the house quickly, without another word, his bag slung over his shoulder like a furtive Santa Claus.

'Well, I hope no-one else gets any daft ideas,' Helen said, looking at Tom, 'he never even wished me Happy Christmas.' Tom went home shortly afterwards, leaving David to sit in the armchair and think of Billy's adventure.

Tom spent Christmas with them, pooling his money with the family he was becoming part of. On Boxing Day David went with him to the Hall. The place was full of men drying out from Christmas Eve, some about to plunge into another bout of booze. They talked of Spain, it was a main topic now. Madrid had still not fallen, the newspapers had been wrong about that, and hopes were raised.

'See, it proves the people can do it,' Tom said. 'They haven't broken like the papers said. They are not a rabble.'

'Aye, and they'll have Billy down there soon,' a Boy added, 'putting the wind up any Fascist he gets near.'

'Wind – a bloody bayonet, more like.'

Billy was a local folk hero. A life of agitation, the riot, and now Spain placed him high in the workers' minds. Moscow Billy was known to everyone, a term of endearment to most, of abuse to some. Billy lived by the code he espoused, that was his strength, David thought, a simple thing, but so very hard to attain. Spain would be full of men like his uncle, some would be stronger. It was a bigger arena than their insular valley, it would draw contenders from everywhere, and there would be champions amongst them. David tottered home more drunk with future hopes than the beer he had consumed.

Snow came quickly after Christmas, fringing the black tips with a gleaming white, and snarling up the valley floor with a grey sludge. Gloom hung over the valley, the clouds were always low, and smoke from the stacks did not have far to go to thicken the dark skies.

David squelched his way to the library. Slush oozed over his boots to extinguish any warmth that hid there, numbing his toes. There had been no word from Billy, so they presumed him in Spain. He had been gone for two weeks, and Tom was anxious to follow him. David met Tom in Conti's and they talked around the stove.

'If we wait any longer, it might all be over,' Tom said. 'We will have done nothing.'

'Oh I think we will have plenty to time to get involved, Tom. It's shaping up to be a full scale war, and they are never over quickly.' David took off his boots and warmed his feet.

'You have come on a bit, Dave, since that march. Never used to go out in weather like this, did you? Like a bloody mountain goat you are now.'

'Stop flattering me, I've a long way to go yet.'

'Maybe, but I don't think you'll be dropping out of anything anymore.'

Tom's compliments were pleasing, and indeed David felt the change in himself.

As David steamed in front of the stove. Tom worked on him to go to Spain. He was determined to get a decision.

'Let's do it now,' Tom said, 'let's go tomorrow, we've got nothing to lose, no jobs, your marriage is over.'

'But Tom we can't just up and go like that, we haven't planned anything.'

'Look David, we might never hear from Billy, we can't wait on that. Besides, he's told us what to do, and we've saved enough to get over there, just about. My tobacco money has been put away these last three months. Look at these hands, shaking for the want of a fag, they are.'

David gave him one. Tom paused, looking for assent in David's face.

'Come on, what do you say? We can get the milk train out of Cardiff before anyone is up and about.'

'What about my mother, and my sisters?'

'Leave them a note. If you tell your mother you know what will happen, she'll try to stop you and there'll be a big hoo-hah. No, leaving secretly is the best bet.' Tom took a deep drag on his roll-up. 'Well?'

David nodded his head slowly, and sucked hard on his own cigarette to steady his nerves. He knew he had to say yes quickly, before funk set in and he created excuses to stay.

'Good man,' Tom said. 'Right, listen, I'll go and get my stuff and come back to your place. I've been ready for weeks. We'll leave before it is light. Make sure you pack plenty of clothes, we might be away a long time. And not a word to Helen, mind. I'll come round about two, when all decent people are asleep.'

Tom winked at David and punched his shoulder. He was barely able to contain his excitement. He left Conti's quickly, disappearing up the street, whistling to himself. Conti looked up from his counter and rubbed his chin with his cloth.

David avoided Helen when he got home, not taking any chance that she might sense something. When she went to bed he crept down from his room with a filled rucksack. It was crammed with as many clothes as it could hold, his town shoes, his father's old clasp knife, and a few books. The weight of the latter was a hindrance, but it was unthinkable to travel without words. David wore two layers of clothing to protect his bony frame. The dead of winter was a bad time to be going, but he knew there would never be a good time, and he tried to put trepidation to the back of his mind.

He dried his sodden pit boots in front of the fire while he waited for Tom. The leather was steaming when there was a faint rap on the kitchen window. David let Tom in, shutting the door quickly on swirling snow.

'It's a fine night to be going, boy,' Tom whispered, 'no-one is about, and it's cold enough to freeze the balls off the pawnbroker's monkey. I see you are well kitted up. Good.' Tom was travelling light, his small canvas bag was not full, he wore an overcoat frayed at the sleeves and a pair of unmatching gloves. A hunk of cheese wrapped in paper was his only supply of food. He looked like a thief returning from a night's work, unshaven, covert, and full of adrenaline.

'Let's get a bit of shut-eye by the fire, and hope your ma don't wake up,' Tom said. They had a few hours to fill before the first train. Tom dozed off easily in the red glare of the coals, and David envied the way in which sleep came to his friend. It was never like that for himself, although gradually he did fall into a patchy slumber.

'Come on, sleeping beauty, time to be off.' Tom shook David by the shoulder, waking him from his dream of deserts and hot sands. David shook himself and made ready to go.

'Hang on, Dave, you haven't written a note for Helen. Better do it or she'll have the police out looking for you.' Tom stood smoking impatiently as David scribbled. 'Ma, gone to Spain with Tom. Don't worry, will write to you – David.' As an afterthought he wrote, 'and tell the girls not to worry either.' He put the paper under the teapot, knowing it was the first thing she touched in the morning. Emma was forgotten.

They took the first train out of Cardiff without any trouble, and light was seeping into the edge of the black sky as David crossed the Welsh border. He had finally done it, left the valley and his country, quickly and easily.

'On our way now,' Tom said. David sank back in his seat and closed his eyes.

'Yes, on our way, Tom,' he answered. He saw Helen finding the note, perhaps running into the street to vainly look for him. She would shut herself into her parlour, and stir the teapot relentlessly, crying noiselessly in that strange way of hers.

David's image was accurate, Helen did just as he imagined; but there was anger, also. She cursed David for being so stupid, that boy of hers going to someone else's war. He was the last man in the family, Daniel had gone, Billy was off on his mad quest, and now David, risking himself when he had no right to, and with no word to Emma, who was still his wife. It is Billy's doing, she told herself, and just a few weeks ago she had thought David free of him. Helen went up to David's room, to see what he had taken. The missing clothes told her that this time he would not be turning back at Chepstow, and she understood those long walks in the rain now. But perhaps they would be caught and sent home, perhaps this same day. Helen's thoughts flitted from hope to despair to anger, then back to hope again as she looked at David's books. She went back to the kitchen and drank the tea she had made, sipping it thoughtfully as she willed David back to her.

David awoke to find it was mid-morning, and the train was winding its way through the outskirts of London. The tenements and flat rows of houses were no better than the valley's, bigger and more numerous, that was all. The railway skirted dwellings that bled red brick into the morning light, gaunt, many-storeyed buildings, blackened by generations of train soot. 'Best way to see a big town,' a waking Tom said, 'coming in on a train, they always cut behind the swanky parts. Look at this lot, Dave, not exactly paved with gold is it? Imagine living here, a man would lose himself, I reckon.'

Tom knew how to get to Victoria station from Paddington, so David followed without saying much. He was too busy taking in London, and fighting the fatigue that was already upon him.

They went on the underground, travelling half the length of the valley in minutes.

'This is amazing, Tom,' David said, 'everything is such a rush.'

'Aye, it is that. It's the quickest I've ever come up to London, I can tell you, and my old feet aren't complaining.'

To David the tube was a miracle of confused order. He had never seen so many people travelling together, a seething mass of them jostled each other, shook the rain from their coats, got out crumpled newspapers, lit a thousand cigarettes, slept, scowled, and watched each other with a studied lack of interest.

They were disgorged at Victoria where they saw yet more people, gathering for their trains in the steam of the readying engines. Small clouds of it hung high up under the station's canopy, the place smelt of wet stone, cafés, and people drying off.

Tom guided David by the arm. 'Keep walking and act natural,' he said. 'Remember, we are going to Paris, for the weekend.' As Billy had warned, there were lots of police about, some of them in plainclothes. It was easy to spot them, there was something clumsy in the actions, they tried to nose secretly, and nothing is more obvious in a crowded place.

They planned to mingle with the trippers to France; and there was a surprising number of them for mid-winter. As he waited for Tom to find the right ticket counter, David caught sight of himself in a café mirror, and saw that he was a very unlikely tourist. He was overclothed and bulky, yet still looked lank and wary. His tan coat and hair gave him the look of a whippet, alert before its race, and he felt like one, starting whenever a stranger stared at him. Tom rejoined him with two tickets for Paris.

'Don't look so jumpy,' he whispered, 'you'll have someone onto us.'

David grimaced. 'Sorry Tom, I'm a bit nervous, it would be terrible to fail now.'

'Don't talk about failing, we've hardly started. Billy would boot you up the arse. We'll be in France soon, think of it, on the continent. You'll have a chance to try out some of that learning of yours. You speak the lingo, don't you?'

'I learned it in school from books, but I've never actually heard a Frenchman talk'.

'Aye, well you soon will.'

They spent the rest of the day in London, waiting for their

overnight boat-train to Paris. The tickets cost thirty shillings each, a sizeable hole in their funds. Paris was hosting a Great Exhibition, and it was this which made their trip without passports possible.

'Come on,' Tom said, 'I'll show you the West End, I've tramped around it on that march.'

'Won't we stick out there, Tom?'

'No more than anywhere else. We'll be all right, it will be full of people.'

Tom was right, walkers and shoppers abounded the wet pavements, the streets were massed with them, it seemed to David, most of them affluent looking. He was used to the few in the valley but here men in fine coats were common, made-up women passed him by, sleek objects that purred along, some even smoking cigarettes. David felt shabby and conspicuous as Tom pointed out various landmarks, an echo of Daniel's dandyism was raised up in him somewhere. This was not David's idea of keeping a low profile but Tom did not seem to be worried, 'Look, Dave,' he said, 'the Houses of Parliament, that's where they decide how we live in the valley.'

The hard London pavements took their toll on David's feet. He thought back to that first disastrous journey and gritted his teeth. At least they would not be walking through France, and there would be time to rest on the trains, he hoped. Tom was indefatigable at his side, chatting away in his soft voice, his reticence left in the valley. 'Streets are hard here, eh?' Tom said. 'Come on, we'll get off 'em, have a bite to eat back at the station. We've walked in a full circle, almost.' David was relieved to follow Tom back to Victoria, where they wolfed down what was left of Tom's cheese, plus a few stale rolls they had picked up.

It had rained throughout the day, cold squalls which soaked them through several times. David looked forward to the sun of Spain, he had read the winter there was warmer than the valley's summer. They waited until six for their train, which they took without incident. After two hours crushed into the corner of an over-full carriage they were in Dover, boarding their ferry. No-one stopped them, no-one questioned them, just their tickets were checked. David could not believe how easy it was.

They saw little of the channel. A low fog blanketed the sea and it snowed intermittently, making passengers hug the interior of the boat. David sat with Tom on a crowded bench until he could stand the stuffiness no longer. He went on deck to clear his head, his stomach churned, but he was glad not to be walking anymore. The night closed in around him, clammy, and smelling of oil. A red light winked in the distance, like a glowing coal. As they neared France David's elation grew, he would soon be in a foreign country, even if they were entering it furtively, in darkness. David would have preferred his actions to be seen and approved, but those black slopes held him no longer, and he travelled towards new lands with fresh hope.

A hand squeezed David on the shoulder, jarring him back to reality. 'Better come in, David, you are too conspicuous out here.' Tom shuddered. 'Jesus, I didn't think the sea would be so cold. Come on, before we catch pneumonia'. Tom led him to a corner of the passenger deck, and murmured there were other 'Boys' on board. 'You can tell them ones the Party has sent over, they all have second hand suits on. There's two over there.' The men winked knowingly across at them but Tom did not respond. 'Best not to talk to anyone,' he said, 'you can never be too sure.' Other men joined the first couple, and they stood at the bar and drank. 'Stupid buggers,' Tom whispered, 'can't help making a show, some people. They're asking for trouble.'

David knew Tom would be a sure and safe man to travel with. With him he was confident they would get to Spain. The more David came to know his dour friend the more he sensed Tom Price would be a ruthless man if he thought it necessary. He had no romantic love for his fellow worker, like Billy had. David wondered what lay at the bottom of Tom's decision to go to Spain, and wondered too at his own reasons. His were undoubtedly selfish, he was searching for answers to himself in someone else's war, using it a testing ground. Perhaps they all were. Sometimes he had felt the undercurrent of bitterness in Conti's. It came from always being the underdog, being on the wrong side of a decent life. Yet some of the men who had gone out from the valley were happily married, and in work. Awkward questions swirled through David's mind, like the fog about the boat, until he slept with his chin nodding on his chest, tapping out the rhythm of the crossing. They were docking at Calais when he awoke.

Their luck held, there was no trouble with the sleepy French customs, and they passed quickly through their first frontier.

David breathed in the salty air of Calais and looked around him. Buildings were appearing in the dawn, no different to the ones he had left in Dover. Docks were not the place to celebrate travel, they were wide open, empty places, indifferent to the transient human traffic that passed through them. David and Tom found the railway terminal, and set their thoughts on Paris.

They reached the French capital by late afternoon, arriving unshaven and dog-tired to mingle with its noise and motion. It was large and full, like London, but it was not the same. Paris had an outdoor aura, despite the chill day. Chairs were stacked up outside cafés, waiting to be spread out on the pavements on kinder days, while redundant tables stood without tablecloths. Paris had an impersonal air, inquisitive but not nosy, disdainful but not unkind. Here all was in the look, a flick of an eye, a glance through slitted lids, the toss of a head. David felt that this place would suit him, it could be a confidant, Conti's café would be one of thousands here, it would be an ordinary bar, holding extraordinary plotters and dreamers.

Billy had given them the address of a place in the Place de Combat, which they found hard to locate. They wandered around for some time in the streets near the station. Billy had said it was around there somewhere. 'We had better ask someone where it is,' Tom said, 'we can't keep walking around like this.' Hesitantly, David tried some of his French on a few passers-by. They seemed to understand him, but they answered far too quickly for David. As he tried to decipher their first words they lost patience and left him.

'Come on, David, get something out of these Frenchies, for Christ's sake. I thought you could speak French.'

'It's not the same as in the books, they talk so fast. I can't follow them.'

'Well, come on, let's try up here.' Tom pointed to an alleyway which led into many others. After many a turn and stuttering street conversation with locals they came upon the place they wanted, as the light was fading and their bellies were crying out to be fed.

It was a small office in a Maison de Syndicates, where they could expect help in getting to Spain, Billy told them. They entered a small box of a room, to be received by a Spaniard who sprang up from his desk and eyed them suspiciously. There was another pantomime of hand waving and pidgin talk before the man asked them for their papers. He wanted documents to show who they were, who sent them, where they came from, and what they believed in.

'*Nous avons rien*,' David said, which ended the Spaniard's interest in them, but not his suspicion. The more they tried to persuade him of their intentions, the more sullen he became.

'Come on,' Tom said, 'we'll get nothing out of this sod. Let's go and get something to eat, my guts are all wind.'

This setback was worrying, more money had been spent than they had reckoned on, and it was unlikely the rest would last out until Spain, even if they had any idea how to get there. David noticed there were other union offices in the Spaniard's block. It was far easier to read French signs than talk to the people. In his first flash of initiative he suggested they walk into one. Tom was doubtful, but for once David led. He chose the office of the metalworkers' union, thinking of Juan Davies, and there they met a Frenchman. This man proved to be the Spaniard's opposite. He looked up a from his desk and responded to David's French with shaky English, to Tom's relief. Standing up, the man clasped each of them by the shoulder, and kissed their cheeks, left then right. He told them to '*restez ici*' and went to confer with someone in the next room. Tom scratched his head.

'Blimey, that's the first time I've been kissed by a bloke. Bloody marvellous, isn't it, the Spaniard turns us away, turns away help for his country, and the Frenchie greets us like long lost brothers.' Tom rubbed his cheek. 'Or sisters. I think these foreigners are going to be a contrary lot, David.'

The Frenchman returned and smiled at them. '*ça va, ça va*,' he said, leading them to the door, pushing them forward with his hands. David thought they were to be given a polite brush-off, but the man took them out into the street, and walked with them to a small pension down one of the cobble-stoned alleys. It was dark now, and it was hard to see their way in the unlit street. There was water nearby, they could hear it lapping against stones and they could smell it.

They stopped outside a dimly lit door. 'Stay, comrades,' the Frenchman said, 'there will be someone for you in the morning.' Their shoulders were clasped again. As he went to leave the man turned back. 'If you are hungry there is a café next door, *la*. Eat there. *Au revoir, et bon chance, eh?*

'Best bit of news I've had all day,' Tom said. 'Come on, let's get a room sorted out, then our stomachs.'

An old woman appeared from a side door as they entered the hotel. She was well over eighty, with knitting stuck under her shawl, and a dress the colour of coal. She had already been told to expect them. They were waved in by her spindly hand and shown up stairs as rickety as she was. At the end of the corridor the ancient one opened a door to a small room, which held a double bed, and nothing else. Then she left them they sank onto the bed in unison, enjoying the lumpy ease it provided.

'I bet this old thing has seen a bit of life,' Tom said. He prodded the bed cautiously. 'Hope we don't go through the springs.'

'Napoleon probably slept here with Josephine,' David said seriously.

'No, I don't think he would have stayed here... eh, you're having me on. Come on, let's see what is in the kitty.'

They spread their money on the bed, a small handful of strange coins nestled in a fold of the sheet, and a few notes with deceptively high figures. They had quickly learned that high denominations meant little here.

'How much have we got then?' Tom asked. 'About two pounds, I think. Not as much as I thought'.

'Will that get us to Spain?'

'I doubt it very much, but perhaps that French chap will help us.'

'Aye, let's hope so.'

The smell of coffee was filtering up from the street below, enticing and promising.

'Come on,' Tom said, 'let's get down there and have something to eat. We'll worry about money on full bellies.'

David agreed – he was all for spending the money on one big meal. His triumph at the union office had swept away his caution, for one day at least. They passed the old woman as they went out. She watched them go, chewing her gums kindly at them, her bright eyes set deep in her face, like a benevolent eagle. David noticed the stove she sat next to, a miniature French sister of Conti's. For a moment he wished himself back there, talking in comfort. The thought of a warm bed stabbed at him, a vicious memory of just days ago. He dreaded to think what it would be like in six months, a year. David nodded to the old woman and followed Tom out.

The café was like the pension, noiseless and dimly lit. The man behind the bar did everything from cooking the food to dusting their table. They had underestimated the spending power of their money. Food was cheap in Paris, and they sat down to platefuls of omelette, and a mound of semi-stale bread. It was devoured seriously; they ate like men possessed, until the plates were clean, stopping only to drink the wine that had been brought for them.

The barman fussed around his unusual customers, glad of any change in his routine. 'Conti wouldn't like it here,' Tom said, 'too much work.' They sat on high-backed chairs that rested precariously on the stone floor, and their table was round and tiny, defying one to rest at it too long. But they relaxed and the food warmed them. After the meal they slumped as much as their chairs would allow, and smoked roll-up cigarettes with satisfaction. 'That was a good blow-out.' Tom said. 'They say an army marches on its stomach, I can see why now. A full belly makes you feel a hell of a lot better.'

From a table at the far end of the café two old men watched them, eyes unwavering with interest.

'Those two are watching us like hawks,' David said.

'Well, they probably don't get many like us in here, we'd be the same, wouldn't we, if two Frenchmen walked into Conti's one night. Anyway, we'd better get back to the hotel, and get some sleep.'

David called out for the bill in his best accent, and was glad to see that they still had a few coins left after they had paid it. They got up to go, returning the salutes of the barman, but a large shape blocked their way, materialising out of the gloom of the doorway. They stepped back with some alarm.

'Don't be concerned, my friends,' a voice boomed out at them, 'I have been sent to look for you, you are the two English, no, who were at the metalworkers' office?'

A large man joined the voice, he stood opposite them, the first man David had ever had to look up to. Tom looked at David. His eyes asked if they should make a run for it.

'No, we are not them,' Tom answered.

The stranger laughed, if the deep sound that rolled from his gut could be called laughter. 'Ah, I see you are cautious, that is good. Don't worry, I am on your side.'

He clicked his heels together and said, 'I am Karpinski, Russian.'

He held out a hand which David took

'And who is this young man, eh?'

'Hicks, David Hicks, and this is Tom Price, my comrade from Wales.'

Tom was still suspicious, he glared at David, but Karpinski ignored him.

'Ah, Welles, yes I know. Coal, mountains, singing. Come, we go drink.'

They hesitated.

'Come, come.' He swept before them, and David led Tom after him.

'Why the hell did you talk to him?' Tom whispered.

'What choice did we have, we've got to trust someone, and he must be from the union, how else would he know us?'

Alexei Karpinski was in his forties, more than sixteen stones in weight, and a good head taller than David. His height was emphasised by a head of thick black hair, escaping from the grease which attempted to hold it in place. The grease ran onto his forehead, giving his brow a perpetual shine. With his heavy, curled moustache Karpinski looked eastern. David imagined his ancestors pouring over the Steppes. The Russian was well dressed, with a fine greatcoat and white shirt and tie beneath.

Tom did not know what to make of him. 'I don't like blokes who appear out of the night, unasked. And look at the way he's dressed, more like a count than a friend of ours, he's a real Brylcreem Kid, his hair is full of the stuff.'

As they walked Karpinski told them he was to watch over them until tickets could be arranged for the south of France.

'We've got no money, mind,' Tom said.

The Russian waved his hand.

'The union pays, my friend. Karpinski led them out into their first Parisian night. They went through twisting alleyways that stank of fish and urine, until they came upon a brightly lit bar, loud voices coming through its open front door.

'This is my favourite place,' Karpinski said, 'so *simpatico*, you will find people here like yourselves, *n'est ce pas?*'

The Russian wandered through various languages making David feel in some awe of him. He resolved to say little and learn as much as he could from Karpinski, who was one of the creations of his books, sprung to life before him.

The bar was awash with alcohol, and people drinking it. A clammy cloud met them as they entered, assaulting the freshness they brought with them. Their guardian led them to the one free table, and ordered wine and cassis.

'Drink my friends, Karpinski pays. I haven't drunk with Welshmen before, enjoy yourself this night.'

A bear-like hand crashed onto David's back, and he smelt the grease on the Russian as he was toasted with a glass of wine the colour of Karpinski's face.

A young German joined them at the table, he seemed to know Karpinski. He too was bound for Spain and he singled out David to talk to. He was another serious youngster, disapproving of the drunkenness around him. Hans Kleinz was not much older than David. Crop-haired and blond, he was how David imagined Germans to be, but it surprised him to know that Socialists existed in Germany. 'I cannot go back,' Kleinz shouted over the din, 'not until Hitler is no more. Wherever there are Fascists to fight, that is my home now.'

David felt the commitment of the men around him, and dared not compare his own confused allegiance with it. The bar was populated with Billys. As the wine penetrated he thought they could never lose, not with men like these; he loved his comrades, drunken men became heroes in front of his own drunken eyes. David's last image was of the Brylcreem Kid hugging Tom as he slumped towards the table. He did not know how they got back to the pension, he was one link in a chain of tottering men, each celebrating a war he had not reached.

David woke to hear Tom retching in the washroom that adjoined their room. He stumbled back into the bedroom, white-faced and bleary eyed.

'Awake, are you?' Tom screwed up his eyes to see David. 'God, I feel bad. That stuff we were drinking, cassis, cat's piss, or some such thing, never again, I'll stick to beer.'

'I don't think we'll get much of that out here, Tom.'

'No, I 'spose not. Didn't come here for it anyway, did we...

though a place should have decent beer, all the same.'

David was hardly listening. His head had a man with a hammer in it, pounding his way out in a merciless rhythm. His mouth was as dry as a stick, with a rug for a tongue, and Spain was a million miles away.

'You look like I feel, boy,' Tom said. 'Best get up, have a wash. That Russian, the Kid, said we would be off today, if all goes well.'

David had to think for a moment to remember what Tom was talking about. The night before was a blur of upturned glasses and talking faces. Shakily, he shaved himself in the washbasin, peering between the cracks in the mirror at his stubbly face. Between commiserations and moans they dressed and went out into the street, where the wind struck at their feeble state. They sought out the meagre warmth of the café and spent the last of their money on coffee and rolls.

'Well, that's it, Tom,' David said, 'no more money. I hope Karpinski's word holds good'. He licked breadcrumbs off his hand and realised he was still hungry.

'We'll soon find out if it does, here he comes.'

The Kid stood in the doorway, beaming at them, completely without a hangover.

'My friends, you are well, no? Hah, I see it is no. You are not used to the cassis. Here are two tickets for you, to Perpignan, and a few francs to help you on your way.' He laughed at the relief on their faces.

'You were not sure of Karpinski, eh?' They were embarrassed at the ease at with which they had gained a free passage, but Tom quickly pocketed the tickets.

'There will be others travelling on the train,' Karpinski said, 'but keep to yourselves, don't talk. The French police are some-times blind to us, sometimes not. It depends on their politics, on their moods. France, huh! She is the whore of socialism.'

The Kid spat out a lump of tobacco, and lit another cigar. David nodded in agreement with him, without really under-standing. Karpinski beckoned him nearer.

'Maybe I see you in Spain, soon they will let me go.' Karpinski stretched and ran his hands across his eyes. 'It will be safer there, amongst the bullets.' His voice lowered, 'Russia, she is not good right now, people disappear, people like me disappear a lot.'

Karpinski seemed to reawaken. He slapped David on the knee, 'Life is hell, no?' and laughed.

Later that day Karpinski accompanied them to the Gare Austerlitz, and bundled them onto their train like a fussing grandparent. Groups of men were embracing on the platform, then scampering for seats, there was little attempt by anyone to be inconspicuous. They did not feel as threatened as at Victoria, but the Kid warned them they could be picked up at any stage of their journey.

'The Spaniards might not let you in,' he told them cheerfully, leaning on their carriage door. I hear the Republic is like a kitten, dancing round and round to catch its tail. In Barcelona anarchist fights Communist. Be careful who you are friendly with, my friends, and say you are on the side of the Republic, when asked, nothing more. *Adieu*, Welshmen.' He raised a hand and lost himself in the platform crowd.

They found a few seats at the far end of the train and settled down for another long journey. Paris passed by through the smeared windows of the coach. They were pulled out of the city quickly, David's taste of Paris was one brief swallow, but it was a start, he felt. Tom was asleep instantly; he slouched against David on one side, on the other a man with garlic breath peppered him with pungent snores. He was caught between the two like a minnow, but eventually David also fell asleep, as the train rattled southwards in cold sunshine.

France was far bigger than David realised. Waking at first light he found that they were still hours away from Perpignan; they had crossed the belly of the country in the night and were well into the south. David felt empty and sick, but it was a feeling he was getting used to. He was not a natural traveller, constant motion wore him down, grated at his nerves until they were taut and strung like cat-gut. Tom had no problems, he shook off a hangover easily enough, and was not much affected by extremes of cold or heat. David, on the other hand, was mercury, reacting to every nuance of his environment.

A weak sun filtered into the carriage, showing up unshaven travellers, still reeking of Parisian excesses. David longed for the train to reach its destination. It had stopped often in the night, to jerk him out of his troubled sleep. A man came to collect tickets, and at one stop a priest joined them. He was a long, rawboned man, who sat like a ramrod amongst them, fingering his hat. His face twitched with distaste, but he said nothing. The priest knew he was in the presence of the unholy. He reminded David of Iolo Hughes – he had the same air of disdain, tempered by the quiet desperation of the outsider.

It was light enough to take in the passing landscape. Flat fields stretched to distant mountains. Arles was in this part of France – cornfields and madness; tragedy lay in the soil. Tom still slept beside David, who gave him a nudge in the ribs, taking some pleasure in destroying his slumber.

'Are we there?' Tom asked.

'No, not yet, but I don't think it's far now.'

Tom scratched his whiskers, and looked around him. He started when he saw the priest, then smiled at the man. The priest flared his nostrils at Tom, as if trying to exorcise him from the carriage, and looked out of the window. Tom shrugged.

'How far have we travelled?' he asked.

'Oh, hundreds of miles,' David answered. 'You have slept through it all, Tom.'

'Aye, I reckon I have, best way to travel though, isn't it?'

They were close to their goal. Perpignan was not far from the Spanish border, and they hoped to cross into Spain by rail or road. The back door entrance across the Pyrenees was a last resort David wanted to avoid, if at all possible. Sleep was leaving the men in the carriage. Most of its occupants were for Spain, that was obvious, all looking as inexperienced as David and Tom, apart from one man who sat in the corner opposite David. Occasionally he looked up and winked at what was being said.

By mid-morning they were moving through the outskirts of Perpignan, passing rows of tall stone houses with shuttered windows too small for them, like eyes. They were painted in pastel colours and looked like the work of an impressionist through the filthy train window, hints of a lost gayness in a town that looked old and faded.

They disembarked in the usual muddle of people moving around in search of other people, directions, or just a quick exit from the mass. David and Tom detached themselves from the other passengers, moving swiftly to the street outside. Karpinski had given them the name of a pension on a piece of wine-soaked paper. The priest stalked past them as they tried to read it. 'I wouldn't put it past him to shop us,' Tom muttered. Other volunteers passed, they all seemed to know where they were going. David thrust the paper at a man on a news stand, who read it and pointed up the street, curving his hand to the right.

'Come on Tom, let's try up there.' They followed the man's hand and found the place they wanted, a small pension stuck between the railway tracks and a busy road. It was anonymous, and suitable. This time they had not wandered hopelessly, as in Paris. David breathed deeply, to expel the fug of the train. The sky here was clear, and of the palest blue, as if the colour had been washed out of it.

Their pension was snuggled against others of its kind, in a dingy side street. A sharp faced man scurried to meet them as they knocked on the door. A beret flattened his head, and glinting eyes scoured them from beneath it. David gave him the note, and mentioned Karpinski's name. The man nodded with a resigned air, they guessed many before them had been sent here. '*Venez*,' he said, and led them up to the top floor, where he let them into a room. He was back down the stairs before they could ask him any questions.

'Looks a bit mean, that one, Dave,' Tom said, 'reminds me of a ferret.'

'We can't pick and choose, and we aren't the most fruitful of customers, are we?'

David sank onto the bed, which had a mattress as hard as iron, but was still a relief after the wooden slats of the train. Tom tried to open the window, but it was stuck fast, glued by generations of dirt and paint. It shook as a train passed.

'Just like back home, *bach*,' Tom said, 'remember the last coal train, chugging down the line before midnight. Set your clock by that, you could.'

'That was only days ago, Tom.'

'Aye, of course it was, it seems longer, somehow.'

David saw that train as he gazed up at the ceiling. In the valley he rarely slept until it had passed, two engines strained to pull the long line of trucks, a great symbol of the valley and its way of life.

'We'll have a scout around tonight, Dave, see how to get to Spain. Perhaps we'll find someone like that Russian.'

'Maybe, but don't count on it, we can't stay lucky forever.'

'No, and we have been lucky, haven't we? Jesus, it's gone like a dream so far. How close are we to the border?'

'About thirty miles, I think'

'Good, not too far.'

They went out as night fell, and bought coffee and rolls with the Kid's francs. When they got back to the pension there were two men waiting for them. The landlord pointed the strangers towards them, winced, and went back to his lair at the back of the place.

'Like a dog coming out of a bloody kennel', Tom said.

They looked at two men who mirrored themselves, the same overdressing, and wary faces, and with these two, unmistakeably British flat caps. They could never be French police.

'Hello there,' the taller man said, 'I'm Bob McCormick.' He stretched out a hand and David looked into the face of a man who was calm and thoughtful. Grey eyes were widely spaced below a high forehead. Closely cropped hair was the same grey at the edges, and thin on top. It made McCormick look older than he probably was. The other man stepped forward.

'And I'm Danny Simpson, ex-pugilist, and docker, from Liverpool. You boys are Brits, aren't you?'

Tom glanced at David and spoke up.

'Aye, Welsh. This is my mate, David Hicks. I'm Tom Price. Going to Spain are you?'

'Of course,' McCormick said, 'like you.' There was a tangible air of relief all round.

'I thought you might have been coppers,' Tom said.

'What, with these coats?' Danny fingered a hole in his sleeve.

'We have come from Paris,' David said, 'come on up to our room to talk.'

David was enjoying his new confidence. They went up the stairs and made a table of the bed. Danny produced two bottles of foul red wine, which they passed around, Paris forgotten. McCormick was large-framed, his voice a soft Scottish burr, sometimes scarcely audible. His cold eyes gave him a steely look, they stared out like a cat's, unflinching and demanding.

Danny was quite different, he was an elf of a man, his round face sat atop a body of sinewy bones, and his ears gave his trade away, they had the thickening of regular bruising and his nose was much-squashed, as if it was trying to go two ways at once. His eyes shone with good spirits and openness. Tom took to him at once. David tried to reserve his often hasty judgement.

Their new comrades were amazed that they had reached Perpignan unofficially.

'A lot of men have been picked up,' McCormick told them. 'Stupid, they went around shooting their mouths off, or came out totally unprepared.'

David and Tom glanced at each other.

'Aye, we seen some of those crossing the channel,' Tom said.

McCormick did most of the talking, quietly asking questions as the wine flowed. They told him of the help they had received from Karpinski. David talked freely, but Tom was wary of the Scotsman.

'Best not to say too much to that fellow,' Tom whispered, when McCormick was in the washroom, 'he asks too many questions for my liking.

'He's a thinker, Tom, he likes to know things, that's all.'

'Maybe.' Tom accepted the bottle from Danny and took a swig from it.

'So, you are a fighter, Danny?' David said.

'Was a fighter lad, was a fighter.' Danny took hold of his nose. 'See this thing, it was disappearing into my face, getting hard to breathe through it, so I got out. I had a few good years, best quit while I was ahead, I thought. I didn't want to end up addle-headed, like the old boys you see around the gyms.'

'Were you a champion or anything?'

'Lord no. I got knocked down too much. They said I didn't have much of a defence. Knocked a few down myself, mind. It wasn't a bad life, better break your head than break your back, I say.'

McCormick came back. 'I've been thinking,' he said, 'it would be better if we travelled together to the border, we might have a better chance of getting help that way.'

'Do you think we'll have to walk over those bloody mountains?' Tom asked.

'Yes, probably so. It's tricky any other way at the moment, I heard.'

'Heard from who?' Tom said.

Danny laughed. 'Oh, you better listen to McCormick, son, knows everything about this lark, he does. I call him the professor.'

David felt his gut tighten at the thought of the mountains.

'The border has tightened up a lot,' McCormick said, 'it would be stupid to take a chance on being turned back, or arrested, after getting so close.'

'Are you sure we can get over the mountains,' David said, 'they are big, aren't they?'

'Yes, they're big all right, but as long as we can get a guide we should make it. Plenty of others have.'

McCormick knocked out his pipe and looked at them. Tom drained the last of the bottle.

'We had better get to bed then,' he said, 'we are going to need all our energy.'

McCormick and Danny went to their own room, and David got into tho bed they had all sat on, leaving Tom to turn out the lamp.

'That's just what you didn't want, eh David?' Tom said in the dark, 'I hope those walks up the Tump have done you some good.'

'We'll soon find out.' David lay with visions of jagged peaks, swirling snow, and a wind that whipped. His body gave an involuntary shiver as he pulled some of Tom's share of the sheet around him. He lay waiting for sleep to come, thinking that the next night they might be crossing into Spain, marching to their glorious war.

10

David and Tom decided to accept McCormick's guidance. The next day he ordered a taxi to take them to the old town of Erle, as near to the border as they dared get by road. They left in the late afternoon, to the relief of their landlord. The Scotsman paid for the taxi himself. He was the only one with any money left, David and Tom were penniless. The taxi dropped them at the edge of Erle at dusk.

'There will be a guide to meet us at six,' McCormick said, 'I have the place here. He stabbed his finger at the makeshift map he unfurled.

'How did you arrange all this?' Tom asked.

'Others have gone this way before us. The Party has made contacts here.'

McCormick put on round, wire-framed glasses to read the map; they added to his scholarly appearance. Tom had decided not to like McCormick, although the man was friendly, and eager to talk politics. David was a little flattered by the Scotsman's interest, but it was this same trait that Tom disliked.

The Pyrenees lay directly ahead of them, looming large as night fell. Mountain peaks stuck up into the sky like huge worn teeth, and there was snow on the higher slopes with trees scattering the lower reaches. It looked tough country. The four men huddled together at their meeting point, waiting.

A few lights glimmered from distant houses, but there was no-one about; Erle was as still as a corpse. Danny Simpson stamped his feet to keep warm, humming tunelessly to himself. He was the least prepared of them. He wore a pair of summer flannels and a thin overcoat, with plimsoles on his feet and a buttoned cardigan under his coat. He looked more like an ageing Mediterranean sailor rather than a would-be mountaineer. David felt his own clothing to reassure himself.

A man joined them out of the gloom, appearing like a ghost at Tom's shoulder.

'Blimey, who's that?' Danny cried, startling every one.

'It's alright,' McCormick said, 'it's our guide.'

He approached the man and said '*camarada.*' The man nodded and smiled a toothless grin at them. '*Si, camarada.*' He was small and wiry, wizened almost, and old enough to be David's grandfather. Before David was the perfect revolutionary of his dreams: he wore a leather jerkin, khaki breeches and high, laced up boots. A heavy pistol was slung from his belt, bandit style.

'Christ, he's a bit ancient, ain't he?' Danny said. 'I hope he's up to it.'

'They would not have sent him if he wasn't,' McCormick said.

Their guide had no English except 'follow', 'fast' and 'silent'. They soon found out it was all he needed for his task. He had a bundle on his back which he unpacked quickly. It contained sandals made of rope, which he urged them to put on, pointing from the sandals to their feet. Each man received a pair. Tom looked at his dubiously and scratched his head.

'What do you think of these, Dave? They must be the best things for the mountains, I suppose. They look flimsy though, our feet will be exposed.'

The sandals were a rudimentary snowshoes, a noiseless way to travel over the snowy passes. The guide wanted them to hurry, he pointed to the sky, and David realised a light snow was already falling. The old man tapped David's boots with his hand and shook his head vigorously, then he grabbed McCormick's wrist and pointed to his watch. They got the message.

'Put these things on,' Tom said, 'keep the old boy happy.'

The sandals were ill-fitting and let the elements at their feet. David tied his boots together carefully, and put them in his haversack. Danny dangled his plimsoles around his neck, and smiled ruefully at his new footgear.

'Follow,' the guide said, and melted away from them, shuffling across the fresh snow in his own sandals. They hurried on after him, clumsily falling in behind the old man, like new recruits behind a sergeant. The guide trudged head down, gliding over the ground with the least possible effort. They tried to copy him with mixed degrees of success. David managed to find a rhythm to suit his sandals. Tom and McCormick got along with occasional curses and flurries of snow, and Danny stepped out of his shoes altogether, stopping the others while he fixed them on again. The guide turned back and clucked at them, pointing again to McCormick's watch.

They were starting to climb the lower slopes, and a familiar stab of pain was in David's calves. They were all feeling the strain, except the guide, who moved ahead of them easily, never changing his pace, never looking up.

'He's a bloody climbing-machine,' Danny wheezed, 'a goat, not bleedin' human.'

'Save your breath, Simpson,' McCormick said, 'we've hardly begun.'

They climbed for two hours, pushing up a few thousand feet. Their way was narrow and rocky now, they followed the tracks of animals. David prayed there would be no worsening of the snow, no storms. He feared that might finish him. The stinging pain in his feet was turning to numbness, his hot, gasping breath froze to icy spittle on his face, he was splashed with hoar, someone was beating on the backs of his legs with sticks, and there was a furnace in his chest. He felt sharp rocks cutting against his feet, and was glad they were losing all feeling.

Their guide stopped and turned back towards them, grinning at the state of the young foreigners, the yellow stump of a tooth gleaming wolfish in the starlight. He waved them to the ground with his hand, and squatted down himself, whilst they flung themselves onto the snow. Ahead the mountains reared as tall as ever. They breathed like over-run horses, but the old Spaniard was still in his first wind.

'How does he do it?' Danny wondered.

'Used to it,' McCormick said.

'Every time we get over one hill, there's another one bloody waiting,' Tom muttered, 'lined up like sentries, they are.'

'Maybe we are over the worst,' David said, without conviction.

The guide passed around a flask from which they all drank gratefully. It contained brandy, which sank its fire into despairing bellies, and rekindled hope. Spirits were further raised when the guide pointed to a high ridge ahead of them, and moved his arm up and over it. '*España*,' he said proudly. He uncoiled a rope he had curled around him, and tied each man into a chain. They started out again, the four Britons struggling along like blind men.

David had little recollection of the climb over that ridge, it was a blur of pain and exhaustion. Years later he saw a photograph of men crossing the mountains into Spain, a small group like themselves. It showed tiny figures, bent by the wind, struggling alongside a mass of rocky peaks in a blue-tinged scene. It was what he always associated with his entry into Spain, the rich blue-black of the night sky, the stars as sharp as broken glass, and the fringe of fleecy cloud around the summits, ready to gather and sink them in snow.

David did not know whether he was still walking or being carried by Tom when McCormick shouted, 'We are there, the old boy says we are over the border.' The guide freed them of the rope, his hands were the only ones that could function; David and the other new recruits were pack animals to the end. They slumped into a hollow for a short rest, no-one talking, then begun to make a descent of the Spanish side of the mountains. A pale light was creeping over the horizon, a thin lemon-yellow making visible the contours of the landscape. Thick woods shaped up out of the mist, deep ravines leading into them.

Their guide was talkative, chatting away at them in Spanish, and clapping each man on the back. He smiled his congratulations at David, who offered him some tobacco. The Spaniard accepted seriously, and rolled a cigarette with it. He lit it leisurely, all haste forgotten now that he was on his native soil again. He led them down slowly, until they came to a clearing with a hut in it. It was roughly hewn, with a mossy, uneven roof, and was a wondrous sight for every man. Smoke curled out of its chimney, and that meant heat, and food, perhaps. Hearts and stomachs leapt in unison. The guide pointed to the hut and said, '*mi hermano acqui*'. As they drew near they smelt coffee, it blended with the scent of pine and leaf mould. David's legs regained a little sprightliness as he walked the last few yards.

Another old man waited for them, rifle cradled in his arms. He waved to their guide and exchanged a few rapid sentences. The brothers laughed and spat at the earth at their feet. Before he entered the hut David turned to look back at the mountains, to confirm his conquest. The sun was hauling itself into the sky, giving the peaks a hard silhouette. Their cold beauty took David's breath away, and he loved them for letting him cross them, for giving him a victory which made him feel so good.

The hut-keeper greeted them with reasonable English. '*Camaradas*, welcome to *España*. You have done well to cross, the *montagnas* are proud, no, they do not let you over easily. You can rest here, eat.'

They stumbled inside, to be met by delicious heat. Everyone was cut and bruised, but their constant moving had saved them from the worst ravages of the cold. Danny's feet were mildly frostbitten, and he had lost his plimsoles somewhere in the mountains. David had various gashes where the rocks had struck between the cords of his sandals, and aches everywhere, but they were all eased by his relief at crossing the border. It made three he had successfully negotiated, and he felt he had grown a little each time.

Their host offered bread with their coffee, but they barely managed to eat it before fatigue overcame them. David let the coffee course through his body, then fell asleep with the others, four men with their heads resting on a rough table.

When David awoke their guide had gone, back over the border to collect another party of volunteers. His hands and feet itched relentlessly as they came back to life, he rubbed them as he sat before the log fire. The snap of the logs reminded him of his own parlour. The others woke up and had the same problems as David.

'We must have been mad,' Danny said, rubbing his feet. He saw the hut-keeper. 'Here, what's your name, then?'

'Manolo. My brother Miguel, he bring you over the mountains.'

'Has he gone back?' McCormick asked.

'*Si*, to bring more over.'

'Remarkable chap,' McCormick murmured. Manolo shrugged, and served them fresh coffee, and bread and cheese. This time they devoured it.

Manolo sat and watched them, like a satisfied innkeeper. 'Me,' he said, thumping his chest, '*marinero*, when I was young. Learn English good, eh?'

They all nodded with their mouths full. Manolo asked them their names, and where they came from, proudly saying something about Liverpool, Scotland and Wales. He knew Britain through its docks. 'Si, Swansea, Cardiff, I know them. Big cities, plenty women, warm women, eh?' The old man's eyes twinkled as he thought back to old memories.

'How is the struggle going?' McCormick asked.

'Struggle, you mean the fight with the *fascistas*? *Quien sabe* – who knows? We are far away from it here, we hear little. Sometimes Miguel tells me something, but he is such a liar, that one. If he not know something he make it up. Maybe we are winning.'

Manolo knew of Franco and the Republic, but it became obvious that vast parts of his country were alien to him, more alien than Cardiff, perhaps.

'I am Catalan,' he said, 'Catalan first, Spanish after. In the south they are savage, barb... barb...'

'Barbarians,' David offered.

'*Si*, savage.' Manolo could have been back in the days of the Cid, warning of threatening Moors. He stoked up the logs whilst they cleared the table. As he did so Manola told them he would take them to Figueras, a small town near the border, where volunteers were processed. They left before the sun went down, limping along on battered feet. David lent Danny his town shoes. The slopes were still rocky and steep, and the cold no less piercing, but they were confident now, and reached a small pueblo in two hours.

'You stay here tonight,' Manolo told them, '*mañana*, someone come take you to Figueras. *Salud, camaradas.*' He left them, and went back to his mountains. David sensed he would never leave them for long, they were Manolo's oceans now.

The village was a cluster of red roofed white-washed houses. They were dilapidated and looked as if they were reluctant to be there at all. The alleyways were deserted, and the place still. If people were watching them they did so very secretly, there were no curtained windows here. David was disappointed, he wanted to meet the people he had come to fight for, he wanted a welcome, but no-one came to greet them. He glimpsed the face of a child spying from a glassless window and waved, but the figure was pulled away sharply.

'Not much like back home, eh boy?' Tom said. 'Imagine a bunch of Spaniards appearing in our village like this: you'd have women on every doorstep.'

Eventually, when they were beginning to wonder why Manolo had left them here, a portly man in an apron appeared out of an alley. '*Señors*, I am Carlo, your host. You stay with me tonight, in my *casa*.' He took them to a house which doubled as an inn for any rare travellers that stepped his way. In a cold and almost dark room Carlo offered them soup, for which he expected money. McCormick paid him. They shared the room with the man's family, and with goats and chickens which wandered freely in and out. After his elation at crossing the mountains David felt flat, and somewhat puzzled by his first taste of Spain. Tom caught his mood.

'Cheer up, Dave. Didn't expect a parade, did you? We are hardly the cavalry, after all.'

'No, we certainly aren't,' McCormick said. 'These people don't know us, and probably don't trust us. And they don't have anything to thank us for, either. We asked ourselves here. As Manolo said, the war is far away, it hasn't touched them yet.'

'They must think we're all cracked,' Danny said.

After their greasy soup they slept as best they could on the two mattresses laid out in front of the fireplace, a cavernous grate that dominated the room. David encountered his first fleas.

For most of the next day they waited for their lift to Figueras. A car arrived for them in mid-afternoon. It was an American Buick, a monster of chrome and polished wood, tarnished but still gleaming. At the wheel of it was a boy of seventeen, a bright-eyed youngster who grinned at them and made the car roar with acceleration outside the inn. For good measure he played a tune on the car's horn, delighting the small children attracted into the street.

'Good God,' Tom said, 'it's like something from a Hollywood gangster film. They must have commandeered it.'

'Maybe it was Jimmy Cagney's,' Danny said. 'We're going to travel in style, lads, or boyos.' He winked at David and Tom threw his cap at him. They were in high spirits as they bundled themselves into the car.

Soon they were jolting over rutted roads, driven crazily by the young Spaniard, who shouted sentences at them as he drove, laughing at their nerves.

'Don't worry, English, I drive good, I talk English good. We go to San Fernando, to the big castille. Plenty people like you there, plenty English, Germans – all.'

'It's an old fort, built in the eighteenth century, I think,' McCormick explained. 'They use it for a base for people coming into Spain.'

'Billy probably went there, Dave,' Tom said.

'Yes, but I think he will be where the action is now.'

'Oh aye, he will, you can be sure of that.'

Danny competed with the cacophony of the Buick and the driver with his versions of popular songs, but no-one minded. As the car rolled over winding country they were enthusiastic again. David forgot the muted welcome of the village and re-lived his crossing of the Pyrenees. He basked in this personal triumph and hoped it would mark a turning point for him.

San Fernando was a sprawling edifice of rock, sitting atop a hill of the same rock, a strong and ugly place. The Pyrenees lay around it, a ring of peaks made golden by the late sun. The Buick deposited them in a courtyard, where a bored Sergeant said '*Salud*,' then added '*camaradas*' as an afterthought. He scrutinised McCormick's papers, but obviously could not read them. He scratched his head and called a soldier, who showed them where to sleep.

The fort summed up David's first impressions of Spain: vast, and roughly put together. They were led deep into the building, to an underground stable, which stank of cavalry mounts. They were to bed down here. There were men already recumbent on the floor, David recognised a few from the train. 'Welcome to the Ritz, lads,' a voice called out of the gloom.

David's belly was empty again and another uncomfortable night loomed. He resigned himself to it and determined not to moan. He made a place for himself beside Tom. They had not talked much together during the day, their new companions inhibited them somewhat, they were not in the valley, and they were suffering infant pangs of homesickness.

For the first time on the journey David thought of Emma. Usually she conjured up feelings of guilt and frustration, a mirror to show him his weaknesses, but this time David felt free of such barbs. In their place was calm, and warmth. For some reason he was able to look back on his marriage without flinching. He wished he had seen Emma before he left, and wondered how much he would be missed. As the clamminess of his new sleeping place took a grip David thought of that old iron bed above the shop and the presence of Emma in it.

They were woken at first light by a Spaniard shouting at them. 'He has the voice of a ruptured bull, that one,' Tom muttered, scratching himself, and sitting upright. David struggled to remember where he was. He went up into the courtyard with fifty other stubble-cheeked men, rubbing his eyes as the glare hit them. The morning was sunny and icy, the mountain cold brought down to them by the wind. A bunch of men of various nationalities stood around, weighing each other up, Britons, Germans, Slavs, a few Belgians, and an Irishman.

They were lined up, to be addressed by the commander of San Fernando. He strode down steps to meet them, short and dumpy, a regular army officer. He was not unlike Franco.

'Welcome to *España*, comrades! To our great struggle against tyranny. We salute you.' He saluted, and the men shuffled an acknowledgment. They were bombarded with flowery phrases of encouragement and thanks.

'You are getting a proper welcome now, Dave,' Tom whispered, 'even if this bloke does go on a bit.'

'They set great store by speeches,' McCormick said.

'Aye, I've heard a few of them before,' Tom said.

The commander stretched out his speech as long as he could, but he never said much more than 'welcome'. After it they were marched off for breakfast. They each had a plate of stew, or grease and hot water, as one man put it, with hunks of bread, fresh this time. David learned at the table that the International Brigades were based at Albacete, a town somewhere in the south. It was there that they would be sent for training.

San Fernando did not inspire David with much confidence. It had a derelict air, more like a mausoleum than a fort. Most of the regular soldiers here were poorly dressed in makeshift uniforms, and rifles were rare, good ones more so: they were old, decrepit sometimes, and in need of cleaning. Sentries carried them proudly, their badges of inexperience. The recruits were allowed to walk around after breakfast. David approached a Spanish guard with Danny.

'Blimey, look at this old thing,' Danny said. 'I thought it was a muzzle loader for a minute. Here, let's have a look, mate.'

The soldier, mistaking Danny's grin of incredulity for approval, grinned back, and handed over his rifle without concern. Danny sighted along it.

'Don't look like its fired a shot this century,' he said. He whistled and the guard shook with pride.

'I hope we get better stuff than that, Dan,' David said.

'Course we will, lad, after that lovely speech of the commandant's we'll have to. We are in a backwater here, that's all, the real troops are away having a go at Franco.'

David nodded.

Later in the morning they were paraded in front of the fortress. They formed two lines beside the castle walls, facing the magnificent landscape. The air could not have been more different to the valley's smog. It had a lung-cleansing freshness, there were no chimneys here to cloud the horizon, which lay before them as sharp as a pin, the Pyrennees etched in outline. If all Spain is like this it will be fought over with passion, David thought. He felt the war would be long and fierce.

They stood downwind from the latrines, the stench of which wafted over them, tainting the mountain air.

'This place is a sea of shit,' Tom laughed, and pointed around him, 'looks as if they go anywhere here.' There had been no provision for the influx of transient men staying at San Fernando, so the ground outside was used randomly to relieve bowels. Faeces would be a lasting memory of the conflict for David, a symbol, the cynical side of him said. Wherever they went in Spain filth would be close by, laughing at any attempt at sanitation.

The commander had a few ideas about fitness, he decided they would run around the castle walls. They did so in straggling bunches, some barely managing a hobble after their exertions in the mountains.

McCormick did not see the logic in it. 'Anyone coming over the Pyrenees must be fit, that's obvious,' he snorted between breaths.

'Aye,' Danny said, winking at David, 'looks like they always do the wrong things at the wrong time here. Still, it's their country, isn't it?'

David remembered McCormick's words. The Scot would be proved right. The Spanish would display stupidity, disorganisation, childishness, murderousness, vanity, brutality and cowardice. All this lay before them, but they would also show courage, kindness and loyalty, and occasionally, the ability to get things done.

'If I had done this much roadwork I would have had a much better career,' Danny wheezed.

'No, you would have been too knackered for the ring, boy,' Tom shouted.

'All this fitness stuff,' McCormick said, 'load of nonsense, it is. It hasn't got much to do with killing Fascists, if you ask me.'

'What chance do you think we'll have Simpson,' Danny shouted back at them, 'what chance if the enemy can move faster than we can?'

Tom sucked in a cloud of air and gritted his teeth. David was lasting the run better than his friend, youth was on his side as his comrades sunk to the ground around him. He ran on ahead, feeling fresh and alive in this new world. He allowed himself the luxury of dwelling on the past week. It was his triumph: he had escaped the valley and reached Spain, when other, more experienced men had been turned back.

They stayed at San Fernando for four days, taking part in desultory exercises, like 'attacking' the fortress. Most of the volunteers could speak some English, and all had tales to tell of the struggles in their own countries. The riot David had taken part in had been fought out all over Europe, in far bloodier form. In Rome, Munich, Vienna, Berlin. Some of the men were desperate to win something from Spain, they had been on losing sides too long, for a generation, in some cases. David met lonely men, bitter men, isolated outposts of unshakeable beliefs. They had prepared for the main stage of Spain by playing out bit parts in their own countries. And there were the Dannys, men drawn by adventure, and a vague sense of doing good.

The thought of driving an ambulance was fading from David's mind, he could not drive, and he doubted if anyone in Spain would be willing to teach him. He would have to fight, be prepared to kill, and be killed. Now he was in Spain the prospect was not quite so frightening: he hoped he would be carried along by his comrades, as he had been in Conti's.

The Spaniards at San Fernando were of a different mood to the volunteers. They seemed resigned to the war, rather than inflamed by it. Few were well informed about the motives of either side, and even fewer were politically motivated. The officers were largely resentful of the influx of foreigners, and McCormick said they were not to be trusted.

'They were caught on the wrong side when it all began, that's all,' he said. 'Their sympathies lie with Franco, if you ask me.

They wouldn't have been in the army in the first place otherwise. It's hardly known for its liberalism here, is it?'

On their third night at the fort they managed to find a few soldiers who had some English. They joined them in the stable for a session of drink and talk. The Spaniards brought in wine, paid for by the volunteers' pool. David was the linkman in the conversation; he was beginning to pick up Spanish phrases, feeding off his French, to the admiration of his comrades, who were nonplussed by the language. The atmosphere was polite, with an undercurrent of shyness as men shared tobacco and bottles of rioja in the faint light.

Like Manolo, their hosts were Catalans, and cared little for the south of Spain, and were hazy about the war around Madrid. On some subjects they were unequivocal.

'If Franco wins, we will be finished, comrades, Luiz and me,' a young man, Jorge, spoke in soft voice.

'Us too,' a German echoed.

'Don't think about that bastard winning,' Tom said, 'its only just started, we haven't got to the war yet, have we lads? He won't win, we won't let him win, the world won't let him win.'

There was a chorus of approval.

'What are you fighting for, Jorge?' McCormick asked.

'Me, *camarada*, it's simple. Where I come from, a village, we had nothing, except for one man, a rich man who had everything. We did all the work, to keep him rich, and his sons rich, and his fat wife. And we starved if we did not.'

'Sometimes we starved anyway,' Luiz said, 'when there was no work.'

'What about the church, your priest, didn't they help you at all?' David asked.

'The church she is rich, no, so she is not on our side. Many of our people left her a long time ago, not God, just the church. The priest in our village, a Castillian, the first thing he do is be friends with the *señor*, to please the *señor*. They eat together a lot, the priest gets much, then he tells us to work hard and trust in God, it is sinful to ask for much, he says. We will get our reward in heaven.'

'And we want something in this life,' Jorge said.

'Are all priests like this?'

'All? No, not all. Some are like us, and have nothing. Sometimes they try to help us, but their church does not like them for it.'

'So you have seen through religion too,' McCormick murmured.

'I did not say we are without God, my friend,' Luiz said, 'I think he is in me, and you, in all of us. You too,' he pointed at McCormick.

'No, not in me,' the Scot said, 'God was invented by the rich to keep you poor, don't you see that? Millions in Spain are doing so, right now.'

The Spaniards looked at each other and smiled.

'Maybe so,' Jorge said. 'These are big questions, eh? We don't know the answers.'

Luiz shrugged and emptied a bottle. 'God, he did nothing to save our priest,' he said casually.

'What do you mean?' David asked.

Luiz looked at Jorge, who said, 'We kill him, that man, the people were angry that the *señor* escaped, so the priest died.'

All other talk stopped.

'Si,' Luiz said. 'He try to lock himself in his church, in the tower, but we shoot him out of it.' Luiz smiled at the memory. 'When he fell, he rang the bell, it rang out over the streets and the fields, it was a good sound for the people.'

'That's a bit rough though, innit?' Danny said. 'I'm not religious, God knows, but killing a priest, I don't know about that.'

'Others have been killed,' Luiz said, 'ours was not alone. The *fascistas* kill many of us. It is war, no?'

The gathering broke up as the wine ran out. Luiz and Jorge went back to their quarters, leaving the volunteers to think on their words.

There were twelve Britons at San Fernando and McCormick assumed unofficial control over them. He became their link with the Spanish authorities, much to Tom's distrust. David talked to the Scot a few times, he was as attracted by his education as Tom was repelled by it. He discovered that McCormick had a surprising past. He had taught at a public school, worked in factories, and been to a university, the first person David had met who had done so. McCormick was a bachelor.

'I've had no time for girls,' he told David, as they walked outside the fortress. 'I've always been to busy with the Party. Are you a member, David?'

'No, not yet.'

'I see.'

'Not sure of us, eh?'

David did not answer.

'Oh, I know Tom doesn't like me, I've had that before with my background, but we all want the same thing. I've always found it hard to be liked, so I've given up trying.'

David felt uncomfortable, but he rather liked McCormick, there was a softly-spoken determination about the man, and he had given up much, David felt.

The next day they were taken to Figueras in trucks to board a train for Barcelona, the Catalan capital. Numbers had swelled to a hundred, mainly East Europeans, a ragged group of men who sang revolutionary songs and indulged in virulent back slapping.

They were crammed into ancient carriages, already filled with troops and civilians. The front of the train was bedecked with flags, and the carriages had all been daubed with Socialist slogans. The insignia of the C.N.T. was everywhere, it was the anarchist union, which, with the anti-Stalinist P.O.U.M., was the strongest force in the area. 'It's the likes of those who will make things difficult,' McCormick said, 'they are all crazy extremists.'

It was less than a hundred miles to Barcelona but their journey lasted most of the day. Posters were everywhere, on the walls of the railside buildings, raised high on billboards hung from posts. They attacked the emotions, the senses, even the intellect, it was heady stuff for the volunteers, each slogan was a welcome, lauding their decision to come to Spain.

'They like a bit of colour here,' Tom said, pointing to a large poster on the station wall. It was the colour of freshly turned earth, and showed a worker in a white shirt, tin hat on his head, exhorting the peasants to take the land: 'It is yours' it said. David felt the pull of that image, the oversized aquiline face stirred him; it was propaganda, and it worked.

McCormick was almost garrulous, 'We could do with a few of those on the streets of Glasgow,' he said. 'Something to crystallise the hopes of the people. That could be our Kitchener.'

'What's he on about?' Danny whispered.

'Oh, he's just excited, Dan,' David said.

'Well, that's no reason to use them big words.'

Every few miles the train was stopped and checked for what

seemed like hours. Several men boarded each time, and once a man was taken out of the carriage.

A Belgian had been placed in official command of the volunteers, and he had the task of explaining his men at every stop, using a collection of papers and passes he had accumulated.

'We are getting to be experts at travelling by train, Dave,' Tom said, as once more they shuffled to a halt.

'Yes, I don't want to see another one for a long time,' David answered.

'Go on,' Danny said, 'marvellous things trains are. My dad was a stoker on 'em for years, till he fell off one. Still drunk from the night before he was, though don't ever tell my old lady that.'

Too many lungs competed for too little air in the carriage, and despite the season they were all in shirt sleeves by the end, like trippers going to the seaside. They shared a warm sense of adventure mixed with anxiety, and the relief that they were doing something at last.

The light was fading as they arrived in Barcelona, a bustling port that dubbed itself the home of the revolution. They passed through outskirts that were a sea of Marxist and Anarchist banners waving their messages to the skies.

'They are out for their own ends, this lot,' McCormick muttered, nodding to the banners.

'Aren't we all?' Tom said. 'If you come right down to it. We tell ourselves that it is for the common good, but it comes from a personal belief.'

McCormick looked at Tom with some surprise. 'What we want will free people, give them a better system.'

'Well, perhaps the blokes who put these posters up think the same.'

David had heard much about Barcelona, but the city was strangely quiet as they disembarked from the train. Most shops and cafés were shut as night fell, to conserve energy, and the bustle of the pre-war days was gone. An official met them at the station, and led them to the hotel at which they were to stay. 'Everybody is equal,' he told those next to him, the bosses are all run away, or hiding, or dead. And their houses,' he pointed to a grand one they passed, 'we have them now, they are the people's.'

The few residents they met on the streets were friendly, calling out to them as they marched by, but there was no great excitement at their coming. Barcelona was far from any front, and the surge of enthusiasm of six months before had waned. In contrast the volunteers' own spirits lifted when they saw their hotel. It was palatial, set in a square near the Ramblas, a great change to the previous stopping points for David and Tom. The hotel echoed the days of monarchy and was a strange mixture of that age and the new era of socialism. A C.N.T. banner was draped over a portrait of some past king, masking previous loyalties. David was allocated a vast room, which he shared with Tom and Danny. McCormick had drifted away on the march across the town, which suited Tom.

They were told not to wander far from the hotel that night, so they contented themselves by stuffing down as much food as they could get. It was rumoured that the café next door served free drinks to foreign volunteers on their first night in Barcelona, and this notion drew them surely to it. In the early evening they entered a long room which rang with noise in the still city, and found a space at a table where they could take in their surroundings. David looked around at a mass of multi-national drinkers: passionate talking faces bobbed up in front of him, the café reverberated with their arguments. For once he felt at home in a hubbub; this was a larger version of Conti's, David told Tom. 'Aye, it is that,' Tom said, 'all it needs is the stove.' Danny got hold of a porron of red wine, and delighted in squirting it at them. They quickly learned how to direct its jet effectively.

A common uniform of leather jerkin and beret marked the men of action, some openly showed pistols, the plotters and back room men wore suits spattered with cigarette ash and wine stains, and talked like jackdaws behind their hands. Bursts of words spluttered from their mouths like machine-gun fire, then they were silent. Some men could not be defined, they hugged the shadows and watched. David saw the faces of his comrades glow the colour of their wine through the haze of the room. Tom and Danny determined to get drunk as quickly as possible. David knew he would follow them, but felt that since leaving the valley, drinking was all they had achieved, drinking and talking. It made him feel uneasy, and not quite honest.

'What else can a man do at a time like this?' Danny cheered. 'Come on David, drink up, here, have a squirt.' Danny drilled the centre of David's mouth with some expertise. Neighbouring tables shouted out to them, and their porron was refilled several times, and beer sometimes appeared on the table, given to them by whoever happened to be passing. As David drank, faces blurred and danced around, he was slipping into drunkenness and dreaded the next morning. He saw a kaleidoscope of images in his head, the slashing rain of the valley faded into the Pyrenees, Helen's face mingled with Emma's, with the peasant's on that poster, with his own; he saw himself running with a rifle, running somewhere and falling. Sounds ebbed and flowed around him, like tide rushing on pebbles.

'Come on boy, time to get you back,' Tom was pulling him up, and Danny held onto his other arm. The café was emptying its load onto darkened streets. They tumbled out in a crowd, a restless wave of shouting men, congratulating one another, loving one another, promising reunions in Madrid, in Franco's sitting room, on his grave. The three comrades slouched back to their hotel, a six-legged pyramid of drunken balancing.

The next day lingered, the minutes stuck in the pit of their hangover, and they sat in their bedroom wondering why they tortured themselves so.

'It's not like the beer back home,' Tom growled, in a voice afraid to raise itself to an audible pitch. 'That stuff flows out easily enough, not long after it's gone in, but this wine, it sinks into your guts, man, saves its dregs there, turning and churning. God knows what's in it.'

'If He does, it's a terrible secret he's keeping,' Danny said, before making another dash to the washroom.

The hotel was awash with rumours, of victories, defeats, great plans to beat the Fascists, *mañana*. In the afternoon David felt able to take a walk outside. The day was fair, lit by a weak sun, a shadow of its summer self, but enough to warm. He managed to find the main thoroughfare of the Ramblas. It impressed him with its spacious ways, so different from his own huddled streets. It was easy to imagine the scenes here when control of the city had been fought for.

David's body welcomed the soothing of the sun, he felt it unfurl, like a leaf shaking off dew, and his mountain bruises eased. He sat on a bench and watched what went on around him. Away from Tom he thought of what lay ahead. He wondered how he might achieve even a semblance of violence, he had never even been involved in a school-yard tussle. Man had a natural instinct for homicide, he told himself, and trusted he would gain his share when the time came.

He rolled a cigarette and smoked it under another banner. This one showed a red-bereted anarchist firing a silver rifle through the huge letters of P.O.U.M. The gun was the antitheses of San Fernando; it was a dream, the hoped-for future. War was sanitised on this board, a stirring affair to be looked up to, and David was looking up. It was cannily placed to catch the eye of the sitter, to send him to the front with a full heart. The other side would have the same banners, and the same exhortations, words would be shed as easily as blood in Spain. David remembered Billy telling him about the Great War once, as they had lazed in Conti's.

'All those fine feelings they pump into you, boy, well they're hard to resist, see. At first you want to believe like all the other boys.' Billy had stopped and tapped his pipe against the stove. 'But when you get out there, go over the top, they're all forgotten. Nothing like machine-gun fire to destroy grand thoughts. You leave them behind, and get on with the killing, and the most important part of any bloody war, the surviving. That's what it comes down to in the end, just trying to survive. I'll never forget seeing thousands of men running to their fate, like demented rabbits. All for words, and a few feet of mud.'

David wondered if Billy felt the same now, now that he had actually gone to a war for his beliefs. He finished his cigarette and made his way to the hotel, smiling at the people he passed.

That night the men were restless, anxious to be gone, the penniless ones like David especially so. The battle for Madrid had ended in stalemate, Franco had been halted, and there had been a lull in hostilities since Christmas. They spent the night quietly in their bedroom, Danny slipped out somewhere, leaving David and Tom to talk. They lay on their separate beds and gazed up at the high ceiling. It was inlaid with a faded mosaic, and edged with wooden carvings.

'Bit like being in chapel here,' David said.

'Aye, or a tart's boudoir. More a tart's boudoir, I'd say, this is too posh for old Iolo's place. It's the biggest room I've ever slept in, that's for sure. David, we haven't had much time to talk alone these last few days, so I haven't had chance to tell you.'

'Tell me what?'

'You did good in those mountains, I was proud of you. I almost didn't make it myself, you know. You've come a long way since that little march we done.'

'Thanks, Tom. Perhaps a little way.'

Tom's words pleased David. He let him talk on about nothing much, enjoying the tone of Tom's soft voice. It placated his nerves and filled him with fond thoughts of home.

'Eh,' Tom said, 'I didn't like the look of those rifles back at that Fernando place, did you? Out of the bloody ark, they were. You don't think they'll give us stuff like that, do you Dave?'

David liked his opinion being sought. 'No, of course not, there's equipment coming from Russia now. It's early days, Tom, don't forget. We'll have just as good stuff as the other side, soon.'

'I hope so, I don't want it to be like back home, our side running around with nowt except guts.'

David hoped reality would bear out his words. Tom fell asleep, snoring in that solid way of his, a snort in the nose, then a ripple of the lips, like an engine dying. David wrote a few lines in the diary he was keeping: 'We have reached Barcelona safely, tomorrow we go south.'

11

The journey down to Albacete took the best part of two days, punctuated by the now expected stops and checks. Carriages grew fetid with cooped up men, what heat there was mixed with tobacco smoke to fray tempers and stifle conversation. Most were surly by the end.

Before leaving the hotel David procured a simple map, trading the last of his tobacco for it. As they travelled he tried to equate the passing landscape with the few details his map showed. Albacete was a town midway between Madrid and the Mediterranean, on the plains of La Mancha. No-one knew anything about it, except that it was remote, and well out of the way of any action.

The landscape became drier and browner as they pushed south. Apart from the odd cluster of sheep, the red dust of the plains was an alien land for the Welshmen. Sometimes they skirted a greener patch of land, oases of growth which heightened the overall impression of desert. David looked for the windmills that Quixote tilted at, but never saw any. He knew this part of Spain would support the Republic; its poverty said so.

'You will be warm down here, boy,' Tom said, 'the land looks well scorched. You'll like that, eh, no more freezing.'

David half nodded as he felt a trace of the Pyrenees in his bones. Tom was right, it would be a cauldron here in a few months. He saw a clump of trees on the horizon, gnarled, stunted bits of wood that were curling back into the soil, abandoning their attempts to grow.

The sun was fat and sinking when they reached Albacete. They stopped at an exposed strip of station.

'We are here, lads,' Danny shouted. 'Gateway to the war.'

Stiffened limbs were rubbed back to life as men disembarked and shook themselves. They looked about dubiously at Albacete. It did not seem to be a gateway to anything other than oblivion. The town was asleep.

The volunteers were assembled and marched to the Albacete

bullring, where a small reception committee greeted them formally. They were split up into groups. The Britons were joined by a few Americans and one Canadian. Before them, piled in the dust, was a collection of clothing, described as uniforms by a Spanish officer. 'Take your choice,' he told them, 'there is one for each.' It was a lottery, a mixture of military curios from all over Europe. Even so the men were glad to take off their civvies, and share a common identity.

David found a khaki shirt and a pair of floppy trousers, bell-bottomed like a sailor's. He knew he looked ridiculous but he was in good company. He scrambled for a beret, which he thought gave him the look of a veteran. Danny had the worst outfit: he looked like a clown deserting from a circus, with trousers that reached to his midriff, and a leather jerkin that stank. He winked at David and looked down at himself with rueful eyes.

'Well, we're in the army now, lad. I'll keep warm anyhow, with this sack on.'

'You didn't look much different before,' Tom said.

With shouts of good luck they were herded off to their training camps, split up by nationalities.

The Britons went to Madrigueras, a smaller town, twenty miles further into nowhere. Things were happening quickly, after the slow torture of the train. Men fingered their new old clothes thoughtfully, they had a shabby uniformity now.

'I didn't like the way that officer was barking orders,' Danny said, 'I had enough of that in our army. I thought this do was supposed to be the people's war.'

'There has to be discipline, Dan,' Tom said. 'I wonder if we'll have British officers?'

'Christ, don't say that, there's nothing bloody worse.'

'It will depend on whether there are experienced men here,' McCormick said.

'I bet the Scot has got his sights set on being one,' Danny muttered. 'I don't fancy him leading me into the valley of death.'

Madrigueras was not much more than a pueblo, a collection of houses, as dry as the plains that surrounded them. Its people were likewise impoverished, they scrubbed out a living on the poor soil from dawn to dusk, using tools which would not have been out of place in the Stone Age. The volunteers pulled into an oblong courtyard, in front of a building which splayed yellow light from its windows. People spilled out of it to greet the trucks. David jumped down, to be immediately patted on the back.

'So you made it at last, did you boy, *bach*?' a voice whispered in his ear. David recognised it, and turned to find Billy's face inches from his own. His uncle stood beside him, grinning from ear to ear. His display of cracked and missing teeth was a splendid sight.

'Well, 'aven't you got anything to say to your old uncle, then?'

They hugged each other, then David pushed him away, embarrassed.

'Huh, you haven't changed. Still the shy one.'

Billy saw Tom. 'Hullo Tom, glad to see you got down alright. Put it there, son.'

There was a round of hand-shaking as the new men were led inside, to spend their first night at Madrigueras in a whirl of gossip, news sharing and mutual congratulation.

David sat at a communal table, a series of small ones had been placed together to seat everyone. Billy and Tom sat on either side of him and for the first time David felt he could relax a little, without rushing headlong into drink, although wine had been procured. The sky was clear, scattered with stars, and a piece of moon was visible through a window. David felt that this was his first real night in Spain. He listened to the swell of Welsh voices around him, and was comforted by it.

On one wall of the room was a poster of Greta Garbo, tattered at the edges, but still colourful.

'Wondering what that is doing here, lad?' Billy asked. 'We're in the local flea pit see, they had nowhere else to put us. They still show pictures next door, if they can get 'em.'

David smiled at the thought of a cinema for a barracks. There was an American hero opposite him, winning some fine war, on a poster not much different from the ones in Barcelona.

David answered Billy's questions about their trip, and the valley. Billy spoke as though he had been away for a long time, not just a month before them. His words slurred with nostalgia as he said them. He took to hugging David in between swigs of any passing bottle, gazing at him with bleary eyes.

'We got to stick together now, boy, you and me. I owe it to your father, to old Daniel. Miserable sod... and Helen, to Helen... a woman and a half... boy if you knew...' He trailed to a halt. 'Eh

148

Tom,' Billy shouted. 'We got to stick together eh, you, me, and the boy.'

David slept in a room with eleven others, on a bunk with rotten slats. Someone went through his in the night, causing a minor alert, and much drunken laughter. David awoke without the misery of a hangover, and was able to study his comrades with a clear head. Billy still slept, rippling his lips with a steady snore. David found it hard to believe they had been reunited so smoothly, that he was in the reassuring presence of his uncle again. The backbone of Conti's Boys was here.

The trickle of Britons in Spain had increased to enough men to form a battalion, part of the Fifteenth International Brigade. The early volunteers had fought in the defence of Madrid; many had already died in that battle. David was billeted with an eager and inexperienced group of men, five Welshmen, two Londoners, the rest northerners, from Manchester and the mill towns of Lancashire. All struggled to cope with their breakfast of beans saturated in oil. Billy laughed at their distress. 'Come on, get it down you lads. You'll soon get used to it, all you need is iron guts and a tight arsehole.' The table spluttered into life, and Billy took his cue to address the new recruits. He told them of Madrid.

'It was a real motley crew there, I can tell you, on those barricades. Waiters in bloody penguin suits, kids no bigger than their rifles, college boys with their books under their arms,' Billy winked at David, 'everyone and his mother were standing together. A united front, that's what stopped them, and us volunteers. There was some good soldiers there, Germans and the like', Billy stopped to shovel down some food, wiping his mouth with a piece of bread. 'Guts was the only thing we had to fight with, guts against tanks. It was hand to hand fighting in the end. We were on the same footing as them then, and we turned the bastards back.'

'What was the equipment like, Bill?' Tom asked.

'We didn't have much. I tried three rifles in all, and none of the buggers was any good. Talk about shooting around corners, I 'ad better luck using one as a club in the end, like this.'

Billy made a mock lunge at Danny, causing him to cough up soup.

'Careful now Billy, I'm a boxing man, you know.'

Billy warmed to his audience, and held them effortlessly, no-one else spoke. David saw how Billy had aged in the few months he had been in Spain. Daylight from the window deepened the furrows on his face. It was crazed with lines and mining scars, and his eyes were prone to water, yet Billy's optimism belied his age. He was the youngest of them, and he had waited for Spain all his life.

'Must admit though,' Billy continued, 'I was glad when our planes come over. Ruskies they were, came across the sky like silver angels, they did, the little darlings. Up till then the Eyties had been bombing bloody hell out of us. They pissed off as soon as they saw our planes, only came at night after that. I hear they are dropping their bombs anywhere now, killing women and kids.'

There was a ripple of disbelief at this.

'I see you lads will have a lot to learn,' Billy said softly. 'This is a new type of war. Come on, eat up everyone, food is short out here.'

The battalion was commanded by Tom Winteringham, an Englishman. After breakfast they marched to Madrigueras square, to hear him address them. They spilled out of their cinema barracks noisily, eager, garrulous and confident that their presence in Spain would greatly change things. David surveyed his new surroundings as Winteringham's words flowed over them. The town had a stale going-nowhere feel, it was cut off, and did not seem to care. Streets leaned into streets, creating havens of shadow amongst blunt architecture, the domain of old men and small children, and cats, watching all with flinty eyes.

David missed much of what Winteringham said, but woke up when he heard the phrase 'not much time'.

'I am afraid that is the picture, men,' the commander said, 'there could be a renewed assault on Madrid at any time, and we will be called upon to help in its defence. You will have to learn quickly and do your best with what we have. Supplies are a problem but the situation is improving. Good luck with your training, and thank you for being here.'

They were dismissed, watched and mimicked by a few local children, wide-eyed and curious, but too shy to approach.

'I'll see you later, lads,' Billy said, 'you new boys are going on a little hike. You'll like that, even in winter here the sun blasts out all impure thoughts.'

'Aren't you coming, Billy?' David asked.

'No, us old-timers have advanced to killing, we don't need any more keep fit stuff. Look after those feet of yours, boy, I'll see you when you get back.'

They were taken on a route march, out onto the plain. A column three abreast was formed, and they covered the road in a semblance of order, under a sun that hinted of a future strength. It was like a warm spring day in the valley, but the peasants they passed in the fields were well wrapped up: cotton jackets were turned up around their necks, and sombreros kept their faces in shadow, just the occasional white of an eye caught the sun. Most of the toilers scrubbed around in poor soil, tending sad-looking crops. Their work seemed aimless. David remembered the words of Juan Davies 'they have nothing', and believed it now. The soldiers' presence caused little reaction amongst the peasants, the men grew tired of shouting greetings that were ignored, or, at best, returned with a dangle of the hand. Fear in these people, and little hope in the possibility of change – a very different attitude to the workers of Barcelona.

Most of the men in the battallion were Communists, officials of the party back home, unemployed workers, a scattering of the middle classes: teachers, students, and a few unlikely recruits: a public-school headmaster and an ex-army officer. David got to know the big-mouths and the sly ones, the back-slappers and zealots, the good men and the confused. Morale was high, there was a real desire to get at the enemy – men wanted to test themselves and be counted.

After more marches, which David lasted easily enough, they were given wooden sticks, roughly shaped into rifles. Some were amused by them, others angered. Be patient, they were told, guns are on the way, good guns. In the night meetings were held, and lectures given by political commissars, men appointed to look after morale, morals and political commitment. They were the Communist Party's chaplains. There were talks on Russia and Marxism, which made those without strong affiliation restless.

'We come here to fight, didn't we,' Danny said, at one meeting, 'not to go to school. When are we going to get proper training, and rifles?' There was a murmur of support for the boxer and again they were told 'soon', and 'be patient'.

On their fifth night they were allowed out into Madrigueras.

David walked with Tom and Billy through the empty streets to a small bar Billy knew. Billy was a sergeant now, promoted for his experience, and his actions at Madrid. There was no sign of their promised six pesetas a day pay, but Billy had some money. The bar was the front room of a house, low ceilinged and airless, lit by a kerosene lamp strung from a beam. Billy ordered a bottle of wine.

'Taste's like cat's piss, but it does the trick,' Billy said.

'Haven't they got any beer?' Tom said.

'Beer! No Tom, you'll have to drink this stuff, or nowt.'

They did so slowly. This was to be no binge, Madrigueras did not seem to be the place for it. Billy talked quietly about the valley, and the miners' past victories. He grew maudlin, and his personal homesickness swept over them all in waves. David felt a fraud, experiencing such nostalgia for a place he had always run down.

'It's funny,' Billy said. 'You don't think about it much when you are there, I never thought I would miss that filthy smoke, and the rain, but I do somehow.' He twisted his pipe in his hands.

'You haven't been here long, Bill,' Tom said.

'Aye, right enough. Daft, isn't it? Pity this lot wasn't happening back home, isn't it? We could have a good clear out once and for all.'

Billy had changed, David saw. Here he wanted everything in a rush.

'You can't stop and debate with a bullet,' Billy told them.

'Talking of bullets, when are the rifles coming, Bill?'

Billy was expecting Tom's question. He glanced over at the barman and lowered his voice.

'Now don't go blabbing this, but supplies are still pretty short. We get nothing like the other side, and half of what Russia sends is stuck at the French border. That bastard Blum keeps shutting it, afraid of upsetting the Capitalists, I suppose. What we have got is needed at the front, and that isn't much. You can count yourselves lucky you weren't pitched straight into it, like we were. All I had at first was a tin hat, and that didn't bloody fit.'

Billy stopped for another glass of wine, and a further look around.

'My first rifle come off a dead man, and the thing wouldn't hit the side of a barn.' His voice dropped to a whisper 'It was slaughter, first off, half our boys died needlessly, wasted lives they were. I was amazed the Fascists didn't get through. The big brass thought they would, they hopped it to Valencia. But we did hold them, in spite of everything we held them, and that gives me hope, boys. Things can only get better now, even if it is *mañana*.'

'What is that Bill, *mañana*?'

'It's that's their favourite word here, they always put off till tomorrow what they could do today, war or no bloody war. We all have to put up with it, eh Sebastian?' Billy turned to the barman, who had been leaning his ears towards them.

He shrugged his belly, making ripples of fat quiver as it settled over his bar. Sebastian looked like Oliver Hardy, the same gloomy interest, the helpless appeal for sanity in his eyes. He mirrored one side of Spain. They finished the bottle and walked back to the barracks, thoughtful and sober.

David had no time to dwell on Billy's words. They were roused before dawn the next morning, jolted out of sleep to face a tumult of men running, and confused messages being shouted. 'We're going to Madrid,' David heard. 'To fight – the Fascists are trying to break through again.' He sat up and rubbed the chill from his bones. A sergeant shook him by the shoulder. 'Come on Hicks, move yourself. We are leaving after breakfast.'

Around the tables there was a buzz of excitement. They were served more food than usual, and there was meat in the stew.

'Is it true, Billy?' he asked as his uncle passed the table, a sheaf of papers in his hand.

'Aye, it's right enough, Madrid is looking dodgy again, they need everyone there, even you lot.'

He placed a hand on David's shoulder and gave it a reassuring squeeze, but there was worry on his face. The plan to give new recruits effective training was discarded, they would be flung into the fire, like the men before them. David did not believe in *mañana* at this moment, and Billy wished he had kept his mouth shut in Sebastian's bar.

There were trucks outside in the courtyard, and a pile of rifles were stacked besides them, jumbled together like a crazy arms bazaar. They were all shapes and all sizes, and they were all old.

'Bloody hell,' Danny said, 'they are like those at San Fernando, worse if anything.' A Spanish captain came with the rifles, he handed them out, first come first served. Tom got a small American Winchester, which he sighted doubtfully against the sky. Seeing David the captain gave him a long barrelled piece, a German Mauser, which was very heavy, and completely filthy. It looked as if it had been lost in the mud of the Somme, and just found. A broken bayonet lay beneath the barrel. Danny whistled when David showed him his catch. 'What a brute, it's almost as big as I am.'

A few of the experienced men dished out some ammunition, they knew what fitted what, for all the rifles were different calibre. David received a handful of greasy cartridges, which he stuffed in his pockets. He had no idea how to load the Mauser, but he was not alone in this. 'You will have plenty of time to practice, comrades,' the captain beamed at them. They boarded the trucks without further ado, bundling their bags and cases on the floor. Madrigueras disappeared in clouds of dust as they began their journey to Madrid. Children saw them off, waving red cloths like skinny scarecrows, and David settled back against the canvas to endure another bone-jarring trip across the belly of Spain.

'This is bloody chaotic, Bill,' Tom shouted over the noise of the engine, 'we are nowhere near ready.'

'I know, I know, but that's the way it is, there's never enough time here, or there's too much. At least the boys are well dug in around Madrid now, and we've got air cover, and some tanks even, I hear. Listen you two, stick by me. You'll be shit-scared when the shooting starts, unless you are mad, but that will pass, see. Some of the boys who bought it the first time, they done something daft, like sticking their heads out in the open, or panicking, and running out of cover. Avoid things like that and you have a chance, they shoot just as bad as us.'

'I'm not sure our guns will shoot at all, Billy,' David said.

'Most of 'em will, when they are cleaned up, not very good perhaps, but they'll kill, if you give them a chance. Let's hope we'll have the time to give them a going over before we go into action.'

Billy glanced around the men in the trucks, steadying himself by holding a piece of rope which hung down from the canvas. 'Listen now, lads, in the last big one we used to go over the top with no hope of winning anything except a mouthful of mud. Mown down like rats, most of my mates was. Didn't really know what the hell we were fighting for – king and country, what does that mean? – but no-one forced us here, did they, we haven't been followed by Kitchener's eyes, only the eyes of our own beliefs. Remember, that, if the going gets hard. Right, end of speech. I'll be sounding like one of them commissars of ours.' Billy nudged David. 'Cheer up boy, too bloody bright to get shot you are, and your uncle's too bloody mean.'

It took them a day to reach the southern edge of Madrid, where they were deposited, covered with dust, cold and exhausted. They shuffled around, shaking stiffness from limbs, and listening for sounds of war. In the distance the odd rattle of gunfire could be heard, hollow sounds, like the whine of wasps trapped in bottles. The long boom of a shell made them all duck, but it landed far away.

The enemy was collecting its forces for an attack on the Jarama valley, in an attempt to cut the Madrid line of communications with Valencia, the government's base on the Mediterranean coast. Six hundred Britons had been assembled, with old hands like Billy spread thinly amongst them. They were in a hilly land, sprinkled with orange groves and bare outcrops of rock, dry but not as barren as Madrigueras. That night they slept in the open, to wake at first light to the sound of heavy firing. Even the greenest of recruits knew that heralded a major attack, somewhere.

It was the second week of February 1937, and they were told they were going into action immediately. Men stood around eating dry bread, apprehensive and excited.

'Come on lads,' Danny cried, 'eat, drink and be merry, isn't that what they say, for tomorrow we snuff it.'

Someone threw a lump of bread at him.

'So much for giving the rifles a going over,' Tom said.

'Don't worry,' Billy said, 'there will be time for a quick practice and clean up. Immediately never means quite that in Spain.'

Billy showed his group how to load their rifles, then handed out an extra fifty rounds of ammunition apiece, to supplement their Madrigueras pocketful.

'That will mean about thirty usable rounds, lads,' Billy shouted, 'the rest will be duds, you'll have to put up with it.'

Spanish ammunition was notoriously unreliable, and scarce, but each man was allowed to fire his weapon several times. They stood in a mass, and loosed off at a mound of rocks fifty yards away. David tried to remember what he had read on the subject. He recalled the need to hold the rifle firmly against his shoulder, to prevent the recoil shattering the collar bone. He did so and sighted along his long barrel. He squeezed the trigger tentatively, very much aware he was on the edge of a new world. He felt the life of the gun as it jerked in his hands, exploding its hot load to send a message of death scudding towards the rocks. The force knocked him back and hurt his shoulder but he tried another shot. This time the Mauser jammed, gagging on the rust that clogged it.

'Let's have a look,' Billy said. He busied himself with the Mauser, fussing over it with some contentment. David watched in amazement; his uncle loved all this. Billy scoured the barrel with a length of cord, until he was satisfied with it. With a rag he polished the gun until it gleamed blue-black through the rust.

'Try it now, David. This old girl is a good piece, killed plenty of us in the last war, didn't it? Take your time, don't jerk the trigger.'

David peered along the sight and fired another round at the rocks. The Mauser reared to the right and missed by yards. Billy tut-tutted.

'Give it here again, it's pulling.' Billy examined the gun. 'Hmm, can't do much about that, its the age of the thing. You'll have to aim a bit to the left to compensate – and hope for the best.'

David took Billy's advice with the next round, and it smacked into the heart of the rocks, drawing the approval of the other novices. Billy gave him a few extra rounds and whispered, 'There you are, hit a target as big as a house and you're a marksman in this war.' David's next two rounds were duds, and the practice was over. Compared to the hapless efforts of most of his fellows he felt he could use the Mauser. Around him men blazed away with their strange guns, enthusiastic but useless. The air rang with the curses of the frustrated, and the rocks lay undisturbed.

'Safest bloody place to stand is in front of the rocks,' Billy shouted. Officers walked amongst them, brave-faced, but resigned. The practice was over.

The night had been cold, with frost seeping through clothing, a foretaste of what was to come as they faced a campaign in open country. David had spent most of it awake, pressed against the wall of a shattered house, the resonance of war in his ears. He heard outbreaks of firing, and sometimes the low thud of a shell, he felt he was being sucked into a vortex, a willing, but unready player.

A steady stream of wounded men were stretchered through the village in which they were camped. David forced himself to look at some of them, holding down the gorge that rose in his throat as he saw the twisted remnants of limbs, pitifully tied up with rags. Stifled moans became screams when stretchers struck the ground. It was like one long mining disaster.

After rifle practice the ubiquitous stew was served. David tried to eat it, watching the procession of pain filter its way to the nearest medical post. He gnawed at his bread, but could not digest the stew. Already he was bitter at their lack of preparation, and aghast at the standard of equipment. Dying needlessly was his greatest fear, and not far away men were doing that, no doubt. He shivered as a lost shell further ruined some buildings just a few hundred yards away. Men shrank into the ground and waited for a bombardment that never came. David sat back up shakily, fear was in him, he was on the fringe of the darkness war always brings, one of the poor bloody infantry.

The new men spent the rest of the day obtaining scraps of knowledge in the art of warfare. They learned how to take cover, dig holes, care for their weapons, their training was being condensed into an afternoon. At dusk Winteringham addressed them.

'We are going in tomorrow men. We will defend an elevated position, a strong point in our defences. The enemy is trying to break through and cut the Valencia road there.'

A murmur spread through the ranks.

'Elevated position? That means a hill, don't it?' Danny asked.

'At least we will be looking down on the buggers,' Billy told those around him.

'Get as much rest as you can men, we move out at first light tomorrow.' Winteringham stood on an ammunition case as he talked to them, his back against the sun. 'You haven't had much time, I know that,' he said, 'but I know you will do your best, and that's all I ask of you.'

'S.O.B.S!' Danny muttered.

'What,' David said, 'what's sobs?'

'Same Old Bull Shit, me son, Same Old Bull Shit,' Danny walked away, without his usual wisecrack.

They disbanded into groups of men talking rapidly, trying to keep nerves at bay. Despite this David slept soundly enough that night, and marched out with his comrades in the morning, alert and apprehensive, and still finding it hard to believe he was marching to war. The Mauser cut a line in his shoulder; he could not find an ideal spot for it to settle against, he was too bony.

Within hours they were in position, looking across open ground to where the enemy would spring from. The rocky scrub resisted any attempts to dig worthwhile cover, but men scoured out hollows the best they could. They had time to do so for the day was uneventful, and they were not called to do anything more than dig.

Billy was in charge of a machine-gun, one of the dozen Maxims the battalion had. They were cumbersome things, mounted on small wheels, easy to jam and brutes to dismantle, but very effective at killing when they worked. Billy's group was a little larger than a platoon, thirty men bunched in the centre of the hill, with outposts on either side.

The only action they saw that day took place overhead, against a backcloth of pastel blue sky. David watched Russian fighters attacking Italian Fiats, like gnats buzzing around bees. They made squawking noises as they raced around the sky, spitting bullets at each other, and ignoring the soldiers below. For a short time the Republic had air superiority, bolstered by the arrival of the Russian planes. It was a war for all nations. Tomorrow Africans would be trying to kill Britons, today men who lived thousands of miles apart fought each other over a land foreign to all of them. Men cheered the action above them, it helped to know they were not the only ones at it. A roar broke out as a Fiat was seen to plummet, smoke trailing from its fuselage. It disappeared over the horizon to an uncertain fate, and everyone wished it dead. 'Chalk one up for our boys,' Billy shouted.

An ex-army Lancastrian was Billy's number two on the Maxim, with Danny, they were the only ones who had fired a shot in anger. Ignorance was shared evenly amongst the others. David tried to work out where they were but his map was quite inadequate. They had no official ones, so knowledge of the terrain was zero.

David's frame was too thin for the harsh ground, the rocks grating against his ribs at all times. He spent a long first night on the hill, a bright night, lit by distant flashes of gunfire. Tom lay next to him in the hole they had scrubbed out, Danny was further down the hill.

'At least we haven't got rain here,' Tom whispered. 'These holes would soon fill up in a storm.'

David nodded but did not reply.

'What are you thinking?' Tom said.

'Nothing much. I was going over my life, back in the valley.'

'Going over your life,' Tom chuckled. 'Anyone would think you were an old man. Still, I know what you mean. We're almost in it now, aren't we, no going back.'

'Aye, no going back. I'm glad we met up with Billy though, it seems better when he's with us.'

'Yes, I know. I'm going to try and get some sleep, David.' Tom turned his back, and snored in minutes. David smiled, his friend never had to try to sleep, it came to him kindly, shutting off his problems and salving his body. With David it was fickle, he sat with his knees hunched against his chest, and prepared for a bout of insomnia. The wind probed his clothing and the night grew icy.

David thought of his mother's parlour, and the glow of its hearth. The valley was a far better place he saw now, a much safer place. The riot came to his mind, it seemed so minor as he nestled the Mauser between him and Tom. Emma would be in bed back in the Vincent house and he was on a hill in a war a lifetime away.

A brisk start awaited the battalion. A message was sent up to them, telling them to move up to the next ridge. An attack was imminent.

'Bloody marvellous that is,' Billy said, 'they wait until we are dug in, then move us. Come on lads, quick as you can, we don't want to be left here.' They packed up in a flurry of action with the Spanish messenger pausing amongst them, telling tales of the Moors who lay ahead.

'Don't let them catch you alive comrades,' the man said. 'They are like serpents in the night, they are not there, until your throat is cut.' He drew his hand across his own throat and made a gurgling sound.

'Alright,' Billy said, 'that's enough of that talk. Bugger off Pancho. Move out, lads.'

In the night the Moors had crossed the Jarama river, another breakthrough had to be prevented, at any cost. It was an hour's march to the next ridge. The Mauser was heavy and David sweated profusely, though the air was keen. He felt his height was a danger, an attraction to snipers, so he tried to make himself as small as possible, walking with shoulders hunched, and legs bent. 'You look like a pregnant crab,' Bill told him, but he did not care. Billy was a good head shorter, nearer the ground. There came a sound of shells, punishing someone up ahead. Waves of men ducked instinctively, much to the delight of Billy.

'Take it easy you lot,' he shouted, 'that's for someone else, they're landing miles away. Don't you know you never hear the one with your name on it. Keep going towards that bloody ridge.'

David was two thirds back as the battalion spread out in a fan shaped procession, a wedge of men moving upwards. David heard a shout ahead of him, a sound that was caught in the throat and snuffed out. He looked up to see a figure fall to the ground, slumping over quickly with the minimum of fuss. Small puffs of dust were rising from the rocks, and there was a rustling in the air, like paper shaking, or dead leaves sifted by the wind. He saw another man go over, then those at the front were falling rapidly, as if punched down by invisible assailants. Billy was shouting in his ear, and pulling at him.

'We're under fire, get down, down on your belly,' Billy dragged David to the left and pushed him face down into the rocks there, the only cover available to them. Men were screaming and running, trying to hide from the bullets. Those at the front were decimated, their bodies strewn on the slopes, some inert, some quivering in agony. From all red streaks appeared, a seeping of colour around the body, then rivulets that coursed freely, marking the victims with their flow.

The enemy was firing down on them from the ridge top, they were caught in a perfect ambush. The high ground Billy had hoped for had been snatched from them. David risked a look up from his hiding place. He saw rifle flashes, and made out the turbanned heads of the Moors bobbing about above. At his side Billy was desperately trying to set up the Maxim. 'Lie on your bellies lads, and return their fire for Christsake. Make a noise or they'll be down amongst us.'

Most of Billy's group were unscathed, they began a cursory

fire as the first shock of combat left them. David rested his
Mauser on a rock and fired his first round in earnest, at no-one,
but it calmed him a little. The round was good and the rifle leapt
in his hands. Billy's Maxim started up, a persistent chatter of
bullets, like the sound of dry sticks being split by an axe. They
were under heavy rifle fire, but no shells came down. David
adopted a technique of firing at distant gun flashes, then burying
himself in the earth. His rifle jammed after five rounds and the
Maxim soon fouled its ammunition belt, but there was a lull in
the firing from the other side.

Billy counted the men around him. He scratched his head.

'A lot must have copped it at the front, we probably haven't
got any officers left.'

'Shall I go and find out?' Tom said.

'Don't be daft, you wouldn't last two seconds out there. No,
we'll keep our heads down here for a bit, see what...'

'They're coming down the hill,' Danny yelled, 'hundreds of
the bastards.'

A sea of Moors washed towards them. Billy galvanised the
Maxim back into action,and he was right, it was good at killing.
It cut a swath through the Moors, a cruel scythe that took many,
yet they came on blindly, crying hatred and pain at their adver-
saries. David fired one shot that he knew hit its mark. He saw a
man fall to the ground, he landed on his back and stayed there,
like an overturned turtle. That man was dead, he was sure of it,
there was a clammy emptiness in his gut, an intoxication of shock
and power. Billy clapped him on the back. 'Well done, young 'un,
you've opened your account.'

In this way David's taking of a life was lauded. Later he
learned that the Moors wore little Christian hearts over their
own, to protect them from the bullets of the unGodly. They made
perfect targets, David had used one to sight the man he had
killed.

Several times the Moors tried to advance, pushing forward
whenever the Maxim stopped firing. Billy's number two was
forced to urinate on its barrel, to stop it overheating. A cloud of
pissy steam drifted over the nearest men.

'Bloody hell,' Danny shouted from his position, 'rather him
than me, he'll have his pecker shot off.'

'Stop mouthing and start shooting Danny,' Billy said, 'we're holding them lads, they can't take much more of this.'

Billy was right, the remnants of the battalion held their position, and the enemy pulled back to the ridge by nightfall. In the darkness the wounded were brought in by the stretcher bearers, and the dead were left to bloat in the sun of the next day. Over a hundred Brigaders had been killed.

David helped Tom and Billy scoop out a hole for the Maxim and themselves, and Danny joined them to share the little water they had. They were all quiet, emptied of emotion. Danny was out of bullets, Tom had a few left, there was just one belt left for the Maxim. Men had been sent for more, but communication with other battalions was almost nil. They did not know if they were ahead or behind their main force. Units were easily cut off as the battle changed its parameters.

'If things are going like this all along the Jarama they must be getting through,' David said.

'We've held out here, haven't we?' Billy said, spluttering out pieces of bread.

'Aye, but look at the cost, all those lads,' Tom said sadly.

Half the battalion had been killed or wounded in their baptism of fire. David sucked on his teeth in an attempt to slake his thirst. He could taste gunsmoke in his mouth, mingled with the sour aftertaste of killing.

McCormick had been killed in the first wave, shot through the lungs. The Scotsman died in a pool of pink blood, snuffed out and forgotten as the battle passed over him.

'Well, McCormick won't be annoying you any more Tom,' David said.

'No, he didn't last long, did he? Shouldn't speak ill of him now though, he was alright, I suppose, just couldn't take to him.'

Billy overheard them. 'He was a good bloke that McCormick, knew what he was doing here. He was a schoolteacher, did you know?'

'No, I didn't,' Tom said.

'Aye, taught young 'uns, wouldn't have thought it, eh? In some posh school too. Well, he died for what he believed in, I'd say.'

'Yes,' Tom said. He had judged McCormick as a type of man rather than a man, and regretted it now.

That night they rested in a heap, knowing that they must fight on in the morning. Danny discovered a small sliver of shrapnel in the back of his calf, unnoticed in the heat of the fight. The Moors had been throwing grenades down the slope, but David had not realised it. He found it hard to isolate incidents in his mind. The images of the day shimmered in a red haze of smoke and screams, they danced in his head, like the horizon on a hot road. He listened to his comrades talking, then let sleep take him, it shut out the day as he sank into its abyss, insomnia temporarily vanquished.

Before the sun came up David was awake, lying on his back, listening to the wind cutting around the crags above, making its rustle his own litany for the dead he viewed. He saw birds flit from a distant orange grove, preparing to welcome the new day. They made sharp cries that matched their darting flights. He thoughts of the swallows back in the valley, they played in the same way over the river, diving at the clouds of midges on a summer day, disdaining the black sludge.

Billy was close by, rolling a cigarette as the sun turned the ridge gold.

'Pretty spot eh, boy? Might as well fight somewhere good to look at. Here.' he handed David the cigarette, immaculately rolled with the minimum of tobacco. 'It concentrates your mind, a good smoke. Helen would kill me, mind, encouraging you with the weed.'

Billy laughed, making a dry rattle in his throat. The smoke sought the void in David's stomach. It was good American tobacco, very different from his Spanish stuff. That fell out of the papers, or exploded into fire. Smoking was ritualised in the battalion, passing tobacco around was an act of sharing, including, and trusting. David adopted it easily with Billy.

Some food and more ammunition reached them before the next attack. It was shared out and consumed quickly as they crouched and waited. 'Let's pray they haven't brought no heavy guns up,' Bill said to himself. Fear returned to David, worse than the day before, if anything. He tasted iron in his mouth, like the penny he had once sucked as a child. Someone was kneading his guts into knots, but he was prepared for the sight of the Moors now. He cleaned the Mauser and sighted it at a spot on the ridge. As the sun rose the enemy recommenced his attack. There were more of them this time, spread out along the ridge top in lines.

Firing broke out.

'Try to hold the buggers as long as we can,' Billy shouted, 'don't waste bullets.'

They kept up a retaliatory fire for some minutes, but rifles fell silent as they were emptied, and then the Maxim ran out of ammunition. Billy kicked it in anger: 'Bastard machine. Come on boys, let's get out of this while we have a chance.'

The Moors walked towards them this time, trancelike and unhurried. When they got to within two hundred yards they scented victory, and realised the Maxim was out. Billy led them back down the slope, every man's back crawling with the expectation of a bullet. They made good targets for the Moors above, and men tumbled past David, spilling their blood as they rolled down the incline.

'Make for that cover down there,' Billy yelled, pointing to a clump of trees.

David turned to see where Tom was, to find his friend sunk down on his knees, blood soaking through his jacket.

'Billy, Tom's been hit,' he shouted. David felt the urge to run but his legs slowed and he went back to Tom. Billy pushed past him and pulled Tom's arm.

'Come on, David, take the other one, before they are on us.'

'Leave me,' Tom moaned, 'save yourselves.'

They ignored him and frogmarched Tom along. Another group's Maxim had been salvaged and set up in the trees. It saved them, scouring the Moors at knee height as they came down, felling them in droves. They gained cover with Tom and sank to the ground. David looked back and saw Fascist officers urging their men on, but the Maxim was too much, and the attack faltered, then crumbled. It was stalemate.

12

Tom had been shot in the back, the bullet going out through his shoulder. It looked a very bad wound but he was conscious as they laid him down amongst the orange trees. He clenched his teeth and breathed in short gasps, his face ashen.

'Don't fret *bach*,' Billy said, 'you have had worse than this down the pit.'

Tom tried to smile, but could only grimace with bared teeth. He was stretchered away to the nearest village where trucks waited to take the wounded back to Madrid.

'Don't bump him now, lads,' Billy said, 'watch out for them pot-holes.'

'Do you think he will make it Bill?' David said.

'Don't know boy, it didn't look good, but then you can never tell with gunshot wounds. I've seen men shot to pieces and live, and others pop off with just one neat little hole in 'em. Depends where it is. At least the bullet went clean through Tom, they won't have to go digging around for it.'

David shared a cigarette with Billy, cupping it with their hands against the wind.

'I find it hard to take stock here, Bill,' David said. 'Our feet had hardly touched the ground before we were here, killing.'

'Aye, it's like that. Fiddling around doing nowt for ages then bang, like today. Just try to remember what we are fighting for and you'll be okay, you'll come through alright, up here anyway.'

Billy tapped his head.

David wondered if Tom had lost sight of what he was fighting for, if he had lost sight of life itself. Billy left to check their new position. He turned back to David.

'By the way boy, you done alright back there.'

David settled down for another bitter night, the day was dying quietly, and the air clearing of smoke. Frost was coming down. He was able to pick out the movements of the enemy as they harvested their dead; small dots peppered the far slopes, like ants going about some gory business. The assault was spent and Madrid safe for now. Franco would look for softer nuts to crack.

In the days to come there was sporadic fighting on David's front, cuts and thrusts which came to nothing as each side probed the defences of the other. Full scale battles were over on the Jarama, cold, hunger and boredom set in, a triple alliance sent from hell for the infantryman. Lines of communication were established, and supplies better organised, but conditions were never less than severe. Men were lousy within days of arriving at the front, and most suffered stomach ailments and skin infections. Every morning David tried to delouse himself, stripping layers of clothing from his body to search for parasites. He crushed lice between his fingers, cursing every blood-gorged body. Some always survived, to torment him the next night. His nerves were stretched like cat gut by the constant fear of attack, but he grew used to the sick dizziness of not enough food, and not enough sleep, and the stink of his own body was lost amongst those around him. The battalion stayed in its holes for the next few weeks, and the Moors stayed in theirs.

Tom was alive, they heard, being tended by British medical staff in a Madrid hospital.

'If things stay quiet I'll see if I can get us a bit of leave,' Billy said, 'go and surprise the bugger, see if he's skiving.'

They were lifted by the news. The lack of action continued, and men grew lousier and more bored. In small groups they were allowed leave in Madrid, their places taken by new recruits sent from Madrigueras. In the capital men filled their bellies and drank as much as they could, spending the few pesetas they were given as quickly as possible, fortifying themselves for another stay on the Jarama. The very lucky ones managed to afford a prostitute, in one of the brothels the Republic said no longer existed.

A headquarters of stone and earth had been built to serve the battalion. On the last Friday of February David waited in it with Billy for a lift to Madrid. They had been granted a weekend there, their first leave.

'Soon be in town boy,' Billy said, smacking his hands together, 'Jesus, I could drink a drop or two I could.'

The old man sighed, as if remembering a love of long ago.

'Tom will be surprised to see us,' David said.

'Won't he just. How long have we been out here, David?'

'Best part of a month.'

'Seems like a bleeding year. Bet you could do with a nice warm bed, eh? You might even get a bit of skirt to go in it, nice looking boy like you.'

Billy dug David in the ribs and laughed. Sometimes David wished his uncle was not so predictable. A rat watched them from the gloom of a dug-out corner. Billy spat tobacco juice at it. 'No use looking at me, you bugger, I'll never be your dinner.'

Winter was flowing out of the Jarama valley, and a warmer sun was creeping into the sky. David felt its glow this day and was glad to be alive. He met each day far more keenly than he ever had in the valley. His first month of war had humbled his hopes and streamlined his dreams: now those dreams were of staying alive, first, last and foremost.

Madrid. They were there at last. It took them two jolting hours from Morata de Jajuna, the village nearest their position. David traced the earlier fighting by the ruins they passed. Whole streets were levelled, houses crazily twisted as they tried not to fall over and add to the rubble. The road was often blocked with debris, or pitted with fresh bomb craters, but as they neared the heart of the city conditions improved. There were taxis and trams, and people strolling about on an afternoon that mimicked spring. Some cafés braved the bombing to serve on the pavements, and the Madrilenos still looked in shop windows, even if they gazed on emptiness.

Madrid was calmer than Barcelona. The people here were just as proud of their resistance, but they did not crow about it. There were fewer posters than in the north, and perhaps less suspicion too, despite Madrid's bitter start to the war.

They went straight to Tom's hospital. It was a rambling building, which looked as if it had been a barracks at one time. They walked up a flight of stairs to find confusion inside. Men and women in white coats dashed around, shouting or following directions. New arrivals were being examined and sorted in the hospital's foyer, like deliveries. They had to step over them to get inside. David stopped a young nurse as she scurried past. She turned to face him, scanning his scruffy outfit with irritation. She was English but tried to say something to him in Spanish. David interrupted her.

'Where would Tom Price be, miss?' he asked.

'Oh, you are English are you? No, Welsh is it? I'm going that way. Mr Price is up here. You'd better come along if you're friends of his.'

The nurse swept past them up the corridor, where men lay on stretchers, awaiting beds. They followed along behind her, hurrying. She had a good figure. Billy winked his approval of it. Fair hair was tied back to reveal a neck dotted with freckles, auburn flecks that matched her colour, and her hips were wide and strong, contrasting with her slender waist. The nurse was thin, pounds had been lost in her work perhaps, but David liked that. He had a sudden yearning for toothpaste, for clean clothes; desire was re-awakened in him.

She led them to a room where they found Tom propped up in bed, reading a newspaper. Others were scattered around him together with a slim volume of English poetry. Tom looked smaller, lost in the folds of his bed, and he sported the beginnings of a moustache which was touched with grey at the edges. It put ten years on him. He started when he saw them.

'Good God, Billy, and David. What are you doing here?'

'Got a bit of leave lad, for the weekend,' Billy said, 'thought we'd better come and see you, see if you are swinging the lead.'

'How are you Tom?' David said.

'I'm alright now, on the mend. It was a clean wound, they told me, I was lucky. They got me here quick and fixed me up good.'

'Aye, you were lucky,' Billy said, 'we thought you were a gonna at first.'

Billy sat on the edge of the bed, and David stood behind him. The older man fingered the book of poems.

'Eh, what's this then Tom? We'll have another college boy here.'

'Someone left it here. You read anything when you are stuck in bed all day, even poems.' Tom was eager to talk. 'I've been wondering about you two, it was pretty bad on the Jarama, I heard.'

'We survived,' Billy said. 'As you can see, the Fascists didn't break through.'

'Yes, that's true, but you think all sorts of things lying here. Most of the lads can't talk very much, I've seen some terrible cases.'

Tom lowered his voice and jerked his thumb towards the next bed. A man lay swathed in bandages, inert as a mummy. 'Got the top of his head missing, he has. Bullet took it off. They don't know what to do about it yet, but the poor bugger is still breathing.'

'Aye, makes you wonder, don't it?' Billy said. He reached for his pipe, filled it, lit it and stoked it up into a tiny inferno. 'To think old Johnnie Reynolds died falling off that bar stool down the Anchor. And he was only eighty-five.'

They laughed, and the shyness caused by the place and Tom's condition evaporated.

David let Billy talk to Tom and allowed himself to savour the quiet of the room. High windows threw streaks of light into it, and it was peaceful and clean, a haven which the moans of the wounded did not diminish. He looked at the row of six beds, and wondered how many of the men in them would survive, and how many would be good for nothing much anymore, put together men, their bodies supported with bits of steel, dead and useless bits carried around with them to the grave they had escaped this time. He thought of the man he had killed. A quick image of him falling back came into his mind, he had dreamt it several times: the flash of the red heart on his jacket, the kick of the Mauser in his hands. There might be others he had shot, lying like Tom, suffering, or slowly dying. David shook the thought from his head and read one of the poems in Tom's book, about green and safe England.

David realised Tom was talking to him.

'Aye, Dave. I had this letter from back home, never guess who from – Conti.'

'Good Lord, fancy him writing.'

'Aye, I was amazed too, but he was always hard to fathom, wasn't he? And he sent ten woodbines, the angel.'

Tom twirled his moustache in triumph and handed the cigarettes around. They were hopelessly mangled by their journey but the three men delighted in them. Billy smoked pipe and woodbine alternately.

'Read the letter to us, Tom,' Billy said.

Tom smoothed the sheet out and did so.

'"Dear Tom Price," it says. "I hope you get this letter safe. I write to Billy and young David also. There was a lot of talk about you going off like that, especially David. I have Mrs Hicks in here, asking questions. She blame me for saying nothing, but I say I know nothing. All men are pigs, Maria tell her. But all is calm now, the café is quiet. I do not have so many Boys in here, more have gone to Spain, perhaps you see them, eh? I try to follow you in the papers, but they are against you here, they like Franco. Maria gets crazy when she reads of the priests and the churches, she thinks words cannot lie. Me, you know what I think about it. Maybe I will be wrong. Anyway, I hope you are alright, and the others. I write to you because I know no-one else will. I finish now, before Maria see this letter. If you see Billy, say '*ciao*' for me – Conti.'"

Tom took a deep breath, reading the letter had tired him. His soft voice blended well with the still of the room, and they received Conti's words as if they were a sermon; the letter's simplicity tugged at their home-sickness. David felt a flush of envy at Tom's letter, and guilt that he had not written one. They sat quietly for a while, letting Tom sink into sleep. A bullet had passed through him, breaking a rib and grazing a lung, but missing vital organs. He was healing fast, and would be back with them soon. Tom had rejected the chance to go home.

The nurse reappeared. She scolded them in whispers.

'Look at all this smoke, that's very selfish, you know. You'll have to go now, you've tired out poor Mr Price.'

They stood bashfully before her, David caught the faintest trace of scent in her clothing, mixed with disinfectant and the dried blood of her tunic. He saw that she was not much older than he, a year or two at most. She relented at their crestfallen faces.

'Well, I suppose Mr Price was glad of a smoke and a chat. You can come back tomorrow, if you are still in Madrid.'

'Oh we'll be here miss,' Billy said, 'got a weekend's pass see.'

He nudged David. 'Come on lad, standing there like a dog with its tongue out he is, miss.'

David's ears burned crimson as the cool eyes of the nurse drilled into his, but they were quizzical not mocking.

'Why did you say that?' David exclaimed, as soon as they were in the corridor.

'Only a bit of fun, don't be so sensitive. She was a bit of alright, eh, don't tell me you didn't notice. Besides, she fancied you.'

'Don't be daft, Billy.'

'She did, I'm telling you. Your old uncle knows a thing of two about women.'

David blushed anew and Billy enjoyed his discomfort.

'Come on,' he said, slapping David on the back, 'let's find that hotel of ours. This way, Romeo.'

They walked along a street cut up into chiaroscuro by the sun. Billy was in good spirits, and anxious to paint Madrid red.

'Did I tell you, Dave, the first time I was here? Met up with a few girls, in between the fighting. High jinks we had. Made socialism worthwhile, they did.'

David let him talk on, and thought about the nurse, and whether Billy was right. He wanted him to be.

Their hotel was filled with journalists and political representatives of all shades. The second floor was used by the actual fighters, and they were given a room there, a place that held a large bed and the smells of former occupants. Billy lay on the bed and smoked whilst David counted their hoard of pesetas, to work out how red they could paint. Billy had saved a surprising amount, and was determined to spend it all.

In the cold water of the washroom they scrubbed themselves as clean as they could, and David put on the few clothes he had saved for the occasion, they were shapeless and crumpled but clean and lice-free. By nightfall they were ready to step out, hungry and adventurous.

Billy knew where to go. He led the way to a large café, a den for volunteers and their hangers-on. They went into it, to be met by a wave of hot air and noise. David was reminded of Barcelona, he heard the same mix of languages as men harangued and tested each other. They found a table and Billy ordered the only food available, a thick stew with pieces of mule meat floating in it. They ate greedily and noisily, soaking chunks of bread in their bowls and washing it down with a bottle of the usual cheap wine. David was living like a soldier, he was alive this night and it was all that counted. He knew what the wine would do to his head, but he did not care.

A few hundred men were packed into the café, with women spread amongst them at the liveliest tables. The electricity was off and the café was candlelit, yellow flames flickering at every table, leaving the walls and corners in darkness. They sat as if on stage, playing the role of soldiers on leave. The first bottle was empty when someone joined them from the shadows. A hand was placed on David's shoulder, and a voice boomed.

'So, my friend, you are here, eh? I told you we would meet again.'

Karpinski stood before David, his frame stretching to the ceiling.

'Who are you then?' Billy said, a little disconcerted.

'It's alright Bill, this is Karpinski, the man who helped us in Paris. He's from Russia.'

Karpinski clicked his heels.

'At your service, *señor*,' he said, then slouched into a chair besides them.

'A Ruskie, eh?' Billy said. 'Pleased to meet you, and thanks for helping the lad.'

Billy poured the Brylcreem Kid a glass of wine, from their second bottle. The Russian smelt it, rolled his eyes, then drank it down in one. David was proud to show off his Russian – a true child of the revolution – to impress Billy.

They talked late into the night. The Kid was always curious, asking about everything from Welsh coal mining to the Jarama. They told him about Tom, and the action they had been in. The Kid nodded encouragement, or frowned sympathy. He said little about himself.

'How do you think the war is going?' David asked him. The Kid shrugged.

'It's a crazy war, a good war, a just war, necessary, but a crazy war. All things are possible in it'.

He paused and chewed on his black cigarette. 'We will win, of course, without doubt we will win, but things must be better organised. That is why I am here, and many like me. To organise. The Spaniards have heart, courage, even ideas sometimes, but we must help them realise them.'

It sounded as if Karpinski had said this many times before.

'I'll drink to that,' Billy said. 'Organisation, unity, that's right. Isn't that what I'm always saying, David, back home? Always saying it.'

Billy slopped wine over the table and had difficulty staying in his chair. The room was starting to spin slowly for David also. He realised he was bored, he did not want one of Billy's speeches. The thought shamed him, but he just wanted to drink and be empty-headed, full-bellied and with his comrades. He stopped listening and was at drunken peace with himself.

David thought Karpinski carried him back to his hotel that night, but was not sure. In the morning there was the now expected roll of drums in his head, and each tread to the wash-room shook him. Yet it was not as bad as in Paris, he had toughened up since then. He washed, dressed and slipped out of the hotel to get away from Billy for a while. He left him still asleep, curled up in the middle of the bed, his mouth open, like a whale basking.

David found a café and bought a cup of coffee, and tried to read a paper someone had left on the table. It was full of the exploits of the army, defeats turned into stalemates and stale-mates into victory. The Brigades were praised with gusto. As the coffee dropped like lead globules into his stomach David read about himself: he was a hero, a brave and expert soldier, a saviour. The Mauser was a ghost in his hands, he felt an echo of panic, mingling with the dregs of his coffee, and last night's wine.

Two Spaniards looked over from their table, one said '*salud, camarada*' as he left, and patted David on the back. It was respectful pat, and David enjoyed it. His stomach warmed by the coffee, he walked out into Madrid in good heart. He passed an apartment block that had been hit in the night, a bomb had cleaved it in two. A team of men picked over the remains as women cried in the rubble. One wrung her hands and appealed to the sky for a personal miracle. She saw David and looked at him hopefully for a moment, as if he could do something. There were no civilians in this war: it was a family affair, incestuous and savage, a salve for old spites. David walked on quickly.

As his head eased he felt hungry, but his hands grabbed at pockets as empty as his stomach. He made his way back to the hotel, hoping that Billy would have a few pesetas left. There was a light step at his side.

'You are out early, I thought all you boys slept it off in the morning.'

David turned to see the woman who had joined him. At first he did not recognise her, her face was shadowed by a wide-brimmed hat, but the scent was familiar. It was the nurse from the hospital. They stopped under a shop awning and David saw her clearly. She was pale in the morning light, with two faint lines stretching on her forehead, highlighting her questing blue eyes. Slightly chiselled features showed determination and stamina, but not arrogance or meanness. David felt a strong and instant attraction; it tied his tongue.

'Have you had breakfast?' she asked.

'Yes,' David lied, 'back there.'

She looked at him sceptically.

'Where?'

David waved an arm vaguely.

'Oh, somewhere, in one of the side streets.'

'Ah. Well I want some. Couldn't you eat some more?'

David shrugged, and cursed his poverty. But he knew he would go with her, he did not want to let this girl out of his sight.

She led him to a small eating place tucked away in a cul-de-sac. The nurse knew her way around, they were in a place the war had not touched. It was old Spain, Castillian reverence was in the architecture, heavy and ornately sombre, defying the new age. At the door of the café the nurse stopped him with her hand.

'Look, you must let me treat you. I know you've had nothing to eat. You will have spent it all last night, I saw you in that place with your friends, I was in a corner.'

She pushed David inside before he could argue; he let himself be pushed.

They sat at a table to be quickly served by an attentive waiter, who eyed the pretty English girl. She thrust a hand at David.

'My name is Celia Kadle.'

Her hand was moist and tiny in his.

'You have strong hands,' she said, 'but they have not seen much work. What is your name?'

'Hicks,' David blurted out, 'David Hicks.'

'Pleased to meet you, David Hicks. Hmm. You don't look much like a Welshman: too tall, and not very dark, are you?'

David felt she was challenging him, and certainly teasing. He had never met a girl like this before, her confidence unnerved him. He tried to hide his shabby trousers under the table as he felt her eyes appraise him.

The breakfast was plain, but a delight for David. He tried to eat as carefully as he could, to belie his hunger. As his stomach filled his tongue loosened, and monosyllabic replies turned into sentences. Celia Kadle put him at his ease, she did not pry and

David liked that. He found himself telling her about the valley, and his family, about most things apart from Emma. Celia came from the edge of London, her family were well-to-do, 'but liberal' she told him.

'I've been here from the start,' Celia said. 'I was on holiday when it all began, and just sort of stayed here. I've been to Spain before, with my parents, and liked what the government was trying to do. I'm not really a nurse.'

'What about your parents?'

'Oh, they were worried, of course, but they know me too well to try to stop me doing anything. What about you David, why are you here?'

David stretched the truth. 'I come from a nest of Socialists. You met my uncle at the hospital. There are quite a few of us from the valleys.'

'Yes I know, but you look very young. What did your family say?'

'As I've said, my father is dead, and my mother, well she didn't know we were coming to Spain until we were gone.'

'Gosh, that was a bit hard.'

'Yes, I suppose it was.'

They talked until noon. By that time David's infatuation was in full swing. Celia had become his ideal woman. His beleaguered senses latched onto her, and he fantasised strongly. Shyness turned to desire and he wanted Celia like he had never wanted Emma. She dashed his senses like fresh water and he fell willingly under her spell, hanging on every word she said, modulating his opinions to suit hers, trying to say things that would please and impress her; doing it all wrong.

'Well, it's after twelve,' Celia said. 'I'm needed back at the hospital. Half a day off is enough. Here's my address, David, you can write to me if you want.'

Celia handed him a scribbled line, which he put in his pocket carefully. Then she left him, striding out of the café and down the street, each step taking her further away from him. The suddenness of their parting was a blow to David, and as Celia faded from sight he wished he had asked her if she had someone.

The clear skies were gone, replaced by a thin drizzle that drifted down off the mountains. Billy was up when David got back to the hotel. He was in the washroom, scraping his face with a razor, and swearing softly as his whiskers resisted the tired blade. He greeted David with a grunt.

'Ah, you've appeared, have you? I was beginning to think you'd done a bunk.'

David sat on the bed and said nothing of Celia.

'Where have you been, then?' Billy asked.

'Just walking about, I had a thick head.'

Billy laughed. 'Mine's booze proof, I reckon. Let me get my clothes on and we'll go and see Tom again.'

They found Tom out of bed, sitting at another man's, one blinded by shrapnel. Tom was reading a letter for him. The man sat with twitching face, trying to put pictures to the words Tom read. Tom waved to them and finished the letter, tucking it back in the blinded man's pocket.

'Let's go outside,' Tom told them, 'we've got a veranda here. You can look out over the city.'

He led them out, walking in front of them slowly.

'Should you be on your feet, Tom?' Billy said.

'Yes, they said I could, I'm healing fast now.'

Madrid lay before them, blanketed in greyness. The drizzle brushed against them.

'Just like the valley, eh lads,' Tom said.

They sat in chairs under a canopy and watched the rain intensify; waves of it drifted down and worked across Madrid. Low buildings stretched away from them, pock-marked by the bombing.

'I'll be back in a few weeks,' Tom said, 'not bad for a man shot up.'

'That's good news,' Billy said. 'You are sure you want to come back, though? You had a bad outing.'

'Yes Bill, quite sure. All the more reason to come back, I'd say. The odds of it happening again must be pretty long anyway.'

'We saw the Brylcreem Kid last night, Tom,' David said. 'Came up to us out of the blue.'

'Did you now, Karpinski eh? What's he doing then?'

'He didn't say much,' David said, 'wanted to know all about us though.'

'Aye, like in Paris. Do you think he's a spy?'

'Who knows?' Billy said. 'If he is he's wasting his time with us buggers, that's for sure.'

David was restless. He turned at every footstep to see if it was Celia, but she did not come. They left Tom after an hour, and by dusk they had left Madrid, travelling back to the Jarama. Solid rain turned the tracks into quagmires, their truck skidded along, full of men boasting of their exploits in the city. 'Old Dicky got off with this girl, fixed her up for a date, and her whole bleedin' family came along, granny and all – that red wine is summat, eh lads, I was pissing it neat by the end of the night, should have bottled it again – Madrid has taken a pounding, planes, they're the future, you mark my words.' It grew quieter as they neared the front, David watched old nightmares creep back into faces, as men thought of death and luck, and getting through it all.

The rains continued for the rest of the winter, allied to a freezing fog that cloaked the Jarama valley. It wormed its way through to the marrow of the best protected bone, and was roundly hated. Men made shelters of their fox-holes, foraging for makeshift roofs, using anything to try to keep out the wet and cold. Clothes rotted on their backs and they were wracked by dysentery and fungus. But they endured, they had no choice. Each side was content to let things lie on the Jarama, and the Republic knew that a stalemate was the best it could achieve here.

Tom rejoined them in March, looking fit and clean amongst his filthy comrades. He appeared as David was trying to write a letter to his mother. It was hard for his chapped fingers to hold the pencil, and raindrops kept finding the notepaper. Tom laughed at David's surprise.

'Don't look so shocked, I said I'd be back. Here, write a letter get a letter.'

Tom thrust an envelope into David's hands and jerked a thumb at the surroundings.

'Jesus Christ Almighty, they didn't tell me I'd be coming back to a shithouse. Come on, move up boy, let me share this luxury with you.'

David saw Celia's name on the back of the letter and tore it open quickly, stuffing his own into his pocket. It was a note rather than a letter, but he delighted in every word:

Dear David,

I hope you are well. You have not arrived here so I assume that you are. Take care of yourself and do write to me. I think of you often, especially when the wounded are brought in. Mr Price will deliver this letter to you. He is a fine man, we have talked several times. He told me you are married, or were married, I am not sure which. That was a surprise. Try to let me know if you can come to Madrid again.

Goodbye David,

Celia.

David damned Tom. Why did he have to tell her that? He squirmed in annoyance and glared across at his friend, who sat giving out tobacco and news in equal doses

'Nice letter is it?' he asked.

'Why did you tell her I was married?'

'Oh, she mentioned it, did she? No harm in that, was there? It just came up when we were talking. I had no reason to lie to the girl.'

'Did she ask much about me, then?'

'No, not really, we just chatted, you know, about nothing in particular. Don't fret, I haven't told her your life history.'

David cooled down. Tom was right, there was nothing to fret about. Emma was his past, there was no need to hide her, and Celia had written to him, there must be interest on her part too. Hope burned inside him, unaffected by the cold in the trench. David retrieved his own attempt at a letter, flattening out the crumpled paper on his knees. He asked Helen to write again, telling her that he had not received anything. David knew she would have written several times by now, and that her letters lay somewhere between the valley and Albacete, lost in the turmoil of war. "I am well and safe" he wrote, adding things about the Jarama and Billy and Tom. "Tell Emma I am alright," he added as an afterthought, "if you see her." He put the paper in an envelope he had been saving and switched his thoughts back to Celia.

After weeks of inactivity the war caught up with David. They were issued with new rifles, a standard Russian model replaced the multifarious pieces of the battallion. David said goodbye to the Mauser gladly. The new weapon was cheaply made and flimsy, but it was accurate and light. He was able to carry it strapped around himself with ease. The men were also issued with a type of Mills bomb, the 'fai', which had a pin held to its side by tape. They were as dubious as Spanish cartridges but the men liked to wear then from their belts, like Mexican bandits.

Death came mainly from the skies now. More Fiats appeared over their lines, and fewer of their own planes. Daily bombings began, and nights were no longer safe. A moon and a clear sky brought the enemy. Many times David crouched with his comrades, listening to the crump of bombs as they fell on someone else. There were few direct hits but when a bomb found a trench the men in it stood no chance, only bloody bits of them remained, like the sweepings of an abattoir.

In late March David was picked for his first night patrol, one of seven men led by Billy. Patrols were sent out often to glean information about their enemy neighbour. It was the deadliest of tasks, hated by all but the crazy. David's patrol moved out at midnight, crawling past their outer defences into no man's land. David brought up the rear of the group, crawling behind Brannigan, a quiet Irishman rumoured to be an IRA veteran.

They passed over ground littered with the debris of war, jagged-edged equipment which lay ready to snare the unwary, to betray the position of the clumsy. Something scuttled to David's right, and the patrol froze, like one animal. A rat appeared, sleek and well fed. It eyed David and melted back into the darkness.

'I wonder how many of our boys that thing has gnawed,' Brannigan whispered.

'Shut up, Irish,' Billy hissed, 'we are getting close to them now.'

They were as near to the enemy lines as they dared go. Each man strained his ears for sounds of his presence, but drifting rain deadened noise. Normally neither side would be too anxious to meet, but this night Billy had been ordered to take a prisoner. 'Vital to the bloody war effort,' Billy had told them before they set off. It would be difficult to find anybody on this foul night, even an enemy patrol might pass them by unnoticed.

The patrol stayed where it was and listened for some time, each man isolated by his own silence. Imagination amplified every sound, every rustle became a throat-slitting Moor, slithering towards them with a knife in his teeth. David was beginning to nod when a 'psst' from Brannigan jarred him back to alertness.

'Someone is coming,' he whispered, 'get ready.'

The message was passed along and they waited. A chink of metal on stone betrayed the presence of men approaching.

Billy had chosen a good spot. David was with two others on one side of a defile, Billy was up ahead. It was an ideal place for a trap, for only one man could pass through at a time. David's hands were clammy, they stuck to the stock of his rifle and his mouth filled with bitter iron again, the first time he had tasted real fear since Tom had been shot.

A figure appeared out of the blackness, head bent, following the track through the defile. Behind him trudged three others. They were hooded with balaclavas which gave them a sinister look, and followed their leader like human vultures. No-one was to move until Billy said so. The enemy was close enough to embrace now, but Billy's patrol lay unsensed behind the rocks. Billy stood up and shouted a challenge in his rough Spanish. There was a gasp from the first man and someone started shooting.

David remembered two things about this night above all else. One was the scream of a man bayoneted in the gut, a ghastly sound that turned into a grating rasp, like a very old woman crooning to a baby. The other was the sight of Billy lying on the ground, life flowing out of him through holes in his chest.

Two of the Moors died instantly in the first exchange of fire. The other two tried to run but were tackled by Billy. There was a frantic melee, fought out desperately amongst the rocks. They had picked a patrol with an officer, perfect for their needs, but tragic for Billy, for he was shot by him, as he closed in. Billy was jerked back with a cluster of small bullets in his chest. He had not expected a pistol, or he would have shot the man at once. The officer was clubbed to the ground by Brannigan, and his Moorish corporal was bayoneted as he begged for mercy. The action was over.

David reached Billy as his eyes rolled upwards, as if beseeching the heavens to take an old sinner. He did not say anything and David did not know if Billy saw him before he died. He shook his uncle repeatedly and called out his name, until Brannigan lifted him away from the body. 'Come on lad, you can't do anything for him now.'

They had one dead leader and a few others with slight injuries, and their captive officer was barely alive. Brannigan had struck heavily, blood poured from the Spaniard's head and trickled from his mouth.

'Finish the bastard off,' someone said.

'No, Billy will have died for nothing then.'

David realised it was himself talking.

'We'll bury him here,' he said.

'There's no time for that,' Brannigan said, 'we've got to get back quick.'

'We'll bury him,' David said, in a voice no-one dared stand against.

A shallow grave was scooped out with bayonets and Billy was left in the soft earth of the defile. David stood over his mound for a minute, choking back tears.

'He was a good bloke,' Brannigan murmured to a quiet chorus of agreement.

They began the crawl back to their lines. Along the front troops woken up by the firing snapped at each other, firing into the night at phantom attackers. When they were sure there was no attack they went back to sleep.

David fought the urge to stay with Billy. He could not take in what had happened. It seemed moments ago that Billy was complaining about his soggy pipe, and telling his jokes with twinkling eyes. Now he lay in an unmarked grave which the rats would quickly find. David crawled blindly with the others, disbelief flooding through him.

It took them the rest of the night to get back, pulling their unconscious captive along the ground, like an anchor. A grey smudge of light was in the sky as they regained their lines, the dawn just beaten. The officer was stretchered away, to be cared for until he could talk. News of Billy's death spread quickly through the battallion. It was bad news to wake up to, for the old man was well known and well liked.

David sank into his trench and vomited in the light of a new day. Sorrow and anger and despair churned into a vile stew in his guts until it imploded there and hurled itself upwards and out of his mouth. David felt his heart was going with it, he was empty, numbed. He cursed the stupidity of the night as he pulled filthy blankets over him, willing sleep to take him away from all this. He heard the call of a bird above him, a doleful sound, as thin and haunting as a curlew's. Tom was bending over him.

'Are you alright, David? I've just heard. I can hardly believe it, Billy gone.'

David nodded but could not say anything.

'I'll let you sleep, that's the best,' Tom said, 'we'll talk about it later. It's a bad business, a bad business.'

Tom began to climb out of the trench, then turned back.

'I'm glad you are alright, boy,' he said softly, pushing the blankets up around David's head.

13

David had plenty of time to think about Billy's death, for April was a tame and actionless month. He saw Billy's staring eyes nightly in his dreams, he dug out his grave, he cried out against his death, and awoke panic stricken with a sense of loss. It was ten days before he could talk to Tom, and Tom, wary of his moods, let David be.

David asked Tom to write to his mother with the news. Tom used the letter as a chance to talk, seeking David out on a fine April night.

'I sent that letter, David,' he said, 'don't know when it'll get there, mind.'

'Good. Thanks Tom.'

'That's alright.'

Tom sat next to David on the edge of a trench.

'You have been very down since Billy caught it. Who hasn't, eh? I've talked to Brannigan and the others. You couldn't have done nothing to help him, none of you could. Meeting someone with a pistol was just bad luck. Billy took the lot in the chest. He wouldn't have known much about it.

'No, but I do. I'll never forget it, Tom, I dream it every night.'

'Yes, I know, I hear you sometimes. Who says you have to forget it? It would be stupid to try, but perhaps it will fade, with time. Billy would not want you to brood too much, he wouldn't think he died in vain, not that one. Have a good drink on me, he'd say, and get on with it. Of all of us, he knew what he was about here, remember.'

'Yes I know, it's just...'

'It's just that you never expect a chap like Billy to go down. You get to relying on them too much; we did that in Conti's. They seem indestructible, but they are not, we know that now. Billy has gone and you must be the stronger for it.'

'Yes, I know. You make sense, Tom, but it's hard.'

'It is that, lad. What did he say, war is hell, and we're bloody in it.' Tom grasped David's arm. 'It's the two of us now, not three. I'll look out for you, if you'll do the same for me.'

'Alright, Tom.'

'Good. You've been sitting around like a lovesick tomcat for too long. Look, the weather is turning.'

Tom pointed to clement skies and clouds that had lost their greyness, and grown kind again.

'Perhaps our luck will turn with it.'

Tom was right, winter was vanquished, the days turned hot and bright, bringing with them something David had not faced before. Flies. Flies that rejoiced in finding thousands of men living in pig-sties. Even in early Spring all manner of insects plagued them.

'See,' Tom said, as he smacked a fly into a red smudge on his arm, 'there's always something that gains. Think what a lovely surprise it must have been for these little bastards, finding us lot here, our flesh just asking to be eaten.'

'It doesn't console me Tom,' David said, 'knowing that I am a provider.'

'Perhaps we should complain to the commissars, maybe these are Fascist flies.'

'All flies are Fascist, Tom, they have to be.'

Lice became virulent again, stretching into life as sun warmed men's backs. They were bad in winter, now they bit relentlessly. Nights were spent scratching at them until skin was a mass of festering sores and rashes. Everyone suffered, men worn down by inactivity let their morale sink. There was talk of deserters, some had upped and gone home, it was said, and others caught had been placed in a special camp, somewhere near Albacete.

Battalion commissars did their best to maintain spirits and commitment. They were a combination of evangelist, miner's agent and cheer leader. Some of the men despised them, others were glad of their presence, David kept out of their way as much as possible, and tried to learn daily from his environment. More leave was given as the front continued to stagnate. David got another weekend pass, as one of the longest serving on the Jarama. This time he was going to Madrid on his own. He wrote to Celia, praying she would get the note before he arrived. He was glad that Tom was not going with him, he wanted to get away from the war and all talk of it. Celia would not know about Billy, and there would be no need to tell her.

David received a month's back-pay, and travelled to the

capital in a truck full of news from the north. He heard that Guernica, the old Basque capital, had been bombed flat by German planes. Women and children were the main casualties. Feelings were running as warm as the day, and many descriptions of Franco were offered. David shared the anger, but not the shock at hearing the news. Guernica had spiritual significance for the Basques; Franco wanted to crush that spirit and the Luftwaffe wanted practice. He remembered the anguish of the women in the Madrid rubble. Death came mainly from the skies now, for the people of Spain. 'Save us from the black birds,' the peasants cried. They would have cried it at Guernica, before they died, shocked and unbelieving in the dust.

He checked into the same hotel, sharing a room with a couple of London men intent on enjoying their first leave. They did not bother David much. He walked over to the hospital as soon as he could. A young doctor directed him through the confusion to where Celia was working. The man talked of her in a way which aroused jealousy in David. The doctor's coat was many shades of red, bright for fresh stains, brown for the older ones, yet David was conscious of his own shabbiness, and lack of worldliness.

Celia was tending a heavily-bandaged man.

'He was trapped in a tank,' she whispered, greeting David with a squeeze of the hand. 'I got your letter. I won't be long here, then we'll be off.'

Celia laughed at his evident eagerness. 'You'll make a lazy woman of me, David.'

He smelt her as she brushed past him, and wondered how she managed to stay fresh in such a place. They exchanged glances; David thought he saw a flicker of desire in her eye, at least he wished he did.

'You had better not stay here,' Celia said, 'the other nurses might get jealous. I'll pick you up at seven. Are you in the same place?'

'Yes, on my own this time.'

'Not with your uncle, or Tom?'

'No, not with them.'

'Come on then, I'll see you out.'

Celia took him to the hospital steps, but he was reluctant to leave her. Take it easy, he told himself, play it cool; but he did not know how to. Celia gave him a gentle push down the steps.

'Go on, don't be a baby.'

She turned on her heels and went back into the hospital. After a few moments to collect himself David walked back to his hotel; war-torn Madrid unnoticed in his excitement. *Baby*. He did not mind the term from her, he wanted to be Celia's baby.

David's room mates were out when he got back, so he lay on their double bed and smoked a cigarette. His smoke curled up to the ceiling, and he watched it twist and turn in the light, a snake of his own making. He wondered how many others had done the same, before going to meet their women. He saw Celia's face in the sun patterns on the wall and fell asleep watching her.

He slept for a few hours then roused himself to wash and shave, taking great care not to cut himself with his venerable razor. He put on his one good shirt, tried to smooth out its creases with his hand, wiped his shoes with newspaper and swept back his hair with the remnants of a comb. Gargling with water he would have given much for toothpaste, but he had to content himself with rubbing his teeth with his fingers.

At seven Celia waited outside the hotel for him. Her hair was down, trailing freely over her shoulders, like an auburn shawl. David's pulse quickened as he neared her.

'Hello, you're on time,' he said.

'Yes, of course, I always am.'

'I should be picking you up, you know.'

'Don't be stuffy. You're not in that valley of yours now. This is the land of new ideas, haven't you heard? Women are equal, and all that, comrade.'

'Of course I know that, I'm fighting for it, aren't I?'

'Oh David, don't be so serious. I'm teasing you.'

David smiled shyly, and let Celia take him to the same place as before. This time there were more people there but the atmosphere was restrained; the diners ate quietly and their conversation was a low murmur. They sat at a round table which was covered by an oil-cloth, faded to the stain of the wood.

The stump of a candle flickered from a bottle on their table, its style perfect for David. He was all his heroes, Gaugin, Baudelaire, Byron, Poe; flawed heroes. Yet Celia Kadle filled him with awe.

'Relax,' Celia said, 'you're not going into battle you know.'

'Sorry, it's hard to adjust to a place like this after the Jarama.'

'It must be, but you are very nervous.'

'What makes you say that?'

'The way you hold yourself, always on a knife-edge, sitting half off your seat. You do want to be with me, don't you?'

If only she knew how much. 'Of course I do, Celia. Yes, of course.'

'Good, let's enjoy our meal then.'

They drank a white wine far removed from the mouth wash David was used to. It came in a dusty bottle and a waiter poured out half a glass for him to try. David loved this, he swirled the wine around in his mouth, feigning knowledge.

Celia became more beautiful as the wine flowed. A dab of colour appeared on each cheek like the afterthought of an artist's brush. They highlighted her features, her skin shone with health, her teeth were pearls. David felt his own teeth with his tongue, they were sound but yellowed by the tobacco he smoked and coated with the grime of the last three months. His skin was ravaged by his stay in his fox-hole, his face was the antithesis of Celia's but she did not seem to mind and he did not care, he was flying on hope and happiness.

They pooled their money to pay for the meal, which had been yet more stew, despite the pretentions of the restaurant. David suggested a walk. 'There's been no bombing tonight, it should be alright,' he said.

They went out into a spring night, and breathed it in.

'It's so much fresher than London,' Celia said, 'all that awful smog.'

'And the valley,' David said, 'the air there is always full of coal, or smoke, or something, unless you are on the Tump.'

Celia laughed. 'On the Tump, what's that?'

She leant against him as they walked, and David put his arm around her, naturally.

'The Tump is what we call one of the hill-tops.'

'Oh. That valley of yours,' Celia said. 'Did you like living there?'

David shrugged. 'Not much, it was a trap, hard to get away from, you know.'

'Yet you married so young.'

David paused. 'That was a mistake. It didn't last, it's over now, Celia.'

'Yes, I gathered that. What was she like, your wife? What was her name?'

'Emma. She was... good. Look, let's not talk about all that, it's another life, and it's gone.'

'Alright.'

The streets were deserted, and eery with echoes. Some were untouched, some were in ruins, the losers in the lottery of bombs. A few cafés spilled out noise and people as they passed. But Madrid was mainly silent this night, with most of the Madrilenos behind closed shutters.

'Do you want to come to my place?' Celia said. 'It's out near the university, not too far.'

'Yes, I'd like to.'

'Come on then, I've got some real coffee there.'

It took them twenty minutes to reach Celia's street. A narrow flight of stairs led to her first-floor apartment. David felt his heart pound as he climbed them.

'It's not much,' Celia said, 'the hospital got it for me. But at least it's private, I don't have to share it with anyone.'

Celia opened the door and showed him into a small room, an all-in-one place which had a bed at one end and a stove at the other. In between was a table and two chairs. David closed the door after him, there was an English calendar nailed on the back of it, showing Picadilly in a Victorian setting; it was marked with crosses. On a windowsill Celia had placed a white flower in a pot; it made the spartan room alive, and hers.

She drew a curtain across the room to close off the bed and busied herself at the stove. David looked out of the window and played the worldly man. The night air fanned him, cooling the wine from his cheeks, but doing nothing to quell the fire within him.

'Admiring the view?' Celia said. 'The coffee will be a few minutes, the stove is very pernickety.'

Without saying anything David turned and kissed her, wrapping her in his arms. He expected her to pull away from him but she did not. She returned the kiss.

'I didn't think you were the impetuous type,' she whispered.

David felt her frame with his hands, running them down her back and onto her buttocks. They were taut and unresisting. Celia pressed against him, her lips played on his face until they found his again. David could not believe her actions, or his own, and knew he would not stop, not now. They stumbled through the curtain onto the bed, and lost what control they had left.

David tore at Celia's clothes clumsily. She laughed.

'Hold on, I'll help you,' she gasped.

In a few moments they were naked and under the sheets. 'Now,' Celia moaned, as she pulled him into her. She gave a small gasp of pain as he entered, and continued to make little sighs which raised in pitch until they were finished. Their lovemaking was a daze of movement and sensation for David; he lost himself in this woman. He saw the light in Celia's eyes, eyes that were moist and deep and knowing, eyes that were in control, even at this moment. It was almost daybreak when they ceased, and slept.

Celia was slight in David's arms, she melted against his ribs, heart pumping next to his. His own body felt strong and wiry. The soft muscles he had brought to Spain were hard sinew now and there was not an ounce of spare flesh on him. Celia's face did not soften much as she slept; her determined lines slackened but did not disappear. They gave her a look of perpetual thought, as if she was pondering a problem barely remembered but never solved. She had cried out many things when they made love, passionate things that David answered with his body. He wanted this new day to last forever: he welcomed the dawn that crept into the room; every minute with Celia would be savoured. David fell asleep with her breath mingling with his, a final intoxication for his senses.

It was noon when he woke. Celia was up, standing over the stove in a dressing gown, a cup of coffee in her hand.

'I had a terrible time with this pot, it boiled dry in the night and it's almost disintegrated. Just as well the stove stopped working.'

Celia smiled and handed him the cup. David drank it in bed, the best coffee he had ever had. He wanted to shout from the window like a schoolboy, he wanted to end the war single-handed. If this was what love was no wonder people sought it so.

Celia spent some time in the bathroom and emerged in a dress the colour of her eyes.

'David Hicks, don't sleep the day away. There's a razor in there, you can do with it.'

David scratched his face, and got up, stretching like a cat. He shaved, making the most of the keen blade Celia provided.

No bombs had fallen in the night. This fact, and some glorious spring weather, enlivened the city. People were out in force on the streets, talking of the Republic's new president. Caballero, the old peasant leader, had resigned to be replaced by Juan Negrin. David wondered if the change would bring an improvement in fortunes.

In the afternoon they went out. David walked the streets proudly, glad to show off Celia. They stopped to buy a newspaper, David asking for it in Spanish.

'You have picked it up well,' Celia said, 'I find it difficult.'

'The French I learned at school helps. I am learning the slang now.'

The newspaper told of trouble in Barcelona as Karpinski had said. Communist was fighting Anarchist there; a Fascist plot was being foiled, David read.

'It makes you think,' he said, 'our lot fighting amongst themselves. What a way to fight a war. There's an old Italian back home who would say he told me so.'

'I don't know much about the different factions really,' Celia said. 'There are so many of them in the Republic, it's all a bit intense. Lots of people disappeared at the start in Madrid. They were taken away at night, 'going for a ride' they called it. Some were found shot, others were never found. Come on, let's have something to eat. I'm starving.'

David wanted to talk more about Barcelona but sensed that Celia was not really concerned about it, so he kept his peace. They sat at a pavement café, under a poster of a blindfolded soldier reading a book.

'What does that say?' Celia asked.

David consulted the Spanish Grammar he kept in his pocket. 'It says, "Illiteracy blinds the spirit. Study, soldier". We could do with messages like that back home.'

Celia smiled. 'Quite the student, aren't you? You know, for someone who was glad to get away, you mention "back home" quite a lot. And you've only been here a few months.'

'Do I? I hadn't realised.'

'I think you are a bit homesick, like Mr Price was.'

'No, not at all. I think about the valley sometimes, that's natural isn't it. But I'm glad I am here, never more than right now.'

He pressed Celia's hand.

She ate her eggs slowly, thinking about David as she did so. He was attractive, there was no doubt about that, there was a little-boy-lost quality about him that would draw many women. But he was wound up tight, like a corkscrew. A lot of feeling had been blocked off somewhere along the line; he had been stunted, she sensed. That might be the reason for his early marriage, and its failure. It was obvious that David was infatuated with her, and Celia did not want that. He had to realise that in Spain relationships had to be casual. It was impossible for her to cope with anything more.

Celia watched David watching her, his eyes on her constantly. She knew he would smother her if given half a chance, he wanted her all to himself and he wanted to rely on her. It's not going to work, she realised, and she regretted last night. David had set so much store in it, and she had not. There had been others in Spain, one of the doctors, once or twice, and a young German, so easy to handle, so unlike David.

'What are you thinking, Celia, you look miles away.'

'Oh, nothing much. Is the food good?'

'Yes, fine. Last night was great, wasn't it?'

'Yes.'

'Shall we go back to your rooms now?' David's hand felt for hers. 'Come on, let's go,' David said, 'I've had enough of this place.'

'No, I think you should go back to the hotel now, they'll think you've disappeared.'

'What do you mean?'

'Everything is going too quickly. Last night was fine and you are very nice, but I don't want you to get the wrong idea about us.'

David looked at her as if she had struck him.

'I don't want you to get hurt. Things change very quickly here, I can't make any commitment, not at the present. I'm sorry if you have misunderstood.'

Celia felt a flush of shame, but kept a steady face. David stared at her in disbelief.

'What are you talking about, misunderstood? You gave yourself to me, I thought you loved me. All those things you said last night, didn't you mean them?'

Celia did not know what to say, he was truly a child to believe anything said in bed. He had no right to think anything of it, no right, yet she felt lousy.

'You are too young,' she said, 'and I am too young. You must see that.'

David's face reddened to the colour of the wine.

'Too young! I've been bloody married! I tell you what I see, I see that you used me, led me on. You've made a fool out of me, Celia, a complete fool.'

David's voice rose and trembled, and tears welled up in his eyes.

'David, I didn't use you, we used each other. I want us to be friends.'

She reached out for him but he brushed her hand away.

Heads swivelled as he lurched up from the table. He left, scattering plates in his wake.

Celia called out to him but David was not listening, her words were shut out as he staggered through the streets. What had happened? How could it change so quickly? David was half sobbing, half gasping for breath when he reached the hotel. He tripped on the steps outside it, inviting the jokes of passers-by.

His room was empty, so he crawled into bed, seeking the solace of the sheets. Anger mingled with hurt in his guts, making him feel light and sick. He went over the weekend, all the things he had said to Celia, how he had opened up to her, trusted her. And she had sent him packing, like a beggar casually fed. Blind emotion clouded David's sense, he was filled with self pity and the bitter taste of rejection. He fell into a troubled sleep, but woke when the others got back, thinking he was with Celia.

Late the next day David was back with the battalion, preparing to move to another area. For once he was glad of the anonymity of the soldier, and glad of the company of men. They were sent back to a base at Morata de Tajuna, to rest and reorganise. It was well into May 1937, and the Spanish summer was on them. Men spent a few days delousing themselves and getting used to sleeping without the fear of attack. David busied himself with these chores and tried not to think. He cleaned his rifle endlessly, and scrounged for the best ammunition and food. He wanted to keep that Madrid weekend a blur, in the hope that it would go away.

He tried to tell himself it was a dream, a crazy few days in which happiness spilled through his hands like sand.

At last a letter came from his mother. David opened it nervously, but it contained no castigation. Helen's words were calm, worry hidden from them. She told of minor incidents in the valley, a few squabbles between miners and police, and that Iolo Hughes had been struck down with a stroke. "It happened in the chapel," she wrote "right in the middle of a sermon, he twisted up like a corkscrew and shook like a leaf, but he's better now and back preaching though his voice is much quieter."

David could not imagine a softly spoken Iolo. Helen had talked to Emma in the village. "She looks older, David, too old for her years. It's such a pity". She asked after Billy and Tom, and David realised that his mother did not know of Billy's death. That brought it all flooding back; Billy, Celia and Emma, three faces swirling in his head.

David shared the letter with Tom.

'What do you think,' he asked, 'surely they know about Billy by now?'

'Aye, I think they must. Your mother's letter has taken a long time to find you, that's all.'

'I bet it shook the Boys to hear about Billy,' David said.

'Shook the whole village probably,' Tom said, 'your mother will be praying it's not you next.'

David thought of the scene in Conti's. Devastation at first, the denial of the fact by the Boys that were left. Then Conti eulogises over Billy, polishing the chrome of his coffee pot as he does so. A Boy spits at the stove and is scolded by Maria. Impenetrable gloom falls on moist eyes, a few noses sniff until someone suggests a trip to the Anchor – 'have a drink on Billy, he'd like that'. In the pub the spirit lightens, Billy's old stories are retold, stretched, enlarged, new ones form as men get drunk. Conti is left alone at his counter, to gaze on chairs a little wistfully, thinking of the man who died so far away.

David wrote back to his mother. He dressed up Billy's death, he did not tell her it was a vile tussle in the dark, over nothing. This time there was no rain to smudge the paper and he kept his words neat, and sent them to the valley in a good envelope which cost him five cigarettes.

The battalion was returning to full strength. The new recruits from Albacete had the luxury of decent weapons and some training. Conditions were changing for the better, but with irritating slowness. The Republic was a dragon, shaking itself into life. At least they had the appearance of soldiers now, in uniforms which matched more or less and tin hats which they wore like upturned basins. David was a veteran after four months in Spain. New men deferred to him as he had done to Billy, he felt he could discard his youth for good.

A few more Welshmen joined them, miners or ex-miners. They formed a Celtic club, a Spanish Conti's where news and ideas were exchanged. David learned of changes in the valley from Huw Thomas, their most garrulous member.

'There's a lot of stuff being organised back there now,' Huw said: 'Collections, Spanish Aid, marches, that type of thing. They are taking refugees from here too, kids mostly.'

'What do they say of us, Huw?' Tom asked.

'Well, I have to admit, a lot of people don't seem too bothered about it, they can't see why we are interested in another country. My own missus is one of 'em. What the hell do you want to go out there for, she says, stay here and do something for your own family. Get a bleedin' job. Women don't understand do they, boys?'

There was a grunt of assent.

'What do the papers say?' David asked.

'Them. You know what to expect there. You lads who came out first are either red scum and criminal elements, or heroes of the working classes. I think that confuses people.'

'What are you, Huw?' someone shouted.

'I'm the hero of the scum, I am.'

Huw was not very funny but they all laughed with him. David liked the club, as long as he was on the edge of it. Its gossipy nosiness was a comfort here, yet he hated those traits in the valley. As he sat and listened to Welsh voices he knew that the valley would always be with him, and that earlier attempts to lock it in a box marked 'past' were fatuous and ill-conceived. The place was a root which lay just below the surface, holding him fast. These men made him feel it; it pumped influence through his veins as vital as his blood; but it was not a threat anymore. If he survived Spain, David resolved never to deny his home again.

The battalion increased to three hundred men, a small core of veterans, the rest fresh from Britain, bristling with enthusiasm and the need to get things done. The air in the camp was tinged with optimism, supplies were better, there was enough food, and the enemy had failed to break through on the Jarama. After a week at Morata men charged up like batteries, a second surge of heart mastered doubts bred in battle.

'Why don't you join the Party officially, Dave?' Tom asked one evening. Tom was heartened by the news from Barcelona, the Anarchists were finished there, their leaders dead or in jail. The Left was now firmly controlled by the Communists. 'You are committed to us, you've proved that, and you'll always be thought a red back home anyway, after this.'

'I know, but I think I'll stay as I am, Tom.'

'Why, man?'

'I don't know, perhaps I'll join later.'

'Maybe there'll be no later, David. My war nearly ended pretty damn quick, didn't it?'

David saw that Tom was annoyed, but he did not want to join anything, even the Communist Party. He was determined to become his own man.

The men's eagerness to have another crack at Franco was soon satisfied. After two weeks rehabilitation they were moved out quietly one night, in a convoy of trucks that took them to the east of Madrid. George Nathan, the Brigade's most adept soldier, was chief of operations in this new campaign. They were going to attack, Nathan told them, to strike southwards to meet Republican forces coming up from the town of Villanueva. Between them they hoped to push the enemy back from the foothold he had in the Madrid suburbs. It was an attempt to divert Franco from the crumbling north, a bold plan and a gamble. Attack. It was a new word for David.

14

David surveyed the new arena at first light. It was a land of deep ravines and gullies, topped by outcrops of rocks. In between lay stretches of flatter country, baked as brown as bread by the sun. There were very few trees, the willow copses that skirted the Guadarrama River presented the only dashes of green for the eye to rest on. Nothing much grew away from the river.

The enemy positions lay beyond a flat plain. The Brigade was to attack the next day, at dawn. David watched columns of men move up, Spanish and volunteers alike. In the distance Russian Chato planes snapped at the enemy's defences, softening them up for an attack. The plain worried all experienced eyes; there was scant cover between the battalion and its first objectives, the villages of Villanueve and Brunete. The whitewashed dwellings of Villanueve glittered like jewels in the flawless morning, beguiling and peaceful.

'This is the one,' Tom muttered in David's ear, 'we've got to win here.'

'Yes, I think we have,' David said.

They would never have a better chance of doing so. Surprise, something David thought the Republic would never manage, was on their side, they had air cover and their best equipment to date.

The battalion was not part of the initial attack in the morning, they waited in reserve, listening to the sounds of war in the distance. After two hours they were told to move out: 'Come on lads,' a sergeant shouted, 'we're on our way. They're having trouble taking that place.'

The attack was held up at Villanueve, and every minute lost was vital. They marched onto the plain, a natural sun-trap that surged and pulsed with heat, and advanced through stubble set alight by earlier fighting. It was a hellish place to fight in.

They were not under fire but the advance sapped energy. Men drank from canteens and tied handkerchieves around their necks as they walked. 'Here, Dave. Your balls will fry here, my son,' Danny shouted. No-one answered him.

The enemy, well dug in around the village, opened up with machine-gun fire as they neared it. Bullets sped past David; he knew their whine and rustle well now, but it still turned the sweat on his back cold. He dropped to the earth and fired mechanically at the buildings. Each round was good, encouraging, but still he fired blindly through thick smoke. Men were hit on either side of him as he lay on his belly, and soon there was a knee-high cloud of dust to ally itself with the smoke of burning buildings. Their sergeant stood up and took a bullet through the neck. It spun him around several times in a dance of death. The man spat bloody foam and died two yards from David. He lay there the rest of the day, spreadeagled on the earth with wide and sightless eyes.

They were stuck, unable to go forward or retreat. David cursed their lack of artillery, always conspicuous by its absence. With heavy guns the enemy's machine-gun nests could be soon winkled out. They were in a hollow, a few hundred yards from the outer houses of the village. David sighted his rifle on a window and fired a few rounds at the black hole, and prayed no-one would be stupid enough to order them to charge.

By noon most men had drained their canteens, and were thirsty. Tom crawled close to David.

'Got any water? I'm dry.'

David gave him a pull of his supply.

'Ta. Where are the guns, eh? We are like fish in a bloody barrel here.'

David drank some water himself and threw the canteen across to Danny.

'Cheers mate,' Danny cried, 'my tongue has fur on it.'

'We could finish that place off in no time, with guns,' Tom said. 'We can't afford to get stuck here.'

'There are women and children there,' David said, 'maybe that's why they are not using any of the heavy stuff.'

'You don't believe that. We both know it's because they've sent the guns to the wrong place. They are standing idle right now, being lent on by the bloody gunners.'

David knew Tom was right.

Danny howled and swore at the top of his voice. 'Bugger me, I've been hit.'

'Where? Are you alright?' Tom said.

There was no reply for a moment then Danny replied, 'I'm

alright, I suppose. They've got me in the same place as before, the bastards – back of the leg.'

Danny had been nicked in the calf by a stray bullet. His humour turned to hatred before their eyes, David watched the Liverpudlian squirm with rage in the dirt, swearing constantly as Tom tied a rough bandage around the wound. He never thought Danny had such anger in him but he saw another man surface now, Danny was diamond returning to carbon, and he was dangerous.

Villanueve defied them. David fired many times at distant gun flashes but he never saw the enemy. In early afternoon the firing from the village stopped and figures could be seen moving forward.

'It's all over,' someone cried, 'they've had enough.'

'Keep your positions,' an officer shouted, as some men began to get up. 'Stay down men, until we know what's going on.'

David shaded his eyes and saw women and children coming towards them. That might signify surrender, but he sensed danger. No-one fired, and the group of civilians moved closer in a curious huddle. As men relaxed their grips on rifle stocks a burst of firing came from the midst of the group. David saw soldiers crouched behind the villagers and they were very close, close enough to throw grenades over their human barricade. One fell amongst then, shattering a woman and child with its steel splinters. Others burst among the front men of the battalion.

'The bastards,' Danny shouted. 'It's a trick, lads, a fucking trap. Fire into them, or they'll be on us.'

Danny knelt and fired repeatedly through the terrified people of Villanueve. Old women fell as others joined him, crumpling and slumping to the ground without drama, and lying there, white undergarments showing against black dresses, like magpies blasted by a farmer's gun.

David fired with Danny, they all did. There was no time to think, no time not to fire. The villagers died, leaving the enemy troops exposed. They tried to retreat but the battalion was amongst them, closing like one savage animal that wanted to rend and tear. David shot an officer at close range through the face, Tom bayoneted a man on his right, a boy more than a man who screamed like one as his guts spilled into the earth. They were out of control, consumed with blood lust, and the fighting was too intense to last long. What was left of the enemy ran back to the village, in a vain attempt to escape. They cleared them all out by nightfall, there were no prisoners and Villanueve was theirs.

David sat amongst a pile of dead people when it was over, his mind slowly beginning to function and fill with horror. He did not want to acknowledge what he had done; he blamed the sun for causing his madness; but awareness came back to him, it would not let him get away. The hand of a dead girl rested against his boot, he shook it off, a guilty butcher. David wanted to hide from this rag of a body, but stayed beside her and tidied her hair with his hand. He pushed it back to see a peaceful face, unmarked and very still, as if she was holding her breath for a joke. He wanted her to burst into life again, and waited for a long time for her to do so. The girl was untouched from the waist up, but below there was not much left of her. A grenade must have landed at her feet. David felt wet and looked up to see if it was raining, but the sky was cobalt-blue in the dusk. It was his tears he felt, coursing down his cheeks. He cried for this child who would never cry again, and knew he would not kill anymore.

They dug in around Villanueve and recuperated. Supplies of food had been left by their foes, and some feasted on them. David found that his stomach rejected everything, and sleep did not come to smother his battered senses. He lay with Tom in a bombed out house, looking at the stars through what had been a roof.

'You can't sleep either, David,' Tom murmured.

'No, I can't.'

'Funny, you'd think we'd all go out like lights after this day. I'm really done in, but I can't sleep. Nerves maybe.'

'Yes.'

'Aye, that's what it is, a bit of reaction. It's hard to get back to normal, after the scrap we had. My guts are all twisted up, as if some bugger's got hold of them and wrung them out.'

'Try and get some sleep now, Tom, it will start up again in the morning.'

Tom began to snore after a few minutes. David lay back and gazed at the sky, so full of light and movement, yet so empty and indifferent. He knew now how horrors were committed and re-committed by ordinary men like those who lay around him. Tom sat up suddenly and spoke what he was seeing in his head.

'Danny went a bit wild today, didn't he? A good bloke like him too. David, we aren't bad, are we, we aren't murderers?'

'Some would say so, but I don't. We are just soldiers, who got caught up in something lousy. We can't change it now.'

Eventually David joined Tom in a light sleep.

In the morning they crossed the Guadarrama River, and spent that day engaging small bands of the enemy cut off by their advance. The time lost in taking Villanueve had given the other side time to bring up heavy guns, and the Republic's planes were challenged by German and Italian aircraft. David looked back from the far side of the river to see Villanueve disappear as it was bombed. They had got out just in time.

Men stopped to fill their canteens, for they had heard the river would dry up in a few days. The water was brown and suspect, but it was all they had.

'Don't worry about this stuff killing you, lads,' Danny laughed, 'we won't live bloody long enough for that.'

The boxer seemed back to his usual self, yesterday's horror cast off with a night's sleep, but David would never forget that inner man released on the plain, and he stayed away from Danny as much as he could.

Once again the enemy was entrenched in positions above them, on fortified heights that rose out of the plain. They faced the worst thing for foot soldiers, an assault on an elevated position. At dawn on the third day they attacked, with fifty men less than they had begun with. The American Lincoln Brigade was on their right, Lister's Spanish troops to their left.

As they neared the heights they came under heavy machine-gun fire. Men dropped to the ground and returned the fire, but the tardy were cut down. The day was the hottest David had ever experienced. As he inched forward sweat clogged his eyes, he continually wiped them, and wondered what he would do if there was hand-to-hand fighting.

Men were dying rapidly. David lost count of those he saw twist like mad clowns as they felt the agony of their wounds, and the ones who sank noiselessly to the ground as if praying or trying to bury themselves. He saw a man's head shatter from a direct hit, showering gore over his comrades. Senses numbed to protect, and each death touched him less and less.

Over the clamour of the battle they heard the whine from the air. Planes were diving on them. 'Hug the ground, lads,' Tom yelled, 'we're going to cop it.' David lay in the red earth, holding his helmet on as tightly as he could. He felt the ground heave as the bombs struck, but they fell away from them.

'Jesus, look at that!' Tom cried. David followed his hand to see the Americans catching it, blown out of their positions like ants. For them there was no escape, and no chance. They tried to shelter under rocks but they were shattered into pieces, and men along with them. Some ran into the open, where they were destroyed by the machine-guns. The Lincoln battalion disintegrated, the heart bombed out of it in minutes. From his high point the enemy saw everything, every act carried out in the clarity of a cloudless day.

With desperate charges they managed to take the lower slopes, but it was impossible to dislodge the enemy from the ridge. They pulled back to stronger positions, and continued to inflict great damage. Without further support their advance was over.

That night they lay in small groups beneath the ridge, cut off from each other by ravines, with no communication with their command. David was one of a group of eight men, half of them wounded. Tom and Danny had survived the day with him. Danny crawled over, in search of water.

'Here, Dave,' he said, 'do you know what they are calling this place? Mosquito Ridge, that's what. On account of all the bullets, see, they comes down on us like flies. And that's how we go down, isn't it, like bastard flies.' Danny was pleased with his simile, he chuckled to himself but he was hollow and desperate. They all were.

Wounds were tended the best they could, but there was no way of getting the injured away. One man from the Midlands kept up a low moan for hours, until death took him. His noise was taken up by others in the darkness, a litany of pain to celebrate the sufferings of the day. David did not talk much with Tom, they shared a bitter disappointment, and that was enough.

In the morning the same moves were re-enacted. Men died in the futile attempt to take the ridge. David fired his rifle, but never at definite targets. He was useless here now, but no-one noticed he had no fight left. By midday they had moved up another hundred yards, only to be caught in a crossfire. A dozen men were trapped in a narrow gully, with scrub burning on both sides. Enemy machine-gunners had pinned them there, now they waited to scour each exit.

'We're going to get fried or shot,' Tom said. 'Christ, this is a bad spot we've landed in.'

Ricochets wormed their way between the rocks, in search of bodies to sink their steel into.

'Looks like it's all up with us, Tom,' David said.

'Maybe. I can't do much with this anyway.'

Tom's left arm hung limply, shattered by the glance of a bullet.

'God, when did that happen?'

'Back there, somewhere.'

Someone was crying, a baby-like sound that rose in a lull in the shooting. Tom went over to the man and shook him with his good arm. 'Shut up, you. Get a hold on yourself, we're not done yet.'

'Here, lads,' Danny said, 'have you got any grenades left?'

He collected five and stuffed them in his pockets, discarding his rifle.

'What are you doing?' David asked.

'The only thing I can bloody think of. Right lads, I'm off up that way.' Danny nodded towards the ridge. 'When I get out of this fucking trench you lot scarper down the other way.'

'Look Danny, that's no good, you wouldn't last a minute,' Tom said.

'Course I will, I'll use me old ringcraft, dance my way past the bullets. Anyway, what chance have we stuck here? Go on, get the wounded boys up, and when I draw their fire bugger off back down. And stop gawping at me all of you, none of us live forever.'

He gave a mock salute to David. 'So long mate, I'll say hello to Billy for you.'

Danny ran out into the open and began to scale the slopes with his bandy legs.

'Come on,' Tom cried, 'we haven't got time to watch.'

They turned and hurried down the slope to a lower, safer place. David could not stop himself looking back, wondering why they were not being fired at. Every enemy eye was on Danny, but for thirty yards he was charmed, the bullets missing him. He stopped to pull the pins on the grenades and was hit immediately, pushed backwards by the force of countless rounds. He tumbled down the slope, blood spurting from the many holes in his body. The grenades exploded, and Danny was gone.

'For Christsake David, get a move on,' Tom shouted.

David responded, lurching into a shambling run. They got fifty yards down, out of the crossfire, but only four of them survived. In a heap they lay behind covering rocks, breathless and hurting. David thought he imagined the ground drifting away from him, then realised that the planes were back again. 'We can't take much more of this,' he hissed, 'we are bleeding away.'

But they did survive, to spend another night listening to the confused sounds around them. Sometimes a crazed man fired a shot into the night for comfort, perhaps, a homage to the savage gods of fear and anger. The battalion had little hope of co-ordinating a retreat but at least the enemy had not chased them; he remained on his hill, content for the moment with the carnage he wrought.

Unlike the Jarama the fighting did not die down. For two weeks there was the cut and thrust of war as each side contested the arid land. By the fifth day the battalion had halved to 150 men, and the remains of the Lincoln Brigade merged with them. David survived, but did not kill. He was never in as tight a spot as the gully again. A bullet splayed into rock near him and cut his face with tiny shards, this was the closest he came to death. He began to get a reputation for being lucky.

Tom never left the front. He was strapped up and he managed to fire his rifle with it propped up against a rock, with David loading it for him. Their day became one long charade of dodging planes and foraging for water. After a week David found it hard to imagine ever doing anything else, almost used to his new life. The Republic's forces spent themselves without making further headway, and on the nineteenth of July they re-crossed the Guadarrama, now a river-bed of mud. They were back where they started, with forty men left alive out of the original three hundred.

Incredibly, their pitiful band was ordered to dig in on the river's bank. 'They want us to hold up the enemy, lads,' a bitter officer told them. David cried out inside at the futility of it. They could hardly hold themselves up and would be brushed aside in the first attack.

'I don't know about this any more, David,' Tom said, 'we are being wasted, so many good men, and I can't see the sense of it.

It's as if they never learn from their mistakes – and it's always us, the volunteers.'

'Everyone fighting is saying that, Tom, it's always us. We are not as strong as the other side, that's the truth of it.'

Few of the men made much attempt to dig in, most barely scratched the soil. They were listless and battle-weary with no fight left in them. They stood around dazed, awaiting their fate. David sat in dried mud and watched ants forage around his feet. They marched headstrong and seemingly wayward, but they had purpose. Each ant had the imprint of a mission inside it, a task to be completed, carried out endlessly until it perished. One came upon the body of a fellow, it probed the corpse with its antenna then hoisted up the larger ant onto its back, holding it with its pincers in an absurd balancing act. It dropped its load several times, but always stuck at it. Another forager came to help it, and between them they tottered back to the safety of their nest. David wondered what they did with their dead.

Hitler had learned what ants had always known, thought David. Order was what he offered; to follow him was to be provided for, to be a given a place, and to know it. Accept your lot and obey the rules, don't think, look straight ahead in your blinkered club. Franco backed it up with religion and netted many souls. David wondered if his side was any different. He understood Billy's clamour for unity now. Billy had recognised the strength of the other side and had sought to combat it. Never had the vagaries of the Left been so exposed as in Spain. Order gained Franco victory, he was helped by superior weapons and supplies, but David felt in his gut that even if things had been equal they would still be disadvantaged.

A further ordeal at the river was only averted because the enemy counterattack faltered and petered out on the far side. Each side had bled itself dry in this campaign. They struggled back to Villanueve as fresh troops marched past them to the river. 'Poor bastards,' Tom said, 'look how eager they are, just like we were.'

Amongst the rubble of the village they tried to take stock of the last two weeks. David's nerves were frayed, he jumped at any sound and had forgotten how to sleep. The others were the same.

'We are never going to win, are we, David?' Tom muttered sadly, 'I can see it now.'

Tom played his bayonet into the earth, sifting the red dust, like a child bored on a beach.

'I don't know, Tom. Spain is a place where anything could happen. We aren't winning, that's obvious, but... I don't know.'

These were the most hopeful words David could offer Tom, but he knew that his friend was right. Weeks of fruitless fighting did wonders for a man's intuition. There was defeat all around him, he sensed the fading of hope in his comrades: it spread from man to man like a plague, first the easily daunted, then the optimist. It settled over them, and they could not shake it off.

When David finally slept he was wracked by horrors. Franco pranced around in his head, carried aloft on the shoulders of Mussolini and Hitler. The unholy triumvirate grinned like ghouls, yellow teeth turned to graveyard tombstones. They were still in his mind when he awoke, to return to Mondeja with the thirty seven men able to walk. George Nathan had died in the night, of wounds received at Brunete. It was a fitting end to their sad campaign. Their fight, in this arena at least, was over.

Tom was taken to Madrid, to be treated again at Celia's hospital.

'Do you want me to give her a message?' Tom asked.

'No, don't say anything about me.'

'What if she asks, though?'

'Tell her what you like, it's no matter to me.'

Tom left in a truck filled with fellow wounded. David had never felt so alone as he watched him go. With Billy and Danny dead, and Tom gone, perhaps for good, he was isolated. And he, David Hicks, was a soldier who could not kill.

Mondeja lay in a valley, a cooler place than the villages of the plain. Trees gave shelter from the sun, and served to mark meeting places and resting spots for different factions. David knew the Marxist tree, the London boys' tree, the Welsh tree. Men grouped themselves according to beliefs and prejudices, but every man shared in the general camaraderie, even in this bleak time. Losing Billy had moderated David's attempts at mixing in. Without Tom he became a loner again, a dour figure to be seen plodding around the perimeter of the camp, head down and hands in pockets.

One day he walked away from Mondeja to the highest hill he could climb, and freed himself from the war for an afternoon. He sat and watched the camp and saw new recruits arriving, Spaniards mostly. The Brigades were becoming less foreign as volunteers were killed off. David welcomed the Spaniards, he wanted to get to know the people they were dying for. So often they hurried across Spain at night, then fought in open country, passing baffled peasants. When they mixed with the Spanish people, most of the men were too strung out to do anything more than drink.

David lay back in the earth, and let the sun warm him. Crisp air kept him from over-heating. He felt it sift over his body, as sure as a lover's hand. He doubted if many had been here before him. Spain was not a country for a man to walk in without good reason. The poor had no time, the rich feared the open: it held the sun, and the poor. Perhaps once a boy had been posted here, to warn of a Moorish attack on the valley below. David saw it, the gasp from the boy as he sighted the black-cowled riders, his desperate scurry down the slopes to the village, the cries of the villagers as they gathered up children and blindly ran, knowing in their hearts they could not escape the scimitars, and worse.

After an hour David made his way back. The sun sank behind the valley's fringe of mountains. He was refreshed by his dose of solitude but as he neared the camp he felt the urge to walk away from it again, to walk home for good. His legs slowed as he passed the Welsh tree, where men were stirring for their evening meal. The smell of stew wafted over from the kitchens, tugging at his stomach and steadying his nerve.

Two messages waited for David. A note from Tom said "I'm alright, see you soon, I hope", another told him to report to the company commander after mess. David pondered on this as he ate. He had not had much contact with the battalion hierarchy. At six he reported to the house which served as company head-quarters.

An Irishman, Paddy O'Daire, was in command now, a man David knew little about. He knocked on O'Daire's door.

'Come in, Hicks, come in,' a voice from inside said.

David pushed open the door to see O'Daire sitting behind a makeshift desk.

'Lovely fresh evening lad, isn't it? I hate it too hot.'

David sat at the offered chair. O'Daire had a strong face; keen eyes peered through a brow knotted with furrows and dents, and he was strongly built, with hard muscle compacted onto a square frame. O'Daire had knocked around the world a bit, and knew the score in Spain.

They lit up cigarettes as O'Daire put David at his ease. David tried to concentrate, but much of him was still on the hill.

'Shame about Billy Hicks,' O'Daire said, 'he was your uncle, wasn't he?'

'Yes,' David said.

'Aye, he was a fine man, we could do with a thousand more like him. It's what we lack, good NCOs.'

David nodded. 'Look Hicks, I've had my eye on you for a while now, this is why I've sent for you – no, nothing to worry about.'

O'Daire took a long pull on his cigarette, and looked David in the eyes.

'How would you like to train at the officers' school?'

David was not sure he had heard correctly, and was not given time to answer.

'You've proved yourself in the field, stayed cool through it all, I've heard, and you are old for your years – nothing like war for ageing, eh? The Republic needs men like you, Hicks, that's what I'm saying. You know what it was like when you came out, bedlam, and it's still bloody bedlam on the fronts. We've got to put that right, and we need experienced men to lead.'

O'Daire paused, and stared at him. 'Well, what do you say?'

The irony of what the Irishman was saying struck David. How little people really saw. "We need men like you". And the last fifty rounds he had fired were un-aimed. He liked O'Daire. He had an honest earnest air about him, like a good teacher, but he was still giving the standard pep talk. An officer, that would please the old school, and horrify Billy. David saw the old man's face curl up with disgust, wherever he was. "You, one of them", the face said. Yet it would be a chance to get away from the front for a while.

'Well lad?' O'Daire said.

'No, I don't think I would want that,' David said.

O'Daire raised his eyebrows.

'Don't want the responsibility, is that it?'

'I just want to stay an ordinary soldier.'

'But you are not ordinary, are you? You have survived, for one thing, and you have an education. That's what we need.'

David shook his head. O'Daire thought for a few moments.

'You aren't too happy about things here, are you? Think they have gone badly.'

'You just said yourself – bloody bedlam. A lot of us died uselessly at Brunete, we didn't receive a clear order for days. It was a bloody shambles, we all know it.'

David heard his voice rise, but O'Daire was unperturbed.

'Isn't that a good reason for becoming a leader, for doing something about it? You'd have the chance to get your ideas across, perhaps.'

'No I wouldn't, you know it. Spain isn't like that, men get swallowed up here. No, I'll not change my mind. It's bad enough being led by stupidity, without having to pass it on.'

O'Daire scratched his head and studied David for a few moments. Someone barked orders outside, a rasping sound that punctured the still of the evening.

O'Daire spread his hands.

'So be it,' he said, 'if your mind is made up I won't press you, but I'm disappointed, Hicks.'

He waved David to the door.

'Don't forget, I'm here if you want to talk again.'

The battalion stayed at Mondeja, readying itself for the next campaign. Tom returned in August, with an arm stiff but functioning. He greeted David with six bottles of wine, carefully wrapped in a cloth sack.

'We'll have a get-together tonight, with some of the boys,' Tom said.

David was glad to see his friend, he saw a rekindling of spirit in him. At Brunete the fire had died in Tom's eyes, but it was back; he had gained a second wind of enthusiasm.

'How is the arm?' David asked.

'Good man, good.'

Tom held it up and stretched out his hand.

'An English doctor, Tudor Hart, he pinned the bone together, said he was trying out a new idea. I'm glad he did, or I would have lost the arm otherwise.'

That night they were allowed to build a fire in an orange

grove. A dozen men sat around it sharing chocolate and wine, some reading letters from the bundle Tom had brought to Mondeja. Two Spanish brothers, new men, had attached themselves to the Welsh group, Alphonso and Ricardo Ruiz, called Dick and Al by everyone. From these two David learned much about the Spanish people and the land which demanded so much of him. Dick was tall and thick set, with powerful shoulders that hunched together when he was perplexed, which was often. His brother was smaller with more nimble body and mind, a dapper man with a quicksilver tongue, a player of guitars and chaser of women. Al had been sent from his village to attend school in the city, and his English was good. The brothers came from a family of small-holders, the slightly better-off peasants of Spain.

David sat as near the fire as he could. Al laughed at his shivering shoulders. '*España*, she is a strange place no? By night the sun run away, she takes all her heat with her.' Al's voice was soft and quick like most of the rural Spanish. Dick smiled and nodded whenever his brother spoke, he had no English and said little in his own tongue. Al did the talking for both of them and each brother liked this arrangement.

Tom lead the discussion, the reticent man of the valleys was gone, in his place was one who men listened to, held by his quiet conviction. David watched his friend in the glow of the fire and saw his face lit with more than its heat. Tom shone with renewed hope

'You men who have just come out,' Tom said, 'you'll be much better prepared than we were, isn't that right Dave?'

David nodded mechanically.

'Bugger-all we had, and no time at all, but we stopped the Fascists in the Jarama valley. Think what we can do now that we are organised. Russia is sending plenty of stuff.'

Tom was repeating Billy's speech of Madrigueras. Russian help was a trickle compared to the torrent of men and supplies from the Axis powers, but men like Tom and Billy made it into a symbol.

David still wanted to be part of the comradeship, but the skies of Castille clouded with enemy aircraft was a powerful memory, and Tom's words did not reach those planes and bring them down. The war was good for Tom, David thought, he had been wounded twice and was a greater man because of it; a leader was being forged from the lonely soul he had been.

'You are quiet down there, Dave,' Tom said.

David raised a mug of wine.

'I'm alright – enjoying the fire.'

Ricardo grinned and said '*Bueno, bueno*' until Al dug him in the ribs. Tom talked on, and more men joined them out of the darkness, with more bottles. Someone began to play the mouth organ. Its thin, shaking sound was perfect in its fragile warmth, an evocation of the comradeship the men felt. They started to sing as David slipped away into the trees. Turning back he saw a circle of heads fringing the fire, moths darting above them, entranced by the flames. Some drifted into the blaze, trapped on the warm currents of air. They exploded like minute bombs as the heat fired them. David put some distance between himself and the party as the tenor voice of Al began to sing out, each phrase followed by the mouth organ. David could not understand the words but knew it would be about a woman.

Someone was near him in the darkness. David relaxed as O'Daire approached him. With him was the battalion commissar, another Welshman. He greeted David.

'Hullo there, lad. Had enough of the do, eh? Walk with me a little, we'll have a chat.'

O'Daire melted back into the darkness, leaving David with the commissar. He was a small man, bow-legged and bright-eyed, typical valley size. He guided David along, barely coming up to his shoulder. For some minutes they talked of nothing much, exchanging snippets of news; the commissar knew Billy, and David's village. David was relaxed with his countryman. 'Aye, Billy Hicks,' the commissar said, 'a magical man, lad, magical.'

The commissar scratched himself.

'Don't want to be an officer then?' the commissar said. 'Shame that, but then we don't like bosses much where we come from, do we? Somebody has to lead though, at times like these. Went to the County School, didn't you, David? Fine thing, education. We fought for it for a long time. Spain could do with a dose of it, perhaps this wouldn't have happened then.'

He did not seem to want answers from David, and David was glad not to give him any.

'Been out here for a while, now, haven't you? Wife back home too. Mine died a few years back.' He talked on, steering David around the camp like a child

The commissar's homeliness lulled David into talking, and after half an hour he found himself doing so freely. His companion had a gleam in his eye now, a clever poacher of words who had drawn his man out.

'What's the matter, boy?' he asked softly. 'There is something up with you, something worse than the usual gripes of the men here.'

'I don't want to fight anymore,' David said bluntly, 'I don't think I can.'

'Ah,' said the commissar, 'that's it.'

'Not after Brunete. I've had enough, something happened to me there, something snapped. I don't have any fight left in me.'

The commissar watched him with owl-eyes.

'You are all mixed up, we all get it, bound to, in a situation like this. But don't give in to it. You're an old hand now, a veteran by the standards of this war. Do you really want to throw that away? How will you feel in years to come, have you thought about that? This type of thing can eat into a man, like cancer.'

David wondered what he meant by "this type of thing".

'I don't want to fight,' David repeated. 'I'll stay, do something else, but I won't fight.'

'You'll have no choice of staying. They won't let you go home, we are part of the Republican army now, been incorporated into it. We have signed on for the duration.'

'What about those men who have deserted? I've heard talk.'

'Aye, there's been one or two. Most of them are not proper deserters, just lads a bit confused, lost sight of what they are fighting for.'

'Well, what happens to them?'

'We have a camp near Albacete, Camp Lucas. Those lads go there, to think things out, rehabilitate themselves.'

'You mean a prison camp.'

'No, I don't. Nothing as bad as that. It's just like another training camp. It's a way of looking after our own, better they go there than land in a Republican jail, and maybe disappear.'

They had walked to the sleeping quarters.

'I've rambled on enough for one night,' the commissar said. 'I'm glad we've had this little talk though. That's what you need, David, to talk to people more. I've seen you wandering about the place, on your own. Don't keep everything bottled up inside you, you'll explode if you do that. You are feeling what most soldiers feel, at one time or another. Fight it, and don't do anything daft. Your record is first class out here.'

The commissar pressed his hand with his own, and left him. David went to his bunk and realised he had received another pep talk.

The smell of pine smoke drifted across the camp, rich and sweet. It gave the illusion of safety and comfort. Men came back to their bunks, satisfied with their night. Tom joined David. He was clumsy with wine, and happy for once.

'Hullo David,' Tom said, 'you are here, are you? I wondered where you had got to. Thought maybe you had drunk too much.'

'No, I was tired.'

'Good get-together, wasn't it? The lads enjoyed it. Here, some say we are moving out again tomorrow, our rest is over.'

'Do you know where, Tom?'

'No, it could be anywhere, I s'pose. Wherever it is, you can bet it will be hot, in all sorts of ways.'

David's heart sank. 'Yes, it will be,' he said.

'Are you alright, Dave? You've been very quiet since I came back.'

'I'm alright. I've always been quiet, haven't I?'

Tom did not seem convinced, but he did not push.

'I'm getting some shuteye, see you in the morning.'

'Goodnight, Tom.'

Tom was woken in the night by David moaning in his sleep. He watched for a while, but did not disturb him, and could not understand his words. He knew that David's mind was crowded with doubts and worries, the lad had strange ways for one so young, but all men were visited by devils in the Spanish night. Tom turned over and went back to sleep, glad that he was through his own test.

Campfire rumours became reality in the morning. The camp buzzed as the men were rushed through breakfast.

'We are going to Aragon, lads,' an officer shouted as he walked through them, 'there's going to be a push there.'

'Aragon, where the 'ells that?' a cockney voice shouted.

'What do you care, Fred?' another answered.

There was the usual laughter to gloss nerves and mask the

tension that was beginning to knot in experienced guts. David knew the formula now.

'Aragon is up north,' he told those near to him, but no-one was listening.

'It's Brunete again, boys. They are sending us back to Mosquito Hill,' someone joked.

The thought chilled the veterans. David tried to digest bread, but he had no spit. He did not rush with the others, he let them return to their sleeping quarters to collect their gear, and stood watching the hill he had climbed. It was a red blur against the deepening blue of the sky. He was walking towards it before he had time to think. He walked like a man in a stupor through the bustle of the camp, but no-one questioned him, no-one stopped him. He was through the outer perimeter in a few minutes, deserting calmly as his comrades prepared to go to war once more.

15

David gained the heights quickly, he was well away from the camp in an hour. Turning to look down as he climbed he saw a line of trucks approaching the camp, the battalion's transport to Aragon. He knew he must be missed now. Tom would have kept quiet, in the hope that he would reappear; he would not want to think David had run away.

A deserter? Was he that? David could not take it in. Fear was on him now, yet he was exhilarated: finally, he had done something. He stopped to rest on a ledge of rock. It was shaped like a man's forehead, the stone swept back by centuries of wind. He sat in a shaded spot, and decided this was a good place to think. A small bird flitted about in the mountain air, delighting in its first year of flight. There was a splash of russet on its breast, not unlike the robins of the valley.

David took stock of his situation. He had no food, no map, no hat to guard against the sun, and just a few pesetas in his pocket. He might walk into the arms of the enemy at any time, and the border was three hundred miles away. He would have to forage for food and live rough. He had as much chance of surviving as a snowball in hell, he thought.

The bird brought others to study the interloper. David felt them laughing at him, as he sat hunched in the rocks. You are going nowhere, they said, you are lost, *hombré*, not free. That mountain you see in the distance we can fly to in minutes; you will take a day to walk there.

The birds tired of David. Whirling away from him they called their goodbyes on the wind as they rode the warm currents down to the valley. David began his own descent of the far side of the mountain. As he walked worry grew; he did not see any future. He was thinking this as he walked straight into the arms of the commissar waiting for him on a dirt road, sitting in his open-topped car in the shadows.

'Hullo, lad,' he called, 'thought you'd be along sooner or later.'

David could have run back to the hills, but he saw the futility of that. They had found him so easily and so quickly he was shamed, and stripped of any further response.

'Tom Price said you would come this way,' the commissar said, 'so I thought the best thing to do would be to wait here, in the car. Phew, it's a hot one, isn't it?'

He offered David a canteen, which he took and drank from greedily, watched by the outline of the commissar's face. It was all he could see, the rest was lost in the shadows.

'Nice little spot here,' the commissar said, 'peaceful, far from the madding crowd. Who said that? Someone famous, I bet.'

He talked like a man meeting another on a stroll and David stood before his car like a recalcitrant schoolboy.

'Where did you think you were going, lad? Look at you, totally unprepared. I should have realised though, last night. You had that rabbit look about you. Scared and excited, that's how you were.'

'I was deserting,' David said.

'I wouldn't use that word,' the commissar said quickly. 'That's a dangerous word to use in Spain. No, mixed up, we'll say. Lucky for you you didn't bring anything with you, that would have made it premeditated. Best thing now is for you to go to Camp Lucas for a while, sort yourself out there. Here, get in, out of the glare.'

He held the door open for David. He climbed in next to the commissar, sitting stiffly on the leather seat.

For the first time David noticed another man, a Spanish driver who looked at him with contempt.

'This is Antonio, my driver. He's a local lad, his farm is not far from here. In fact I think we'll stop there on the way back. There's no rush now, your comrades are well on the way.'

'I suppose there will be a lot of talk about me,' David said.

'No, not that much, you are not important enough for that. Only your unit will miss you, they'll be a man short, won't they?'

The accusing eyes of Antonio bored into David as they stopped on the track nearest to the farm. He resented this foreign deserter coming to his home. Antonio Cuesta was the youngest son of a hill farmer, his land no longer worked. They walked up to his farmhouse, a building faded to a dull yellow. The place had an abandoned look; its stone walls needed mending, the outbuildings were dishevelled.

'No men here, see,' the commissar said. 'Antonio's father and brother were killed in the early fighting, so there is no-one to run the place until the war is over.'

They were met at the door by an old woman, Antonio's mother. David caught the word 'prisoner' but the woman looked on him kindly enough. She was not so old now that he could see her face – in her late fifties at most, but aged by hard work, and sorrow. *Señora* Cuesta walked slowly, with a premature stoop.

Three bowls of stew were laid before them, small bowls that held a watery liquid with lentils floating in it. David sat without looking up. He feared shame would show in his eyes.

'These are the people we are fighting for, David,' the commissar said. 'Simple enough, aren't they? Simple in their lives anyway, their brains are as good as yours and mine, or better. Don't worry, they have no English.'

The commissar waved his spoon around the room.

'Haven't got much. The downtrodden masses, you might say, but they aren't any more. They have pride and self respect, they always did have and now it's had a chance to surface. They have a voice now, and we have helped them shout a bit, volunteers like you and me.'

The eyes of the commissar burned.

'It's a wonderful thing to have achieved. These folks have a flicker of hope now and I'll tell you one thing, it will last no matter what the outcome of this war. I won't be around to see how it all develops in later years, but I hope you will, David. That's why your actions here are so important. It's your future as much as theirs.'

The *señora* sat away from the table, but she watched David with unwavering eyes. They were the only un-aged part of her, as sharp as flint and blue as birds' eggs. She was not typically Spanish; her hair was streaked with fair strands; there was a hint of northern lands in the woman.

'Why has this boy run away?' she asked her son.

David answered her himself, surprising everyone with his Spanish.

'I don't know why, *señora*. I was tired, very tired.'

It sounded better in Spanish. 'Tired, *si*, all this killing, it tires the heart.'

She thumped her breast with her hand. 'My man is gone, my son also, that tires me, but don't give up English, you did a great thing to come to Spain, to help us. I would not have come to your country to help you. You are young... don't give up.'

The commissar was shrewd. *Señora* Cuesta was David's personal Passionara, her words moved him and he felt less of a stranger. They finished the meal and drove back to Mondeja. Antonio left them for his next driving assignment. He managed a half smile at David as he drove off, hostility melted by a little understanding.

'*Adios, camarada*,' he said, after a little thought.

'*Adios*,' David said.

By nightfall he was on his way to Camp Lucas with two other men who had demanded to go home. There was a hard fist in David's stomach at the thought of the camp, but not the same as going into battle. Apprehension took the place of fear. In the truck one man talked a lot, a curly haired man with a Midlands accent. He had the eyes of a ferret, they darted everywhere like daggers. The Ferret had an air of desperate artifice about him, as if he had bluffed his way through his life without ever knowing who he was, and now was trapped by his own deceit.

'They won't keep me,' he said. 'I'll be off, the first chance I get. It's a con this lark is, and no mistake, eh mates?'

David did not answer, and the other man was also silent. This one sat upright with his head nodding against the tarpaulin, averting his eyes from the other two. The Ferret did not mind, he ignored their reticence and talked for most of the journey. His nervous bursts of words matched the jolts of the roads. He would tell 'em when he got home, oh yes boy, he would tell them.

David arrived at Camp Lucas as stiff and as crumpled as the truck's canvas. He was nervous, but there was no-one to meet them. The Spanish driver waved them carelessly towards a small group of buildings and roared away into the night. Eventually a man came out of the largest building as they approached it.

'Hullo there,' he said, in an English voice, 'you must be the new men. I've been expecting you.'

He read their names from a piece of paper and David acknowledged his. He told them his name was Angus, and that he was in charge of the camp. David saw a man in his early twenties and wondered how he could be in charge. Angus was a quiet-faced man, with eyes that were calm and strong, eyes that weighed people up, but did not judge in haste.

'Most of the men here are British,' Angus said, 'there are a few Frenchmen and other nationalities, but most are like yourselves.'

Angus's tone was not accusing or threatening, and tensions eased as he led them to a low building. It was gloomy inside, the windows were too small to let in much of the dawn. A few tables were laid with cutlery, wooden spoons and a few worn knives.

'You are in time for breakfast,' Angus said, 'we haven't got much here but no-one goes hungry. Sit down there, the others will be in shortly.'

They sat at one end of the largest table, self-conscious new boys.

'This is a rum do, innit?' said the Ferret. 'I thought there'd be barbed wire, guards, all that stuff. This Angus fella is more like a bleedin' vicar than an officer. We've struck lucky, lads.'

David was surprised at the openness of the camp himself. Men began to drift into the room, in ones and twos, without order. A few gave them a muted greeting, others did not glance an eye at them. They sank down in their allotted seats and waited for their food. An air of apathy was instant, and pervasive. David's own troubles were echoed in this room, he felt them mix with like minds. One man he recognised, from the Jarama campaign.

'Hullo there. It's Petersen, isn't it?' David said.

'Oh, it's you, is it, Hicks? You are here.'

'I thought you had been killed.'

'No. I suppose that's what people would think when a man disappears. I ended up here. My nerve went.'

The table fell silent.

'Nerve,' the Ferret muttered, 'fuckin' rubbish that is. Nothing to do with nerve. Plain common sense, that's all it is.'

Angus sent for them when the meal was over. They stood facing him in front of two tables placed together to make a desk. The Ferret whistled aimlessly and stared at the floor.

'There are about sixty of you here,' Angus told them. 'I've been given the job of helping you along. There hasn't been much done here yet, most of the men are pretty fed up.'

'Yeah, I noticed,' the Ferret said.

'I hope to change that,' Angus continued, 'but there will be no inquisition, no lectures, just new training to help build up your confidence again.'

'Where did you fight then, sir?' the Ferret asked.

'I was at Brunete. Nasty spot, wasn't it?'

Angus thumbed through a sheaf of papers looking for details of his charges. He glanced up from time to time, matching the man with the information.

'What's it say about us, then?' the Ferret said. 'Bleedin' heroes, eh?'

He laughed and turned to the others, but they kept silent. David felt an urge to strike the man and clenched his fists in his pockets. Angus ignored him and put the papers aside.

'Well men, is there anything you want to ask?'

David and the silent one shook their heads, but the Ferret stepped forward.

'I don't think it's right,' he said. 'I done my bit out here, no-one forced me to come out but now they are forcing me to stay. I want out, what's wrong in that?'

'It's probably been explained to you that the Spanish government won't allow it. And we need you, the Brigade needs you, you know how things are at the fronts.'

'Aye, that's why we are here.' The silent one spoke for the first time, in a soft Yorkshire voice. Angus was uncomfortable.

'As I said, no pep talks, you'll have plenty of time to air your views. Take it easy today, meet the rest of the men. You'll know some of them, perhaps.'

David did see a few faces he recognised. They acknowledged him in a half-hearted way, embarrassed and resigned to their new roles. Camp Lucas was a place of slouched shoulders and despondency. The Ferret summed it up. 'This place is a right knacker's yard. I'm hopping it, first chance I gets.'

A Spanish cook brought news of fighting around the town of Belchite in Aragon. David's comrades were fighting and dying there, he said, as he dished out the stew.

'You will join your *camaradas* again, *sí*? You will help *España* again.' The cook was very old, but young with enthusiasm. He waved his arms. 'It is a great attack. The *Fascistas* will be swept away this time, *camarada*.'

Always this time. The Ferret told the old man to piss off, but he kept on smiling and cooking.

Days dragged at the camp. Angus's policy was one of gradual rehabilitation. Commissars came down to help morale with talks.

They tried to relight flames of commitment, but at first their pleas fell on stony ground. The men were too fed up to be told anything. The only time they listened was when one man talked of Joe Louis's last fight.

The peace of the camp did help, however. They were in a cul-de-sac of the war, protected by their remoteness from any conflict. The food was poor but plentiful – the peasants who grew it for them had far less. A change came upon some men gradually. They were free from lice and dysentery, they could sleep without the fear of a slit throat, the ground did not heave apart under them, and the only things that flew through the air were the local birds. As bodies improved nerves healed with them, and spirit crept back into fragile souls, timidly at first, then stronger as confidence returned.

David kept to his solitary role, watching what went on around him, weighing himself up against the others but never joining them. There were a few other ferrets in the camp but most were like himself, men a little more prone to self-doubt and question; men more likely to crack. All were looking for answers to their actions and even their lives. A few men began to see Angus, asking to be returned to their battalions. Usually they were the ones who had been at Camp Lucas the longest.

David avoided Angus as much as he could, he continued his habit of walking and was allowed to do so as long as he stayed within the camp's perimeters. David tramped along the edge of a waterless land, passing peasants who nodded at him and pointed fingers at their heads after he passed. Sometimes he found a place to sit and watch the drab camp.

On Friday of the second week David talked with Angus. It was a cloudy day, blue sky was squeezed into strips by massed cumulus. David was about to make his circuit around the camp when Angus appeared.

'Can I join you, Hicks?' he asked. 'I feel like a stroll myself.'

David shrugged.

'This is a bit more like home, eh?' Angus pointed to the clouds.

Angus was a strange commander, always asking and never ordering. They walked alongside ruts left by generations of carts.

'Just like sculptures, aren't they?' Angus said. 'Things seem so permanent here. I suppose that sounds strange with all the upheaval Spain is going through but the sun seems to burn everything into eternity, into your mind. Don't you think?'

'It's a very different land to the one I came from,' David said.

'That's the Welsh valleys, isn't it? We have a lot of good men from there. You came out in '36, didn't you?'

'Yes, not long after Christmas.'

'About the same time as myself. I was a student in London.'

'I was a shopkeeper in Wales.'

'Really, you are young for that.'

'Wasn't my shop. It came with the girl I married.'

'Oh, I see, you are married.'

'Separated now.'

'Not because of Spain?'

'No, it happened before that, before I decided to come out.'

'I see.'

They lapsed into silence and walked on.

'I've got a girl back home,' Angus said. 'I met her when I was studying. It's hard on her, me being here, and all the other women waiting for news. It's often the reason men get fed up over here, they get letters begging them to go back. It's easier for the single chaps.'

'Maybe.'

'Why do you want to go back, David?'

Angus used his first name easily.

'Don't your notes tell you why? I'm no different to the others, I'm fed up too, had enough, washed out, afraid, call it what you will. I've seen too much blood spilt for nothing. What's the phrase, "lack of moral fibre". Perhaps that's the best description.'

'No, I don't think so.'

Angus stopped by the ruin of a tree. It lay sideways in the earth, its broken branches stretching out to the horizon, like skeletal hands.

'The war does seem crazy at times,' Angus said, 'but a civil war could never be anything else, here especially. I was at Brunete. A good friend of mine was shot just in front of me. I managed to carry him back to the medics, but he was dead. That's when I got my injury. They must have shot through John and into me, his body must have saved me. Now I'm "*inutile por el frente*", as they say.'

Angus pointed to his lower back.

'Still got a piece in there, impossible to get it out, they said. A permanent momento from Franco.'

Angus was not bitter, that was what was different about him. It was a rare quality at Camp Lucas. They sat on the tree and shared tobacco. It was good stuff which David inhaled deeply, relishing the searing of lungs and throat.

'As I said when you came here, I don't believe in talks to gee people up,' Angus said. 'I think they are insulting. It seems to me that the ideals that brought men here should withstand any trial. I was tested at Brunete, greatly tested, and it was tempting to think of going home, to make reasons for doing so, tell myself it's all useless like you have done. But I don't think it is, you see. Win or lose, it isn't useless or hopeless. I believe I am on the right side and losing won't change that.'

Angus touched David's arm lightly but David looked away, out across the fields to the black specks of the peasants who dotted them. Angus continued.

'A few of the men came to see me yesterday, they want to rejoin their battalions. That chap who arrived with you, the quiet one, he was among them. It was good to hear them say they wanted to go back, it takes courage to try again I think, it proves their belief...' he paused. 'Whatever happens here now I've gained by being a part of it.'

'You are lucky then,' David said.

'Haven't you gained anything?'

'I thought I had when I was part of things, but something slipped away from me, I couldn't face killing any more. So, not much gained really.'

'This business is difficult for all of us.'

They smoked more cigarettes as flies buzzed around them.

'Only mad dogs and Englishmen would be out walking on a day like this, eh?'

'And Welshmen.'

'And Welshmen. Let's make our way back.'

Perfectly timed to match his thoughts, a letter waited for David. It was a few lines from Tom. He told of the campaign in Aragon. "Stuttering to bloody defeat we are again" he wrote. "All the plans have gone wrong here, men are dying in droves. What tanks we have are wasted in stupid advances over bad ground. We still can't seem to get things right – but we go on, David, we go on. I hope you are alright boy, and will be joining us soon. I'll see you."

David felt a flush of affection for Tom. He had not mentioned the desertion, there was no admonishment in the letter. Tom had found time to scribble something down when he was undoubtedly in danger. It was half a year since they had left the valley together, the merest fraction of time but an age for David. He was twenty, having passed secretly out of those traumatic years that a later age would dub "teenage".

David went through his retraining at the camp and listened to the talks. Outwardly he was calm but inside there was a daily struggle for self belief. He slid memories through his mind, sifting through his past and his many mistakes. Each piece of selfishness and deceit he marked no matter how painful it was. Sometimes he felt his face burn as he thought how he had been, but he kept to his task. It was his way of exorcising that part of him and coming to terms with it; David tried to lay a foundation for a better person to stand on. Emma was often in his thoughts, she became a constant memory with much guilt surrounding his vision of her. Celia's face was there also and he struggled to see through her and on to the goodness that was Emma, goodness he had so abused. The loneliness in his gut told him how precious that quality was. He knew that he did not deserve to get her back. Yet David felt the flicker of a premonition that they might be together again, one day. He struggled to keep it faint, mistrusting any optimism. Just weeks ago he had told himself Emma was over, the valley was past and that he was glad of it.

David saw himself as less of a deserter and began to accept Angus's view of the men at Camp Lucas. He never talked with Angus again to any great extent but was asked several times to act as a translator.

After six long weeks David came to a decision. He went to see Angus, who received him cordially, without surprise.

'I thought you would be along before much longer,' the commander said.

'I don't want to fight again,' David said, 'I'll never change my mind about that. But I do want to help, rejoin the battalion. I thought I might be able to help in the medical services. It was what I originally wanted, before I came out.'

'I see,' Angus said. 'Can you drive an ambulance?'

'I can't drive anything but I could help with the wounded. There were never enough stretcher bearers at Brunete, were there?'

'No. Well, it's an idea but I'm not sure what Command will think of it. You are an experienced soldier by this war's standards, they'll want you back with a gun.'

'No,' David said flatly, 'never that. A stretcher or nothing, even if I have to stay here for the duration of the war. That's what this tells me.'

He pounded his heart, *Señora* Cuesta style. Angus smiled.

'It's obvious your mind is made up. Quite an improvement on the chap who first came here. I'll see what I can do. No promises mind, I don't have much say in anything. You realise, don't you, that medics are often in more danger than the actual fighters?'

David nodded and hoped his determination showed. Angus stretched out a hand.

'So be it then. Leave it with me and I'll let you know.'

David walked to the door. 'By the way,' Angus said, 'welcome back.'

He watched David walk to the barracks, a quick, long stride that suited his frame. Angus rubbed his back and frowned. 'Don't know what training he'll get,' he muttered to himself. He went back to his tray of jumbled papers.

David's decision had been a quick one. He was grateful to Angus, the man had reached him in one gentle talk. Self-hate was gone and a sliver of self-respect was in its place, a waif inside him that he wanted to nurture. For some, Camp Lucas was a backwater filled with washed-up men, but it was a turning point for David. Angus had stood at the crossroads and pointed the way, but David was taking his own steps.

That evening he sat watching the sun's display with a few others. The Ferret sidled up to him. He had made no attempt to make good his escape. 'Why should I mate, this is easy street, ain't it?' he explained.

The Ferret no longer annoyed David for he no longer saw himself mirrored in his shifty eyes. At that moment he felt almost tenderness for a man who had nothing. He saw the Ferret for what he was, without judging, and that was enough.

Angus worked wonders; within a week of David's request he had rejoined the battalion as a stretcher bearer. It was late Autumn 1937 and they were back at Mondeja, recovering from their trials at Aragon. David met Tom on a rain-soaked October day, the first time they had seen each other for eight weeks. David shook hands with his friend with some embarrassment, but Tom greeted him warmly.

'Good to see you back David, I heard you were coming. Welcome, you poor bugger. Fancy wanting to come back to us lot of layabouts and scoundrels.' Tom looked at him closely, 'Alright now, are you boy?'

'Yes, I think so. I got your letter.'

'Aye. Wrote that in between the bullets. It was rough in Aragon.'

'When has it not been?'

The commissar came up to them. 'So there you are David, back with us again, eh? Angus has been in touch, it's a stretcher bearer for you.'

Tom scratched his head.

'Are you sure about that, Dave?'

'Yes. I've had plenty of time to think about it. It's the best thing for me I reckon, and for the battalion.'

'You know best. As long as you are back, that's the main thing. Right, let's get down to more important things: did you bring any fags with you?'

Tom led David to the sleeping quarters, where he had a bunk ready for him. David had not been grilled with questions, his comrades were extremely tolerant of men like him. That night he caught up with the news from the front. Little of it was good but David was prepared for that. Tom noticed the change in him.

'You seem a lot calmer,' he said, 'older as well.'

'Don't make an old man of me yet Tom, or I'll never be able to carry those stretchers.'

'Aye. You know how difficult that job is, don't you? It's a hell of a thing. I couldn't manage without a rifle.'

David laughed. 'I don't think that would be quite the thing Tom, dumping some poor sod off a stretcher to start shooting.'

'I'm glad to see you can joke about it. You've obviously given it a lot of thought.'

'Yes, there was plenty of time to think. You see Tom, this is an easier thing for me to do than fight, so don't worry.'

Tom did not question him further on his decision.

They sat amongst a group of recent arrivals. Tom talked to them paternally and David saw how like Billy he had become. The quiet valley blacksmith was still there but Tom led men now, and men looked to him for guidance.

David heard of the death of the Ruiz brothers.

'Poor buggers,' Tom said. 'They never had much of a chance. Dick broke cover and caught it in the guts, and Al wouldn't leave him. There was nothing we could do for Dick. We left them a packet of fags and got out of there. We were retreating.'

'So you don't know if Alphonso is dead?'

'Must be. At least I hope he is, the Moors were just behind us. I hope they shot him, you know the alternatives.'

Tom pointed to his eyes, and his crotch. He sighed. 'Good baccy this, David. So you're going to be a doctor's runner. There'll be plenty of work for you. Hey, you might meet up with that...'

Tom stopped himself, but David knew who he was going to mention. The chance of meeting Celia in his new role had crossed his mind, but he did not dwell on it. There was much to learn, without brooding about things over which he had no control.

The north of Spain fell to Franco that autumn: the enemy gained the coalfields of the Asturias and the land of the Basques. There would be no separate state for Juan Davies. In the south there was another of the strange lulls which punctuated the war. The battalion trained and retrained as winter came on, chilling the nights and tinging the mornings with frost. This time David was well prepared. He had not forgotten his frozen entry into Spain and had picked up various items in the summer. From a Czech he had scrounged a balaclava of thick black wool which stank despite repeated washing. He had numerous layers of socks and vests, and his outside trousers were baggy enough to let him wear a second pair beneath. David had little spare clothing, for he wore it all. It gave his sparse frame a solid look, yet he still suffered as the nights grew icy.

'It's going to be a corker this year, the locals say,' Tom said. 'Worse than the buggers we have back home. You haven't forgotten those mountains, have you Dave?'

'No, can't you see how much I have on?'

'Aye, I have noticed. You look like a bloody polar bear. It would take half an hour to strip that lot off.'

'I won't be doing that for a while.'

'You'll keep the bugs nice and comfy in there, anyway.'

Tom strolled off to teach the new men, a sergeant now, and happy.

David was also learning, with a handful of stretcher bearers. They were given instruction in basic things: how to carry a man on a stretcher, how to dress simple wounds and stop bleeding.

'Keep your own bodies in one piece, that's the main thing,' their sergeant told them, 'you'll be shot at by both sides sometimes, when things get confused. Those little red crosses make lovely targets, especially from the air.'

David learned what he could. His experience was appreciated by the medical corps and they made him a corporal.

The battalion was to see Aragon again. As Christmas approached Republican forces attacked Teruel, the old city of the region, a place noted throughout Spain for its melancholy air. It was another surprise move and gained an early initiative as the Republic had done a number of times before. Tom's weather forecast was correct; the winter proved appallingly bad and they moved to the battle zone through snowdrifts deeper than a man. Once again the battalion was held in reserve.

David travelled with a small medical team at the rear of the column. They would meet their nurses and doctors at the front. 'They're coming up from Madrid,' the sergeant said. As they huddled under canvas and blew on numbed hands he entertained them with tales of gore. The sergeant went into great detail about the death of a young doctor blown up at Brunete. 'Blown to bits he was. Them bastards will bomb anything from the air, don't ever forget that lads. Don't prance about in the open unless you have to.' David remembered the doctor, called Sollenburg, a brave little man who had insisted on being in the thick of the action. He had saved Tom's arm with a makeshift splint.

Many times they stopped to dig out trucks. Men cursed as they heaved at the beleaguered vehicles; each time they succeeded in getting one free they were sprayed with freezing mud which formed an extra coat on each man. The country they passed through was featureless, its contours disguised by snow.

Heavy drifts of it lay everywhere, a huge off-white blanket lit by the pale echo of a sun which gave the snow a yellow hue. David thought of the powerful god blazing down at Villanueve and wondered at the change, so different to the mildly turning seasons of the valley. When new storms hit, vision fell to a few feet and the trucks crawled through driven snow until it was impossible to go on.

David knew the weather did not favour his side. Any impetus they had gained would be slowed by the elements, and there was a danger the attack would slither and freeze to a halt. He put his hands under his arms and looked around him in the truck. There was just enough light to see his fellows, a dozen men, most under thirty, red-faced and freezing, talking with mock cheerfulness. They looked unlikely saviours as they shivered and stamped their feet.

After a slow haul the battalion arrived at Mas de las Matas, a village of stone buildings on the edge of the campaign. Here they were greeted with good news: Teruel had fallen and Republican troops occupied the city. It was the best possible Christmas present for everyone. They could celebrate the season intact, there was no immediate fighting to face. There were food parcels from home, wine was plentiful and they received a sack of mail.

Warmed by his best meal in months, David watched his comrades open their letters. This time there was nothing for him or Tom; their Christmas letters would be lying elsewhere in Spain. He made the news of others his own, searching for signs of good or bad tidings, watching the face of one light up as he read the scrawl of his kids, catching the crease of worry in another as he read that his wife was desperate for him to return from his stupid war. David saw eyes mist up, cheekbones grow mysteriously moist and men dab at them slyly, daring others to notice.

'A proper Christmas this is turning out to be,' Tom said, as tables of men smoke and drank, sending up clouds into the roof. They were billeted in the largest house in the village, that of the local landowner.

'Do you realise, David,' Tom said, 'we have been here a year, almost. What a year. What do you think they'll be doing in Conti's now? Are you thinking of your family? I would, if I had one.'

Tom drew breath and smiled into his mug. He caressed it with his large hands, tracing its cracks with his fingers and sighing as if it was alive and had a soul. 'I miss my Mary,' he said quietly.

'What did you say, Tom?' David asked. 'I couldn't hear for all this din.'

'Nothing boy, nothing. I was thinking of the village and that.'

'Me too. Funny, isn't it, how a place changes when you are far away from it. It doesn't seem so bad now, despite the troubles. I shouldn't say this, but even the likes of the Reeses and the Vincents don't seem so bad after what we've seen in Spain.'

'Better the devils you know, eh?'

'I suppose so.'

Tom lowered his voice, and ran his mug along his brow.

'Tell you what, boy,' he said. 'This must never happen back home, what we've been at here. It doesn't solve anything in the end does it, not this kind of war. The losers will always hate the victors, and where does that leave everybody? Back at square one.'

Tom topped up David's mug, then his own, though David drank little from his. He no longer needed the wine.

'I've learned a lot of things out here,' Tom said, 'you have too. It was easy to see things in black and white back home, them and us, like Billy used to. But I've had my eyes opened here a bit. I saw Karpinski when you were away – I forgot to tell you. Well there's a Russian Communist at the forefront of it all, and do you know what, he was frightened to go home, just like the German lads. Remember what he told us in Paris, about people disappearing back there? Well he reckoned he would be one of them. They're having purges of anyone Stalin thinks is a threat, or just doesn't bloody like. No better than what has happened in Germany. So what goes on, eh? That shook me.'

'Yes, poor Brylcreem. I don't know what goes on, Tom. Some would say the end justifies the means.'

'Aye, I did. But what end though? I'm not sure the workers are any happier under Uncle Joe. To me, now, it seems there's always those on top, whatever they call themselves, and there's always us crushed underneath. The frightening thing is that no matter what they say on their way up, they all seem to become the same when they give orders.'

'Maybe you are right Tom, but I thought you knew where you were going when you came out of hospital. You were a new man.'

'I am, that's the daft part of it. Being with the lads, helping each other is great, as long as you don't think of the future too much, because even if we win here I can't be confident about the final outcome.'

'Maybe only money wins wars, Tom.'

'You could always coin a good phrase, boy.' Tom drained his mug with a slurp. 'Well I don't know what the answers are but...'

'We keep going,' David finished the sentence with a salute of the hand.

'Aye, that's right,' Tom said, 'Billy would be proud of you.'

Tom slipped into drunkenness, and he had that in common with most of the men. They slumped over their tables and banished stress for a night. David thought of Karpinksi, sent home, his bulk trapped in a railway carriage. He was a free spirit gloomily foreseeing his own doom, like Yeats's airman, as he sped towards the cold east. Unlike the Russian, Tom had benefited from Spain – he needed the togetherness and the spice of danger and hardship. Perhaps that was the attraction of war, the Boys' Club gone mad, a seasonal male blood-letting, a rut for darker needs: the need to release energies trapped in factories and offices and families, the need to be free of them for a few years, or perhaps forever.

'Here Tom,' someone shouted from another table, 'save us some booze, you're like a bloody syphon.'

'Aye, I have drunk a drop, haven't I?' Tom belched with relish. 'I'll probably see Father Christmas in a minute, coming down that chimney.' He pointed to the vast fireplace, hewn out of rock, and long disused until now.

'Nah, it'll be a Moor, Tom, come to cut off your nuts.'

Men awoke to join the laughter, they were all in good heart. A solid meal, messages from loved ones; simple things, but enough to change a mood completely.

Outside the weather grew steadily worse, touching them all with its cold. When it eased they would be called into the battle, David had no doubt; they would fight and die in weather so oppo-site to Brunete. He was a figure of fun now, with his layers of clothing, but he did not mind. They would be needed. The wind howled through Mas de las Matas and David shivered, despite the heat of the room. The party broke up and men stumbled to their corners. It would be the battalion's last celebration in Spain.

In the next few days David learned what extra he could about medical matters. Skin diseases became part of his life. 'Try to stop them scratching' was the sergeant's motto, as most were affected. Scratches turned to sores, then to congealed scabs as dirty fingers probed. It was as if the whole battalion had a layer of pus under its surface, waiting to break out and suppurate. Men tried to delouse themselves by putting their clothes outside for the lice to freeze, but some always survived. Treating sores was all David had to do for a week, until the enemy counter-attacked.

They were ordered up on New Year's Eve, to dig in on one of the slopes of Sierra Palomera, a mountain as high as any in Wales. Teruel was set among crags, approached by treacherous roads, often with sheer drops on one side. They tried to dig holes in the iron hard earth but could not get any depth. 'Just enough to bury your head in,' said one man, 'like them big birds in Africa.'

Attack came immediately from the air, and the Brunete sequences began again. To survive, a routine of moving out of their holes at night to any building they could find was soon devised. This enabled the men to withstand the cold. In the morning they slipped back to their positions. There was no risk of a night attack, when the sun went down no-one could do anything but shelter. There were occasional casualties from long range sniping, but the weather forbade full scale fighting.

In another attempt to keep the cold at bay David wore a blanket with a slit in it for his head. He moved yeti-like through the snow and others envied his protection and wished they had collected like him in the summer. David was assigned a stretcher with another man, an Englishman called Jackson who came from a Lancashire mill town. Jackson was under fire for the first time and ducked every time he heard a shot, just as David once had. Their first customers were men shot by stray rounds, or picked off by snipers. The mountain was a good place for men to shoot each other secretly. David and Jackson carried the wounded over frozen tracks to a makeshift hospital set up close to the lines.

As the weather did not relent the enemy attacked anyway, probing the Republican positions in strength. The battalion came under increasingly heavy artillery fire; they were being softened up but they held their position and hid the best they could in their shallow holes. David was not so fortunate. His job was to brave the open on the trek back to the field hospital. Every time a shell came over, Jackson hunched his shoulders and jolted their wounded charge. One man suffered particularly in this way. He was gut-shot and screamed every time they bumped him. David watched his face from the back of the stretcher, to see if life would run out of it. The man's face was whiter than the snow they trudged through, and a thin trail of blood had frozen on his chin. David did not tell Jackson that few survived stomach wounds in Spain.

'Go easy with this one, Jackson,' David shouted, 'for Christsake.'

16

A small operating theatre was housed in an old farm building, dangerously close to the action. This was where they took the wounded. Inside the temperature was not much higher than zero and the only source of heat was alcohol, which was burnt in tins. The place reeked of it, searing David's lungs each time he stumbled in with a new load. They took nine men there in the first two days of fighting; three died on the way, the others took their chance under the surgeon's knife. A few would survive, to go home, or to fight again. Each time he helped save a life David felt those he had taken on the Jarama and Villanueve were offset a little.

On the fourth day of 1938 David needed treatment himself. His hands had frozen to the handles of the stretcher and were mildly frostbitten. He sat on a stool in the hospital waiting for someone to see them, cursing himself for his carelessness. He had taken off his gloves for just a few minutes to search in his pockets, and that had been long enough to punish them. He huddled as near as he could to a tin of smoking fuel, a pool forming under him.

'Are you the one with the frozen hands?' a nurse said to him.

David jumped at the voice, it was so like Celia's; every visit to the hospital she had been in his mind. But he turned to see another woman looking down at him. This nurse was similar only in voice, but that was enough to bring it all flooding back.

'Well, are you the one?' the nurse said. 'I haven't got all day.'

'Yes, I've got trouble with them.'

David held up his hands. She looked at them and scolded. 'You should never have exposed them. Still, not too much damage done.'

David sat still as the nurse probed his hands. Slowly, feeling was returning to them. They started to glow with pain and he was glad the balaclava hid his wincing face. She put a salve on his hands and bandaged them up, leaving the fingers free.

'You won't be able to carry a stretcher for a while, try to keep them out of the cold.'

'How do I do that?'

'Sorry, I know it's impossible. Well, keep them in your pockets as much as possible.' She stared at him and tapped his head. 'I suppose this thing is to keep you warm as well, is it?' She lowered her voice. 'It's a bit smelly you know. Take it off, you're warming up now.'

David took the balaclava off and returned the nurse's stare. She shared Celia's determination, but that was all. This one was dark-haired, round-faced and kindly. She busied herself with her tray of bandages, looking at him all the time.

'You were in Madrid, weren't you? Visiting at the hospital?'

'How do you know that? Yes, I had a friend who was treated there.'

'Yes, I thought so. I saw you there a few times. I was stationed there a few months.'

There was a silence. She must know Celia, David thought. Don't ask.

The nurse seemed embarrassed, she fussed over his hands, pinning the bandages together. His hands felt as if they were gloved.

'I'm very sorry,' the nurse said.

'What?'

'I'm very sorry. I know you spent some time with Celia Kadle, she told me about it. It was awful, an awful thing to happen.'

David looked at her in amazement, surely Celia wouldn't have...

'It happened not long after, didn't it? I was in the hospital. We thought we were going to cop it at first, the bomb fell so near. Then we heard in the morning, they had flattened Celia's area. She was one of three we lost, two nurses and a doctor, a friend of Celia's, funnily enough. We were all terribly upset.'

David just looked at her.

'I'm sorry,' she said, 'perhaps I shouldn't have brought it up again, there's so much of it here...' She saw the look on David's face. 'Oh God, you did know, didn't you?'

'Yes, of course, we heard about it,' David said. 'I'm a bit tired...'

'You've got the job for it. Stay here for an hour or so, get warmed right through, if that's possible with these tin things. Good luck out there.' She carried her tray off to another room.

The throb of his hands mixed with shock. David sat as still as he could, lest he fall off the stool. Celia dead. He did not know what he felt: numbness, despair, even anger, were all present in him. It made his time with her even more of a dream. He thought of that room with the curtain, and the blast striking. He hit his hands together and almost fainted with the pain; he hit them again, then was calm.

David stepped into the night, struggling to put his headgear on with his thickened fingers. Emma's face came floating into his mind like calm waters, and stubbornly stayed there. The news of Celia brought awareness as sharp as the frost. Emma had offered the sweetness of life, and he had seen dull responsibility and chains. It was he who had been bound, how well he knew it now. David walked back to his unit with blazing hands and mind, sad, but light in spirit. Love cuts death short, he had read somewhere, and he wanted to believe it now.

He had little time to dwell on Emma or Celia as the fighting escalated. The enemy still had pockets of troops in the centre of Teruel which Republican forces tried to winkle out, before Franco sent reinforcements. The battalion was positioned on cliffs overlooking the river. Tom was in charge of a machine-gun, David was part of one of the few stretcher units in the hills.

'By Jesus, it's cold,' Tom said, as David joined him in his dug-out, a cave where twenty men sheltered. 'They fixed your hands up alright then, Dave,' Tom said.

David held them up for inspection.

'I bet a nice little nurse did that for you,' one man muttered, in hope.

'These guns are going to be no good,' Tom said, giving the Maxim a boot, 'the bolt freezes every time we put it back in. Must be hot down there, though.'

Tom gestured towards Teruel which was lit by gunflashes and the occasional flare. Smoke hung over the city, and it gleamed through it dully like a badly polished jewel.

'They are keeping us back here,' Tom said, 'we're in reserve again. Remember when we all used to moan about that, eh? Don't hear anyone doing that now, we're all too bloody wise – anyway this place isn't worth fighting over.'

'What do you mean?'

'I was talking to one of the Spanish lads, comes from round

this way. He said there is nothing there, it has no strategic value just a useless old town in a barren hunk of land. The commissar says we are trying to draw Franco away from other places, but I don't know. Seems we are always fighting over useless objectives, like we did in the big one.'

'Ideas can be fought over anywhere, Tom, I don't think the place matters anymore.'

'Maybe, but it's good to have some results you can see, touch, feel, hold in your bloody hand. That's what the ordinary bloke wants.'

'At least we've captured a biggish town.'

'That's right boy, keep cheering me up – and there's the chance to kill more Fascists.'

The enemy was determined in his attempt to retake Teruel and the battalion advanced under heavy shell fire to counter the threat, descending from the heights they occupied, using the ruins of shattered buildings as cover. David dressed the wounds of many men before his small bag of supplies ran out. He worked in dense fog made worse by the smoke of battle. It was an eery atmosphere as David found himself in the town's bull-ring with Jackson. They had lost touch with their comrades as they stopped to help a dying soldier.

'God, this is an awful place,' Jackson said, 'it's as if all hell has broken loose and come here.'

David pulled him lower. 'Keep down while this stuff is going over, dead stretcher bearers are no good to anyone.'

They sheltered against the bloated carcass of a horse. The cold had turned it to iron and it lay like a toppled statue, lips frozen back from its mouth giving it a mocking grin. Shells fell close to them, shaking the ground.

'We can't stay here,' Jackson shouted, 'let's go back.'

'Go back where?' David said. He pointed to the dense fog around them. 'Do you know the way out?'

Tom and their unit had disappeared some time ago; they were isolated and David knew his partner was feeling the urge to run. He sympathised with him, remembering only too well that feeling in himself. His own gut was tight and he was afraid and jittery, but he had stopped running. He did not know where his new strength came from but he welcomed it, it was a comfort.

'Best move on a bit,' David said, 'see if we can find the others.'

As they did so the ground behind shattered from a shell burst, scattering pieces of horse into the sky, and over them.

'That was almost us,' Jackson cried, as they stumbled forward.

They found Tom and his men sheltering up ahead.

'Where have you been?' Tom said, 'I thought you had bought it back there. Try to keep up David.' Tom was angry and relieved. 'Look, there's lads bad hurt here.'

Two men lay on the ground, bloody and unconscious. One was beyond any help they could give, the other's legs hung like sticks from his waist, lacerated with shrapnel.

'A shell landed on the wall they were hiding behind,' Tom said.

They laid the man on the stretcher.

'Go back through the bullring, the way we came,' Tom said. 'There will be people coming up to meet you, they are bringing up a mobile surgery. Just keep walking as straight as you can, away from the shells.'

They carried their charge back as steadily as they could, but Jackson's hands were shaking freely.

'Keep the stretcher steady, mate,' David yelled at him, 'or we'll never bloody get there.'

He knew Jackson was on the point of cracking. Stretcher bearers had a special torment, they had to walk upright under fire presenting slow-moving targets that the most cock-eyed of Spaniards had a chance of hitting. In a city there was the added risk from shrapnel and falling debris. Jackson was going over a thousand possible deaths as he walked.

As they got further back the firing lessened and David relaxed a little. 'We're out of the worst of it now, Jackson. Keep your pecker up.'

It was the last thing Jackson ever heard. The stretcher lurched suddenly and they were over. The wounded man groaned as he was tipped into the snow, and David swore loudly as his shins grated against rubble.

'What happened?' he shouted, 'did you fall?'

Jackson did not answer. He lay a few feet from David, in a pose that suggested sleep. David knew that pose, and knew Jackson was dead before he turned him over. A bullet had shattered the base of his skull, probably an errant round looking for no-one in particular. Shock was in Jackson's eyes, frozen there in a split second of realisation that he was killed. Warm blood seeped through David's gloves as he lay Jackson back on the ground.

The wounded man was still conscious. 'What's going on?' he asked, through gritted teeth.

'My mate has caught it, but don't worry, I'll get you back, somehow.'

David tied the man to the stretcher with Jackson's scarf, then pulled it, Red Indian style. He tried to shut his ears to the groaning that went on behind him, and stopped whenever it stopped, to check if the man was still alive. His will to live was strong, the man clung to the thread of life tenaciously, enduring jolt after jolt.

David made ground very slowly, but was not under fire. The action was in the distance, where he had left Tom. The noise of war came through the fog in bursts, harsh cadences of gunfire and the heavier boom of explosions. He stopped to shelter against a wall and tried to light a cigarette. The wind snuffed out each match the instant it flared, so he gave his charge the unlit cigarette, sticking it through his frozen lips. They set off again, David pulling the stretcher along the most even course he could find. Teruel was full of echoes, of gunfire, burning buildings, falling masonry. It was a fitting place to perish in.

David found his surgery, after two hours of plodding. He saw a red cross painted on a door and stumbled through a heavy curtain into the arms of a startled orderly.

'I've a wounded man outside,' he said, 'if you'd care to get him in.' He felt hands reaching for him as he sank down to the floor.

David came to on a heap of sacks which someone had placed under him. A man stood over him with a mug of steaming liquid in his hand. He took it gratefully.

'You passed straight out mate, we thought you had been hit until we realised you were just knackered.'

'How's that chap I brought in?'

'Didn't make it. We had to take his legs off, and the shock was too much. Never mind, old son, you did your best, eh?'

David drank his tea and said nothing.

'Was he a friend of yours?' the medic asked.

'No, I didn't know him, just another customer.'

The man shrugged and turned to go, then the obvious question hit him. 'Eh, where's your oppo then, how are you on your own?'

'Jackson, my partner, got it back there, shot through the head.'

'Good Lord, I'll have to report that. Do you know where your unit is?'

'Don't be stupid. Out there somewhere, the same as everyone else.'

'Right. Drink that now, and rest up.'

David drank the tea and went back out onto the streets before anyone could stop him. He knew he was stupid to do so, night was falling, rubbing out the few bearings he had, and the whereabouts of friend and enemy were changing all the time, but he felt he had to find Tom, and his unit.

He walked a few hundred yards in the direction he had travelled with the stretcher. He knew where the bullring lay, so he headed for that, in the hope he would meet up with someone. David stopped to light a cigarette, sheltering against a wall riddled with bullet holes. This time he managed it. He cupped his success in his hands and dragged in smoke, lighting up the pock marks of the wall with his glow. Next to him an apartment block was carved in two, sliced down the middle like a cheese. A bicycle hung crazily from the third floor, as if it was trying to find solid ground again for its buckled wheels. From another room a double bed protruded, twirling its sheets to the ground at David's feet.

David stubbed out his smoke on the wall and made to move on, but was stopped by a challenge. '*Quien es?*' was hissed at him from an alleyway. His hands reached instinctively for the rifle he no longer had and he tasted iron again. He did not know who asked the question, so did not answer.

'*Quien es?*' the voice came again, this time accompanied by the sound of rifle bolts being drawn. David thrust his arms into the air and prayed they would respect the red cross. Five men came out of the alleyway and clustered around him. He talked to them rapidly in Spanish, and this increased their suspicion. One prodded him with a bayonet, making him close his eyes, in anticipation of the plunge.

I am going to die, he thought, stupidly and uselessly.

'I am a *camarada*, a *medico*,' he said, as strongly as he could. There was a silence and he wondered why they didn't shoot him.

'You have papers?' one asked. David fumbled for identification with fingers that took a lifetime to work. Each second boomed in his head and his back crawled with cold sweat, but he managed to hold out his papers to the questioner. The man stepped forward and snatched them away, then held them up to the light of a smouldering building. David saw the Popular Army insignia on his overcoat.

'*Si, si, camarada*,' the man said. He waved a hand and the others lowered their rifles. David leant firmly against the wall, afraid he would fall down if he left it.

'What are you doing here, *Ingles*, where is your unit?' David waved his hands in a very Spanish gesture of ignorance, then explained his situation. The Spanish troops listened, nodded and flung forward wildly conflicting ideas of what David should do, and the direction he should take.

'The city is dangerous,' their sergeant said, 'the situation changes all the time. We ourselves do not know where the *fascistas* are. We hear their shells, but shoot at shadows. Teruel is a place of shadows, and death.'

'Why not come with us?' another suggested, 'we need doctors too.' David was tempted by the comfort of numbers but refused.

'No, comrades, I must find my own people.'

The Spaniards shrugged and bade him '*Salud*'.

'You were lucky, English,' the sergeant called back as they left, 'we would have shot you for sure, without questions, if you had been armed.'

David went forward again, through the streets of a quieter Teruel. The shelling had ceased, but smoke hung acrid in the air. Abandoned houses cracked and sighed as they settled to their new shapes. Teruel had become a symbol of the whole war; the grin of the dead horse was the perfect masque of death – even the abnormal cold derided a saner Spain. David walked through a place that Torquemada could have designed, and approved.

The night brought temperatures down to new depths. It was vital that David found a decent shelter, for he could not find Tom. He scanned every likely opening as he passed, but they were all hopelessly bombed out. In the second hour of darkness the shelling began again, incredibly, insanely. What were they firing at in this blind night, he wondered. Any wise rat would be tucked away safe, he was the only one on the streets.

A building fell apart on David's right, showering him with dust and bricks. He sank to the floor, groggy with the blast. Cold and exhaustion kept him there. They are firing at me, he thought, as consciousness drifted away from him, the whole world is firing at me. A voice inside said 'you'll die if you sleep, die if you sleep'. The black shroud of the sky hung over him, shot through with pretty colours.

There was a roaring in David's head, like a wild sea dashing itself on rocks. He was carried with it, swirling along with the white horses, and there was someone shouting at him, pulling him back with brutal force, pulling him back to Teruel. He was being kicked. David came to, and saw the figures hovering over him, he heard guttural Spanish barked at him. His vision cleared, a thin face looked down at him, its nose like a dagger. It was the face of Spain's old enemy. David had fallen into the hands of Moors.

He had no doubt he was going to be killed. Ice tingled on his spine, he hoped they would finish him quickly, no more than that. As he braced himself for a bullet Emma flashed into his mind, then Helen, the Tump, Conti's, all crowded into a few seconds, but the bullet did not come. They pulled him to his feet, like children who had found something tiny to torture. They stood around him, jackal-like, wiry men with eyes the colour of the night. One pulled out a butcher's knife and David thought of a Spanish boy he had seen near Villanueve, wandering with gouged out eyes.

'I'm English,' he said weakly, 'not Spanish. *Extranjero, extranjero.*'

The man raised his knife but someone pushed him away. They had been joined by an officer.

'English, eh?' he murmured. He searched David whilst two Moors twisted back his arms. Another held a bayonet against his side, anxious to fillet him like a fish. David sensed him waiting for just the slightest flicker of approval from the officer.

The officer found David's papers, and for the second time that night they were examined. David cursed himself for not going with those Republican troops. He was fully alert and thinking now, thinking of anything that might delay his death. The officer took off his leather gloves.

'So, International Brigade. A volunteer, a Red come to destroy *España.*'

He spoke in English, a clipped accent. David could taste the salt of his blood as it trickled from his mouth. The officer shouted a command to the Moors and they moved out rapidly, dragging

David along with them. Whenever he faltered they kicked him in the ribs, but he lived.

David was taken to a building half a mile away, where soldiers milled around, setting up a command post, he guessed. He tried to stay conscious, knowing that his life depended on this. Being a foreigner had saved him back in the street, he was sure of that. They hauled him through doors and down steps to a cellar, where he was flung face down on the floor. He was locked in and left. He lay still for some time, listening for footsteps, but no-one came. His body was one collective pain but he did not think anything was broken. It was not just the cold his layers of clothing had saved him from. David let sleep take him, surprised how easily it came.

He did not know if it was night or day when he woke. There were others in the cellar with him now, he heard them groaning and shuffling in the dark, but he could not see them. No chink of light penetrated his prison, and it was as cold as death. He rubbed stiff joints, and tried to keep his thoughts warm, at least, not knowing whether he wanted anyone to come or not. He thought of those rare summer days on the Tump, the fire in his mother's parlour, and Conti's stove, ordinary things that were wondrous now. Muffled sounds of war filtered down to the cellar, sometimes the room shook, and he heard the whine of shells going over. Teruel was being fought over once again.

As a stretcher bearer it had not occurred to David that he might be captured. To be shot and killed, those fears were always present, but falling into the hands of the enemy, that had been beyond his pessimism. And now they held him. He tried to work out how many hours had gone by when the cellar door was thrown open and light flooded down the steps, blinding his eyes. He screwed them up and glanced around him for a moment, and saw four other prisoners, all Spanish, and all wretched.

'Which one is *Heecks*?' the guard called out. He filled the doorway with his outline, black against the light.

David roused himself and got to his feet stiffly, stifling a gasp of pain as his body protested.

'Ah, *si*, there you are, *Heecks*.' The guard hissed the name with contempt. David stepped forward as resolutely as he could. As he neared the steps a second guard reached out and yanked him up by his hair. There must have been a wound on the back of his head, for he felt it begin to bleed. This annoyed the Spaniard; he wiped the blood off his hand on David's coat, and dug his fist into his side a few times.

David tried to retain consciousness as he was dragged out of the cellar, but it was difficult. His wound, hunger, cold, and ultimate capture, had drained his vitality to a faint spark. He gritted his teeth as he was pulled up several floors. He wanted to live. This flooded through him, pushing all his past life into perspective. He concentrated on this one thought, he wanted to live.

They got to street level and stopped outside the double doors of a room. The guards rapped on these and waited for an answer. A voice from inside said 'come', and David was pushed into the room, to face a man sat behind a desk. He wore a bright uniform, with pince nez on his nose.

'Ah, the Englishman, yes?'

He motioned David to a chair, and the guard pushed him into it. The pain in his head seared and the floor moved in front of him. The officer made a clicking sound with his tongue, as if he was trying to flick something from his mouth.

'You are wounded, I see. No matter. So, the International Brigade.' He fingered David's papers. 'A Welshmen. I know that country. You are a long way from your home, *señor*. You are a Communist, no?'

David did not answer. He kept his eyes focused on the edge of the desk. It was ornate, with intricately carved legs that looked too slender to support it.

'*Si*, you are a Red, you all are. And so young. How long have you been in my country, *señor*?' He spoke slowly, picking at his hands with a file. They were well manicured hands, used to giving orders. David felt the guard closing in on him but the officer waved him away.

'We don't want unpleasantness, do we? Leave that for others, it is tiresome, and messy. Besides, there will be much of it coming your way, later.' He paused and got up, walking to the window. 'Listen, Hicks. Teruel is peaceful, you have lost it, as you have lost the war. It's only a matter of time now, soon *España* will be rid of your kind, the dregs of my country will be cleared out, once and for all. We will be great again, we will have another golden age.'

David saw a pink-faced little man, with a waxed moustache, in a tin soldier's uniform, dreaming of Armadas, conquistadors, and the Inquisition. Suddenly he felt pity for this one who had the power of life and death over him. Beneath the fervour he sensed fear, and hysteria not faith, tyranny not courage.

'You are running away like rats,' the officer said, 'and those we have trapped in Teruel will be hunted down like rats, for that is what you are, rats without God and without victory. How could He let you have *España*?'

As David's diminutive questioner walked around his chair he lashed out with his ringed hand, a cobra-like strike that split David's cheek. It burnt but he did not cry out, he was too exhausted to waste precious breath. The officer kept walking, as if unaware of his action. It was the gut deed of a man not in control of himself, and this made David strong. This man was twisting on his own hatred, a caricature of it, and a prisoner just as much as David; more so, for he would never have the chance to escape. David had the centre stage, not him, and he had not uttered a word.

The officer drew close to him again, and David braced himself for another blow, but it did not come.

'Be silent, *señor*, I do not mind. Soon you will know the error of your ways, we will teach you.' He beckoned to the guard and David was jerked up again. The interview was over – though in fact it had been a one-sided monologue rather than an interview. Torture must lie ahead. The guard took him back to the cellar, where he resumed his place against the wall, and resumed his freezing. The wind screeched over Teruel, like a thousand curlews crying at once. It was a desolate sound, as bleak as David's future.

At least they had not killed him. He tried to hang on to this thought, to convince himself that it was a good thing, yet images of mediaeval tortures loomed in his mind. They appeared easily in his Spanish dungeon. He wished he had never read Poe. After some time one of the other prisoners talked to him.

'My name is Miguel Rivera, comrade,' he told David softly, in Spanish. David shook the hand that reached out for him.

'David,' he answered, 'David Hicks.'

'Are you German?'

'No, Welsh.'

There was a pause.

'British?'

'Yes. Like English.' How that explanation would gall the Boys.

'Ah, *si, Inglés*. I have been here for three days, I think. It was my first battle, but I did not kill any *fascistas*.'

Miguel was young, younger than David, a baker's assistant from Madrid. He was impressed with the presence of a foreigner, it lessened his loneliness.

'Will they kill us?' Miguel asked. David felt his panic rise with the question.

'No,' David said, 'why should they do that?'

'I am not a member of anything,' Miguel said eagerly, 'they made me fight. My father did not want it. It's nothing to do with us, he said, stay here and make bread, he said, let that be your war effort. But they made me come, to this place of death, of *el diablo*. I don't belong to anything.'

'You must tell them that.'

'I did, but they just beat me.'

No-one else spoke in the cellar. Miguel fell silent, and each man waited for his fate to walk through the door. Thoughts and fears worked away at them in the darkness. They lay like beasts in an abattoir, scenting death but hoping they were wrong. David knew he would be missed by now; he hoped Tom would not think he had deserted again.

David was kept in the cellar for several days. A few times the iron door was opened, and a jug of filthy water placed on the floor. Around it they scattered pieces of bread. On what David thought was the third day one of the Spaniards died, quietly, in the corner. He heard the last struggle for air, and the death rattle in the throat as the final gasp escaped, and the absolute silence that always followed. David wished he had spoken to the man. No-one should have to suffer such a solitary end, but they were all close to it, and past talking.

When the guard came with the water David told him, and the body was dragged out. It was the widest the door had been opened. David saw Miguel, the frightened baker's boy, and two others, older men bloodied like himself. These had not said a word, they just stared ahead of them, at unknown devils.

David set his thoughts as far back from the present as he could. All memories were sweet, for they came from a time when death was just a faint spot on a distant horizon. He was still not twenty-one, an age when youth should laugh at death. He understood those ants on the Brunete plain. Their lives were short, so why should they not rush through them? Time, or the lack of it, gave them order, and purpose.

They came for David on the fourth night. He was taken up the stairs into light which made his head whirl. He wanted to fall but dared not, for they would kick him until he got up, or was dead. They took him to the same room, but this time it was a different officer. This one was large and square jawed, very different to the tin soldier. He looked like a pugnacious beagle.

'So, the English. Not much more than a boy, if you take away the face fuzz.' This man spoke in Spanish. 'You speak our language, I think.'

Thin bile escaped from David's stomach, if there had been any more there he would have spewed it out over the desk.

'*Si*, you are frightened, my little rabbit. Did you think the likes of you could stand against the *Generallisimo*?' Like the other one this officer ended his sentences in questions he did not need answering. He thrust his face at David, dog-like. His breath smelt of garlic, and malice. 'I think you must talk to me,' he said.

This time David did so. Silence had taken him as far as it would.

'You have my papers, so you know my name, where I come from. I am a stretcher bearer, in the International Brigade, a non-combatant.'

'Hah, the rabbit talks. A stretcher bearer, any coward could say that. I think you are a killer who is too afraid to say so.'

'I wore a red cross. Anyway, does it make any difference?'

His interrogator smiled, and clicked his knuckles. He lit a black cigar, striking the match on the sole of his polished boot.

'You are a criminal against the true Spain, against the *Generallisimo*, against God.' He raised his eyes upwards. 'This is punishable by death.'

'I was a stretcher bearer.'

'You are against us, you have committed treasonable acts, you are lucky to be alive now, Englishman.' The man's face turned the colour of ripe plum, and he showered David with tobacco spittle as he leant on his shoulder. 'Put all hope out of your mind. You will be shot, there is no doubt of it, and no escape.'

Despite his preparation for it, the news of David's fate fell like a hammer against his sense. He struggled to keep his voice steady and his face blank.

'You can't shoot me,' he said, 'not without a trial. There are rules, even here.'

'Rules? Rules for you? You should have thought of this before you came to Spain, to kill. And who knows you are here?

David began to say something else but the guard cuffed him off the chair. He sprawled on the floor, too weak to rise.

'You see, rabbit, you have no strength, no will. You have nothing. You will be taken to a place we have for your kind, until it is time. It might be a few days, or weeks. We are very busy with so many to deal with. Take him back.'

The guards frogmarched David away. He doubted if he would survive to face a firing squad.

17

His last night in the cellar was spent alone, there was no sign of Miguel and the others. David was certain of their fate. From the moment they had taken him out of the cellar he expected to join them, first against a street wall or in an obscure field, but they brought him to a new place, a prison to the north of the city. It was a low slab of a building, old and slit-windowed, like San Fernando.

They thrust him through a doorway and helped him on his way with a few kicks. He fell into a room filled with men. There were several hundred, heaped around the floor, some living on top of each other. David gagged at the stink which rose to meet him. He tried to breathe as lightly as possible, until it no longer troubled him; until he was part of it.

Faces looked up at him but he did not recognise any of them. A tattered man made a space for him and he flopped down into it as the door clanged shut behind him. This place was no warmer than the cellar, despite the many bodies. Here the wind whipped through the slits, but it was lighter. David was able to look around him; he was in a charnel house. Many men here were badly wounded, dying before their captors could do the job. 'Welcome, comrade,' said the tattered man.

David's first night was a nightmare filled with the cries of despair of the men around him. It was never silent. Someone would start moaning and another would take it up, until it passed around the room in a pathetic chain of suffering. It was as if the prison had one collective soul to which each man contributed in his turn. In the morning a number of bodies were removed. 'They have cheated the *fascistas*,' the tattered man said. 'That is good.'

When the dead were removed a pile of mouldy bread and a large urn of water were deposited on the floor. A few frozen vegetables floated in the urn. Those who could crawl to the food shared it with the inert. Word spread that there was an 'English' among them. David was the only foreigner here. He began to talk to José, the tattered man, who was from Figueras, another proud

Catalan, with a hint of gypsy in his features.

'Did they say they will shoot you?' José asked. 'Si, me too. All of us they say they will shoot. But you, my friend, they cannot do it. You are an English, they will be afraid.'

'I do not think so,' David said. 'And why should I be treated differently to you? We share the same cause and fight.'

'*Si*, but not the same country. You are not Spanish, it would not be right to shoot you, it would not be polite.'

In the icy gloom of their cell David discussed many things with José; they became friends. In the nights they hugged each other for warmth, as all the prisoners did. At first this was hard for David, but his reserve was broken down by the proximity of death, and the respite of a little heat from José's body. It occurred to him that for the first time he was really sharing himself with someone, a Spaniard he could barely see, who was covered in filth.

This was when they talked most, locked in each other's arms like lovers. José had a wife and two children in Barcelona. He described them in minute detail.

'That is the worst thing, comrade,' José said. 'I know I will never see them again, I knew it as soon as I was taken. Conchita will not know if I am alive or dead, every day she will expect me to come home, every night her worries will begin afresh.'

'They have your name here, José. There will be a record.'

'I don't think you know, comrade, how many of us they have shot. Very many. Very many. You have a woman, in your country?'

'Yes, a wife.' David did not want to disappoint José. He was not the kind of man who would understand separation, and David wanted to link himself to Emma, he realised.

'What is her name, your woman?'

'Emma.'

'Emma. *Si, es buena.*'

David told José about the valley and the lives of the people there, his people, he called them. It was a solace to do so, it gave him kinship with the valley and put a seal on the feeling that had been growing for months. David experienced loneliness blended with the loss of belonging, yet felt he had never belonged to his community more than in this dismal hole.

A man can only be threatened by death so many times, and David learned not to flinch when they received the evening visit.

Each night an officer came to them and read out six names, the ones to be executed in the morning. This man was their harbinger of death; he loved his role and played it well. His voice was sonorous, it rang out like a girl's as it savoured each name mouthed. The officer searched the room as men answered, some defiantly, some calmly and sadly, with the resignation of brave men doomed. Once a name had to be repeated into the silent room until a man was found to match it. This one cowered against the wall and tried to deny his presence in the ruthless play. 'Please, please,' he wailed, 'I have done nothing, why me, why me?' They let him cry on for several minutes, letting his noise work on nerve-ends. Then he was silenced with a rifle butt. It was the only victory the officer had.

'*Pobrecito*,' José murmured, 'it is hard for some to wait like this, there is too much time for thought. A bullet in battle is sudden, a man should not fear that so much, but this...'

José leant away from David and spat into the darkness. Someone swore out of it and José whispered apologies.

'Why did you come to Spain?' he asked. 'What did you know about us?'

'Not much. I read some books, and talked to others.'

'Ah, books. *Si*.'

'I wanted to help. The poor struggle in my country too, but not like here. They have it better, for they have fought longer, perhaps. But like here it is the few who decide, and they do not decide for the poor.'

'You are right, comrade. You dream also, eh?'

'Why do you say that?'

'You see the easy side of it. I am not very poor, the government is not run by poor men. Negrin, Caballero, all of them, they are not poor. And they would not give everything away, no-one wants to return to nothing. They deal in words, fine words, speeches that we all listen to, words that change little, in the end.'

'Do you say we are wrong to fight?'

'No. There was no other way, but then I did not expect much with victory. In Barcelona, in '36, it was beautiful. You could feel the heart of the people beat in the streets, one great, simple heart that felt things clearly, together for once. When we took to the Ramblas many thought things would be swept away forever, but not I, comrade. I saw the bosses go, *si*, and the police, but more came. They were from our side but, I don't know, there is something about a man who controls other men, it changes him. And soon we fought each other.'

'I heard about that.'

'*Si*. After that time I knew it would be no different to other times. I am glad we fought, never doubt that, and if we may yet win it will be better for my people, but there will be no paradise, no heaven on Spanish earth. This killing makes me see it clearly. Change for Spain is like a snake trying to glide up a wall of glass. First it gets a little way up, then it slithers back, always forward and back.'

'You speak wisely, José.'

'Maybe – or foolishly, it is all the same, no, in the end.'

José laughed, a low gurgle in the throat that made him quiver. David laughed with him, not knowing why.

José spoke without despair and was not burdened with hate. He had done his best for his side in the war and was satisfied with that. It was all a man could do. David understood that now, and much more. The nightly visits of the officer were powerful stimulants to knowledge. The knowing of himself grew each time the names of the doomed were read out, honed and distilled by the spirit of the men with him.

David watched the sky change through a slit in the wall, a blue piece became a fragment of cloud, a dash of winter sun, or black thunder-clouds. It was a salve to his senses, and a personal window on a world all but taken from him. He looked back on the valley through this slit. Each day spent in his hole made his home more attractive, a place that nurtured, not enchained. Breathing the foetid air of his fellows, and lying in his own filth, he felt free inside.

They called José's name on the fifth day. David knew it was the fifth for he had five marks on the floor in front of him. A piece of stone had served as a chisel, and each morning he chipped another line. José stiffened against him for a moment as his name rang out, then he relaxed.

'José Francisco Martinez, which are you?'

The officer's voice probed the cell, cajoling, mocking. José raised a hand and the guards came over to him, marking his face and position.

'At seven, Martinez,' the officer said.

David dared not say anything to his short-lived friend.

'Don't be so sad, my friend,' José said, 'it had to be. I will make a path for you to follow, if they decide to be impolite. I grieve for Conchita and the little ones, but for myself...'

With this José fell asleep calmly, his head resting on David's chest.

David wept silently for José, and Billy, and McCormick and Danny, for all of them, for Emma and Celia, his father, the valley, even the Vincents. Love was being prised out of him and he gave it freely to José, as he had never given it to those who had reached out for him.

José filed out with the others in the morning. Two men had to be helped. José turned for a brief glance back at David picking him out from the sea of watching faces. Their eyes met, José's bright and full of fire as they caught the light from the door. They said '*adios*, comrade'. David nodded his head and looked away.

There was a wait of fifteen minutes before a rifle fusillade rang out, followed by a single pistol shot. It was the most forlorn sound David had ever heard, an echo of the first ragged volley. It sounded like paper being torn quickly. The men in the cell were taut, straining for this moment. After a minute they relaxed audibly, expelling air, coughing and murmuring, like a throng dismissed from church.

If one listened carefully enough, it was possible to hear the whine of the bullets as they chipped into the prison wall, passing through men on their way. David could not prevent himself from doing this. He heard a man shout this time, in praise of the Republic, and hoped it was José. Someone passed him a piece of bread and said 'José was a brave man.' David chewed mechanically, and answered yes.

The bodies would lie outside, stiffening with frost and death. Eventually they were carted off to some field, where they would be buried in unmarked trenches, still clutching each other, as they had in prison.

New captives joined them, bringing bad news. It was true, the enemy had retaken Teruel, in the last week of February. The Republic was on the retreat once more. David found he could no longer keep down what food he was given, his stomach rebelled against it, and in a fever he drifted in and out of consciousness. Any attempt at sanitation was impossible. Within a few days, he lay covered in the faeces of the men around him, and his own.

Sometimes he walked the ridge in the valley, making things right with Emma. Sometimes Billy was with him, telling him 'it won't be long now, boy, and it's nice here'. Once he tried to get up to follow his uncle, treading on the man next to him, who pulled him back down. 'There is nowhere to go, comrade,' the man said. 'They will shoot you for sure if they see you are sick.' It did not feel so cold anymore. David was used to being frozen, it was fine being frozen; he was fiery hot, and freezing.

Someone was shaking him, very hard. David struggled into consciousness to see a face looking down at him, it was the Beagle.

'Ah, *señor* Hicks, I see you have settled in well.'

He wiped his hands on his boots. 'Filth.'

It is to be my turn, David thought, but he did not hear any names called. He tried to kick out at his tormentor, but the effort made him dizzy and he had the strength of a kitten. The thought of breaking away came into his head, he would make them shoot him in his mad dash for freedom. Then he remembered he could not stand. Hands pulled him up and carried him out of the cell. He imagined the courtyard outside, an open and windswept place littered with debris, and a bored firing squad blowing into cupped hands, anxious to be out of the cold. Their officer would examine his pistol, stroking it with love, and marching up and down. The last glimpse of the world would be so sweet, and so bitter.

David shut his eyes and waited for the cold blast of air that would announce his presence there, but it did not come. They did not take him outside, but to an interrogation room. His eyes tried to adapt to the light, and smarted from heavy tobacco smoke. Warmth hit him like a blow to the face, and the floor rushed towards him.

'Leave him,' a voice said, 'you will make him worse. Let us alone now.'

David focussed his eyes on a tall figure in front of him, a man in a suit. It was finely cut, the colour of burnt wood. The man stepped back and studied David, his face pensive but not hostile. David managed to crawl back into his chair, and sat on it like an invalid. He was alone with the man with the elegant suit.

'My name is Merry Del Val, Mr Hicks. I have been asked to

talk to the British prisoners. You are something of a rarity here.'

Del Val thumbed through a pile of documents on the desk, letting them fall through his fingers idly. 'So much paperwork.'

His accent was refined, and his hands soft with nails as finely cut as his clothes. He wore a shirt as white as the window light, and had the look of a man who had wanted for nothing. David could not believe such a figure was in the room with him. David smelt his own stinking state and was glad of it; he wanted to oppose Del Val in every way.

'Why are you in Spain?' Del Val asked.

David sighed at the familiar question, but was glad to hear a voice that did not bark. He shrugged and looked at the top of Del Val's head. Del Val asked David questions casually, without enthusiasm.

'Why do you throw your life away? You are young and have everything to live for. Yet you are here, meddling in our squabbles, things that should not concern you. And you haven't changed anything, you know. The International Brigade is a minor irritation, nothing more.'

David did not argue or talk much at all, but he could see Del Val was different, far more casual and human, he did not sense hate or fear in him. Fever made the scene dreamlike: Del Val's head floated above his body and his satin tie became a red flower.

'They have told you that you will be shot?' Del Val asked.

David's eyes flickered a response. The Spaniard got up from his chair and David saw tiny flecks on his collar, specks of imperfection. Del Val placed his hands on the back of David's chair.

'I have the power to save you, you know,' he said softly. 'You will have to behave in a certain way, of course. You were deceived by the Republic, Hicks, you did not know what they were like. If you sign a statement saying this they will not shoot you. You might even be sent home.'

So they wanted him to renege, turn traitor. David was surprised they thought him important enough for this. It was hard to think clearly.

'Why should I trust you?' David said.

'No reason, but that you want to live. I think you want to live very much.'

'I thought people like me were a minor irritation, surely they can't care about anything I sign?'

Del Val smiled and pulled at his tie.

'No, but the *Generallissimo* wants the world to know that he is fair and just. He bears no grudge against the likes of you, he sees you as misguided dupes.' Del Val made little attempt at seriousness when he said this. 'I will give you a day to think it over, a day to think about all the years that could lie ahead of you. It is your only chance, you know.'

Del Val called the guards in a tougher voice and David was taken to a new cell, an empty room of bare stone walls. He was thrown to the floor, to recommence his freezing.

In the other place his comrades waited for the shots to come, and wondered at the silence.

That night David was woken by guards kicking him. At first he thought it was a dream and tried to think them away, then he felt the stabs of pain breaking through the fever into his brain. He tried to curl up into a ball but the boots always found soft places. There were strange noises in the cell and he realised it was him, shrieking. A guard pulled him upright, so they could get at his face. David kicked out himself, with pitiful force, yet he heard one draw breath and curse. They renewed their assault with greater vigour and struck at his face with their fists. He felt teeth splinter before the void came. His last thought was that this was what Del Val must mean by thinking things over.

David never saw Del Val again in that place, he never knew if he was playing with him or making the standard offer. Del Val had been right about one thing: David did want to live, but most of the time he spent fortifying himself for his death, staring at the walls of his solitary cell. His life hung on the finest of wires, for an eternity, it seemed to him, yet he could not extinguish hope, it flickered within him somewhere, ready to leap up at the slightest encouragement.

David missed the closeness of the large cell; suffering together was easier to bear. His new place was high-ceilinged, with a roughly hewn floor, damp and ancient. There was one high window, gashed out of the rock like a scar. It scattered weak patterns of light on the walls, the one changing aspect of David's day.

When he came to after his nocturnal beating he was free of fever, but he was in pain, evenly divided throughout his body. At first he lay inert, not daring to move, then he began to feel himself, checking for broken bones. He could not find any, but he found gaps in his teeth as he probed around his mouth with his tongue. Two or three were gone from the left side, the holes they left felt huge, vast craters of torn flesh. He was glad it was not the front ones. After an initial burst of hurting his body grew vague again, as if resigned to the ill treatment. It had detached itself from all messages from his brain.

In a moment of complete lucidity David realised the war inside himself was over. And he had won. He hoped others lying in this stinking prison nourished similar victories inside them. He loved his comrades, how could their foes compare? They were strong, but it was a meagre ascendancy of mercenary armies and conscripts frightened by the religious threats of the cynical. Franco was shrewd, he tapped the fears of men and would win. David knew it now, but it would be the outcome of just one struggle, one strand of struggle that would be re-enacted over and over, perhaps forever. The enemy had not conquered his guts and did not sit in his soul, or Billy's, Tom's, or José's, and there was fear in his captors. He felt it strongly in his inquisitors, they would always have it, they were born with it, it made them vicious and resolute for a time, but it would gnaw away until they crumbled. David sat on the floor, hunched up to protect his bruises, and read the moods of the sun on his private wall.

He was alone for six days, waiting for the door to open and his presence be demanded. In the courtyard outside the executions continued unabated, they marked the start of David's day. If he slept at all he woke to the same volley of shots. One morning he confused them, in a half-sleep, with the valley's coal trains, the early ones that trundled down from the top pits. They were two-engined monsters pulling long lines of trucks, each engine snorting into the damp Welsh dawn. It was a sound that always heralded action, the dreaded action of going to school, or opening the shop.

David was given soup to eat, rather than bread and water. He kept hope to a sliver at this better treatment; he knew his captors delighted in dangling carrots in front of the doomed, and to reach out for one was to be undone. After a week two officers came to his cell. They held papers in their hands, confirmation of his death, he thought.

'You are to be moved,' one of them said, 'in the morning.'

'Where am I going?'

'To join the rest of your kind. You are still under sentence of death, of course, but it will not be carried out yet. We don't know when it will be.'

The rest of his kind, did they mean other Britons?

'Am I being taken from here?' he asked.

'You don't need to know any more,' one snapped back at him.

They left him, and the door was banged shut again. David slept soundly that night, in the dirt with his myriad lice. In the morning they gave him a large bowl of soup that was almost hot, and fresh bread to dunk in it.

For the first time since his capture he was allowed to wash. The water was ice but he thrilled to its touch. In a piece of mirror he saw a haggard ghost looking back at him. It blinked as he blinked, stared as he stared. David did not want to believe he was the ghost. His beard was matted with dirt, black rings encircled his eyes like targets, his teeth had yellowed and his gums had receded perfectly to display two gaps on one side. The teeth had been knocked out cleanly and the craters he had imagined were small holes. He probed them gently, then gargled, spitting out a putrid mess from his mouth. He did so again and again until it felt fresh, and alive. Then he stripped off his clothing, layer by filthy layer, until he reached nakedness, a multi-hued nakedness: his body covered in different shades of brown by bruises and drying cuts. His ribs were very sore from the kicking, but he was in one piece.

The guards shouted for David to get a move on. He dressed after throwing some water over the top half of his body. He discarded the worst of his underclothes. It was March, the weather would be changing in his favour. David had one last look in the mirror and the ghost looked a little better. A new David Hicks confronted him, looking ten years older than the one he remembered, with lines of resolution furrowing its brow. It was not a weak face anymore, he saw the face of a man who had won through against himself.

By noon he was out of the prison, heading for the next unknown place in a truck. David could not gauge the direction but he rejoiced in the fresh air. He gulped it down eagerly, letting its edge scour his lungs and exhilarate his system. It was better than the finest tobacco smoke. His hands were bound behind him with fence wire which chaffed at his wrists and cut off the flow of blood, but it was a trivial thing after the prison. He looked at distant hills and thought of the valley and Emma, and smiled. The guards looked at him strangely, he had no right to look happy. One cuffed him around the head. '*Stupido*' they said to each other.

They passed through snow-spattered country, open country which shrieked its freedom at David. The far hills were tinged with blue, and topped with the snow of a long winter. Further down the slopes it was melting in streaks, revealing slabs of green and brown land. David smiled again but the guards did not strike him this time, perhaps they had some sympathy for the crazy English.

For some hours they travelled on roads crowded with supply vehicles. David was able to look out of the back of the truck and see the strength of the enemy. Everything the Republic so desperately wanted was here in abundance. Every town they passed through had German and Italian equipment backed up on side roads, waiting for the final push towards Barcelona. They swept past rows of pristine armour, unused tanks and artillery, and, outside one town, an airfield bristling with the latest bombers and fighters.

David saw a sign for Burgos, the city of old Castile, and knew they had been travelling north and west. By this time the guards were tired and surly, bored with their charge and wanting food. They had stopped briefly, but David had not been given anything to eat. His hands had lost all feeling, and the familiar ache of hunger settled in his gut. It was dark when they stopped, somewhere near Burgos. The last hour they had travelled dangerously, slipping on the rough roads. The guards were anxious to unload David, and be gone.

The truck crashed to a halt and a head thrust through the canvas. It belonged to a Spanish sergeant. 'So, another Englishman, eh?' He shone a torch in David's face and prodded him with a cane, like a farmer inspecting a new arrival from the cattle-market. The guards pulled David out and stood him in front of the sergeant. The man looked merciless, but David expected nothing else. He was prepared to match sadism with his new self, to see if it was strong.

They marched him across a road to a small building, set amongst larger ones. David thought he glimpsed a church in the gloom. Light blinded him as he stumbled through a door, and he swayed unsteadily. The sergeant cut the wire from his wrists with a pair of clippers and David let his hands hang at his sides, afraid to move them. The man examined his papers, peering at them closely and muttering 'Si, si' to himself. He looked up and gave David another poke with his stick, smiling a smile of broken teeth and malice. He gestured to the guards and David was taken back outside, to another door. This one was heavy, and bound in iron. David knew he was in a religious place. The door creaked open and he was thrust inside, to sprawl in the darkness over unseen bodies.

He was in the presence of many men: he could smell them and hear their noises, but he could not see them. At first the dark was absolute, so he stayed where he was, waiting for his eyes to get accustomed to it. After a minute he was able to make out figures lying and sitting in front of him. One of them got up and came towards him. 'Hello mate,' a voice whispered, 'welcome to San Pedro, me old son.'

18

David Hicks came again to San Pedro, forty years after that cockney voice first welcomed him. The prison drew him back to Spain after the death of Franco. It was the symbol of his catharsis. He found it still there, a little more weather-beaten but standing resolutely, defying time and war, oblivious to the men who perished in it. He walked away from it for the last time, re-emerging from his past into the present, and the audience of small boys who had followed him, unnoticed by the day-dreaming old foreigner.

'What are you doing, *señor*?' one asked, 'where do you go?'

David wondered how much these boys knew about those times. He thought of telling them that the convent had once been a prison for men like himself, but did not do so. That was a job for their fathers, and grandfathers, if they had survived. It was their country, he had learned that long ago.

'I am seeing the sights,' he replied, to the nearest boy. This one repeated the answer to his friends and they all laughed.

'The sights, *señor*, here? There is nothing here for you. San Pedro is an old, empty place. There are no nuns anymore.'

'No, there are no nuns.'

The boys followed their mysterious tourist for a while until they grew bored and scattered, running into alleyways to chase cats.

Emma was coming to meet him. He could see her walking up the street, picking her way carefully over the cobblestones. Her hair caught the sun as it always had, holding its light for a moment, and she looked young again, her figure not much altered down the years. She had not grown stout or bent; David liked that. He did not see his own age mirrored in her, Emma kept them young. They met at the corner of the street, in the shadow of San Pedro.

'Have you seen all you wanted, David?'

'Yes. There was not much to see. Just an old empty building.'

He tapped his head. 'All the pictures are locked up in here, Em, that place started them off again, that's all.'

'You must be tired.' Emma pushed the hair away from his eyes, it grew thickly still.

'A little,' David said. 'It's a long climb, I hadn't realised.'

They stood together quietly for a while. David had not wanted Emma to come to the convent. He did not want her to share in that place of so much misery, and as the boy said, there was nothing there now.

'Well, you finally came back,' Emma said. 'I never thought you would, you know. How do you feel?'

'I don't know. Sad, happy in a way, it's hard to describe. It was such an age ago, yet it is so real, so close. I can smell the same smells, see the same faces so clearly I half expect some of those lads to come round that corner.'

'Yes.'

'They were good men, Emma. They deserved better. They deserved to be on the winning side.'

'Weren't they, in the end?'

David smiled. They walked back to the café.

'Being on the streets here is strange,' David said. 'I never saw them before. I arrived at night and left in the night. It was often like that in Spain.'

Emma let David talk on, he had earned the right to reminisce, and had never made the mistake of constantly reliving the war as some of the veterans had, living on bitter memories of what might have been. She had worried about their visit to Spain, so soon after Franco's death, but David had been so excited by it, as if the old Republic had finally won. David thought Spain might have another chance now. The country had never left his heart; most of them were the same, the ones who went out from the valley and came back. They never stopped loving the place. Emma was not jealous of the country, it had changed her man and given him back to her.

'I'm glad we are together here,' David said, as they walked. 'The place where I realised how stupid I had been about us, about everything back in the valley.'

Emma squeezed his hand. 'Yes, I know,' she said.

The café had emptied its young men onto the streets, and lay deserted and waiting for them. They ordered coffee and sat at the talker's table. It was still littered with cigarette butts and spilt liquid. How well Emma remembered the day David came home, a cold February one, in 1939. He was one of the last they let go, because he was political, they said.

For a time they thought him lost. Helen Hicks got an official letter. John Hughes, postman, knocked on her door one morning and handed her an envelope as thin as a wafer, adorned with an oversized stamp. Hughes was solemn, he always was when delivering letters from Spain, they so often brought tragic news.

'One from over there for you, Mrs Hicks, don't know who from, mind.' Hughes the nose hung around, hoping Helen would open it in his presence. But she bade him good morning and shut herself into the house, retreating to the parlour before she dared tackle the letter.

It had got wet along the way, and she had to trace the words with her fingers, peering through the new spectacles she had picked from a box in the Emporium, when Mrs Vincent wasn't there. They regretted to inform her, the letter said, they regretted to inform her that David Hicks was missing in action, at a place called Teruel. She sat down calmly, and nursed the cat in the armchair. It began a cracked purr at the unexpected spoiling.

Helen's mind was blank for some time, she did not want it to be otherwise, then she began to go over David's short life, from baby onwards. His changing face flashed through her head in a rapid history. It was not a happy history, riddled with wrong turns, and weakness. She must take blame for that, David was her flesh and blood, she had moulded him into what he was, cossetted him against the harsh valley, she could admit it to herself now. And he had gone to war, that weak boy of hers, and was missing.

Other men had gone missing and then turned up, and David had survived over there when Billy had fallen. Helen often wondered at that. She did not feel the certainty of her son's death, so she decided to hope, against the odds, until it was proved to her. The tom-cat's battle scarred head was soft in her hands, pulsing with life, life that could resist stubbornly all that fate brought against it. Helen hummed to herself, pushing away the emptiness that threatened.

Then came the rumours. A man wrote to her saying he had seen David in a prison camp called San Pedro. She had not dared to believe it, but people began checking and finally it was confirmed that David were indeed alive, a prisoner.

It was with this news that Emma began visiting Helen. She did so hesitantly at first, but was warmly welcomed, and a bond grew up quickly between them. In the Hicks parlour Emma found the warmth that had always been absent in her own house. They shared a mutual loss, and talked often through that long winter. Helen was impressed by Emma's lack of bitterness. 'I couldn't blame you if you hated David,' she said once, 'you've lost him twice over, but I think you're a bit like me, girl, you don't judge too quickly.'

Sitting in that parlour with Helen became Emma's only social activity. Her mother tried to discourage the liaison and attempted to introduce her to suitable young men, but she spurned them all and was eventually left alone. Emma never divorced David, resisting the pressure to do so until her parents tired of that too.

The two women were together when news came of Tom. A letter was sent to Helen, there being no relative. Emma remembered her clutching it to her breast, as if it was a child.

'They've killed poor Tom Price, girl,' she said breathlessly. She read out the letter, turning it in her hands. 'Poor man. He was always so quiet. I thought he would get through it. It was meant to be for our Billy, I always felt that; if it wasn't Spain, it would have been here, in some riot, or rotting down Cardiff gaol. But Tom...'

She sniffed and attacked the fire with her poker, showering the grate with sparks as she shaped the coals.

'He was a bit like my Daniel, that Tom, the opposite to Billy. I don't know Emma, we are losing our men, over something I can't quite understand.'

'At least David is out of the fighting, in that prison,' Emma said.

'Aye, there's that.'

Helen sat down heavily, to think, as she put it, and silence fell. They listened to the splutter of the new coals, and the rumble of the old cat. Emma knew Helen was thinking that the letter might have been about David. She tried to imagine such news herself. David's leaving for Spain had surprised her. She had thought it was another of his dreams, something he would talk about a lot, but never do. She had been proud of him, in a way, for going through with it.

Following the war became a preoccupation for Emma, and

she discussed the events with Helen. Relying on newspaper reports they formed their own Conti's in the parlour. In their ignorance of Spain they were equal, but they strove to improve their knowledge, for they respected the fact that it drew local men there. For each of them it was a way of staying close to David. Emma no longer tried to deny her need for that.

Helen placed Tom's letter under the teapot.

'Which one is David like, Helen?'

'What's that girl?'

'I said which one is David like, Billy or Tom?'

'Certainly not Billy. Neither of them really. David is different again. Who knows with him? I'm his mother and I'm not sure what type of man he is. He was so deep, that boy, it was like having a stranger in the house sometimes, even though I doted on him – oh, I can see that now girl, I did dote on him, waited on him hand and foot, spoiled him. And when Daniel went I did it all the more. David was everything to me then, I put it all into him. If I had not done that he would have been better with you, Emma.'

'Don't blame yourself. I have thought a lot about it since he left. David was looking for something else, something he thought he could not get from me. You did not put that there, there was a restlessness inside him, churning him up all the time. He was never satisfied with anything.'

'Aye, that was David alright, always looking over the next hilltop. Let's hope he's found a bit of peace over there.' Helen dozed off in front of the fire, unaware of the irony of her last words.

Emma watched her nurse the cat in her sleep, sifting mechanically through its warm fur with her fingers. She was ageing quickly; lines were etched in her face like the cable of the pit wheels, her hair was all grey now, and tiredness had rubbed the shine from her eyes. The last few years had weighed heavily on Helen. Quietly, Emma got up to leave, scanned by the slitted eyes of the cat. Helen woke when she got to the door.

'Oh, off are you, Emma? I must have nodded off.'

'Yes, I didn't want to wake you.'

Helen looked her up and down.

'We've had a lot of chats now, Emma, you and me. Tell me one thing. If David – when David comes home, would you want him back, would you have him back?'

The question startled Emma, though she had asked it of herself many times.

'I don't know. I don't think he would want that, he would have to change so much.'

'Well, men do change sometimes, even if they never admit it. We can change them. You love him still, don't you?'

Emma coloured, and nodded her head slowly.

'Yes, I knew so. It's as plain as that ridge out there, that is why your mother is like a bear with a sore head. She knows she cannot break that, only you can. You think David never loved you, don't you?'

'What else can I think?'

'You could think that he didn't know what love was. Oh, he read all about it in them fancy books of his, but he knew nothing about it, I could see that. It might be that he has had time to think about it all, being so far from home. They say you see things clearer from afar. Maybe David realises how lucky he was to have married you.'

Emma tried to interrupt but Helen waved her silent.

'Yes, I know. Why should you think this, why should you give him another chance, why should you hope? It hurts the heart fit to bust it, I know that. Perhaps you should expect the worst, that he won't be coming back to you, or he's been killed, but I feel in these old bones of mine that David is alive out there, and has changed. I can't explain it, don't ask me to, but I feel it as clearly as I feel the heat from these coals... Well, I've had my say about that son of mine, Emma, you'd best get off now, before I have your mother down here, shouting the odds.'

Emma walked home through the village to the hill, crunching the snow under her boots. It was just as cold in Spain, the papers said, soldiers were freezing to death out there. She let herself into the house quietly, taking care not to disturb her father. Yellow light leaked under his study door; he was up all hours, planning another shop.

Helen's words struck deeply into her, and Emma was lightened in spirit that night. Perhaps the old lady was right; David must have changed to survive so long, when so many tougher men had fallen. She slept with this mood, and dreamt of her distant husband. They were happy and starting afresh, their problems swept away, everything solved. The wind howled David's name. He was alive, David was alive. But the dream turned dark. She saw the ceiling of their old bedroom over the shop, and felt the pain of her child tearing his way out of her. That lead-grey ceiling bore down on her, smothering her. She fought it, pushing it away from her until she woke, in a cold sweat.

Emma started into consciousness with Mrs Hicks's question on her own lips. 'Would I take him back, will he come back?' She thought of the turmoil David's return would cause in her family, and told herself it was not worth going through again. Then she thought he would not be back anyway, and it was pointless to go over it all. But David would not go away.

She punched the pillows in frustration. If only she could stop loving him, that would be a release. It was unwise to love him, he was not a good bet, and her experience with him was far more tangible than Helen's intuition. It was she who had suffered the hurt and humiliation, it still coursed through her with vigour. Helen's words disturbed her. She had convinced herself that David would not be back, but she was not sure anymore. Meeting with him, talking to him, she did not know how she would react.

Her room was cold but Emma got out of bed to pull back the curtains. There was a moon, about to sink over the ridge. It lit up the valley with its pale light and highlighted the shadowy rows of terraces; the river was turned into a silver snake, gliding past snowy banks. Emma shivered as she felt the icy breath of the night. David hated the cold so and he was out there somewhere, and she was worrying about him, whether he thought of her or not. She went back to bed and tried to sleep again.

Throughout 1938 Helen lived on rumour and counter rumour, dismissing the bad, letting her hopes rise with the good. Some of the valley's volunteers came back in the October of that year, but David was not among them. Helen decided to see one of these men, travelling to another valley to do so, a long bus journey for her. She told no-one of the trip, any news of David she wanted to keep to herself, at first, if it was bad. She got the address of the man from one of Billy's friends, and found him living in a terrace like her own. A woman answered her knock, a child hung from her hip, and others called from inside. She was hostile, glaring with mistrust at Helen.

'You are not from the welfare, are you? No, you are too old for that.'

'I want to see your husband, please.'

'What do you want with him? He's only just got back from Spain, stupid bugger that he is.'

'It's that what I want to see him about.'

The woman went to shut the door on her, but Helen blocked it with her leg, hurting herself in the process.

'I want to find out about my boy, that's all,' Helen said. 'He's a prisoner out there.'

The woman's anger softened.

'Oh, I thought you were one of them political women, come round nosing, causing trouble. I don't want my Jack doing nothing more with politics.'

'No, I understand.'

A man's head popped around the door. 'What's all this then woman, who have we got here?'

'Helen Hicks, David Hicks's mother. Do you know him?'

'Aye, I've heard the name. Related to Billy, wasn't he? You'd better come in.'

He led her to the parlour where his wife left them to join her brood. Children's clothes lay everywhere.

'Six of the buggers we have,' Jack said, proudly and ruefully, 'the missus hasn't forgiven me for leaving 'em yet.'

'Did you see my son in Spain? Were you in prison too?'

'Aye, I was. Nice little place called San Pedro. Nice for rats, that is. David Hicks, yes, tall, I remember him.'

Helen hung on his every word.

'Was he alright?' she asked. 'Was he wounded? How was he?'

'Hang on a bit. Yes, he was alright, bearing up like. He hadn't been hurt bad, as far as I can remember. Don't worry, the young boys last the best.'

'Why hasn't he been sent home, like you?'

'Dunno. We were exchanged for prisoners our side had. Perhaps they run out of them. Nothing is sure out there, but your boy will get through it, if he's lasted this long.'

'How did they treat you?'

'Oh alright, see.' Jack walked around the parlour, and scratched at his vest. 'I'm here, aren't I?'

Helen saw a man spare framed enough to be called emaciated, with yellowish, sunken cheeks and eyes the colour of nicotine stain. He was probably not forty, yet looked her age. Helen could not get more out of Jack, he would not open up about San Pedro.

Helen returned home elated, and in a fine temper. She damned the secretive, schoolboy nature of all men, and cried inside with joy at Jack's news. The man had seen David, in the flesh. He had confirmed the rumours. Be patient, she told herself, it is just a matter of time now, it has to be. Helen could not understand why some were set free and others kept, she was jealous of the freed. She hummed to herself as the bus bumped along the valley road. That Jack, she thought, he was only trying to spare my feelings. She felt a fondness for the harassed father of six souls, and resolved to send them some of the clothes of the children she had kept. Perhaps David could go to college when he came home, become a teacher, something safe like that.

San Pedro kept David a prisoner for a year, a year which was a long rack for his virgin self-belief. All his sufferings of the Teruel cell were re-enacted and stretched out over days and months, but this time he was with his comrades and countrymen, men he could talk with, and pool miseries with. They shared the same indignities and lousy food, the same lice and scabs, the same typhoid and the same beatings. Always beatings. David's height marked him out, one small sergeant took a particular interest in him. David's body became his personal punchbag, but he survived. Ribs were cracked, he lost another tooth, and a small scar appeared under his right eye, but he survived. His captors did not reach into his soul, and the longer he stayed alive the more his determination grew. Pessimism was isolated to one corner of his mind, and he thought of living, and the future.

David helped the men around him as much as they helped him. There was no room for loners at San Pedro, so he ceased to be one. He had never shared so much, or belonged so much, and he cajoled the weaker ones, as Billy had him. Many men died from disease, others simply disappeared, taken away for questioning never to reappear. David involved himself in the various classes of learning that sprung up in the prison. He passed on what knowledge he could, and was a member of the secret committee that was formed to maintain morale.

The first men to leave San Pedro were exchanged for Italian prisoners held by the Republic. The hopes of all were boosted by this but David was not in the first batch. The prison authorities were especially suspicious of him, he had good Spanish and an education. What his father had so desired for him was dangerous here. David underwent more interrogations than most. German officials visited San Pedro from time to time; they were the worst of the questioners. They asked questions softly, as Spanish guards tried to beat information out of men who knew nothing. German prisoners were filtered out, to be shipped back to Germany to face torture and certain death. David wondered if Hans Kleinz, his companion of Paris, was one.

Old comrades met at San Pedro, but Tom was never one of them. David never saw his friend again and could only guess at his fate until he returned to the valley. There he learned that Tom had survived Teruel, and had lived through everything until the last days of the International Brigades. Tom died re-crossing the River Ebro, as the remnants of the last Republican effort streamed back from their attack, beaten and in disarray. David never learned more of Tom's death or found where he was buried, but he hoped it was on the river's banks, that final place of expectation for the volunteers. And he hoped Tom died still believing in it all. Then he was shamed for doubting it could ever be otherwise.

What was left of the Brigades paraded through Barcelona on November 15th; the Catalans said goodbye to them. La Passionara, the woman who had symbolised what had drawn most of them to Spain, sent them home with her emotive words ringing in their ears. She too was to leave Spain, living out the rest of her life exiled in Russia, even after Franco died. A month later the British contingent arrived at Victoria Station, three hundred of them left. They marched to a solitary drum, and a bugle. One man made a speech saying they would fight on at other fronts, but David was not there to hear it.

It was February of the next year before they let him go, he was one of the last to leave San Pedro. He crossed the border by train two years after he had walked over the Pyrenees. There was no need for secrecy this time, he journeyed openly, watching all he passed with eyes that were sad, for they were knowing. On the

French side he saw the trains laid up at sidings packed with war goods for the Republic. They had not reached their destination, the machinations of politics had halted them. David gazed through the window at their defeat, he saw it in the unused tanks and guns sent from Russia, paid for by Spanish gold. It was the last bitter pill he was required to swallow, and his last memory of the war.

In days David was in London, catching the Paddington train for Cardiff, marvelling at the suddenness of it all. The British government had repatriated him; he had their bill in his pocket, but would never pay it. It was a final act of rebellion.

A woman and child sat opposite him in the carriage, noses wrinkled at his state. The child was curious, and asked why a tramp was on the train. He would have talked to David, but his mother held him firmly and told him to be quiet. David wanted to tell the boy he was just a man returning home from a war they had heard little about, and cared less, but he did not speak. He sat in the bent attitude he had grown used to in San Pedro, his eyes blinking continuously in the light of southern England, amazed by the sea of green outside the window. He had managed to shave in France but the clothes he wore were vintage rags, held together with pieces of string. He was a tramp on the outside, and a new man within.

David caught the last train up to the valley and went straight to Emma's house, before he had time to change his mind. He wanted to see her first, he had decided this a long time ago. In San Pedro he had lain with hundreds of other men and thought of her for hours. As it became likely that the enemy would not carry out his threat of execution he thought of her all the more. Emma had every right to refuse his offer of another go; she ought to throw it back in his face, and might do so. But he had to try, he had lived the past six months with this decision.

He stood in the dark before Vincent's oak door and rapped on it several times, firm strikes of the hand. After a minute Vincent himself opened it, cigar in hand. He blinked at David in disbelief.

'Good God, Hicks.'

His mouth opened and he tried to say something else, but he just mouthed air, such was his surprise. Emma appeared, her hand on her father's. She stared at David and Vincent stared at each of them.

'Yes, it is me, Mr Vincent. I've come to see Emma.'

The old man's face was beginning to flush as he searched for words.

'You've shocked us, David,' Emma said, in a weak voice, 'turning up like this. Come in, come into the study please.'

She pulled him past her dumbfounded father, who stood frozen at the door. Emma led David to the study and helped him take off his coat, which almost fell apart in her hands.

'You are shivering,' she said.

'I'm not cold,' David answered.

They stared at each other, their eyes insatiable. David saw a woman unbelievably lovely, one discarded by him, by a man who seemed hateful to him, from another lifetime, another world. Emma saw a man reed-thin, ravaged, hollow-cheeked and aged before his time, not unlike the men who sometimes knocked on their kitchen window. It was David, but in disguise, and there was something else very changed about him.

They sat down shyly by a fire of layered logs.

'My father will be in now,' Emma said, 'when he regains his composure. You gave him such a shock, he's gone to tell mother, probably.'

'Sorry to barge in like this. There was no time to write, I've just got back, on the train.'

'You haven't seen your mother?'

'I haven't seen anybody.'

'You came straight here, from Spain?'

Emma looked at David with wide eyes. The fire snapped and the room charged with their feelings, two years of thoughts were brought to life. She stared at him, and he returned her look calmly. This was the difference in him, she realised, his eyes no longer flickered around, like they used to. David had always reminded her of an animal trapped and wanting to run. That nervousness was not there now, his eyes met hers frankly. Emma thought of Helen's words, and wanted to believe them.

There was a smallish scar under David's bottom lip, like a tiny blue worm curled up, and another nestled in the crows' feet of his eyes. And he had teeth missing, she saw the gaps when he talked. His eyes had always enlarged so at night, Emma saw David's recent history of suffering in them, and yet they did not ask for pity, that quality was gone.

'I was not sure I would ever see you again, David,' Emma said, as calmly as she could.

'There were times when I was sure I would never see you.'

'Did you want to see me?'

'Yes. Not at first, but as time went on, I had time to think, lots of it. I went over everything in my mind, you know me, always thinking.'

'Yes, but you never used to find any answers, did you? Not for us anyway.'

'No, not then, not when we had the shop.'

'Why did you leave like that? It hurt your mother so.'

'Yes I know it must have. But it was the only way I could go, Emma. I took the easy course, as I always did.'

Mrs Vincent was shouting in the hall, gathering her indignation as she prepared to meet her enemy.

'I am a changed man, Emma,' David said. 'Different to the one you had to suffer. Spain has changed me.'

'Has it?'

'Yes, I'm not running away anymore, I never will again. I was always doing it, I can admit it to myself now, running from responsibility, from you, the shop, from myself. Perhaps I can start being honest now. I know I don't deserve another chance, you should have divorced me, but I'm asking for one. I have nothing to offer, I'm penniless, I even owe the government money, but I'll do my best for you, this time... I'll do my best for us. I give you my word on it, and that means everything to me now.'

It seemed an age to David before Emma spoke. She rose from her chair as she did so, her eyes glittering in the fireglow.

'You must mean it, David. I could not stand it again, if it went wrong, you must mean it this time... I still want you.'

Her hands reached for his, and she rested her head on his shoulder. David was afraid to touch her at first, then he put his arms around her waist and drew her to him. They confronted her parents like this.

Vincent burst open the door, pushed through it by his wife. She had prepared herself well.

'I want you out of this house, Hicks,' she shouted, 'coming here like a thief in the night. Look at him, like a bloody tramp he is, a gypsy. A thief, a thief who stole our Emma once, and now is at it again.'

David rose to meet the silent Vincent, who supported his wife's rage but was unsure. He too, sensed the difference in David, this older man was a stranger, not the dreaming boy he had once employed.

'Go on,' she urged, 'throw him out, and Emma too, if she bothers with him.'

'I've a right to see Emma, Mrs Vincent,' David said, 'she is still my wife.'

'Wife. That's a laugh. Fine husband you turned out to be. Scum, that's what you are, a bloody bolshie.'

'Stop it,' Emma shouted, the first and last time David ever heard her do so. 'I am going with David now, to start our marriage again.'

'I knew it,' her mother shouted.

Vincent was stunned, and blustered 'You don't know what you are saying, girl, going back to him.'

'I do, dad, my mind is made up.'

'But he can't keep you,' Vincent said.

'And he'll be off again,' his wife added, 'if they go once, they go again.'

'Emma will stay with me at my mother's, until we are on our feet,' David said.

'On your feet, you'll get no work around here, Hicks, my husband will see to that, you... you damned agitator.'

Vincent did not respond to his wife's threat.

'I'll get my coat,' Emma said.

She brushed past her parents. David did not want to let her go, he did not want to let her out of his sight, now that she was won again. He felt a little pity for Vincent. The old man would have to live out the rest of his life with a wife who would never let him forget, or forgive. She would keep the wound open and suppurating down the years. David hoped he might talk to Vincent later.

Emma rejoined David, and they left the Vincent house for the last time.

'You'll be sorry, Emma Vincent,' her mother cried after her, 'just you wait and see, you'll be sorry.'

David felt Emma shrink a little as she held on to him, and resolved to never give her cause to be sorry. He held her tightly as they stumbled down the road, and she relaxed in his grip; he was strong enough to protect her now, and she knew it. The shouts of her mother became ever fainter as they made their way down through the terraces. David was practicing what he had learned in the arms of José, sharing himself with Emma for the first time. He liked the feeling.

As they walked along the streets a man passing recognised David. He stopped to take a long look from the other side of the street, then called out a hesitant greeting which David returned with a wave. This Conti Boy hustled away to tell his tale, the café would know in minutes.

They did not hurry. The lines of the ridge merged with the night clouds, its outline was blurred to the dark mass which used to look so menacing to David. He had left hating its confines, now it was welcoming, an old friend. They stopped to watch the sluggish river, and hold each other.

'Never thought the old place could look so good,' David said, 'and I've never seen a river dirtier or darker, but it's beautiful.'

It was past midnight when they got to David's house.

Helen was waiting for them, David heard the kettle simmering on the hob, the most exquisite sound of welcome he could imagine. His mother came to the door.

'There you are, then,' she said calmly, 'took long enough walking down here, didn't you? Ronnie Osmond said you were back, ran over here to tell me he saw you in the street, walking along as calm as you please, with Emma at your side. I thought he'd been drinking at first, but then I sat down, and felt that it was true. And here you are.'

'Hello, ma.'

Mother and son stood motionless.

'Haven't you got a kiss for your mother, then?'

David went to kiss her on the cheek and she held him for a few moments.

'You've given me a lot of trials, lad,' she whispered. 'An awful lot of trials.'

'I know ma, but it's over now. I'm back, and safe.'

Helen gave him another hug and showed them through to the parlour, giving Emma a kiss as she passed.

'So, went to get your wife first, did you? Thought as much. I hope all that nonsense between you is finished now. I've got the front room ready for you, it's too big for me. Had it ready a long time.'

David and Emma looked at Helen with some awe. David knew the roots of the strength he had found lay in her. She was moulded in bed-rock, and unshakeable.

'Well, let's have a look at you,' Helen said, 'by the lamp.'

She stared into David's face. 'You were always a bit of a rake, so not much difference there.'

Her hands reached for his face and felt over it, as if she was blind.

'Aye,' she said, 'I see a man in front of me now.'

Emma started to cry but Helen hushed her. 'Shush, shush, no tears now. I'll make the tea, Sit yourselves down, and talk to each other.'

Helen turned to the kettle, and dabbed at her own eyes with her tea-cloth. David sat in the old armchair and knew he had a home.

'Left in a hurry, didn't you, lass,' Helen said to Emma. 'Perhaps that's the best way, once your mind was made up. There are some of the girls' things laid out for you upstairs. I didn't think you'd stop to pack a bag, not tonight. Go up for your own stuff in a few days, when things settle.'

'How did you know all this,' Emma asked, 'that I'd be coming here?'

'I didn't for sure until Ronnie told me, but I always had an inkling it would end up this way – remember our talks, girl.'

Helen attempted a wink, but only succeeded in screwing up her face. She poured the tea, and laid out bread and cheese.

'That's all that's here for the moment. Right, I'll leave you now, I'm up far too late for an old woman. David knows where everything is, if he can remember.'

She squeezed David's hand, and placed it in Emma's.

They drank their tea quietly, there did not seem any need to talk, they had all their lives to do that. The tom-cat eyed them suspiciously, trying to make up its mind if David was here to stay or not.

'Doesn't remember me,' David muttered, 'two years is a long time for a cat, a lifetime.'

They made their way upstairs, to the bedroom David had slept in as a child. The cat accompanied them to the foot of the stairs, slouching after them like an idle guard. It scratched and turned back to the warmth of the parlour, yawning and satisfied that David really was back.

David pushed open the bedroom door, expecting the wheeze of the hinge to greet him, but it did not do so. It had always reminded him of his father's chest, a reincarnation of it, but it was gone, oiled and cured.

There was much for David to sort out with Emma in the coming months, but they had plenty of time, for David did not work until war came to his own country. Like many of the Spanish veterans he was not trusted to fight against Hitler, against the same forces he had resisted in Spain. That was a bitter irony for some, but a great relief for the women in the Hicks family. They felt David had chanced his life as much as any man ought.

David served his war working in the last place he would have imagined a few years before, the dreaded pit. It caught him at last, in 1940, but he went into its maw willingly enough. It was a final test for him, and a formal sign of his acceptance of the valley and his acceptance in it. And it was not such a dread place if one learned its moods and conditions, and did not try to go against them. This was David's war effort, and it brought in good money. He was a provider at last.

David's five years underground was the perfect breeding ground for the ideas spawned in Conti's and hatched in Spain. He became active in union affairs, but never led. At night he studied, in true mining tradition, aiming to get to that damned training college when the war ended. He went to see the retired Lewis-Jones, who agreed to help him. David got to his college in 1946, ten years later than he planned.

Three years later he began to teach in a small primary in the valley. He lived with Emma in the Hicks house, they never saw the need to leave it. David arranged with his sisters for the house to be his when Helen died, in the last year of the turbulent forties. Emma was with him at her bedside at the end knowing, like David, that death was imminent, but still trying to will it away from the indomitable old lady, wondering how it dared call on her.

Helen gave up her ghost as calmly as she had always lived, her eyes turned towards the ridge. The new young doctor had been called to attend her in her last weeks. It was old age, he told them.

'Mrs Hicks got very tired,' he said, 'I've seen so many like her since I came to the valley. Women not so very old, but worn out. It must have been a hard life here, in the old days.'

The doctor wrote 'old age' on the death certificate, and something about the chest. They no longer had to pay him.

'She looked so peaceful,' Emma whispered.

'Yes. She knew we were settled and happy; all her children are happy. That meant so much to her, life's greatest gift to me, she said. If she had gone ten years ago, it would have been very different, Em.'

'Yes.'

David looked down on his mother with great sadness, but it did not echo in the emptiness he used to carry inside him. He was not pricked by guilt. And he had the warmth of the woman beside him for solace. The doctor was right, Helen had not lived to a ripe old age, though she had deserved to. She had barely crept to seventy, but what times had she lived through. Hard times indeed, but lively times, vibrant with hope and change. And Helen had died in the midst of so much of it. She had seen despair conquered and hope return to the valley, and she died knowing that a future had been secured for her family, and her people.

David pushed a sliver of hair away from her face, smoothing it back in place with his hand. He felt the warmth fading from her cheek, and the lines of her face had relaxed, as if the years were leaving her. He thought he saw just a tinge of pink in her cheeks, an echo of her youth, before the dull mould of death settled on her and she became cold to the touch, that absolute cold that marks the passing of a soul.

Helen Hicks was buried next to Daniel, on a day when winter returned for a last rail at spring. It was the lot of the Hicks to be buried in the cold, not one of them had died in the summer, ever. A few yards away from Helen lay Iolo Hughes, who had succumbed to a second stroke during the Normandy landings. Iolo was with his flock permanently now, watching them. The old guard of the village was fading, leaving the young to their new age.

On cue, the pit whistle called out as they lay Helen next to Daniel. It called out to David, and Emma, and the whole village, announcing its continuing reign: 'I'm here to stay,' it said, and David wondered if it would always be so. He could not imagine the village without it, or the valley stripped of the dozen pit-heads that scarred it, each one a sentinel for a community, and a symbol of the lifeblood of the place.

The whistle was no longer a cruel sound. David had served

his time under its sway and heard it without fear now, accepting it as a part of him. He knew it was calling him, he was a working man and his heart responded. Helen was earthed over as mourners drifted away like leaves. David turned at the chapel gates to see the two gravediggers bending to their task, and said a last farewell to his mother. He walked home with Emma's arm in his, firmly in his.

They remained a childless couple. That first tragic attempt had stilled any hopes of further offspring. Emma involved herself with the children of others, and the school, and many came to Mrs Hicks for sundry help and delights. David never left his first primary, he became a fixture in it. Some said there was a lack of ambition in him, but he left that to others and was content with his small world. Spain had shown him enough of the larger one. Waves of children came before Hicksie, then old Hicksie, and he was liked well enough, without ever losing his innate sense of privacy. It was a good profession for him, for he could mix warmly with the children, but keep the distance that age gave him.

David had boundless patience as a teacher, and if he had a fault, it was occasionally identifying too strongly with a pupil. Every few years a boy would come along who David thought had a different kind of spark, one which he could ignite into a good future. He delighted in sending these to the grammar school, and took pride in his record of doing so, but it was never to the detriment of the other boys. Each one was a surrogate son, he realised in later years, and balanced his own lack of one.

The rift with Emma's parents was never bridged, but passions cooled as time passed. David's respectable job made it easier for Vincent, who saw them from time to time. His irascibility turned to sentimental nostalgia for a past that never was as he aged. In a way David became almost fond of his old adversary. Mrs Vincent never came near, but she survived her husband to run his now numerous shops with shrewdness and an iron hand. She accumulated more wealth and, to the amazement of the village, a new husband. An Englishman took her away to London when she was past sixty, where she lived for many years, hissing her way to ninety. Charlotte went with her, and never married; she never found anyone good enough for her. The cobra died not long before Franco, but Vincent died in his club, a few years after Helen, comforted by the return of Conservative government.

David and Emma grew together over the years, passing into modern times with confidence. Their's was an equal partnership, their greatest traumas came early, and did not return. When David sometimes sank into a trough of worry Emma was always there to pull him out of it. He never lost his way again, and the flame of self belief kindled in Spain was not snuffed out by advancing age; nostalgia did not turn to bitterness. In the village they were accepted as being a little different, they were educated, 'political', and without children. This gave them a position they would rather not have had, but they got used to it, the village was their home.

David's sisters Ruth and Mary married, aborting their route to spinsterhood, and confounding David. Ruth married a man David introduced her to, someone he had worked underground with. She had two daughters with hair as black as hers. Mary became a shopkeeper, keeping that business in the family. She prospered at her counter, with a Cornishman who had been drawn to the valley by the mines and ended up captivated by Mary, a meek giant who doted on her, without any children for rivals.

Men no longer gathered at Conti's, but David still called in there, to wrangle with the Italian over anything, and drink espresso coffee from the polished machine with the eagle on top. That place changed with everything else, it had a jukebox in the fifties, and boys on motorbikes roared up and down the newly widened road to feed coins into it, tempting it to blast out rock and roll for their leather-clad girlfriends. Conti was gone by then. He died in his bed, while Maria served ice-cream below. 'He was too idle,' she wailed, at the funeral, 'his heart grow fat, like his head, then pouf, it bursts, stupid man, stupid man.' She never recovered from her loss and could be seen years later sitting in the gloom at the back of the café, still clothed in black, watching her sons run the business. It was they who moved in the jukebox, shooting up the profits, ending the talks, and an era.

David retired early from his classroom. An arthritic back cut short his teaching, a legacy from the frozen stone of Teruel and the beatings of San Pedro. Yet he did not mind it overmuch, there was more time to spend with Emma, and his books – they were always there. And the pain kept a little anger burning away somewhere inside him; a man needed that, he thought, it kept one honest.

On good days he was still able to walk up to the Tump. It took him twice as long now, but he had the time. He saw the same sea on the same horizon and the valley floor was terraced the same. Only the pits had gone. One by one in the sixties they fell empty, until sheep or new factories stood over their seams. David welcomed this in a way, working below ground one was nothing to cherish – but he hated it also. They were symbols broken, and with them went much of the heart of the valley. Communities were being replaced by individuals who had no time.

On the Tump he still read in the sunshine, sometimes Emma was with him. She read too now, and that gave David the greatest pleasure. He loved to introduce her to his favourites. Even his most private occupation had become a shared one.

Emma watched David drink his Spanish coffee. He always held cups in both hands, never by the handle, as if he expected them to run away from him. She felt a flush of love and gratitude for the life they had shared. It had been a good life, forged out of that terrible start, and she still looked forward, at sixty. Others she knew had drifted apart, after the initial rush of union, leaving children and broken hearts in their wake. They had survived, and grown steadily closer to each other. She reached out for David's hand and held it, and he smiled that calm, depreciative smile of his.

The Spanish boys were coming back, noisily announcing the end of the fiesta. They looked in at the café door and saluted David, surprised to see him in their lair again, and this time with a *señora*. One doffed his cap to Emma, and they walked on, clicking their heels on the cobblestones, in love with their own youth.

'What are you thinking?' Emma said.

'Oh, that they are the future going by, care-free like we never were, or their parents. Those are the sons of the people I fought for, fought for and against.'

David pressed Emma's arm, kneading the loose skin with his fingers. 'And I was thinking that my war has finally ended, Em, just now, the last piece of the jigsaw up here –' he tapped his head '– has fallen into place. Those lads will be my last image of it. They are the first generation that can look forward with hope here, as we did in '45. Billy and Tom would have liked that.'

Newport Library and Information Service

Also by Roger Granelli...

Dark Edge

"Roger Granelli's *Dark Edge* is a novel where the personal echoes the political. The dramatic events are played out against a back-drop of proportions so large that the memory of those twelve months of struggle remains undiminished." Tony Heath, *Tribune*

"*Dark Edge* is a gem amidst the slag-heaps of Thatcher's legacy."
The Big Issue

"Granelli has a gift for making character emerge, for letting actions speak for themselves... this is a serious and intelligent book." Victor Golightly, *New Welsh Review*

£6.95 pbk, ISBN 1-854111-204-X

Status Zero

"Granelli's brilliant *Status Zero* is one of the best two books I've read this year." Phil Rickman, BBC Radio Wales

"Granelli paints a powerful and poignant portrait of Mark Richards' condition and thought processes which inform his actions." Harold Williamson, *Young People Now*

£7.95 pbk, ISBN 1-85411-255-4

Out of Nowhere

Roger Granelli's *Out of Nowhere* is the real thing. He writes fluently and vividly and involves one in his story, creating characters and atmosphere effortlessly."

John Pikoulis, *New Welsh Review*

£6.95 pbk ISBN 1-85411-120-5

Resolution

"I really enjoyed *Resolution*... brilliantly moody and suspenseful."
Phil Rickman

"Granelli's ability to paint a picture and to subtly raise question you want to know the answers to make this novel incredibly hard to put down. A subtle and compelling examination of human motives." *The Big Issue*

£6.95 pbk ISBN 1-85411-333-X

The Author

Roger Granelli's *Dark Edge* was the first novel to emerge from the miners' strike. His other books are *Out of Nowhere*, a tale of murder and jazz in the USA, *Status Zero*, a bleak examination of crime and deprivation, and the paranoid literary thriller, *Resolution*. He is also a prizewinning short-story writer and a professional musician and composer.

ROGERSTONE

4/9/06

Z658015